HOODWINKED ~IN~ HOTLANTA

E. R. JENSEN

ACKNOWLEDGMENTS

Hoodwinked in Hotlanta really pushed me to step outside of my comfort zone of middle grade fantasy. The premise for the book began with a family discussion about COVID-19 and the lasting impact it has had on society. At the end of the conversation, I had a lot of what if questions on my mind. Then I realized, what if I wrote a book about it?

I began to write and was filled with uncertainty about whether anyone other than me would like this story that was begging to be written. So, I started telling people about my idea, friends, family, and strangers. They were intrigued, most said they would read it. Encouraged, I continued working on what is now *Hoodwinked in Hotlanta.*

Many thanks to friends and family who have offered encouragement throughout the book creation process.

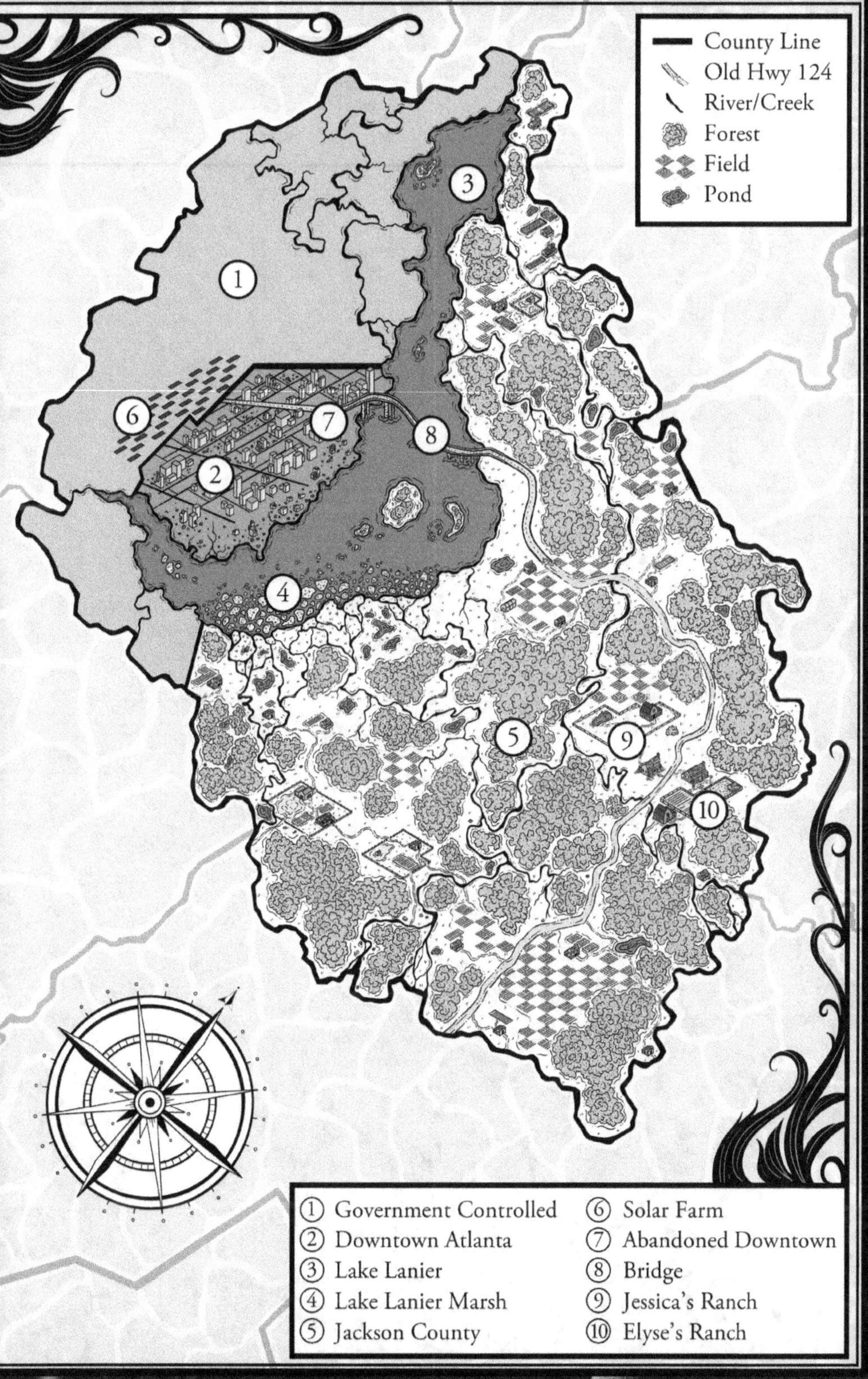

County Line
Old Hwy 124
River/Creek
Forest
Field
Pond
1
2
3
4
5
6
7
8
9
10
1 Government Controlled
2 Downtown Atlanta
3 Lake Lanier
4 Lake Lanier Marsh
5 Jackson County
6 Solar Farm
7 Abandoned Downtown
8 Bridge
9 Jessica's Ranch
10 Elyse's Ranch

ONE
ELYSE

On a Wednesday morning in July of the year 2125, in Jackson County, Georgia, in the pearly gray dawn light, Elyse Hutchinson was riding her golden-colored horse, Honey.

A tall, solidly built, twenty-one-year-old woman with long red hair in a single messy braid, Elyse was wearing a well-used tan cowboy hat, a green long-sleeved button-up shirt, jeans, and cowboy boots. She had inherited the horse ranch from her parents. Her great-great-grandmother had started the family horse breeding business over one hundred years ago, before even COVID-19 had happened. Petting Honey's neck, Elyse took a deep breath. A few weeks ago, the most important thing to her had been discovering more about her family. Part of her regretted the decision to dig into the past. She should have just accepted what she knew and left everything alone. *Except then I would have never met Josh Everly or discovered I have a magical talent*, she thought.

Honey nickered, drawing Elyse back to the task at hand: checking the fence line that bordered the old Highway 124, one of the few paved roads that was still safe for a car to drive on. Elyse had been hoping to get an early start before the sun and the humidity made it almost impossible to be productive. And yet here she was, daydreaming instead of taking advantage of the cool morning temperature.

Elyse clucked to Honey, urging the mare to continue forward at her steady walk. The sun began to peek over the top of the tallest grass-covered rolling hills when a sudden feeling of foreboding hit Elyse, causing her to sway precariously in the saddle. Honey reached back with her nose and nuzzled Elyse's boot, as though checking to make sure she was okay.

Elyse shook herself to get rid of the bad feeling. *Magic,* she reminded herself. *What I am feeling is my magical talent doing… something.* Even after everything that had happened, she still had these feelings—premonitions, or whatever Catrina had called them. Supposedly, she would eventually be able to fully control them so they would only come when bidden, but Elyse was skeptical.

Giving Honey a quick hug, Elyse returned to the task of checking the fence line, eyes expertly going over each post, looking for weakness or loose barbed wire. Honey tossed her head slightly, causing Elyse to look up just in time to see something shiny coming toward them on the worn-out highway. With the scarcity of cars since long before her birth, she never paid much attention to the highway other than ensuring that her fence was secure. The fence bordering the far side of the highway was the property line for the thousand acres that belonged to her good friend Jessica's family. This section of the pasture she was currently assessing was a fairly flat field, bringing the fence a mere ten feet from the edge of the highway.

Raising her hand over her eyes to block out the bright sunlight, she squinted, trying to see the winding highway better. "Look, Honey, it's an actual vintage car!" she said, disgust tinging her voice as the roar of the combustion engine got louder. It was one of the old models that were around long before COVID-50, before the automobile industry and the US government forced everyone to have exclusively electric vehicles. *And yet look where that got us. Now over half of the population in the US can no longer afford enough electricity to power even the most basic things—a lightbulb or hot water heater.*

Honey snorted and flicked her ears, bringing Elyse out of her thoughts as another wave of foreboding hit her. This time the feeling was accompanied by an image of the car in flames. Rubbing her eyes with the palm of her hand, Elyse shuddered. *The car is clearly not on fire. Honey can run fast, but not as fast as a car, so I can't do anything about the flames. Catrina might be able to teleport, but I can't.* She giggled at the thought of teleporting herself on Honey somewhere, wondering what the horse would think of that.

The driver of the bright red sports car sped up, blasting past Elyse before the highway disappeared around a curve and the rising hill in the pasture. Honey pawed the ground.

"I know, girl. I'm not impressed either. C'mon, we've got work to do." Elyse clucked, and they continued their trek along the fence. When they got to the top of the hill, she'd be able to survey almost all of this pasture's fence for any major defects. Elyse kept her eyes on the fence with Honey dutifully following the well-worn path. Twice a year they checked the perimeter fence, unless there was a bad storm or other disturbance. Over the years, the trees had been cleared away from the fencing so that when they did fall, they would land in the middle of one of the fields instead of damaging the fence.

Boom!

Honey jumped sideways at the unexpected sound.

"Easy, girl."

Boom!

Honey danced around. Terror rushed through Elyse as she realized that a sound like that could mean just one thing. Her feeling of foreboding and the vision had just come true. "C'mon, girl, let's go!"

Elyse dropped her hand and gave the mare her head. Honey leaped into a full-speed gallop up the hill. Elyse shifted her weight, and Honey slid to a halt at the top.

On the highway below was the red sports car they had seen minutes before, crumpled and smoking.

"Shit," Elyse whispered before urging Honey down the other side of the hill as quickly as they could manage. The horse eagerly found her way down the rocky southern side of the hill, their speed sending the occasional cascade of rocks tumbling ahead of them.

Safely at the bottom of the hill, Elyse maneuvered Honey as close as they could get to the car before throwing herself off her horse, concerned about whoever was driving the car. She rushed forward and immediately regretted doing so. She started coughing as the dark black smoke billowed toward her in waves. Rolling her eyes at her stupidity, she reached into her back pocket for a bandana and tied it over her nose and mouth before continuing closer. She easily jumped over the fence and headed across the road to the car. Dark smoke poured out of the back half. Crossing her fingers, she hoped that someone would come along and find them. She wasn't sure how much help she could be with only a few fence repair tools at her disposal.

When Elyse was close enough, she could see what the car hit. A black steer. She rolled her eyes at the thought of a stupid city person who had gone out for a joyride without considering that there could be loose livestock wandering around. The smoke cleared for a moment around the steer, and she was surprised to see that it looked more like a hunk of metal than a dead black Angus. The steer was the least of her worries though. The vintage car had a driver. Of that she was certain.

"Hello?" Elyse called. She walked around to the driver-side door. She grabbed the handle and tugged. It wouldn't budge. She tapped on the window but was having trouble seeing the driver as the smoke was rapidly filling the inside of the car.

Elyse scanned the ground and found a big rock; she quickly grabbed it.

"If you're awake, shield your eyes!" she warned before throwing the rock as hard as she could against the window. The rock bounced off and clattered to the ground.

Flames licked around the edge of the car. Cursing to herself, she knew her window of time was rapidly disappearing. *The other door, duh!* Elyse rushed to the other side. The passenger door handle was almost too hot to touch. After a moment's hesitation, worried about getting badly burned, she gripped the door handle firmly and tugged. Much to her surprise, the door opened.

Coughing, Elyse waved her hands, trying to clear the smoke to see who was inside.

"Are you okay?" she called. No answer. Elyse climbed into the car, smoke stinging her eyes, trying to see the driver.

Realizing trying to see was futile with the smoke, Elyse gently searched with her hands for the driver. Her fingers finally met firm, well-muscled human flesh. Running her hands over what she assumed was an arm, she slid her hand down to the person's wrist to check for a pulse. Whoever it was was currently alive, and she intended to keep them that way.

Gently reaching around the person, she successfully found the seatbelt and was able to follow it to the buckle.

"Please work," she whispered before pushing down on the seat buckle's latching mechanism. *Click.* With a gasp, she let go of the seatbelt as it released. Wrapping her hands around the arm, feeling certain the person was shaped wrong to be a woman, she gave a big tug. He didn't budge. Growling to herself, Elyse wrapped her hands more firmly around his arm and tugged again. This time it worked, and she fell backward out of the door and onto the pavement with the stranger half on top of her.

Elyse struggled, trying to get out from underneath him. She finally freed her legs and stood, then grabbed the man by the arms and dragged him to the other side of the road. She felt as though this stranger was somehow familiar, almost like Josh. But Josh didn't have a car like that, did he? *I'll figure out who I just rescued as soon as we're far enough away from the car,* she thought, but before she had a chance to get a good look at the stranger's face, the car exploded. The blast threw Elyse backward into the fence, and she blacked out.

TWO

ELYSE

Three weeks earlier, Friday, June 2125

Elyse emerged from the last stall at the end of the aged but well-maintained ten-stall barn with a faded blue horse halter in her hand. Pieces of hay and shavings were sticking to her yellow T-shirt, which had seen better days. She slid the stall door shut and hung the halter on a hook nearby. Running a hand through her hair and coming back with a handful of hay, she smiled and shook her head ruefully.

"Bye!" called Mya from atop her brown horse, just outside of the barn. Mya's short blonde hair was barely visible under her worn dark-brown cowgirl hat. Mya had been working for Elyse for just over a year now, a highly recommended replacement for Juanita, the sole employee her ranch had had for over forty years.

"Bye!" Elyse yelled back with a wave as she headed up to the house for the evening. Elyse paused for a moment to admire her house. It was large by building standards in 2125, but before COVID-50 would have been considered tiny. The house had weathered wood siding and trim with three bedrooms, a kitchen, and a living area in eight hundred square feet. The roof was metal and covered in ancient but still-functioning solar panels that had been installed when the house was built in 2035, as a residence for the live-in stable manager, Juanita's father, Pablo. In 2070, the main farmhouse burned down, and with the scarcity of materials, instead of replacing the farmhouse, Elyse's grandmother, Brianna, decided to move into the house and build a small cabin for Pablo. With one last glance around the yard and pastures, Elyse headed inside.

Walking toward the fridge first, she prepared a light meal, undecided yet if she was going to meet up with the locals at the club Cubed in town or if she wanted to go into Atlanta tonight. Shaking her head, she wondered, not for the first time, if the effort of keeping her city persona separate from her everyday one on the ranch was worth it. *But no one out here in Jackson County would understand.*

After COVID-50, the division between farmers and city dwellers had deepened exponentially. Even though the city dwellers and the government relied heavily upon the farmers for their survival—as providers of the primary source of food—their interaction was minimal. Farmers didn't go into Atlanta, or any of the other remaining cities, and the city dwellers stayed in their high-rises.

In Georgia, most of the smaller suburban cities had disappeared completely. Some had been reclaimed by the forest, and others had been turned into farmland. Even downtown Atlanta had shrunk significantly. The east side of the state was made up of three counties. The west side of the state was a large government-controlled solar farm. Elyse had heard that it was one of the largest solar farms in the whole country, but she wasn't sure how reliable the source was. What she did know was that it was heavily guarded.

No, it's better if my two lives stay separate—and safer for everyone.

Her meal finished, Elyse was still undecided on her plans for the night. What she really wanted was to be able to let her worries about the ranch disappear for at least a few hours. Walking into her bedroom, the heels of her work boots echoing across the smooth, well-worn wood floor, she opened the top drawer on the nightstand and pulled out her cell phone—a small flat piece of glass—and turned it on. It was one of the "luxury" items she had to have if she wanted to go to the city. No one in Jackson County could afford a cell phone. They all used landlines. But everyone living in Atlanta was unwilling to give up the convenience of a cell phone. So, they paid whatever ridiculous price the government demanded to have access to the cellular network. Scrolling through her contacts, she found the one labeled Quinn and touched the phone to call.

"What's up, girl?" Quinn answered in excitement before the first ring had finished.

Elyse laughed at Quinn's enthusiasm. "Are you busy tonight?"

"Hmm…nope! Want to meet me at Three Dragons in an hour?" Quinn asked in a singsong voice.

Smiling to herself at Quinn's eagerness, Elyse said, "I need two hours." She hesitated before adding, "I have a few things to wrap up here." She knew that Quinn would accept the excuse for needing more time without question.

"Okay. I'll see you in two hours!" Quinn replied before hanging up.

Shaking her head, Elyse returned the phone to the nightstand before heading into the bathroom to take a shower. Her uncle Albert, who lived in Atlanta full time, introduced her to Quinn's family more than ten years ago. Since then, the girls had stayed in contact. Three years ago, Elyse decided to start spending time in the city on a regular basis, as though she were living there. Craving the opportunity to forget about the hardships of being a rancher a couple of days a week, Elyse knew that if her parents, especially her mother, were still alive, she likely wouldn't feel the need to get away from the responsibility of running the ranch on her own, but she couldn't change the past.

The car accident that had killed both of her parents had happened five years ago, on their way back from dinner in the city, when Elyse was sixteen. Although her uncle thought Elyse should give up the ranch and move to Atlanta full time, Elyse couldn't bring herself to abandon the life she grew up in. There was no one else on either side of the family left to keep things going if she quit. Her mother had not raised her to be a quitter. Elyse's only living family was Uncle Albert, who she thought was likely in his eighties, and her aunt Grace, who was her father's sister. After Elyse's parents died, her aunt had stopped coming out every summer to help. She cited being too old as her reason, but Elyse suspected the loss was much harder to bear when Aunt Grace was at the ranch. Elyse couldn't blame her aunt, though, because it was much the same reason that she felt like she needed to get away to the city.

Elyse turned on the water, waiting for it to heat up. Just as she set her first foot into the shower, the landline phone rang. Sighing, she turned off the water and walked back over to the nightstand. People who knew her in the city had her cell phone number, as did Uncle Albert and Aunt Grace.

At this time in the evening, Elyse anticipated it was her best friend Jessica calling. They had grown up together. Their mothers had been best friends since they were toddlers and had encouraged their daughters to become close as well. Elyse and Jessica used to spend hours at one ranch or the other. Jessica's family raised beef cattle and Elyse's, horses.

"Hello?" she said, wondering what Jessica wanted tonight. Sometimes, they would just talk on the phone for hours; others, they'd get together.

"Hey. I was wondering if you wanted to come hang out at Cubed tonight. I'm having a rough time with Beau and really need a girls' night and time away from my brother," Jessica begged.

Elyse sighed. So much for going into the city. Jessica always knew the right things to say to get her to go anywhere. "Sure, I'll come. I just need to shower, and then I'll head to your house and we can ride together?"

Jessica giggled. "Perfect. Can't wait to see you!"

As soon as they hung up, she reluctantly called Quinn. "I know we just made plans, Q, but something came up and I can't tonight. Rain check for tomorrow?"

"No problem, Elyse. Just don't bail on me tomorrow, okay? This guy I want you to meet, Josh, he's perfect for you. I'd hate for you to miss out if someone else decided to snatch him up because you're too busy," Quinn teased, although Elyse was certain Quinn was serious that someone else might snatch up Josh.

Not wanting to care about this Josh fellow, whom she knew nothing about, Elyse shrugged and made a kissing sound into the phone. "Tomorrow at seven p.m.!" Then she hung up, wanting to focus on taking her shower and getting ready to go to Cubed.

Beep. Beep. Beep. Elyse reluctantly shut off the shower and reached for her towel. Wrapping herself in it, she stepped out of the shower and turned off the timer. She gave herself ten minutes a day to take a shower. Another sacrifice she had chosen to make to ensure when the big southern storms hit, she would continue to have the basics that many were without. The hot water heater had its own dedicated solar panel and battery pack, as did the heater for the house.

Elyse dried off and hung the towel on its hook before walking to her closet. Flipping through the clothes, her hands hovered over a black cocktail dress, one of her favorites. Unfortunately, riding a horse in a short dress could be uncomfortable. Not wanting to shock anyone at Cubed by wearing a dress, she selected one of her best pairs of jeans, black denim with a floral design and metal studs going down the legs. Riffling through her tops, she smiled when she came across another one of her favorites, a light-beige metallic halter top. She held it up to herself in the mirror. *Perfect.*

Gazing around her closet, her eyes settled on a pair of cream-colored boots—one of the pairs she reserved for going out in an attempt to keep them from getting too dirty. A difficult task, given she had to ride to her destination.

An hour later, Elyse rode up to Jessica's house. She let out a piercing whistle and waited. Moments later a matching whistle sounded from near the barn. Grinning, Elyse guided Honey over to it. Jessica came riding out on her brown mare, Moon, barely visible in the dark except for an oval patch of white hair on her forehead.

"Ready?" Jessica said, riding up alongside Elyse.

"Yep!" Elyse smiled.

Without being prompted, the two mares leaped forward into a lope. Laughing, Elyse urged Honey to speed up even more. As they raced around the bend in the driveway, the moon rose above the tree line, shedding light on the road ahead. Elyse glanced over at Jessica, debating if they should slow down or keep running. They'd have to slow down when they approached Cubed, but Jessica's family owned most of the land between where they were and the bar, so no one should be on the road that late in the evening.

"Race to the bridge?" Elyse challenged.

Jessica answered by speeding up and pulling ahead of Elyse. Honey let out a big snort and gave a small buck before digging in with her hindquarters and shooting forward.

They raced neck and neck until they could see the wooden bridge ahead. On the other side of the bridge was their destination.

Laughing, Elyse took a deep breath as the horses walked over the bridge. "We should do that more often. Sometimes we really do need to just let go."

Jessica nodded in agreement but stayed silent. Glancing over at her friend, Elyse wondered what Jessica wasn't saying. She decided to see if Jessica would open up to her on her own without prying. When they reach the hitching post farthest from the bar, they dismounted and tied the mares.

Walking up to the door of Cubed, Elyse was finally able to get a good look at her friend. Jessica had her curly black hair tied back in a ponytail, and she was wearing a button-up denim shirt with the sleeves rolled to the elbows and white jeans. The white jeans set off her dark skin perfectly, but Elyse had never understood how Jessica could keep white jeans clean. Every time Elyse tried wearing white jeans, they always got a stain within a few minutes, even if she stayed inside the house. As they walked through the door, several groups of people saw them and tried to wave them over. Elyse decided since Jessica had invited her, she would defer to her.

From the outside, Cubed was a plain building with white-painted wood siding. A large sign with a cube painted in black was over the door. Inside, it was rather rustic. The walls and ceiling were encased in tongue-and-groove pine wood. The tables and chairs were all made of rough-cut lumber. Dim candlelight flickered in the room. Mounted on the wall at set intervals were glass candle holders. Past the dance floor was a stage where the band would play. That night, there was a pianist and a guitar player. Behind the bar were shelves full of alcohol from the handful of local breweries and distilleries. Like most businesses in Jackson County, Cubed didn't have electricity, but they did have running water. The patrons of Cubed weren't bothered by the lack of electricity, as that was the norm in Jackson County, and in fact in all of Georgia—except for Atlanta.

Instead of heading over to their friends, Jessica made a beeline for an empty cocktail-height table near the bar. A waitress saw them and came over with their usual, two beers.

"Thanks," murmured Elyse before focusing on Jessica. "You did invite me tonight...so are you going to tell me what's on your mind? On the phone, you mentioned Beau..."

Jessica took a deep breath. "Yes, Beau...I love him, but both of us are still living in the house with our parents. He feels like he is allowed to have an opinion about everything I do, from how I clean stalls and feed to whether or not I bring friends over. It is getting old."

Elyse made a face as she remembered growing up when Beau had tried to boss her around. Two years older than the girls, Jessica's brother sometimes decided he could treat them like servants.

"Maybe you should move out?" she suggested.

"I discussed it with my parents, but they are worried if I move that I won't spend as much time working on the ranch as I do now. It's just the four of us. They can't afford to hire an employee," Jessica said quietly.

Elyse sighed. She didn't think she would be able to afford an employee either after her parents had died. Luckily, she had been able to find Juanita, who was the granddaughter of the ranch's first stable manager, Pedro. When Juanita felt she was no longer up to the strenuous tasks, she found a replacement, Elyse's current employee, Mya. At the time she hired Mya, it was just after her parents' accident, and she had had two choices: hire someone or sell everything. "It's your life. You should be able to choose what you do."

Jessica glanced sharply at Elyse. "I have known my whole life I would be a cattle rancher. What else is there? It would be too expensive to start over doing something else out here in Jackson County. Even if I wanted to move to the city, the cost of rent alone is prohibitive. I also don't have any skills the people in the city want. They don't care about cattle or horses."

Elyse bit the inside of her lip before she responded with something that would surely give away her ties to Atlanta. Uncle Albert lived in Atlanta, and although they had a healthy relationship, there were times where it really felt like she didn't know much about him or her family at all. Most of the residents in Jackson County despised the city dwellers. The feeling was mutual, Elyse was certain.

"I thought I heard that the Johnsons are looking for a renter for one of their cabins? That wouldn't be too far away," suggested Elyse.

Jessica looked at her in surprise. "The Johnsons would be close enough. Maybe I should go check it out tomorrow."

"I can come with you if you'd like," offered Elyse. She had clients coming Sunday to pick up a horse, but other than her plans with Quinn tomorrow evening, she would be available the rest of the weekend.

"Sure!" Jessica said with relief in her voice.

"You know…once you have your own space with four walls and a roof, you won't have to worry about your parents or brother having an opinion if you were to bring someone home with you for the evening," Elyse said and wagged her eyebrows.

Jessica rolled her eyes. "How can you even think about that? I barely have enough energy for when we hang out together, let alone enough to consider a romantic relationship with anyone."

Elyse laughed, gazing around the bar to see who had decided to show up. "Once you discover what you're missing, trust me, you will find time." She was glad she had decided to come here instead of chancing a meeting with her ex, Derek, in Atlanta. They had broken it off over a month ago, but whenever she ran into him, he seemed to think they were still dating. How she hated clingy guys like that. Most of her guy friends who were here tonight weren't intimidated by her running a ranch on her own. A few she had dated, but they had discovered they were better friends than lovers.

Jessica tapped on Elyse's hand. "Did you hear me?"

Elyse shook her head. "No?"

Jessica laughed. "I was asking if you'd like to dance or get another drink?"

"Mmmm…dancing would be good," she murmured just as they started playing one of her favorite line dancing songs. Most of the people who had been sitting and drinking stood up to go form four lines of dancers.

THREE

JOSH

Josh Everly, a tall, muscular man with dark tan skin, short blond hair, and piercing blue eyes, gazed out the window of his apartment in downtown Atlanta. He admired the view as the lights of the city were just beginning to become visible and the sun dropped below the horizon. He reveled in how at night the city could once again be beautiful as the many abandoned buildings were hidden in the darkness.

A wave of relief washed over Josh as he realized how lucky he had been when Victor Pascal had found him just after his seventeenth birthday—the day he had discovered he had a magical talent when it unlocked and set his father's apartment on fire in Manhattan, New York. Taking a deep breath through his nostrils, he could almost smell the smoke.

"I hate you!" shouted a small boy, fists raised.

"Don't do this, Ben," Josh warned. His fists were up too, but he really didn't want to hurt Ben. To most, Ben looked as though he was a boy of about ten, but Josh knew better. While he wasn't entirely sure what Ben was, he was certain it was not a ten-year-old human boy. Josh wasn't afraid to

fight Ben; they had tussled many times before, as best friends tend to do. What he was worried about was fighting in his father's apartment and what would happen if his father showed up before the mess was cleaned up.

Instead of backing off, Ben charged. Josh dodged to the left and spun. Ben overshot him, and Josh stood up with relief on his face when he felt a sharp pain in his side. Looking down, he was shocked to see metallic claws in his side, attached to Ben's dark-brown, human-skinned arms. Growling, Josh tried to pull himself free, but the claws not only stayed in, they sunk in deeper.

"Get off of me!" he shouted, trying to dislodge Ben, panic rising. Josh had no idea what Ben was, but those claws hurt. Blood trickled down his leg. Josh tried grabbing Ben's arms and immediately regretted it as his hands burned as though he had touched a hot plate.

"Ben, please!" he begged, throwing himself to the floor and rolling. Unfortunately, it seemed as though Ben's whole body had the ability to burn Josh. As they rolled, every time he came in contact with Ben, his flesh burned. The burning was too much to bear, and Josh screamed uncontrollably.

The next time he opened his eyes, the room was full of smoke and flames. He shuddered and realized that the claws were no longer in his side, but he could barely move. Every inch of him had blisters from where he'd come in contact with Ben.

Suddenly, Mr. Pascal appeared in front of him. The fires went out, and the smoke cleared. When Josh was able to see himself, he noticed that his skin didn't look like it had been burned. The wounds from the claws were definitely real though.

"What the hell was that?" Josh demanded from Mr. Pascal in a shaky voice.

"You will mind your tongue," rasped his father's voice from somewhere.

Shit! So much for keeping the fight quiet. Josh groaned.

Mr. Pascal offered Josh a hand to stand. Josh took it.

"That, Josh, was…not human," Mr. Pascal said.

Josh rolled his eyes. "No shit, Sherlock." As soon as the words were out of his mouth, he regretted them. His father would beat him later, he was sure of it.

Mr. Pascal continued as though Josh had not interrupted him. "How do you feel?"

"Uh…like I was just in a fight that I lost terribly," Josh said.

The memory faded. Josh shook his head. He still to this day had not identified a creature anything like Ben. Nor did he know what had happened to Ben. Once he went with Mr. Pascal, he never returned to Manhattan.

With Hugo Everly's permission, Mr. Pascal had taken Josh out of Manhattan and into a small compound in upstate New York that was dedicated to training people with magical talents.

Josh's stay at the compound was supposed to have been only a few months, "like summer school," but it turned into four years. He traded the wall that had been barricading him and other families carrying magical talents within Manhattan for a wall around a much smaller place with stricter rules.

At first, he had believed Mr. Pascal, that they only wanted the best for Josh and the other teenagers there. But then it became obvious it wasn't what was best for them. It was what was best for the government organization providing the funding. Largely, the training followed the curriculum of the military academies dedicated to creating the next generation of officers. Participants learned practical skills, such as navigation and tracking, weapons, how to work as a team, and more.

Anyone who arrived without their magic unlocked was put in a building that all participants were forbidden to enter. Rumors circulated about what happened in that building, but those who survived seldom spoke about it. The participants were split into groups based on the type of magic they had. Before long, Josh had figured out that people with certain types of magic came from different regions of the country. Shapeshifters—people who could turn into animals—came from the Pacific Northwest. Vampires from California. People with magical talents that involved the mind, such as telekinesis, predicting the future, and telepathy, tended to come from the Southeast, although a few, such as Josh, originated in the Northeast. The middle part of the country from north to south seemed to be home to elemental magic.

Everyone at the school was from the United States. Little was shared about the rest of the world, although Josh knew from his parents that COVID-50 had ravaged the world, not just the US. Most likely, it was yet another thing that the government was hiding from its citizens.

At times, he hated what he had allowed them to do to him over those four years without complaining or questioning it once. There were other times where Josh was forced to admit the training he had received had played a critical role in preparing him to become a very good FBI agent, honing his magical talent and teaching him how to use it with his other skills.

Ring. Ring. Ring.

The sound of his phone snapped him out of his thoughts. Josh moved away from the window and picked up his phone.

"I'm sorry, Josh, but Elyse had something come up. We'll have to try the date another night," Quinn told him apologetically.

"Thanks for the heads-up." Josh sighed in disappointment before hanging up the phone. Quinn had really hyped up Elyse to him, and he was eager to meet such a compelling woman. Work had been particularly brutal lately, with long hours and not much progress made on his current case. Although he was not looking for a long-term relationship, having a casual girlfriend was something he missed.

The last girlfriend he'd had, Patrice, had broken up with him six months ago. She claimed he wasn't willing to make enough time for her. He had not fought the accusation because it had been true. Often, he wondered why he had even bothered; he was married to his work. Sure, he had one-night stands. But there were times he missed having someone he could just talk to, someone who cared. Quinn…Quinn was a good friend, but they had very little in common. She wasn't the type of person he'd call to tell her he'd just had a bad day. Or if he was experiencing any issues with his magical talent. He just had to keep those to himself too. If he told the coworkers that he was friendly with about his magic problems, they would relay the information to his boss, who would likely pull him out of the field.

As much as he liked having his magical talents—speed and strength were his primary two, but he could also block his mind and prevent it from being read or put under compulsion—there were also times when he wished that more people knew about it. When magical talents were first discovered, during COVID-50, the United States government decided to keep the information for themselves. Seventy-five years later, the majority of the country's population was still unaware that people with magical talents existed. Josh was still surprised that people who knew that there were supply and material shortages that made technological advances come to a screeching halt after 2050 didn't bother to question how some of the luxuries they had were sustained.

I guess no one cares where things come from or how they're made, only that they can have it. I wonder what would happen if it became common knowledge that magical talents exist. Would anyone protest using magic to operate cars or cell phones?

Sighing, Josh pulled out his work computer from his briefcase. The computer was a thin piece of glass about the size of a sheet of paper. The technology had been developed just before the

COVID-50 outbreak. With the scarcity of materials, no one had deemed it important enough to develop more advanced computers in the past seventy-five years. He held it in front of his face, and his face appeared on the screen. A red line ran over it.

"Identity confirmed," a female voice said from the computer.

The computer screen went black before a series of documents appeared on it. Running his eyes over the titles of the documents, Josh hovered his finger over one, and it zoomed in. He started reviewing the file from his current case, capturing a thief who either had the ability to teleport short distances or had an accomplice, hoping maybe he would find a clue that he had missed. The FBI had gotten a few anonymous tips, but the thief always disappeared just when Josh arrived on the scene.

Finally, feeling defeated, he glanced over at the clock. Midnight. He hadn't thought he'd been sitting there for that long, but apparently he'd gotten lost in his thoughts. Putting the computer back in his briefcase, he pushed off from the couch and walked into his bedroom, quickly stripping to take a shower before going to bed, hoping sleep would come easily tonight.

Ring, ring, ring. Ring, ring, ring.

"Shit!" he growled. He hastily shut off the water and grabbed a towel off the bar, slinging it around his hips. He hurried into the bedroom to grab his phone.

"What?" he grumbled.

"Josh," purred the voice of Catrina Fox, one of two vampires Josh had met in his lifetime, although he knew there were more. Vampires had somehow come into existence because of COVID-50. He wasn't sure if vampires had also been born from pregnant women who had COVID-50 and died in childbirth, like the other people with magical talents, or if something else had happened. What he did know was that Catrina came from California—Los

Angeles to be precise—but beyond that he didn't know much about her and wasn't sure he wanted to.

Combing his fingers through his hair, Josh considered his next words carefully, knowing his temper would only get him into trouble. "Catrina, what can I do for you?" he forced out, trying to keep his voice as neutral as possible.

"I have a job for you," she uttered through the phone. He felt the towel slipping from around his hips, even though he'd secured it. As the towel slid, he could feel phantom hands teasing his cock.

Sucking in a deep breath through his teeth, Josh squeezed his eyes shut, trying to fight his body's arousal. "What kind of job?"

Catrina laughed, then the phone went dead. Josh gasped in relief as the phantom hand disappeared. He laid back onto the bed, legs dangling over the edge, trying to get his breathing to become more regular and under control. He hated when she manipulated him like that. Not for the first time, he wondered how he could have been so stupid and naïve when they met, to think she cared about anyone other than herself.

He gazed at the ceiling, taking deep breaths to force himself to let go of the memories of what had happened between him and Catrina. His eyes widened in surprise when Catrina materialized, straddling his hips. Concentration broken by her appearance, he made the mistake of looking at her. Because he was already lying on the bed, his eyes went straight to her breasts. A tight red corset pushed them up so they were barely restrained, leaving little to the imagination. Before he could stop himself, his eyes followed the V of the corset down to where she was straddling him. A red leather garter belt with matching straps crisscrossed down her legs to hold black fishnet stockings in place.

Growling low in his throat, Josh forced himself to look away, even as his cock betrayed his arousal to Catrina. This was what she did.

Don't let her control you again, not like this, he reminded himself. Sweat broke out on his brow as he struggled to ignore Catrina grinding herself against him.

Suddenly, sharp fingernails grabbed his chin, forcing him to turn his face back to hers. Grimacing as the nails drew blood, Josh shut his eyes.

"I thought you enjoyed being with me, Josh," Catrina said in a silky voice before she leaned down and ran her tongue around his ear. A shiver ran through his body.

Reluctantly, Josh opened his eyes and glared at her. "I was stupid. I know better now."

"Do you?" she whispered before dipping her head down and kissing him.

Josh yanked his head to the side and twisted his torso, deciding that if he let her stay on top of him, he was going to lose control completely. Catrina hissed. Her legs tightened their grip around his waist, and she grabbed his shoulders with her claws. Grunting, Josh thrust with his arms to push himself off the bed. He barely moved an inch. He had forgotten how strong vampires really were.

Catrina dug her claws into his shoulder, piercing the skin. Josh sucked in a sharp breath as the claws went deeper into his shoulder. He could feel the blood flowing out of the wounds. She slowly released her hold on his shoulders and jumped backward off Josh and the bed. Her wings, hidden earlier in their encounter, flared wide. Iridescent black, with silver veins. Josh sat up and gave the top sheet a tug. The sheet came free from the bed, and he used it to apply pressure awkwardly to the wounds on both of his shoulders.

"I could give you anything you desire," Catrina whispered as she slowly licked his blood off of her claws.

Josh stood up once the blood from his shoulders stopped enough. He grabbed the towel from the floor and wrapped it around his hips again before leaning against the wall. "I am not interested," Josh said firmly, wondering how, after what had just happened, Catrina could possibly think he still wanted her. "We had an agreement, a business agreement. You called me saying you have a job for me to do. Is there a job? Or were you just going to see if you could get away with raping me?"

Catrina gasped. "I am not raping you!"

"Are you sure? Because in my book, if I don't consent to your sexual advances, then it's rape," Josh said matter-of-factly. Maybe vampires didn't have to consent when they had sex with their own kind. He wasn't that well versed on the nuances of vampire culture. But he did know that in the human world he belonged to, it was a big deal. He also wondered belatedly what she had labeled her actions as when she tortured him two months ago.

Catrina twisted a strand of her hair in her fingers. "Yes, I have a job for you. I need you to put these trackers on the vehicles of your FBI colleagues James Valdez, Gerald Fernway, and Hector Babit." She reached out her hand to offer him three tiny tracking bugs that were each about the size of a peanut. "You have to put them under the front hood of their cars."

Josh raised an eyebrow. "Under the front hood? Do you have any idea how difficult that is going to be?"

Catrina shrugged. "I'm confident you're capable."

Josh laughed uncertainly. To open the front hood of a car, a person had to be one of the people the car recognized as its owner. Which meant he'd either have to attempt to hack into the car's computer when hacking was not his strong suit, or somehow get the owners to open the hood and then put the tracker inside while they weren't looking.

"Why can't I just put it underneath the car?" he demanded.

Catrina glared at him as though he should just follow her orders like a puppy. "It can't work properly from underneath the car."

Eyebrow arched, Josh kept his next thought to himself. *What does it do that it has to be in that spot? Maybe I don't want to know.* Instead, he responded, "When does it need to be done by?"

"In the next week," Catrina said dismissively.

"This couldn't have waited until morning?" Josh appealed, still trying to wrap his mind around the assignment.

This time Catrina rolled her eyes. "I prefer to sleep during the day. Sunlight is uncomfortable. Besides, you work for me, not the other way around. I give you a job when it's convenient for me. Call me when you're done."

Josh opened his mouth to ask another question when Catrina vanished. Cursing her and himself, he closed his fist around the trackers and walked into the kitchen to stick them in a drawer. Trackers secured for the moment, he wandered back into the bedroom and glanced at the clock. Five a.m. It hadn't felt like Catrina had been there for almost three hours, but sometimes with vampires it was hard to keep track of time. Part of their glamor or something.

No point in trying to go back to sleep. Josh sighed. If one thing was for sure, life as an FBI agent was never dull. Now he had to figure out how to get the trackers in place without notifying the FBI that he was also doing Hellfire and Chaos's bidding.

Glancing at the clock again, Josh decided to go to the gym early. A couple of times a week he would meet up with his friend Todd and practice kickboxing. He shrugged. A workout was a workout. He didn't need a second person to work on his technique. Decision made, he pulled on a black T-shirt and red gym shorts, then grabbed a water bottle off the counter and his gym bag. Since it was the weekend, he could come home to shower and didn't need to take anything else.

The gym was conveniently located in his building. He poked the elevator button and stepped out into the gym's lobby when it reached the tenth floor. In addition to the usual sets of weights and workout machines, there was also a regulation-sized platform for kickboxing.

He headed over to one of the mats and began stretching. The last thing he wanted to do was pull a muscle from not warming up properly. The gym was mostly empty, not surprising given it was 5:30 on a Saturday morning.

Stretching complete, Josh wrapped his hands and put on his gloves before heading over to one of the punching bags and doing a slow sequence of punches. Afterward, he repeated the sequence except with kicks. Muscles warmed up, Josh increased his speed and mixed his punch and kick sequences, settling into the relaxing rhythm of his usual workout routine.

His mind drifted back to when he was sixteen in New York. His friend's dad had just pulled him out of another street fight. His knuckles were bruised and bleeding, and his lip was split.

"You must learn discipline. Come with me," Mr. Truman had told him, taking Josh by the elbow and leading him across the street and into a building with blacked-out windows. To Josh's surprise, inside was a gym with not one but two boxing rings.

Shaking his head, he stepped to the side just in time to avoid being whacked by the bag. Taking a step back, Josh spun and did a roundhouse kick with enough power behind it that the chain broke and the bag went sailing across the mat.

He heard clapping behind him. Josh spun, fists up, before dropping them when he saw it was just Todd.

"Maybe you should have waited for a partner today instead of taking it out on the bag."

Josh shrugs. "I was distracted, and then…"

Todd chuckled. "At least the bag didn't split at the seams…I remember the mess that made."

Josh rolled his eyes. "Don't remind me." He walked over to the fallen bag and picked it up awkwardly, then set it down below its hook. He would need a stepladder to get it reattached.

"Did you want to spar?" Todd asked, eyebrow quirked up.

Josh shook his head. "I'll have to take a rain check. Tuesday morning?"

Todd nodded in agreement. "I will see you then."

Josh quickly pulled off his gloves and unwrapped his hands before stuffing his gear back into his bag and heading out of the gym.

In the elevator, he decided it was late enough now, at eight a.m., for him to be able to call Frank without making him too angry.

Dropping his gym bag just inside his door with a thump, Josh made a beeline for his kitchen. Sliding open the top drawer, he reached into the far back and withdrew a phone. He waited a moment while the phone turned on before telling it, "Call number two." The phone was untraceable by the FBI and HAC, but he still wasn't willing to take any chances. None of the contacts on it were identified by name, only by a number.

A strange melody came across the phone line. Leave it to Frank to have something other than a normal ring. Josh thought it was silly to care enough to change it. At least it wasn't unbearable.

"It's early. This had better be good," grumbled Frank.

"I guess I should have waited longer," apologized Josh.

"Just get on with it. Then I can go back to sleep."

Taking a deep breath, Josh spoke slowly. "I have a task that I need to accomplish, and I have to be able to get under the hoods of some *agent* cars."

"I will need more details than that. Each car has a unique identity, and I can't just give you a universal key," Frank replied, sounding more alert than when he had started.

Josh shrugged to himself. "I can send those over shortly."

"Goodbye now," Frank said firmly.

Josh heard the click signaling Frank had hung up on him. Chuckling to himself, he thought, *I guess I deserved that. Didn't Frank say last time to not call before noon?*

Josh turned the phone back off and returned it to its hiding place in the drawer. Rolling his neck from side to side, he decided to take a shower before sending Frank the information.

FOUR
ELYSE

Elyse rolled over and off the bed. Her eyes flew open in shock as she landed in a heap on the wood floor and bumped her head on the nightstand. Her book fell and hit her on the head. Still trying to figure out what was going on, Elyse pulled herself up and was surprised to see sunlight coming in through the curtains.

Glancing down, Elyse realized she was dressed like she had been the night before when she went with Jessica to Cubed. *Apparently I got home and was too tired to even get undressed.*

Dropping the book on the bed, Elyse quickly slid out of the clothes, revealing a matching white lace bra and thong. She removed those too, knowing she'd be more comfortable in her practical daily ranch attire. Walking over to the dresser, she paused in front of the mirror. Her red hair was a tangled mess, and her arms, face and neck were tan from all of her time spent outside. The rest of her was a few shades lighter. She had gotten lucky that she wasn't pasty white and didn't burn easily like her mother had. Other than her height, the rest of her was what most would call average. She had muscles but wasn't excessively muscled. Her breasts were ample enough that she didn't have to worry anyone would mistake her for a boy, but not so large that they would cause her back pain from the excess weight over the years.

Average. She turned away from the mirror and rummaged through the dresser for a clean pair of jeans and a button-up shirt.

The landline rang.

"Elyse Hutchinson speaking," she said calmly into the phone.

"Can we head over to the Johnsons' cabin in an hour?" Jessica replied.

"Eager, are you?" Elyse replied, smirking.

"Beau was even worse after we got back from Cubed. He wouldn't leave me alone until I told him I just went out with you," Jessica said, almost whining.

"I'll go feed the horses and then head over," Elyse said, then hung up.

Elyse rode over to Jessica's at a ground-covering trot. When she arrived, Elyse rode through the open gate, hoping Jessica was ready to go.

Unfortunately, Beau walked out of the house at that moment. He raised his hand in greeting. Elyse had no choice but to wave back. He then beckoned for her to come closer. Inhaling deeply, she guided Honey over to Beau instead of the barn.

"Hello, Elyse. Long time, no see," Beau said, grinning.

Elyse smiled back. "Yeah, it has been awhile."

"What are you up to today?" Beau asked.

Elyse shrugged. She wasn't sure what Jessica had told Beau and didn't want to be the one to inform him that his sister might be moving out. "Just going to go hang out for a bit."

"Well, have fun. Don't keep her too long. We still have some chores left today," Beau said.

Elyse nodded. She would have to clean stalls and feed the horses later also. She thought he might ask her another question, but just then Jessica whistled.

"I gotta go. See ya," Elyse said and spun Honey around in the direction of the whistle.

As she pulled up next to Jessica, her friend gave her an assessing look. "What did you tell him?"

Elyse raised an eyebrow. "I'm not stupid enough to tell him what we're doing without knowing what *you* told him."

Jessica grinned. "So, you just told him the usual? Going for a ride?"

Elyse giggled. "Yes."

"Perfect. Until I know what I'm doing I don't really want to get him all worked up. I want to be able to make a decision for myself," Jessica said, then clucked to her horse, Moon, and they headed back out the gate.

It took about fifteen minutes to ride to the Johnsons'. When they reached the main house, they dismounted and tied their horses to the hitching post. Lucy Johnson was waiting for them.

"Good morning, Jessica and Elyse," Lucy said.

"Good morning, ma'am," they replied in unison.

"I will show you the cabin and then let you have some time to look at it alone. Then, I can answer any questions that you have," Lucy explained.

"Sounds good to me, ma'am," Jessica replied.

Lucy nodded and led the way. Elyse followed Jessica in silence. It had been over a year since she'd been to the Johnsons'. Since her parents passed, she didn't find much of a reason to visit. The Johnsons' children were her parents' age, and they didn't have any grandchildren.

"Here it is," Lucy announced as they halted in front of a small cabin. Elyse gave it an appraising look. From the outside, it looked like it was probably one-third the size of her house. She couldn't recall ever being inside of it, so when Lucy led the way through the door, Elyse didn't know what to expect.

It was a single large room. There was a double bed and a dresser straight ahead, a small sofa to the left, and to the right, a round table for four and a small kitchen with a stove and a couple of cabinets. On the wall between the kitchen counter and the bed was a tub. Elyse was surprised to see a tub.

I'm spoiled with my shower, she reminded herself, then took a few steps toward the tub before stopping in her tracks. *I need to let Jessica lead this. I'm not the one that might be living here. She is.*

Lucy cleared her throat. "I'll leave you to explore it. Just come find me when you're done, and I will answer your questions." With that, Lucy walked out, leaving Jessica and Elyse alone together.

Elyse watched as Jessica walked around, opening and shutting cabinets and drawers. Finally, she flung herself onto the couch.

"Well, what do you think?" Elyse asked.

"I think anything would be better than living with Beau a moment longer," Jessica said, frustration bubbling up in her voice.

"Does that mean you're going to take it?" Elyse questioned.

Jessica nodded in confirmation. "I'd be stupid not to. I don't think my parents will object since it's only a fifteen-minute ride. I can easily manage that. As far as amenities…it's just going to be me. Which means it doesn't matter that it doesn't have a separate formal bedroom. Nothing else is really any different than home. If we want a shower, it's outside in the barn with cold water. The tub in the house is the only way to get clean with hot water…using rocks."

Elyse tugged on the end of her braid. She had forgotten Jessica's family didn't also have a solar hot water heater. They really hadn't been spending that much time together. Or at least not in Jessica's house.

Elyse assumed if Jessica had made up her mind that they were going to go tell Lucy. Instead, her friend wiggled deeper into the couch and beckoned to Elyse.

Elyse obliged and sat in the chair opposite the couch, wincing at how hard the cushion was. "Yes?"

"I know you've been going into Atlanta," Jessica revealed.

Elyse's mouth dropped open in shock. Before she could figure out what to say, Jessica continued, "Mya told me about the car you have in the shed, and I did recall that you have family in the city. What I don't get is why you haven't told me."

Elyse face flushed in embarrassment. "I thought…I thought that you wouldn't understand."

Jessica frowned. "You're right. I don't really understand why you would want to go there and hang out with people who hate ranchers as a rule. But it doesn't change that you're my best friend. Nothing says we must do the same things all the time."

"They don't know," Elyse almost whispered.

"Who doesn't know what?" Jessica coaxed.

"The people I know in the city…they don't know I'm a rancher," Elyse confessed.

Jessica's mouth formed an O. "Ah, so that's how you fit in. You pretend you're one of them."

Elyse shrugged. "I don't feel any different. My friends know I paint and enjoy dancing…which isn't any different than what people here know."

"But what about the horses?" Jessica inquired.

"I just tell people I paint horses."

"How can you leave out such an important part of who you are?" Jessica said, frowning again.

"I just do. As you said, I don't think the reception I receive would be the same if they knew I was a rancher. But sometimes it's nice to pretend I'm not. To temporarily forget about all the responsibilities we have here," Elyse explained.

"Is there a guy? Is that why you go there?" Jessica blurted out.

Elyse raised an eyebrow. *Am I that obvious?* "There was, and now there's not."

"And?" Jessica begged, clearly wanting more details than Elyse had originally wanted to give.

Elyse dove candidly into her explanation. "Derek…his name was Derek. The attraction was there. Still is, if I'm being honest. But he was too possessive and demanding. He wanted to see me all the time, and it got to the point where he'd get jealous of me even talking to my girlfriend Quinn. You know how easily I make friends. Having a relationship with a guy who can't handle when my life isn't exclusively about him, I can't do. I can't even pretend. So as soon as I realized that is what his expectations were, I ended it."

Jessica smirked. "Yeah, I know how easily you make friends… friends with benefits."

Elyse reached over and smacked Jessica. "I do not!"

"Should I list them all off?" Jessica teased.

"No. Please spare me," Elyse said with a groan. Then she got a wicked glint in her eye. "Maybe what we need is to take you into the city. I mean, when was the last time you had sex?"

Jessica's eyes got wide, and Elyse was pretty sure her friend was blushing, but her skin color was so dark it was hard to be sure. "I see…so does that mean that I was your one and only?"

Pursing her lips together, Jessica shook her head.

"Are you going to speak or just be mute now?" Elyse asked before pushing Jessica's legs off the couch and snuggling next to her friend.

"I have been with someone other than you," Jessica said so quietly Elyse had to scoot even closer to hear her.

"Who?" Elyse inquired. Jackson County was tight-knit, and usually it was everyone's business who was sharing whose bed. Elyse was surprised no one ever found out about her and Jessica. Of course, they had been fifteen at the time. That was when they realized that Jessica was attracted to women and Elyse to men.

"You wouldn't know her. It was right after your parents died. Alice was temporarily working for the Webbs during the fall harvest. When the harvest was over, she moved, heading toward Texas or something," Jessica said.

"That's it? Just Alice?" Elyse implored.

Jessica nodded.

"The last time you had sex was…almost five years ago?" Elyse demanded.

Jessica cringed.

"How can you survive?" Elyse said.

Jessica laughed. "Survive? I don't need sex to survive. Do you?"

"Maybe if you had experienced some of what I have, you would understand better." Elyse rolled onto her side, balanced precariously on the edge of the tiny couch. Her body pressed tightly into Jessica's. Giving Jessica a wicked grin, Elyse leaned in, and before Jessica could protest, kissed her. To her surprise, Jessica wrapped her arms around Elyse, pulling her in closer and deepening the kiss, exploring Elyse's mouth with her tongue. Suddenly, Jessica let go. Elyse lost her balance and fell off the couch.

"Oops," Jessica said apologetically as she peered over the edge at Elyse. "Are you okay?"

"Just my ego is bruised. Why'd you let go?" Elyse asked.

"Well, we are in Lucy Johnson's guest house, which I am not currently renting," Jessica said, pausing. "I am also not sure that we should go there again. I mean…if you are serious about us possibly dating, then yes, I am interested. But if you're just doing this so I know what it's like to have mind-blowing sex, then…please don't. I don't want to make our friendship weird."

Elyse pulled herself up to standing and offered Jessica a hand, which she took and stood up. Face-to-face, the top of Jessica's head was at Elyse's nose, forcing her to tip her head up to look at Elyse's eyes.

"I wasn't trying to make things weird. I just…couldn't help myself," Elyse said and wrapped her arms around Jessica, pulling her into another kiss.

There were some heavy footsteps. Elyse sprang away from Jessica and straightened her shirt.

"Is everything okay in there?" asked Lucy Johnson.

Jessica hastily answered. "Yes, everything is fine." Giving Elyse a sideways glance, Jessica headed out the door and to Lucy.

"I need to talk it over with my parents, but if they agree, I would like to rent the cabin. If you're open to it, I could do a two-month trial and then sign a longer lease?" Jessica inquired.

Lucy nodded. "Yes, that would be fine with us." She gave the two of them a knowing look. "I did want to say, I don't care if you have guests, even if you have guests who spend the night. I just don't want any loud parties. It needs to be relatively quiet after nine p.m. Just like you, we keep ranch hours."

"That won't be a problem," Jessica said firmly.

Lucy smiled. "Okay, then just call me later after you've spoken to your parents. If everything works you could move in within the week if you'd like."

"That sounds wonderful. Thank you." Jessica smiled, and Elyse followed her back to the horses.

Elyse and Jessica rode down the road away from the Johnsons'. When they reached a fork in the road, Elyse paused. "Now what?" They technically had three choices. They could both go back to Jessica's parents, they could both go to Elyse's, or they could go their separate ways. Ever since she took the risk in the cabin and had kissed Jessica and her friend had kissed her back, not once but twice, Elyse's emotions had been roiling. Jessica was right about one thing. Elyse was attracted to men. But there were a few exceptions to that rule. One was right next to her, and the other was Quinn. What Elyse found funny was that it was not like she had a type when it came to women. Quinn and Jessica were very different, both in looks and personality. She also had to admit that Jessica had a point. If they were going to try the romantic relationship, then Elyse needed to be all in.

"I have chores. You have chores…I should go home. I'm going to be in enough trouble as it is when I break the news to my parents and Beau that I am going to move out," Jessica said.

"You told Lucy you had to *ask* your parents," Elyse reminded her friend.

"I'm twenty-one. I'm going to tell them that I am moving. It's my life, my choice. I just wanted a little bit more time to think it over on the ride home," Jessica explained.

Elyse nodded in understanding. "Okay. Just let me know when you're moving, and I'll come help."

"I will!" Jessica smiled and reached over, giving Elyse's hand a quick squeeze before kicking her horse into a canter and heading home.

Elyse waited until she could no longer see Jessica before turning Honey the direction of home. *Dating my best friend would be stupid,* she thought. *Besides, what would Beau have to say about that? Do I really want him to be even more in my life? No. Maybe I should introduce Jessica to Quinn somehow. Quinn knows lots of people. I'm sure she could help Jessica find that special someone.* Mind made up, she urged Honey into a canter, deciding the quicker she got home, the quicker she'd be able to get her chores done and then call Quinn.

Elyse smiled as she slid the stall door shut. Her chores for the day were done, and now she could go get ready for her rescheduled sort-of-date with Josh Everly. Because Derek, and now Josh, were men who lived in downtown Atlanta, Elyse had been hesitant to provide Jessica with any details about her relationships, afraid that mentioning a guy who didn't live in Jackson County would force her to share that she went into Atlanta at least once a week.

Now that Jessica knew, maybe it was time for Elyse to go back to being open. They had been so busy lately. Neither one had had much time to spend together either. But Elyse missed being able to tell her anything and everything. *Maybe I should just tell her everything next time I see her …I just don't want to ruin our friendship if she doesn't understand.* Rubbing her hand over her face, Elyse grabbed the box of brushes and deposited them in the tack room before heading up to the house.

I will worry about Jessica tomorrow. For now, I just need to think about tonight. And what to wear.

Excited about finally having time to go to Atlanta, Elyse took a much quicker shower than usual. When she hopped out, she still had half of her time left. Shrugging, she shut off the timer and quickly toweled herself dry.

Elyse finished getting ready to see Quinn and finally meet Josh Everly, who, much to her surprise, was still available for a date, even though Quinn had been so adamant that he would be snatched up by the next available woman.

Elyse took one last glance in the mirror. She was dressed in a tight black cocktail dress with a halter top and low back. The dress showed off her ample curves and her very solid and muscular build. At six feet tall and two hundred pounds, Elyse was not a dainty woman. To those in the city, the assumption would be that she worked out hours each day to develop and maintain her muscles, which was an assumption that was easier to live with than telling them the truth: that she got them from hard hours of working on a horse ranch.

Her makeup accentuated the green of her eyes, with help from her carefully chosen emerald stud earrings and matching necklace. Her shoes, a far cry from the boots she typically wore, were green satin stilettos. Red lips curved in a smile, Elyse grabbed her clutch off the dresser and headed out the door.

Thrilled that she had mastered the ability to hide her rancher origins, she walked out to the shed out behind the house. She pushed open the doors to reveal a car, the only logical way to go into the city. Riding Honey into Atlanta would be foolish. It would take too long, and the mare was more likely to get stolen than not. With the car, she would at least blend in. The car was a dome-shaped piece of metal on the bottom half, windows all the way around the top, capped with a black roof that was also a solar panel. Since the car was off, it was resting on the gravel floor of the shed; as soon as it turned on it would lift off the ground and hover silently.

Elyse tapped a finger on the outside of the car. The headlights turned on, and the car slowly lifted until it was about eight inches from the ground. The car was fully electric and autonomous, making the engine completely silent. In the center of the dash was a large piece of glass. Elyse tapped it, causing a list to appear. She selected her destination—Three Dragons—from the list and hit the big green button labeled *GO*. Then, she leaned back and shut her eyes as the car drove her into the city.

The lights within the car turned on as it pulled to a smooth stop in front of Three Dragons Restaurant and Bar. A doorman in a black suit opened the door for Elyse.

"Thanks," she said with a smile. Elyse headed inside and looked around for Quinn. She was a few minutes early and wasn't sure if Quinn would be there already or not.

Arms wrapped around Elyse's waist, making her jump. "Derek," she said in surprise, recognizing a move he favored while they were dating. At one time, she had thought it was hot, until she realized he used it to indicate she was his possession. He twirled her around to face him. Derek was two inches shorter than Elyse, with chin-length, tightly curled brown hair, green eyes, and coffee-colored skin. That evening he was wearing a dark green button-up shirt and black slacks.

"Hello, Elyse."

Elyse sucked in a breath and tried to take a step back, but his hands held her firmly in place. "Let me go," she hissed.

Derek reluctantly released her waist. "I thought you came to see me. Why else would you be here?"

Anger blazing in her green eyes, Elyse barely resisted the temptation to slap him. "I do have other friends. Besides, why do you care? We broke it off last month, remember?"

He stepped toward her again, reaching for her hands. "I miss you."

"Do you really?" she fired back.

Derek sighed and stuck out his lower lip in a pout. "Yes, I do miss you. But if you don't want to see me, then I'll go. See you around, Elyse." He turned and headed outside, calling for his car to be brought around. Elyse shuddered, sincerely hoping she wouldn't see him again anytime soon.

"Elyse!" a woman shrieked from across the restaurant. Elyse spun toward the voice and smiled broadly, making her way over to Quinn. A tiny blonde bombshell with blue eyes, standing a mere five feet and one inch tall, wearing a tight white dress that accentuated all her luscious curves. Quinn hugged Elyse. "Where have you been? I missed you."

"Busy with work," Elyse stated, hugging her friend back before slipping into the booth. Quinn slid in next to her.

Quinn flagged down a server. "Two cosmos." When the server walked away, Quinn's attention returned to Elyse. "What was that about?"

Elyse sighed. Nothing got past Quinn. She shook her head. "Derek doesn't seem to understand what it means to break up."

Quinn pursed her lips, then smiled. "Well, I am sure Josh is capable of scaring Derek off if it comes to that."

Elyse smiled back to keep herself from blurting out that she was fully capable of taking care of herself. Sometimes it seemed as though the women she encountered in the city were no longer considered valuable contributors to society, instead mere decorations. She knew Quinn wouldn't care about her thoughts on the matter, but other people at Three Dragons would care, and the last thing Elyse wanted was to draw unnecessary attention to herself.

Their cosmos arrived. Elyse took a small sip. "This is really good."

Quinn winked. "I've got you, girl."

The server came back. "Are you two ordering food?"

Elyse gazed at Quinn, questioning. "I'm open to whatever you want."

Quinn handed the server a fifty. "Just the drinks. We're going to go dance." Quinn drained her glass and stood. Elyse finished hers and took Quinn's hand as her friend wove between the tables to the back of the restaurant, then through the doorway to the bar and dance floor.

"Oh, I love this song!" shrieked Elyse, dragging Quinn out to the dance floor. They found a little pocket of space in the crowd and danced.

A while later, when Elyse decided to get another drink from the bar, she left Quinn on the dance floor. She felt a gentle squeeze on her arm and turned around to see Quinn with a guy in tow.

"Josh, this is Elyse," Quinn said breathlessly. Elyse sipped on her drink while covertly examining Josh. He was surprisingly taller than her six feet. He had blond hair, blue eyes, and a smooth shaved face. His white polo shirt hinted at the muscular abs beneath. Elyse tilted her head to the side. She had to admit he was extremely handsome, but so were most of the men who chose to live in the city. Or maybe it was just that the men in Atlanta chose to make more of an effort to clean up than those who lived out in Jackson County.

Her mind drifted back to her dance the other night at Cubed with Colton, a handsome ranch hand who had only been around Jackson County for a few months. Although she had politely declined to go home with him that night, she had been tempted.

Josh lightly brushed his fingers across her hand, sending a shiver down her spine and bringing her focus back to the man in front of her.

"Nice to meet you, Elyse," Josh said in a baritone voice.

Elyse offered Josh a breathtaking smile and sat down her glass on the bar. "Would you like to dance?" she said and offered him her hand, feeling strangely drawn to him.

"I thought you'd never ask," Josh whispered before he took her hand and followed her onto the dance floor. The band had just finished a slow song and was launching into one of their most popular songs. Turning to face Josh, so that their legs momentarily brushed, Elyse flashed him another smile before starting to dance.

Closing her eyes and letting the music guide her, Elyse continued to dance, facing Josh, close but not touching. Her eyes opened slowly as Josh ran his hands along her bare back, sending shivers down her spine. As he settled his hands on her waist, she took a half-step closer, causing her hips to brush tantalizingly against his. Eyes locked on his, Elyse continued to dance. She let the tension from the week slip away as they danced to song after song. To her surprise, Josh kept up with her, not asking to take a break or get a drink. He was able to keep time with the music and even spun her a few times, much to the dismay of the other dancers. Elyse found herself unable to stop smiling.

The band slid from a fast-paced number into a much quieter slow song. She settled her arms on his shoulders and they stood, gently swaying. Elyse took the opportunity to try to catch her breath. As she shut her eyes and took slow, measured breaths, she noticed how well-muscled Josh's shoulders were under her hands. *Maybe that is why has enough stamina to keep up with my dancing, because he's physically fit.* She began to wonder if his whole body was this fit.

"Penny for your thoughts," Josh teased.

Elyse found herself blushing deeply, for once not sure how to respond. Just as the words came to her, the song ended and the band ceased playing.

"We're taking a ten-minute break," announced the guitarist.

The crowd quickly dispersed, leaving them in the middle of the now-empty dance floor.

"Do you know what time it is?" Elyse wondered, letting her arms slide off Josh's shoulders and taking a step back.

Josh raised an eyebrow at her question. "It's one a.m."

"One!" Elyse gasped. It hadn't felt like that much time had passed. No wonder the band needed a break.

Josh chuckled. "Yeah. I guess they're right that time flies when you're having fun, eh?"

Elyse ignored the comment and frowned. "I need to go to the ladies' room," she said and vanished before Josh could respond. Wondering where Quinn had disappeared to, she rushed toward the bathroom, hoping to get in since the band was close to starting again. She felt a hand on her shoulder and turned.

"Quinn!" Elyse said with a laugh. "I was just wondering where you were."

Quinn smiled. "Oh, here and there. How's it going with Josh?"

Elyse blushed. "He's nice."

Quinn arched an eyebrow. "Is that all you're going to tell me?"

Elyse giggled and stepped forward in the line. "I'm not sure that there's anything else to tell. We've been here dancing, same as you. I do need to leave though. I have clients coming tomorrow."

Quinn shrugged and didn't reply. They'd known each other for long enough that Quinn knew sometimes Elyse had clients arrive on weekends. Elyse walked into the next available stall. Walking out of the bathroom stall to the sink to wash her hands, she saw that Quinn was gone. Tonight had been a great first date, and she was hoping Josh felt the same and wanted to go out again.

Decision made, Elyse quickly exited the bathroom and searched the dance floor for Josh. She finally spotted him by the bar and headed back to him, stepping in close before apologizing. "Sorry about that. I should probably get going. I have to work tomorrow."

Elyse watched as Josh gazed at her in surprise. "Tomorrow is Sunday. Why are you working?"

She shrugged. "Weekends are better for some of my clients. I am willing to accommodate their requests when needed."

"If you need to go, then I respect that…I had fun tonight. I hope you did too," he said softly, his eyes locked with hers.

"I did. Maybe we can go out again sometime?" she suggested, taking a step toward the exit. She knew she could probably stand there gazing into his mesmerizing blue eyes forever, but she needed to get *some* sleep before her clients showed up.

"Absolutely," Josh replied.

Elyse nodded and headed for the door. *And…I just made that really awkward.* Rolling her eyes at herself, she wove through the people hanging out around the bar.

FIVE
JOSH

Josh watched as Elyse turned and walked away. *What the hell just happened?* he wondered, trying to wrap his mind around Elyse saying she wanted to see him again and then just leaving. Rubbing his hands over his face in indecision, he debated if he should follow her or not.

Shoving away from the bar, Josh followed Elyse toward the door, keeping a respectful distance, worried she would think he was stalking her or something, when all he wanted was to get to know her better. He watched her walk through the door of the restaurant and wait at the curb for her car. He walked outside.

"Elyse," he spoke just loud enough for her to hear his baritone voice. She whirled around, fists up. He looked at her hands before their eyes met. "Are you going to punch me?" he teased. His words were met with a glare.

Josh put his hands up defensively. "When you left, you said you wanted to see me again, but I don't know how to get ahold of you. Do you want my number?" he asked, offering her a napkin.

Elyse stretched out her hand to take the napkin and peered at it, a slight smile on her lips. "I guess it would help to have your phone number."

Josh nodded. "Exactly." Just then, a black sedan pulled up to the curb and the front door opened.

"This is me," Elyse said quietly. She hesitated a moment, and then to his surprise closed the gap between them and planted a light kiss on his lips before sliding into the car.

Josh watched in stunned silence, mouth agape, as the car drove off to wherever it was she called home. Before she went to the bathroom, he had felt like the date was going fairly well, but she hadn't tried kissing him or making any other moves; all they did was dance. So far Elyse seemed a lot different from most other women he knew. Usually, they either wanted to just talk all night about themselves, have lots and lots of sex, or they got weepy. *The weepy ones are the worst.* Maybe things had gone even better than he thought.

Running his hand over his face, Josh walked around the corner of the building to a side entrance and headed toward the elevator that would take him up to his condo. Just as he was about to step into the elevator, a ghostly hand caressed his cheek.

"Don't forget I'm watching," a honeyed voice said into his ear. A moment later, the voice and hand were gone. He stepped into the elevator and glanced down at his hand, noticing that he was shaking. *Shit.* Catrina sure did know how to get him riled up.

Frustrated with himself for letting that encounter with Hellfire and Chaos get under his skin, he clenched and unclenched his fists, waiting for the elevator to deposit him at his condo. Three months ago, he'd made the mistake of unknowingly getting entangled with Hellfire and Chaos, or HAC—the organized group that opposed everything the United States government was working toward. Now, he not only answered to the FBI, but to their biggest enemy as well.

As the elevator doors opened into his condo, Josh felt too wound up to sleep, especially after Catrina had appeared. He snagged his work computer out of his briefcase and turned it on. Skimming through the files, he had no plan for what he was looking for—

just something to let his mind settle. His finger hovered over one file, labeled *Unidentified #00911*. Josh rolled his eyes. This file likely wouldn't settle his mind, but it had been a while since he'd reviewed it.

As Josh pressed down with his finger on the glass, the file opened and revealed a long list of documents labeled *Unresolved Case #*. Josh selected Open All and waited for everything to load. His boss didn't agree with some of the unresolved cases Josh had included in here, but Josh thought that it was highly likely they were all tied to the same person. Most of the cases were violent murders where there was a sole recognizable body part or identification left at the crime scene. The state of the bodies was inconsistent. Some were shredded as though attacked by an animal while others were just pools of blood with a couple of fingers or a set of teeth. Witness accounts mentioned seeing a cloaked person in the vicinity within a few hours of the murders. Occasionally, red eyes were mentioned too.

Serial killers typically followed a precise pattern to their kills; the variation with these made most agents unwilling to consider them connected. *Except for the hooded figure.* The locations were also scattered. None of them were even within the state of Georgia; the closest one was in North Carolina, with a dozen on the West Coast, a couple in New York, and the rest across Europe.

Josh wasn't convinced the murderer was human either. What he did know was that the couple of crime scenes he had the opportunity to see in California seemed to be very meticulous. As though everything that had happened was staged after the fact or planned to have a very specific outcome. Most of the criminals he'd dealt with while in the FBI didn't care enough to take the time, and the few who did usually got sloppy and ended up caught. This felt bigger to him, like someone was toying with the FBI, and no one was willing to admit it.

As he skimmed through the files, a thought occurred to him. In the top corner of his screen, he had the option to sort the cases in a variety of ways. He selected oldest to newest. As the computer re-sorted everything, he wondered why he hadn't thought of looking at it chronologically before.

Josh's mouth fell open in shock as he saw the first date. April 12, 2025. Snapping his mouth shut, he scrolled to the very last case: January 4, 2124. "If I'm right and it's the same person, then they are over one hundred years old."

Josh tossed his computer to the side before standing up and beginning to pace. "Which means that whoever it is isn't human and existed before COVID-50. How the hell is that even possible?"

Before he could answer his own question, a wave of exhaustion hit him. He realized he had no idea what time it was, but it had already been late when he had left Elyse and Three Dragons. *I should probably just go to sleep.* He made sure the computer was shut off and slipped it back into his briefcase.

Josh walked into his bedroom and glanced at the clock. Three a.m. It was crazy late, or early, depending on how someone looked at it. Stripping, he deposited his clothing in the hamper before wandering into the bathroom and turning on the shower. When the steam rose from inside the glass enclosure, he knew it was hot enough to get in. The water sluiced over his head and back. Closing his eyes, he tilted his face into the water. As it ran over his face, he found himself thinking about Elyse. He had given her his number. Now he just needed to wait for her to call him. He couldn't call her, or he would breach whatever trust they had created tonight. Quinn wouldn't give him Elyse's number. She would hook him up with women she thought might be a good match for him, but it was up to the woman to decide if they wanted to see him again. Even though Quinn knew he worked for the FBI and could get Elyse's number, Josh also knew that if he did that, he would violate whatever relationship he had with Quinn.

As the hot water ran over his back, his mind drifted to a few hours ago when he first saw Elyse. How her black cocktail dress skimmed the top of her thighs, just enough of her lush breasts visible to make a man want to explore them. And the dancing, her hips swaying in time with his to the music and the occasional brush against his groin. A rush of desire flooded through his body as he imagined Elyse there in the shower with him.

Somehow, he made it out of the shower and into bed. He lay there with his eyes wide open. Usually on weekends he was exhausted enough from the week's work to fall asleep. Not tonight. The only thing he could think about was Elyse. Growling at himself in frustration, Josh finally gave up.

Reaching over, he turned on the lamp and snagged a pair of boxers out of his dresser. Debating what to do, Josh decided perhaps doing a workout would help get Elyse out of his mind. Dropping to the floor, he proceeded to do fifty push-ups, followed by fifty sit-ups. He repeated that until his arms were shaking so badly that he could barely lift himself up.

Probably not the smartest choice, he thought. Sweat dripping down his back, he took another shower, this time a quick cold one, before climbing back into bed. He was practically asleep before his head hit the pillow.

SIX

ELYSE

Beep. Beep. Beep.

Elyse rolled over and smacked her alarm hard before standing up. Five a.m. It felt like she had just climbed into bed. Fewer than four hours of sleep was not enough if she had clients coming. She shook her head at her stupidity for staying out late dancing the night before. Groggily, she went through the motions of getting ready. Red hair in a braid, well-worn jeans, blue T-shirt, and work boots.

She had wanted extra time this morning to make sure ZuZu would be perfect for her client. Snagging a bagel from the counter, Elyse walked out of the house and headed for the barn.

Horse whinnies filled the air as they greeted her, demanding breakfast. Giggling at their eagerness, Elyse headed to feed the horses in the barn first, before she began the trek with the hay wagon to feed the horses in the dry lots.

When the morning feeding was completed, Elyse checked on ZuZu in the barn. The four-year-old mare was just eating her last mouthful of grain. Elyse snagged a halter from a hook and opened the stall door. When the halter was on, she led the young mare outside toward the wash rack.

"You're going to love your new owners. I don't know if you are old enough to remember TaterTot, but he is one of their horses. Maybe if you're lucky, he'll be one of the horses they're riding here to take you back." Elyse spoke quietly as she went through the motions of rinsing off the mare, followed by soaping her up with a sponge, paying extra special care to her one white sock. When all the dirt was scrubbed away, Elyse turned on the hose again for the final rinse.

Just as she was reaching for the sweat scraper to get the excess water off ZuZu, the horse decided to shake. Tiny water droplets sprayed everywhere.

"Ugh," grated Elyse. "Couldn't you wait to do that when I wasn't standing so close?"

ZuZu gave her a look and then shook again. When the mare finished shaking, Elyse hastily used the sweat scraper to get the rest of the water off her, then double-checked the tie knot.

"You will stay here to dry. I'm going to go work on the stalls. Be good." Elyse chuckled. ZuZu was almost always good, one of the only reasons she agreed to sell her a year earlier than normal. That and the fact that her clients got burned when they tried to buy from another horse breeder.

An hour later, Elyse heard the whinny of an unfamiliar horse coming down the road.

"Howdy!" called a voice.

Elyse stuck her head outside of the barn and smiled when she saw Brenda riding TaterTot, a buckskin, and her husband, Gordon, riding a brown horse.

"Howdy!" Elyse yelled, waving. She returned the pitchfork to its hook before heading outside to where Brenda and Gordon were dismounting. "Was the ride uneventful?" Although Ohio was just under five hundred miles, it was still a long trek on horseback.

Brenda and Gordon exchanged a look before Brenda responded. "The ride was fine. I'm just glad we're here and that you could help us. As I mentioned when I called you the other day, the other breeder we tried…I guess I was lured to believe that the convenience of the horse being only one hundred miles away would be worth it not being one of your horses. Boy, was I wrong," Brenda said, shaking her head.

This was not the first time Elyse had heard of issues with that particular horse breeder, but she kept her mouth shut. While she greatly appreciated the repeat business, she was not one to gossip about others.

"Are you going to stay for the night or head out?" Elyse asked. The offer was part of the deal when horses she sold went to buyers who must ride home, as a courtesy more than anything. She waited while Brenda and Gordon whispered to each other in discussion.

"If you don't mind, we'll just stay for a couple of hours. Take a short nap and then be on our way," Gordon replied.

Elyse shrugged. "It's completely your decision. The paddock over there has hay and water." Elyse waved her hand to the paddock closest to them with a wide-open gate. "You can put your horses in there so they can relax while you nap." Brenda smiled in thanks. "Now would you like to see your new girl? Then we can get the business stuff finished?"

They both nodded and quickly untacked their horses, setting their gear on the hitching post rail and then leading the horses into the offered paddock.

Elyse waited patiently and found herself grinning when Tater Tot took a flying leap into the middle of the paddock and proceeded to bounce and kick, while their other horse found the hay and ate. When Brenda and Gordon were satisfied their horses were settling, they turned and followed Elyse into the barn.

"She's in the wash rack." Elyse paused in the doorway, wanting to give Brenda and Gordon a chance to meet ZuZu without her interference.

As she stood there at the end of the dusty barn aisleway, her thoughts drifted back to Josh, dancing, and how much fun she'd had with him last night. A wave of desire crashed through her. Gasping, she tried to get ahold of herself. Glancing around, Elyse walked into the tack room and pulled the door almost shut before leaning against the wall, trying to get her thoughts to focus on the task at hand.

I have clients to take care of. I can't be daydreaming about a guy I don't even really know! Rubbing her hands over her face, she considered dunking her head in a bucket of water before rejecting that idea. Although they were repeat clients, she didn't want Brenda and Gordon to think there was something wrong with her. Pinching her arm hard, Elyse finally snapped out of her reverie.

"Elyse?" Brenda called from the aisleway.

Quickly, Elyse emerged from the tack room. "Here I am. Do you have any questions?"

Brenda shook her head. "No, she is perfect and just as you described her."

"Would you like to ride her?"

Brenda laughed. "Honestly, no…I really would just like to take a nap and then head home. Gordon is going to ride her back though. His horse is getting old and would handle the trip home better without the weight of a rider."

"As you wish," Elyse said quietly.

"Can we do the contract now?" Brenda asked as she started to head toward the house.

Elyse laughed. "Absolutely. It's sitting in my dining room." She glanced back toward the wash rack.

"Gordon's going to stay out here. He's smitten," Brenda replied to the unasked question.

Elyse led the way up to the house. She indicated the stapled papers in the dining room. While Brenda read the contract, Elyse headed into the kitchen to fill three cups with water.

"Any questions?" she called over her shoulder. Precariously holding all three cups, she walked over to the dining room table and set them down before one could drop or tip.

"No questions. The contract is clear as always," Brenda said before pulling out a pen and signing the bottom of the contract with a flourish. Reaching into the pack at her hip, Brenda pulled out a fat envelope and handed it to Elyse.

Elyse took the envelope and thumbed through it, counting the bills. A hundred thousand dollars for a single horse. Had Elyse waited another year to sell ZuZu, she could have gotten another fifty thousand. Sometimes she still couldn't believe how in 2125 she could sell a horse with this much training for one hundred thousand when one hundred years ago her great-great grandmother could barely sell them for a few thousand. But that was long ago, before the COVID-50 virus destroyed the "modern world" that relied on electricity and computers for almost everything, when horses had become not much more than a hobby. After COVID-50 hit, the massive supply shortages coupled with the loss of so many lives sent the majority of the world careening back, forced to live like they had in the 1800s without the benefits of electricity and the technological advances it had brought.

A few big cities still existed in the United States, Atlanta being one of them, that used electricity and had technology that was scarce everywhere else. Those cities were powered by huge solar panel farms that were heavily guarded by the US government, just like the one to the west of downtown Atlanta. The government charged exorbitant amounts for the use of the electricity it generated, which made living in Atlanta only attainable if you were one of the elite super wealthy, which typically meant your family had to have been in that category before COVID-50 happened or have skills that the government valued enough to sponsor them to live in the city.

"It's all here," Elyse said and signed the bottom of both copies of the sales contract. "Let me show you where you can rest."

A few hours later, Brenda and Gordon had departed. While they had napped, Elyse tackled all her chores. Stretching her arms, she debated what to do as she walked back toward the house. The clock chimed four o'clock as she entered, still rolling possible ideas around her mind. Heading into the bedroom, Elyse spotted the new book she had begun reading a week ago.

A nice quiet evening in, she thought.

Taking a quick shower, a refreshed Elyse slipped on an oversized sweatshirt and sweatpants, snagged the book, and went out to the couch for a relaxing evening of reading.

SEVEN

JOSH

Trying to blend in with the light Sunday crowd at the Mall of Georgia, Josh was wearing a beige suit with a black shirt and tie. His blond hair was slicked back in the latest style, and he was wearing glasses and had a black leather briefcase in hand. He was at the mall to meet with the hacker, Frank. Frank had designed a device that Josh could use to get under the hoods of the three agent cars.

Josh checked his watch and peered cautiously around the corner. He headed toward the planned meeting spot, the wood bench by the fountain at the center of the mall. He sat down and pulled out an e-reader from his briefcase and pretended to read it. E-readers were small pieces of glass about the size of a person's hand and only allowed the user to read books or digital documents. He knew that someone from HAC was likely observing him and reporting his movements to Catrina. He just hoped that he was successfully remaining off the FBI's radar.

The minutes ticked by. Finally, he spotted someone he was fairly certain was Frank: a short man in medium-wash jeans with messy black hair sticking out of a dark green beanie, and a unicorn lunch box on a strap slung over his shoulder. Frank meandered through the mall, pausing here and there to peer at the wares being sold by the small pop-up merchants that were scattered throughout the middle of the walkway between the bigger stores. Covering his mouth to hide his amusement at Frank's lunch box, Josh tried to keep his focus on his e-reader.

Finally, Frank slid onto the bench next to him and set the lunch box down between them. "Everything you need is in there," he said as he proceeded to clean his glasses.

"Do I need to keep the lunch box?" Josh demanded quietly, fervently hoping the answer was no.

Frank shrugged. "If you open the lunch box, you can remove the inner case and take that instead. I would just recommend not opening the inner case until you're somewhere safe."

Josh nodded and gently slid the lunch box toward himself, carefully opening the clasps holding it shut. Inside, as Frank had stated, was a black leather pouch. Before grabbing it, Josh opened his briefcase. In a swift motion, he took the e-reader and used it to hide picking up the leather pouch and slipping both into the briefcase. Under the pouch was a bag with two cookies. Josh removed one and took a bite before offering the other one to Frank.

"These are great. Thank you," Josh said, standing up. Whipping a handkerchief out of his pocket, he wrapped the cookie in the cloth and shoved it into his suit pocket before setting off through the mall.

Although he knew he had been abrupt with Frank, he also knew the man did not want them to draw extra attention to their interaction any more than Josh had. Other FBI agents would have jumped at the chance to arrest Frank. Josh valued Frank too much as an informant and hacker to jeopardize Frank by turning him in.

Josh walked swiftly through the mall. Now that his business was concluded, he had no reason to dally in one of his least favorite places. He paused once or twice to pretend to peruse a pop-up stand for a moment. The last one he paused at was selling candles. Trying to fit the part of a businessman shopping for his wife or daughter, he picked up a candle and turned it this way and that, when someone brushed past him. He whirled, but whoever it had been had vanished. *Odd.* Hastily setting down the candle, he made a beeline for the door, deciding he had role-played enough. He strolled casually around the corner to the mall doors and exited.

Tilting his head back, he took a deep breath of the refreshing air after being inside the mall. He glanced down into the briefcase. With Frank's help, he would be able to get the hoods of the cars open. Now all he had to do was figure out when and where he could gain access to the vehicles of James Valdez, Gerald Fernway, and Hector Babit without drawing undue attention to himself.

Josh pulled out his phone and called his car before he briskly headed down the street. He had predetermined the pickup point as being around the backside of the mall, different from where he had gotten dropped off. Once the car pulled up, Josh slid in. The car began to drive. It was preprogrammed to drive a winding circuit around the city if Josh did not give it alternative directions. The winding circuit would allow it to appear as though he were going somewhere on business while permitting him to work from within his car if needed, instead of parking suspiciously in front of one building or doing a loop around one or two buildings.

Josh reached into the back seat and retrieved his briefcase. He opened it, pulled out the black leather pouch, and removed the device from inside of it. About the size and shape of a silver dollar, it would easily fit in his pocket without being visible. He set the coin on the center console of the car, then slid out his computer and held it up for the facial scan.

As soon as it booted up, a new blue screen appeared.

HELLO, JOSH.
TO UNLOCK THE HOOD OF THE VEHICLES, YOU
NEED TO HAVE ME WITHIN SIX INCHES OF THE
HOOD. IT WILL TAKE ABOUT TWO MINUTES. IF

THE PROCESS IS DISRUPTED, IT WILL HAVE
TO START OVER AGAIN.

Josh groaned. *Two minutes?* That would be tough if he was not able to get near the vehicle without an audience. *I suppose it could be worse. It could be ten minutes.*

He closed the screen that the coin was using to give him directions and opened a file he had started on the three men whose vehicles he was supposed to put trackers on. He knew that Gerald would be a challenge, and he would probably have to place the tracker while at the office. James Valdez was often out on assignments. Although tracking down his exact location and the location of his vehicle might be difficult, Josh felt that the actual tracker placement could be fairly easy since James was often on the street far away from his vehicle.

He clicked on Hector Babit's file, the FBI agent he had spent very little time with. He knew who Hector was, but other than some very general information, Josh didn't think he knew anything particularly useful.

Josh typed Hector Babit's name into the FBI database and pulled up his personnel file, scrolling through it and looking for anything that would prove useful. He saw something.

WIFE: VICTORIA BABIT
LOCATION: ATLANTA NORTH HOSPITAL
NOTES: COMPLICATIONS WITH DELIVERY OF
      CHILD, HAD SURGERY, IN ICU.

Concern washed over Josh. "His wife is in the hospital. How terrible," he whispered to himself. His eyes got wide when he realized that if Hector's wife was in the ICU at the hospital, then likely Hector would be at the hospital too. Or at least spending as much time there as possible. Some of the FBI agents, himself included, only had the FBI vehicle to drive. While the FBI salary was not terrible, it was still not enough to cover the abhorrent costs of purchasing a personal electric vehicle. Thankfully the government permitted its agents to use their FBI vehicles for two personal hours a week.

It's Sunday. The hospital is my best bet. "I should go check it out." He glanced down at himself, taking note of what he was wearing, his undercover clothing to fit in at the mall. Not exactly the best disguise for the hospital.

Josh shut off the computer, slid it back into his briefcase, and replaced it in the back seat, then retrieved a duffle bag. Since he often needed to be undercover to complete his assignments, Josh got into the habit of having a duffle bag with a small assortment of disguises stashed in his car.

"Darken the windows and drive to Atlanta North Hospital," he ordered the car. The windows went pitch-black so no one could see inside. He shrugged out of his suit jacket and rapidly undid the tie and the black dress shirt. He pulled out a stained white T-shirt, some holey jeans, a faded red baseball hat, and a pair of thick glasses.

After slipping on the shirt and pants, he grabbed a comb out of the bag and deliberately messed up his hair before smashing the hat onto his head. Glancing in the mirror, he nodded, satisfied he no longer appeared to be a wealthy businessman.

Phone set to go straight to voicemail so he wouldn't be disturbed, Josh strolled into Atlanta North Hospital through the emergency room entrance. Someone handed him a clipboard with documents to fill out. He nodded in thanks before sitting down to presumably fill out the form. When he was sure the assistant handing out clipboards wasn't paying attention to him anymore, Josh stood up and headed toward the double doors that led out to the main lobby.

The lights in the lobby were insanely bright. *What a waste,* he thought with a shake of his head. Keeping his head down and holding the clipboard, he skirted around some people waiting to be helped at the information desk and ducked into another hallway. Slowing his pace, Josh read the labels on each of the doors until he reached one marked "Employee Exit."

He opened the door and sighed in relief when it led him into the parking garage. Big blue signs with white letters read "Employee Parking Only" over every row. Josh glanced around to ensure that he was on his own in the parking garage before he headed off at a jog, up the levels of the parking garage, until he reached the first level that had a green sign with yellow writing labeled "Visitor Parking."

If one knew what to look for, FBI vehicles were not too difficult to identify. Standard issue was a four-door dark-blue or dark-gray sedan. They were made with a bulletproof carbon fiber body covered with a thin layer of fiberglass to disguise them as a "civilian" vehicle. Since the cars didn't have tires or wheels, they had few weaknesses. All cars, including government ones, were required to have a barcode etched into the back trunk. The etching process involved magic, making it impossible to change or hide the barcode.

Josh jogged his way through the parking lot, appraising each dark-colored sedan he passed as he searched for Hector's car. He was starting to regret his decision to try this in the hospital when a car was backing out directly in front of him, bringing Josh to an abrupt halt. Much to his surprise, the vehicle next to the now vacant spot was definitely an FBI-issued one. Josh waited for the departing vehicle to be well away before he cautiously approached what he assumed was Hector Babit's vehicle.

First, Josh circled it, making sure there were no additional alarms he might trip. Satisfied that there were not, he double-checked the barcode against the one he had memorized as Hector's. Then, Josh pulled the device Frank had given him out of his pocket and walked over to the hood of the car in the precise location Frank had instructed. The device had a red light on it. Holding it in his hand, Josh was somewhat annoyed when he realized that his hand was shaking slightly.

There is no one here that is going to see what I am doing. This is the perfect place to accomplish the task that Catrina set for me on Hector's car.

The device vibrated in his hand, and precisely two minutes later the light turned green. The hood popped open slightly. Sighing in relief, Josh slid his fingers under the hood, lifting it farther. He pocketed Frank's device and removed one of the trackers, rolling it around in his fingers indecisively.

Remember the consequences if I don't do this. The stakes are high if I succeed or fail. This is not a time to question myself. Rolling his shoulders back, Josh took a deep breath and gently placed the tracker in the exact location Catrina had ordered. Then, he quietly shut the hood of the car.

Adjusting his hat, Josh strolled away from the car and peered around, looking for the nearest stairwell out of the parking lot. When he was about five cars away from Hector's car, an alarm went off.

"Shit!" he griped to himself and took off at a dead run for the door at the end of the row of cars, a bright red exit sign flashing over it. Josh slammed into the door, expecting it to pop open. It wouldn't budge.

He pushed into it again with his shoulder. Nothing. Deciding he should give up on that door and try for the one on the next level, Josh ran full speed through the parking garage. The decline allowing him to run even faster than normal. Just as the next exit door came into sight, strobe lights in the parking garage began to flash.

"What the hell?" he gasped. With just the barest touch on this exit door, it flew open and crashed into the wall behind.

Without hesitation, Josh leaped down the stairs two and three at a time, hopping over the end of the railing to the next level below. Anything he could do to get the hell out of there. His mind kept trying to distract him, wanting to figure out what had happened, whose alarm had gone off and what the flashing strobe lights had been triggered by. But he was on the run, and this was not the time or place for him to do anything other than escape.

Finally, when there were no more staircases to go down, he was at the exit. Josh opened the last door and stepped out onto the sidewalk and into chaos. Police cars were blocking off the entrance to the parking garage, black smoke was pouring out of the top level, and a fire engine was just pulling up.

"You, sir!" an official-sounding voice called. Groaning, Josh turned back around. To his dismay, it was not only a police officer, but Captain Joe Palmer of the Atlanta Police. Josh schooled his face into something neutral. Although he knew of Captain Palmer, he had never had the opportunity to meet him. According to Hector, who had had several cases that required cooperation between the FBI and the Atlanta Police, that was a good thing.

Captain Palmer walked over to Josh, eyeing him. "I'm Captain Palmer…you're Agent Everly of the FBI, correct?"

So much for being anonymous.

Josh nodded. "Yes, sir. I am Agent Josh Everly." He offered his hand, but the captain just gave him a look of distaste and ignored it.

"I saw that you just exited the parking garage. Were you by chance on the top level?" the captain inquired.

Josh shook his head. "Sorry, sir. I wasn't up that high."

The captain tugged at his lip with his finger, deep in thought. Josh held his breath, waiting for the question he didn't want to answer.

Dropping his hand, the captain spoke, "Did you see anything strange while you were in the garage?"

Once again, Josh shook his head. "Everything seemed normal as far as I was aware."

"Very well then, I will let you go to wherever you need to go. I'll call Assistant Director Fernway if I need to get in touch with you again," Captain Palmer declared.

Josh inclined his head in acknowledgement. He ducked under the police barrier and headed across the street, determined to get as far away as possible before he could incriminate himself.

EIGHT

ELYSE

Elyse sat down on the wood bench outside of her house and yanked her boots off. They were caked in red mud. It had been pouring rain nonstop since Sunday night, and after twelve hours everything was coated in the red mud that Jackson County was well known for. It was a pain to get off any surface it touched, so she did her best to keep the red mud outside of the house.

She glanced around, more out of habit than anything, realizing that she had watched Mya ride off in the rain and she really was alone here, except of course for the horses. Chuckling to herself, Elyse quickly unbuttoned her jeans and attempted to pull them off. Unfortunately, they were also wet. The soggy denim clung to her legs. Shimmying this way and that, she finally got out of them. Her shirt thankfully came off easier. With one last glance, she leaped over the threshold into the house.

An odd chill went through her. Ignoring it, Elyse made a beeline for her bathroom, wanting to get the rest of the red mud washed off before it started to make a mess in the house, the very thing she was trying so hard to avoid. Elyse quickly turned on the shower and hopped in, not waiting for it to heat up all the way.

Lukewarm water washed over her, then slowly reached the temperature she'd set it at. As she went through the motions of showering, she let her thoughts drift.

> *Elyse was wedged in between Tory and the saddle horn, her sister a comforting weight behind her as they cantered through the pasture. Glancing to her left, Elyse saw their mother grinning from ear to ear, riding a black mare with not a speck of white on her. To the right was Aunt Grace, riding a red gelding, smiling just as broadly.*
>
> *"Faster, Tory, faster!" Elyse begged.*
>
> *Much to her delight, Tory stretched her hand forward even more, giving the sure-footed gelding, Thumper, his head. They shot forward, momentarily in the lead, before both adult women, laughing, took off past them. Try as the sisters might, they could not get Thumper to go any faster.*

Beep. Beep. Beep. The timer went off, alerting Elyse that she'd been in the shower ten minutes. Pulling her thoughts back to herself with a groan, she stuck her hand out and shut off the timer, deciding that just this once she would indulge herself in a longer shower.

Closing her eyes, she allowed the hot water to sluice over her neck and shoulders to relieve the tension she had been holding in. She savored the memory of those races, the four of them galloping across the pasture, the half-hearted scolding they got from her father when they came back, saying the horses would be of no use tomorrow since they worked them so hard. Taking a deep breath, she filled her hand with shampoo and scrubbed her hair, shaking off the old memories and making sure all the mud, hay, and shavings were good and gone.

What is my plan for tonight? she wondered. Although going back to her book was enticing—it really was a wonderful story—something a little more exciting might need to be on the agenda instead.

Rolling ideas around, she remembered that Josh had given her his number. *I could call Josh Everly…for a second date. Hmmm.*

Elyse finished rinsing out her hair, then shut off the water and cautiously opened the shower door, trying to avoid the rush of cold air. Her hand snagged a big fluffy pink towel off the hook and shut the door again. Smiling at the softness of the towel, she took her time drying off, still trying to decide if she wanted to call Josh or come up with a different plan.

Body dry, hair firmly wrapped in the towel, Elyse grabbed her phone off the counter and tried to remember what she had done with the napkin that had Josh's number on it. Having no luck digging through the nightstand, she wondered where else she might have put it. *Purse?* She slapped her forehead with her hand. *Duh!* She wandered over to the closet to where her collection of purses hung. She found the one she had been wearing that night and was pleased when she found the crumpled napkin just inside.

She dialed the number, and it went straight to voicemail. Taking a deep breath, Elyse left a message. "Hey, Josh. It's Elyse Hutchinson. I was wondering if you'd be interested in going out tonight? Call me back on this number if you do." Hanging up, she muttered, "Wow, how lame did that sound. I really do need to practice leaving messages for people."

Elyse raised her arms up and stretched before setting down her book on the dining room table. After waiting for Josh to call back for an hour or so, Elyse decided she would head to Three Dragons and just hang out. It sounded more appealing at the moment than going to Cubed or continuing reading.

Thirty minutes later, Elyse peered out the window as her car started across the two-mile-long bridge that connected Jackson County to Atlanta. The bridge spanned the marshy area that hadn't existed seventy years ago but had been created when Lake Lanier continued to overflow year after year. As the population of Georgia declined rapidly after the rampage of COVID-50, the lake's spread went unchecked, forcing the development of this bridge for anyone trying to approach Atlanta from the eastern side of Georgia. For those brave individuals who didn't own a car but felt the need to travel to the city, sometimes airboats could manage to get across the marsh, but that was highly seasonal. The depth of the water varied on a month-to-month basis, highly influenced by how much rain the area got.

The sun was beginning to set with gorgeous pink and orange hues, giving the marsh a soft glow. *Ring. Ring. Ring.*

Elyse glanced down at her phone. At first, she didn't recognize the number. Then she realized it was Josh's number. *I guess I should save him as a contact.*

"Hello?" she answered.

"Sorry, Elyse, I was working when you called earlier," he said in a smooth voice. "I would love to go on a date. When where you thinking?"

"Now?" she said hesitantly, hoping she didn't seem too eager, calling the night she was hoping to go out and not preplanning it. She could hear his breathing on the other end of their connection. Moments ticked by, and she wondered if he was even interested if it took this long to respond.

"Tonight is good. Where would you like to go?"

Elyse took a moment to consider. Originally, she had been hoping for dinner somewhere. A chance to talk and get to know one another. Dancing was fun but didn't always provide the opportunity to chat.

"Smokies?" she suggested. It was a quiet restaurant that served authentic Georgian food.

"If that's what you would like. I can meet you there…in thirty minutes?" he offered.

Elyse checked the map on the car's screen. The screen was proposing a new route, one to Smokies instead of Three Dragons. All she needed to do was hit Go and the car would change its route. She lightly tapped the Go button, and the car announced she should be there in twenty-five minutes.

"I will see you in thirty," she said before hanging up. Twisting the end of a piece of her hair through her fingers, she wondered why she suddenly felt nervous.

I did just run off last time. That must be it. She tried not to dwell too much on the end of her last date with Josh, vowing that tonight would end less abruptly.

NINE

JOSH

Josh had been surprised when he heard Elyse's voicemail asking if he wanted to go out on a date tonight, a Monday. He was used to women only wanting to go out on weekends, claiming they were too tired after a day of work to do anything on a weekday.

He waited until he made it home to call her back, wanting a chance to get his mind clear of the case he'd been working on—tracking black market sales of magic items, specifically a device that was rumored to be capable of hacking into the government-run solar farms. If such a device existed and got into the wrong hands, it would be devastating. Or at least devastating to the populations that relied on those solar farms to function, such as Atlanta. Josh hurried through a shower, wanting to be sure he didn't smell gross when he saw Elyse.

Towel wrapped around his hips, Josh headed into his closet. He selected a pair of khakis and a dark-blue button-up long-sleeved shirt. Once the pants and shirt were on, he unbuttoned the sleeve cuffs and rolled them up almost to his elbows, his white undershirt was slightly visible at the collar. He wanted to have a polished yet relaxed look.

Dressed and ready, Josh pocketed his phone and headed for the elevator.

Once at the door, his car pulled up and took him a few blocks away to Smokies.

One of the hosts was at the door and held it open when Josh appeared at the curb. Nodding in thanks, Josh stepped into the restaurant. He had been here a few times over the years, but it was not a place he frequented. Although he had to admit the food was usually amazing.

"How many?" asked a young dark-skinned woman at the hostess stand.

"Two," Josh said, glancing behind him to make sure Elyse hadn't come in yet.

The hostess gazed with a frown for several moments at the screen showing the tables. "I have one table, but it's small," she said uncertainly.

"I'm sure we can make do with a small table," he replied quietly.

The hostess hesitated before making some marks on her screen. "Follow me please." She took off at a brisk walk.

"Josh?" he heard a familiar voice say behind him.

He turned around and waved to Elyse, hoping the hostess would notice he was no longer following. Before he could prevent it, a big smile broke out on his face as he took in her light-pink crop top that showed just enough of her toned abdomen to have him wanting to rip it off her. As his eyes traveled lower, he wasn't disappointed by the amount of leg her thigh-high skirt left bared. When she was close enough, he reached out and gently took her hand and squeezed it. *Behave*, he reminded himself.

"Our table is somewhere over here," he said with a vague wave of his other hand. Elyse stayed quiet but allowed him to lead her to the table the hostess was waiting at.

He peered at the table in the dim candlelight. The hostess had not been wrong; it was a very small table.

"Will this be okay?" he inquired, deferring to Elyse. He wouldn't mind being in such tight quarters with her, but he didn't know her well enough to know if she would share his indifference.

Elyse shrugged and slid into the booth. He watched her before sliding in next to her. The booth had the single bench, which made it rather intimate. Trying to not crowd her too much even with limited space, Josh turned to face Elyse.

"How was your day?" he asked, deciding to start with something simple.

Elyse shrugged. "About the same as most of my days. You?"

"I've had a long day. I hit a wall with one of my cases and keep thinking that I've missed something, but I'm not sure what," he replied, giving her more information than he'd originally intended.

"What is it you do again?" she prompted, eyes bright with curiosity.

Josh turned his attention to the menu, skimming over the entrees before answering her question. "I'm an FBI agent."

"Do you enjoy it?" Elyse asked, surprising Josh. Most people would not ask if he enjoyed his work.

Josh shrugged. "There are times when it can be enjoyable. Nothing like the adrenaline rush of chasing a bad guy. But mostly, I sit behind my desk trying to find enough evidence to go after the bad guys."

Elyse had her hands folded on top of the menu, as though she might already know what she wanted to order without reviewing it.

She must come here often, he thought.

The waitress appeared and took their orders. When she departed, Josh gazed at Elyse again, twisting so he could see her better instead of just out of the corner of his eye. The small booth was awkward. They would fit better if she was sitting on his lap, but that was hardly something he could suggest on their second date.

"Where are you from?" he asked her, trying to come up with a neutral topic.

"Here," she said simply.

He raised his eyebrow; he hadn't been expecting her to say she was from Atlanta. Although it did explain why she would be familiar with the menu of Smokies.

"What about you?" Elyse asked.

"New York," he said.

"Upstate?" she asked.

He shook his head. "No, I was born in Manhattan."

Elyse's eyebrows shot upward in shock. "I thought Manhattan was walled off after COVID-50?"

Josh scooted backward and almost fell off the booth bench. Elyse reached out to steady his arm. "Thanks," he mumbled, debating how much to tell her. It was not like what happened in Manhattan was really a secret. It just wasn't talked about much anymore.

Finally, he decided since they were trying to get to know each other, it wouldn't hurt to divulge the information. "Yes…it was walled off, but people still live there. The government turned it into a place to hold people who developed magical talents from COVID-50. They felt that removing them from the general population would be in everyone's best interest."

Elyse gazed at him, her curiosity clear. "People have magical talents? That's not just a fairy tale?"

"Yes, it's fact, not fiction," he confirmed.

"Does your family still live there?" Elyse queried. He opened his mouth to say something else when their appetizer arrived, bringing the discussion to an abrupt halt. He eyed the fried green tomatoes with some apprehension. Not a huge fan of tomatoes, he had never actually tried the dish. Elyse, who had ordered the appetizer for them to share, clearly had no such reservations. She was eagerly devouring one and was about to reach for a second before he had even selected his first.

Giving himself a mental push, he took a deep breath and chose one of the smaller green tomatoes and settled it on his plate before glancing up and realizing Elyse was watching him with amusement. Shrugging, he took a large bite. Forcing himself to chew, he was surprised by the slight crunchiness and tart flavor.

"Never had a fried green tomato before?" she asked with a smirk.

"That would be correct," he confirmed.

"How many years have you lived here?" she questioned.

"I've been in Atlanta almost five years," he said, not sure where she was going with the question.

"Where did you live before that?" she cajoled, taking a bite of yet another tomato.

"California," he replied before deciding to at least finish the one tomato. It wasn't half bad. He just would have preferred something else if he had been given the choice.

Elyse opened her mouth to say something else when the waitress appeared with their entrées. He could see the steam rising from both plates. His mouth watered as he inhaled the savory spices of the half-rack of dry-rubbed ribs he'd ordered.

The waitress set down Josh's plate of ribs with fried okra and a side of mac and cheese, followed by Elyse's fried chicken and fresh field peas. Both became absorbed in eating the delicious food. Josh couldn't believe how amazing his ribs were. The pork was smoked to perfection and was melting in his mouth.

The companionable silence stretched on with only the clink of the silverware and the hushed sounds of conversations from the other tables.

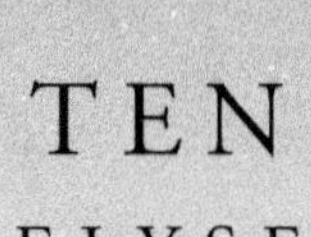

TEN
ELYSE

Elyse leaned back. Her shoulder brushed against Josh's. The chicken had been juicy and not tough. Even though one would assume that most restaurants in Georgia would know how to properly fry a chicken, it was surprising how many truly failed at it. Although to their credit, how many restaurants had Elyse gone to during her lifetime to be able to compare? It wasn't as though she went out to eat on a regular basis.

Closing her eyes and tilting her head back, Elyse's thoughts drifted before settling on the conversation they had had before the food arrived. Josh stating that people with magical talents existed. Still not sure she really believed him, Elyse wanted to at least ask Uncle Albert about it when she got the chance. He would be able to answer her question, and she knew he wouldn't lie to her. Josh… Josh she didn't know well enough to trust that he was not making things up. It was not like she'd seen people randomly using magic before.

Elyse's eyes fluttered open when Josh took her hand in his again. She was enjoying getting to know him better. Taking a breath, Elyse leaned over and gave Josh a quick kiss on the lips, curious about what his reaction would be. She knew from his mannerisms that he was just as attracted to her as she was to him. But he appeared content to not rush their relationship, whatever it was. *Because he's interested in more than just a date or two? I could ask him...*

Opening her mouth, the first word was on the tip of her tongue when the waitress returned.

"Would you two like any dessert?"

What is it tonight with the timing of the staff? Every time one of us is about to speak, we get interrupted. Elyse glanced sideways at Josh, not sure if she was hungry enough for dessert. She had probably eaten too much of the chicken, but it was *so* good.

Josh shrugged his shoulders. "Whatever you would like to do, Elyse."

She bit her lower lip, debating the best course of action. Finally coming to a decision, she said, "We are going to pass on dessert tonight. Thank you for offering."

As the waitress disappeared again, Elyse settled her gaze back on Josh.

"Is there anything else you would like to do tonight?" he asked quietly, holding her hand in his.

Elyse took a shaky breath and lowered her eyes, trying to collect herself. He was being very sweet, but she was somewhat taken aback by how much she wanted to be with him physically. What she really wanted was to get to know him better, before going any further than a kiss or two and dancing. While not her usual plan, she admitted, if she wanted to have a relationship that had more to it than hot sex, then she would need put in necessary effort to make it happen.

Giving Josh's hand a squeeze, she gently tugged hers out of his and returned it to her lap. Hopefully having her hand back would allow her to focus on Josh. "I'd like to know more about you. For example, how have you lived in Atlanta for five years and you've never had fried green tomatoes?"

Josh laughed at her question. "As I explained before, I am from New York. When I do eat, I will admit that I often find myself eating food that reminds me of home. I'm not particularly fond of tomatoes."

"Okay, I can understand wanting food from home," Elyse said with a smile. "What do you do for fun?"

"I go to the gym," Josh replied.

Elyse gave him a look, eyebrow arched. "You think the gym is fun?"

Josh shrugged. "Well…I kickbox, so yeah, it can be fun."

Elyse pondered his revelation for a moment. "Anything else?"

"What about you? What do you do for fun?" Josh asked, effectively dodging her question.

"I paint." She hesitated wondering, if mentioning horses was safe or not. "I paint landscapes and horses." While true, it gave her a way of including her connection to horses without alluding to anything else. Although if she was being honest with herself, Josh was an FBI agent and knew her first and last name. If he wanted to find out that she didn't live in Atlanta but in Jackson County as a horse rancher, he clearly had the tools at his disposal to do so.

"Horses? You don't see many of those around Atlanta," Josh teased.

Elyse shrugged. "I don't need to see a live horse to be able to paint it."

"Does that mean you have a dead horse in your apartment that you paint?" Josh questioned with a straight face, although his eyes were dancing with laughter.

Elyse bumped him with her shoulder. "No, silly. I don't have a dead horse in my apartment. But I am pretty good at memorizing details and painting from memory." She paused, debating if she should tell him more. She wanted to discover who he was, which would also require her to open up more. "I don't know if you go to the North Atlanta Hospital very often, but the painting that's behind the reception desk when you first walk in, that's one of mine."

Josh looked at her, startled. "That's your painting?"

Elyse gave a nervous laugh. "Yes."

"That's really good. It almost feels like you're there in that valley against the mountains," Josh declared.

Elyse blushed and lowered her eyes somewhat. "Thanks."

"Do you have other plans for tonight?" Josh asked. Elyse could hear the hesitation in his voice. She wondered why he was hesitating. Was it because he wasn't as attracted to her as he was acting, or because he thought she wanted to leave?

"I don't have plans for tonight, but I do have an early morning tomorrow," Elyse replied, wondering if he would invite her to do something else after dinner or just let her go home.

"Would you like to come over for a drink?" Josh offered.

Elyse smiled. He did ask, which made her hopeful that the attraction she felt was mutual. But after Jessica had implied that all Elyse did was have sex with any man she was attracted to, Elyse felt reluctant to have whatever this was with Josh be the same. She *did* want a long-term relationship in her future. With someone she could tell everything: that she was a rancher, and sometimes went to the city. Perhaps the best route for her desired outcome was not to start in the bedroom.

"I really do appreciate the offer, but I should get home," Elyse said, keeping her voice light. Then on a whim, she leaned over and kissed him. This time it was more than a light brush of their lips. She could tell he was not expecting her to kiss him after rejecting his offer of coming over, but he also didn't seem to mind being kissed either.

The waitress coughed. Elyse reluctantly slid out of Josh's arms. "That's my cue. I really should go."

Josh scooted off the bench seat to allow her to get out. Out of the corner of her eye, Elyse saw the waitress wink to Josh, as though she thought they were indeed going somewhere for an after-dinner activity. Elyse gave a mental shrug.

Why do I care what the waitress thinks? I made up my mind and I'm sticking to it.

She smiled slightly when Josh snagged her hand in his, and they walked out of the restaurant. Elyse pulled out her phone and put in the order for her car to come get her.

"Are you sure you don't want to come back with me?" Josh offered again before leaning in for a light kiss on her lips. Wanting to stick to her plan of going home, Elyse did not let him deepen the kiss.

"Maybe another night," Elyse replied, just as her car drove up to the curb. "Thank you, though, for being willing to go out last-minute."

Josh opened the car door, and Elyse slid onto the seat. The door swung shut with a click. She shut her eyes.

"Take me home," she said quietly to the car, taking a deep breath to settle herself.

The next morning, Elyse had just come inside to take a quick break from farm chores when the landline rang.

"Hey, can you come help me move?" Jessica said with no greeting.

"I can…do you have that much stuff?" Elyse replied.

"Dad is driving a cart for me," Jessica responded.

"Okay, I will meet you there. You're lucky you caught me. I was coming in for some water. I do still need to finish up a few things in the barn," Elyse answered.

"Okay, not a problem," Jessica said and then hung up before Elyse could get any more words out.

Shrugging, Elyse took a long sip. Cold water sluiced down her parched throat. Of course Jessica had to pick today of all days to move. It was already ninety-five degrees at nine a.m. Elyse didn't want to know how hot it would be later in the afternoon. The humidity was high as well. Draining the last of the water, Elyse put the glass in the sink and headed back out to the barn to finish her chores.

A few hours later, Elyse was tying Honey to the hitching post right outside of Jessica's cabin at the Johnsons' ranch. Jessica was unloading the second-to-last box from the cart.

"What happened to coming right over?" Jessica teased.

Elyse shook her head ruefully. "You know how it goes sometimes. You start one task and then realize that you also need to do X, Y, and Z too. The two-year-olds somehow flipped over the hay manger in their pasture. That thing is so heavy. It was a challenge to get it righted without someone else to help. I was worried they would get stuck in it if I left it as it was."

Jessica nodded in understanding. It had been ingrained in both of them as soon as they were old enough to start helping their parents out at the ranches: animal safety was the highest priority. Downed fence, troughs that were flipped, or other hazards could easily result in severe injuries. The only thing that trumped the animals' safety in priority was if a human was in trouble.

Elyse grabbed the last box and followed Jessica into the house. She set the box on the table with a thud.

"Do you need anything else?" called Jessica's dad from outside.

Jessica smiled at Elyse. "I'll be right back."

Elyse peered around the room. There was a small stack of boxes on the table. The furniture was the same as when they had checked it out a few days ago.

Jessica walked back inside and shut the door firmly behind her. "He's heading home. Would you mind helping me put these things away? I didn't bring much because I don't have much. And, well, as you can see, the cabin is furnished with all the major things."

"Sure, no problem. What would you like me to start on?" she asked.

"How about the dresser? Most of these boxes are clothing. I can put away the few kitchen things and then help you with the clothes," Jessica suggested.

Elyse opened the top of the box she had carried in and confirmed it was indeed clothing. She carried it over to the bed and started pulling the clothes out so that she could sort them before deciding what drawers to assign to things. The first box emptied, Elyse searched for another box of clothing.

"Aside from going into Atlanta, what else have you been up to recently?" wheedled Jessica, breaking the silence that filled the room.

"I've been trying to find out more about my family," Elyse replied.

"Why now?" Jessica asked.

"I've never known much. I mean, you've met my aunt Grace, but no one talks about anything other than horses. I know that not all my family has been exclusively into horse breeding. Take Uncle Albert for instance. He lives in Atlanta and works for a lab doing research," Elyse explained.

Curiosity clearly piqued, Jessica asked, "What kind of research?"

Elyse shrugged. "I'm not sure. Only that sometimes he talks about retiring, but for whatever reason his employers keep talking him into staying longer."

Jessica carried the last box of clothing over to the bed and dumped it out, adding more shirts and pants to Elyse's stacks. "Have you tried asking him before?"

Elyse shook her head. "No, he always seems to avoid my questions, so I have learned to stop asking. Aunt Grace mentioned something about journals at the house. But I'm not completely sure what she's talking about. I've never seen any old journals."

"Well…if you ever do find them, I'd be happy to help you look through them. Sounds more exciting than figuring out what bulls to pair with each herd of cows for next year," Jessica said eagerly.

Elyse laughed. "Okay, I will let you know if I find them. Now let's finish getting you unpacked."

When the last piece of clothing and kitchenware was safely in its new home, Elyse pulled out one of the dining table chairs and sat on it backward, resting her elbows on the chairback. "What next?"

"You seem…different than when we came here. What's changed?" Jessica inquired.

Elyse considered what to say. "I went on…I guess you can say a blind date with this guy named Josh."

"And?" Jessica coaxed, intrigued.

"And…I've been thinking about everything you said, and I decided that this time I want it to be different. Not just for the sex, but a real relationship. Someone I can talk to and just hang out with," Elyse said softly, slightly embarrassed.

"Is it working? Have you slept together yet?" Jessica asked.

"I think it's working. I mean, we've been on two dates and are getting to know each other. He's an FBI agent and goes to the gym for fun," Elyse said with a giggle. "The attraction seems to be mutual. We've kissed a couple of times." Elyse blushed.

"When are you going to see him again?" Jessica inquired.

Elyse shrugged. "I am not sure. I have dinner with Uncle Albert almost once a week. I'll just have to see what fits in. The problem with Josh living in Atlanta is that even if we did, say, get more serious, do I even really have time for that? I mean, you know how much time it takes to run the ranch. I can't imagine going into the city every evening for dinner. I'd never get anything done around here."

"You are right about the time thing. I guess the best option is to just hope that when you reach that point in your relationship, you feel comfortable enough explaining to him about the ranch. Maybe he could even come out here some. Besides, do you really want to marry a guy who thinks you should give up the horses completely?" Jessica inquired.

Elyse was surprised her friend brought up marriage. When they were much younger, they talked about it frequently. They would design their weddings and plan their futures. But since Elyse's parents' deaths, those conversations had stopped, and if she was being completely honest with herself, she hadn't allowed her thoughts to go there, to planning some dream future. She wasn't even sure if she wanted to get married or have kids anymore. Not after losing her parents.

ELEVEN

JOSH

Tuesday morning, Josh settled himself at his desk in his apartment. He found in a typical week he would spend one or two days working on his computer doing research and filing paperwork for his cases. The rest of his time was spent in the field.

Josh was surprised when an email came from his boss, Gerald Fernway, assistant director of the Federal Bureau of Investigation, a dark-brown-skinned lean man with short, curly brown hair, hazel eyes, and a clean-shaven face. The email stated that Josh's newest assignment was Elyse Hutchinson, a horse rancher in Jackson County who happened to also be the great-granddaughter of Archibald Cornelius, the man who was at the forefront of the research on COVID-50. Josh stared at the computer, his mouth hanging open in shock.

Does Gerald know that I have already been on two dates with Elyse? His nostrils flared as he inhaled through his nose and skimmed through the contents of the email.

Most of the information was the same as his usual assignments. Elyse was apparently on the list of descendants of babies born to pregnant women who went into labor and died from COVID-50. All descendants of such women that had been found to date had proven to have some sort of magical ability. Prior to COVID-50, magic hadn't existed in the world. The federal government wanted to have control over everyone who had magic, and agents such as Josh had spent the last fifty years hunting for and collecting those individuals.

Some of the people Josh had found and recruited over the years disappeared. The younger ones ended up at the academy in upstate New York where he had spent four years, and others he still actively had contact with. The email didn't provide details on what Elyse's supposed magical talent was, only that her full abilities had not yet been unlocked. That tidbit of information was mostly a warning. Josh had seen firsthand what happened when talents were unlocked, and the results could be devastating. His last partner had died from being too close to an explosion that was released.

Shuddering at that memory, Josh sighed and opened the attached file on Elyse, deciding if he couldn't meet her that night in person, he would at least do more research. The odds of her being open to recruitment if she didn't at least somewhat trust him before he popped the question were slim.

NAME: ELYSE HUTCHINSON
BIRTHDAY: SEPTEMBER 9, 2103
PHYSICAL DESCRIPTION: LONG RED HAIR, GREEN EYES, SIX FEET, TWO HUNDRED POUNDS
JOB: HORSE BREEDER AND RANCHER IN JACKSON COUNTY
MOTHER: FRANCESCA HOWARD HUTCHINSON
MOTHER'S FATHER: WALDON HOWARD
FATHER: CONNER HUTCHINSON
FATHER'S MOTHER: BRIANNA CORNELIUS HUTCHINSON (DAUGHTER OF ARCHIBALD CORNELIUS)
FATHER'S FATHER: FREDERICK HUTCHINSON

FATHER'S SIBLINGS: GRACE HUTCHINSON
OTHER RELATIVES: ALBERT CORNELIUS (OLDER
BROTHER OF BRIANNA CORNELIUS)
FRIENDS: JESSICA OAKWALD, QUINN FRIERSON
EMPLOYEES: MYA RANDALL

A few photographs were included in the file. One showed Elyse somewhere in a club in Atlanta with Quinn. Another was of her uncle, Albert Cornelius, who was employed by the lab Archibald Cornelius had worked for and lived in Atlanta a few blocks from Josh.

Josh gazed at the picture of Elyse, focused on how at ease she seemed with Quinn in the city. He struggled to imagine her looking just as comfortable in a ranch setting and hoped he wouldn't have to go to her ranch. A few years back, he had had an undercover assignment on the rodeo circuit. He closed his eyes and took a breath, remembering the cheering of the crowds, the thrill of adrenaline as he came out of the chute and roped the calf, the smell of horse flesh. He remembered losing his balance and then waking up in the hospital. He shuddered and absentmindedly rubbed his left arm, the five-inch-long scar surprisingly visible even after all these years. It still ached sometimes.

Being around the horses had come more naturally than he expected, but given a choice, Josh much preferred driving a car. Specifically, his red 2025 Corvette C8. Most people thought he was crazy to have a car that old. Especially one that required gasoline to run and for a person to actively drive it. Because of that, few knew he had one. Parts were impossible to come by, making every drive he was able to take precious because he knew one day the car would have a problem that he wouldn't be able to repair, and then it would be nothing more than a decoration.

Knowing that Elyse is a rancher, I wonder what she would think of my car or if she would like to go for a drive. Shaking his head, he realized how stupid he was being. *Why would Elyse like my car? She's a horsewoman. That's about as anti-car as you can get.*

His phone rang, and he was surprised to see Todd's number flashing on the screen, since they'd just gotten together that morning to spar. "Hello?" he said, curious why his friend was calling him in the middle of a work day.

"Hey, Josh. I know sometimes you like participating in those underground fights. Well, there is one going tonight if you don't have plans," Todd suggested.

I was thinking of seeing if Elyse was available tonight, but a fight might help me clear my head more. He considered his options before answering. "Sure, I'm in. Fifty percent, right?" Josh demanded, confirming his share if he won.

Todd chuckled. "Yes, of course. I'll let Curt know that you're coming tonight. He said to be there at ten p.m. Fight starts at eleven p.m. Please don't be late."

"I promise. That was a one-time thing," Josh muttered.

"If you say so. Just remember, these guys don't care who you are or where you come from until you screw with their fights. Then, they will hunt down you and everyone you know," Todd chided.

Josh growled, "I said I got it. Now, I don't know about you, but I do *have* work to do today. I'll see you tonight. Goodbye." Josh hung up before Todd could distract him any longer.

Elyse was not his only assignment. He was narrowing in on the primary suspect for the black-market sale of small solar panels. Scrolling through files on his computer, he noticed a new one. The Atlanta FBI office had one in-house technology genius, and it appeared as though Sergio Marchello had been successful in his search for video footage that could help Josh pin the black-market sale of magic items on his primary suspect.

Clicking on the file, Josh found several video clips and still images. He opened the still images first. They were sharp and surprisingly clear. His suspect, Kiara Velez, an eighteen-year-old girl from Puerto Rico, was in the first one, although he had no idea how she'd actually gotten to Atlanta since airplanes didn't exist anymore, to his knowledge.

Kiara was shaking hands with a burly man with short black hair, who had his back to the camera. The next photo was from the side, which gave partial views of both Kiara and the man. Josh sucked in his breath when he recognized Octavien Boutin. Octavien was another individual he had been tasked with bringing in. Unlike Kiara, Octavien had a year's worth of cases he was believed to be responsible for, but they only had circumstantial evidence. Depending on what else they contained, these photos could very well be the proof Josh needed to get Octavien.

He clicked on the next photo, which showed Kiara handing over a briefcase, and Octavien giving her a wad of what Josh presumed was cash. The fourth and final photo was Octavien walking away, but he glanced back and up as though looking directly at the camera.

How odd, Josh pondered. He'd never known Octavien to deliberately want to get caught before, but he clearly knew that the camera was in that spot, even though Josh knew that unless someone had seen where it was placed originally, no one should be able to detect its precise whereabouts.

Rubbing his chin in contemplation, Josh decided to look at the videos and see if they shed any more light on Octavien's strange actions.

"Ah-ha!" he shouted to his empty apartment. A video showed Octavien, his back turned to the camera, with a piece of paper laid out on the hood of the car. The paper had a series of numbers: 70-724-58-909. Josh pulled out a piece of scratch paper and scribbled the numbers down, not sure what to make of them. He searched through the entire file on Octavien using the numbers and came up empty-handed. Josh stared at the numbers awhile longer.

"What if it's a phone number?" he wondered aloud.

Pulling out his phone, Josh punched in the numbers and hit the call button. Much to his surprise, the phone rang.

"You are not as stupid as I thought," Octavien's gravelly voice came over the line.

"Thank you for the vote of confidence," Josh grumbled. "Now, why did you want me to call you?"

"I have all the evidence you need to put Kiara Velez away, and my boss too," Octavien said in a hushed tone.

Josh quivered in excitement. "What do you want from me?"

"I need immunity, and I want to relocate to Paris," Octavien replied softly.

"Why Paris?" Josh asked, curiosity piqued. Even as a veteran FBI agent, he didn't know much about what was going on in the world outside of the United States.

"That is not your business. Meet me tomorrow with the paperwork, and I will give you the information," Octavien said curtly before the line went dead.

Josh stared as his computer in disbelief. Octavien Boutin was going to roll on Kiara Velez *and* his boss? What had him scared enough to do that? Then it came to him. *His boss must be here.*

"Fuck," Josh growled and shoved his computer from his lap, leaping to his feet. Running a hand over his face, he realized he was shaking. There wasn't many people he'd come up against during his career as an FBI agent who truly scared him, but Octavien's boss definitely did. Knowing he wouldn't be able to focus on anything else until he cleared his head, Josh changed into his workout clothes and running shoes and headed out the door of his apartment. Instead of taking the elevator, he ran down the stairs and out the side door, taking off down the sidewalk.

Josh glanced at his watch and did a double take. Seven p.m. He needed to get back home if he was going to make it to the fight. There weren't very many things that scared Josh, but Octavien's boss was near the top of his list of people to avoid at all costs. He'd never met him and prayed that he never had to. Unfortunately for him, if Octavien was telling Josh the truth and did want to give up information on his boss, then Josh was going to be right in the middle of a conflict he was trying desperately to avoid.

He laughed. *Or I am just that stupid to think I'm not knee-deep in the middle of it already? I work for the FBI, and HAC has me by the balls. I am totally fucked.* Glancing up at the street sign, Josh decided that since he was only a mile from home, he'd walk instead of calling his car.

The elevator doors slid open, and Josh stepped inside his apartment. It was exactly how he'd left it hours earlier. He snagged his work computer off the couch and straightened the cushions, then put the computer away. Glancing around, he verified everything else was in order before stepping into the kitchen to prepare a protein shake.

Leaving for as long as he had after the call with Octavien was probably a mistake he'd regret after the fight tonight. Over the past year, he had developed a routine that worked well when he stuck to it on the day of a fight. Eating meals at very specific times, thought-out exercise the morning of, and making an effort to not wear himself out before he ever set foot in the ring.

Going on a ten-mile run should have never been on the agenda, but it was too late to back out now. If he did, then not only would he have to worry about Octavien's boss getting ahold of him, but also the organizers behind the underground fight circuit.

He finished off the protein shake and then headed into the bathroom to take a shower. As the hot water ran over his back, Josh wondered not for the first time that evening what he had gotten himself into. If he had called Octavien before he agreed to the fight tonight, then he wouldn't have agreed to fight. Typically, Octavien's business steered clear of the underground fight scene, but Kiara often conducted her business during the fights. If anyone knew that Octavien had spoken to him, there was no telling what he'd be walking into when he showed up. His best bet was to just let the cards fall instead of making assumptions.

Todd was glaring at him when he swaggered through the door into the underground club where the fight was going to take place.

"What?" Josh demanded. "I'm not late."

"But you're cutting it pretty damn close," Todd groused, grabbing Josh's arm and dragging him over to a bench. "You better be ready because you're up next."

Josh shrugged and unzipped his bag, pulling out the tape. He quickly wrapped his wrists, then stood up and started some stretches. He had warmed up before he left his apartment, not wanting to give anyone insight to his fighting style beforehand. Todd knew that was his routine, so Josh wasn't sure why his friend had his panties in a twist.

After running through his warmup, Josh glanced over at Todd. His friend still looked like something was bothering him, which worried Josh. Closing his eyes, Josh took a deep breath. He had to focus, or he was going to be in trouble when he got in the ring. The only thing he could afford to think about now was himself and his opponent. Everything else was just background noise.

Josh's eyes popped open when he heard the roar of the crowd even this far away.

"It's time," grunted Todd.

Josh nodded and followed Todd down the hallway.

"Shredder!" shouted the announcer. A throaty shout went up from Shredder, who was already in the ring.

"Tonight, challenging Shredder is Badger!" the announcer screamed. The crowd went wild. From what Josh had picked up on his way in, Shredder had won every fight he'd ever been in, with half of his opponents dead from internal injuries before they left the building.

90

Typically, there were three fights per night, so Josh hadn't been sure if he would be facing Shredder or someone else. As Todd thrust Josh into the ring, Josh struggled to keep his face a mask. *Shit.* He could feel the power radiating from Shredder now that they were in close proximity to one another. Unfortunately, Josh couldn't tell what Shredder was, only that he wasn't human.

As the announcer prattled on about both of their successes in the ring, Josh let his gaze move around the crowd. He saw Kiara first and kept his eyes moving. When he came to Octavien, he hesitated as he caught sight of a hooded figure behind him. Realizing it was a mistake for his gaze to linger, Josh let his body turn and continue his assessment of the crowd.

Josh took a deep breath and slid his robe off, handing it to Todd, who was on the outside edge of the ring.

"Be smart," Todd whispered.

The bell rang three times, and just like that, the fight was underway. Shredder wasted no time launching himself at Josh. As much power as Josh could sense on his opponent, he was surprised when the punches and kicks were not delivered with more strength than what Josh possessed. *Very strange.*

Josh found his thoughts drifting when Shredder's fist connected with his jaw. The force caused Josh to stagger backward into the railing.

"Get your mind in the fight!" Todd shouted at him.

Josh rolled his shoulders and tried to focus again on Shredder. He watched as Shredder came toward him. Straight right, left uppercut, straight right. Then, just before Shredder started the right roundhouse kick, there was a slight hesitation. Josh grinned and pivoted, executing a left roundhouse kick. Shredder dropped his arms. Josh jabbed a straight right hand. Shredder seemed out of his element, and Josh's next right roundhouse kick left him in the exact position Josh wanted. Before Shredder could regroup and get back on the offensive, Josh continued to pummel him with combinations of punches and kicks.

Josh watched as Shredder continued to stay off-balance. At first he had thought Shredder was faking that he was having trouble, but as the fight continued and Shredder did not recover, Josh wondered how on earth Shredder had been winning for weeks. He also knew that if he beat Shredder too easily without putting on a show, the organizer would be angry and might decide not to pay him just out of spite.

Scooting out of Shredder's range, Josh slid around the ring, staying just out of reach. He glanced over to Todd, who was frowning at him. As his eyes caught Todd's, Josh noticed the hooded figure was standing just behind him. Unable to help himself, Josh stared at the hooded figure. Suddenly, he could see bright red eyes. Josh gasped and tried to turn his face away, but he couldn't. A name was on the tip of his tongue, but he wasn't sure how it got there. He'd never heard it before. *Dariusz Sierzęga.*

As quickly as his gaze had been caught, Josh was let go. He stumbled to the side and groaned as Shredder's fist connected with his ribcage. As he fell onto the mat, Josh peered back toward Todd, but the hooded figure was nowhere to be seen. Todd, on the other hand, was frantically motioning for him to get up.

Just as Shredder was about to stomp on his stomach, Josh flipped himself up to standing and spun, doing a right roundhouse kick followed by a jab, then a straight right-hand punch. Shredder lifted his hands to block as Josh intended, and he threw a right kick, faking Shredder out before whipping around with a left spinning back kick.

Shredder stumbled backward, off-balance. Josh quickly followed up with a jab, straight right punch, and left uppercut to Shredder's jaw. The uppercut connected with Shredder's chin and whipped it up, causing him to lose his footing and land on his back. Josh grabbed Shredder in a headlock and held him until the announcer called the fight.

"Badger wins!" shouted the announcer.

Josh let go of Shredder and backed up, breathing heavily and desperately wanting to get out of there to figure out who Dariusz Sierżęga was. Unfortunately, Josh couldn't leave yet. He had to let the announcer parade him around like a trophy for everyone to see.

When the announcer finally let go of him, Josh was barely holding on to his temper.

Todd grabbed his shoulder. "What happened out there?"

Josh shook his head. He couldn't talk about it here. He probably shouldn't be considering telling Todd anything at all, given his friend had no connections to HAC or the FBI. When they got back into the staging room, Josh quickly unwrapped his wrists and shoved his stuff back into his bag. He pulled on a hooded sweatshirt on before turning to face Todd.

"Did you get my money?" Josh demanded gruffly.

"Yes, now…can we go?" Todd asked.

Josh nodded in the affirmative, and Todd led the way out.

"My place or yours?" Todd inquired once they were outside.

"We could just talk in the car," Josh suggested, not sure he had the energy for a long talk.

"Right…okay. Let's just talk in the car," Todd agreed as Josh's car pulled up and the doors popped open.

Josh climbed in first, then Todd followed.

"What happened?" Todd demanded as soon as the doors were shut.

"A lot of things happened during the fight. Can you be more specific?" Josh muttered.

"You got distracted a few times. It almost seemed like once you determined how easy Shredder was that you forgot the deal is to put on a show, not just demolish your opponent," Todd said.

Josh tilted his head from side to side considering his next words. "Shredder isn't human."

"That explains some things I noticed," Todd commented.

"There was also *something* there. In the crowd. Is that what you were worked up about before we started?" Josh asked.

Todd nodded. "Yes. While I was waiting for you, I saw red eyes under a hood, and I swear they were watching me." He shook his head. "I don't really know, other than I have survived here by listening to my gut. I didn't want you to go out there without at least a warning. Do you know what it is? The thing under the hood?"

Josh pressed his lips together. Of course his friend had to ask the question he wanted to answer the least. "I might," Josh whispered.

"And?" Todd responded.

Josh shook his head. "It's not something we can talk about. Besides if I'm right, you really don't want to know anything. The more you know, the more danger you will be in."

"I can handle myself," Todd replied tartly.

"Not against this," Josh said, squeezing his friend's arm.

Todd did not have magic. He was, however, comfortable with people who did have magic and had a much greater understanding of them than many did.

Todd handed Josh an envelope. Josh took it before pulling the cash out and counting it.

"Ten thousand," said Todd, anticipating Josh's question. "Not too bad. I don't think that's the highest-paying fight you've done, but it's not the lowest either. How do you feel?"

"Like I got lucky that Shredder wasn't using his powers," Josh replied, staring out the car window. "I had some weird news on a case right after we spoke, and I went on a ten-mile run."

He could hear the hiss of Todd sucking in a breath sharply. "That was beyond stupid," Todd chided him.

"I know, I know. I just got lucky Shredder was not as great of a fighter as he had been hyped up to be," Josh said.

"Or..." Todd began, then paused. "Or someone wanted you to win."

Josh turned to look at Todd. "Why would someone want me to win?"

Todd chuckled darkly. "Money, if they were betting on you to win…but there are other reasons. You're in the FBI. Shouldn't you be able to figure that out?"

"I wonder…" started Josh before clamping his mouth shut. "I need to go. Thank you for inviting me to the fight, and I'll see you tomorrow for our workout."

Todd nodded and opened the car door. "See you tomorrow."

When the door shut, Josh leaned against the seat and closed his eyes. "Go home," he told his car. *Todd invited me to fight, and then I was reviewing videos on Kiara and saw Octavien's message. On the phone, Octavien said he had information. Then there was the hooded something behind him at the fight. Too many of those things are happening at the same time for it to just be a coincidence. Which brings me to a question. What the hell is going on?*

When Josh reached his apartment, he tossed his bag on the floor and took a rushed shower. His ribs were mottled in bruises, but otherwise he had come out of the fight unscathed. Towel wrapped around his hips, he pulled out his work computer and sat on the couch. After logging into the FBI database, he typed in *Octavien Boutin*, and a list of known associates came up, as well as places sightings had been reported on the West Coast and East Coast. But there was no Dariusz on the list or anything with an even remotely similar name.

Josh knew he should just put Dariusz's name into the search, but he was hesitant, and he wasn't sure why. Growling to himself, Josh typed in the name *Dariusz Sierżęga* and hit the search button.

To Josh's surprise, the name was in the database. But the file was minimal. "Possible ties to HAC. Red eyes." Josh snorted. It said the things he already knew. Closing the FBI database search, Josh decided to try the dark web. It was risky, but perhaps he'd gain additional information. Just as he finished typing the name and hit search, his computer flickered, then went dead.

"You don't want to know what you'll find," Catrina said softly from behind him.

Josh shifted so he could see her. "I'm surprised you care."

Catrina gave him a scathing look. "You are a useful asset. It would upset me if you no longer existed because you were noticed by…people…you don't want to notice you."

"It's too late for that," Josh muttered.

Catrina clicked her tongue in disapproval. "It's only too late if you keep going down the path you're on. Forget about your meeting with Octavien Boutin tomorrow."

Josh stood up so he could face her. "That video is in the FBI database and my notes are on record. If I don't meet with Octavien, then Gerald is going to be breathing down my neck asking why I backed out of a meeting with a much more important criminal than Kiara Velez."

"Even if I handed you Kiara on a platter? You could take her in Wednesday morning," Catrina offered.

Josh considered her words. The fact that she was warning him away from Dariusz made him want to know more, but he knew he would have to be cautious. He wasn't confident that bringing Kiara Velez in would appease his boss, but it might give him some breathing room. He didn't know enough about Dariusz to know if whatever punishment Gerald could come up with would be better or worse than a confrontation with some unknown HAC member.

"If you bring me Kiara on Wednesday—tomorrow, not a week from tomorrow—then I will take her in. I cannot promise that Gerald won't order to me to set up a new meeting with Octavien, but at least I will postpone it," Josh stated.

Catrina nodded. "Fine. Just do whatever you can to *not* talk to Octavien for as long as possible."

Josh wasn't given a chance to say anything else. The vampire simply vanished.

Yawning, Josh glanced at the clock and was startled to see it was two a.m. already. Quickly stowing his work computer, Josh climbed into bed and fell asleep as soon as he was under the sheet.

TWELVE

ELYSE

It was Wednesday, and after a rough twenty-four hours on the ranch, Elyse was craving another quiet evening with her book. Several of the horses had gotten into some bad grain, and she'd been sharing a round-the-clock watch schedule with Mya, but it was still exhausting.

In the bedroom, Elyse reached for the book when something glinting on the ground caught her eye. Bending over, she realized it was her grandmother Brianna's emerald necklace that she wore last week.

A couple of weeks ago, Quinn had demanded to know if Elyse was attending the annual masquerade ball at Three Dragons. At the time, Elyse had been reluctant to decide, but now the idea of going and possibly seeing Josh again held some appeal.

"I would need a new dress. Maybe I can find one in green to match the emerald necklace," she uttered to herself. She'd only been to the masquerade once and could only vaguely remember it, likely due to the amount of alcohol she had consumed. Tilting her head from side to side, Elyse considered her options: feeding the horses early and going into Atlanta to go dress shopping to attend the ball in two weeks or reading her book.

She reached for the book again, deciding a night in sounded better than the drama of Atlanta, when her phone rang. She opened the drawer and pulled it out. *Uncle Albert* scrawled across the screen.

"How odd," she mused before answering, in a cheery voice. "Uncle, what a surprise!"

She heard a gravelly chuckle on the other side of the line. "Aren't I allowed to call my favorite niece?"

Elyse giggled. "I'm your only niece." Meant in fun, she heard her uncle suck in a sharp breath. *Shit…* the last thing she had wanted to remind him of was Tory's horrific accidental death on the ranch. It had happened when she was five, but she didn't remember much about her sister, though she had heard stories from her family members about Tory. What she did remember was after Tory died, her uncle stopped coming out to the ranch and always seemed to get upset when she was mentioned.

Coughing to presumably hide his sadness, Uncle Albert began to speak again. "I was wondering if you would like to have dinner with me tonight. My car is being repaired, so I can't come to you."

Her eyes opened wide as he suggested the possibility of coming out to the ranch. It had been sixteen years since he'd been out for a visit. The Uncle Albert she knew was a city person through and through. While he thought her stories of the ranch were amusing, she didn't think he had any interest in being on the ranch, not when she could just as easily go see him in a place he was comfortable.

"I got done with my chores early, so I can just feed and head out if that works…or if you want to do a later dinner, there are some errands I can run in Atlanta."

"A dress for the masquerade ball," he said quietly.

Elyse gasped in surprise and almost dropped the phone. *How could he possibly know that?* They'd been on the phone less than two minutes, and she hadn't said anything about the ball.

"We could do dinner at eight p.m. I'll alert the cook it will be dinner for two tonight. Then you'll have sufficient time to run your *errands*."

Elyse tapped her finger on her chin before responding. "That sounds like a wonderful plan. I will see you in a few hours." She debated asking if there was anything else, but after hesitating for a moment, he didn't say anything, so she hung up and returned the phone to the drawer.

"That was so strange," she said aloud to the empty bedroom. Sighing, she walked over to the closet and selected a long dark-blue lace skirt with matching lining and a shimmering silver button-up blouse. *Both modest and "appropriate for a girl her age,"* she thought, remembering a conversation a few years ago that had arisen when she arrived for dinner in Atlanta with Uncle Albert with plans to go dancing afterward. With her mind on dancing later, Elyse had worn a short green pleated plaid skirt and a sheer white blouse with a black under-the-bust corset that laced up the front. When she had walked in, her uncle had turned white as a sheet and had had the butler find her a large sweater to wear during dinner. After she was covered up, she had gotten a very heated scolding from her uncle about dressing appropriately. Since then, she tried to dress extremely modestly and would always bring a change of clothes if she had plans afterward.

Just over an hour later, Elyse stepped out of her car to the entrance of the Mall of Georgia in downtown Atlanta. Before COVID-50, the mall had been located outside of downtown Atlanta in Buford. After COVID-50, it relocated to be closer to the city center and the customers it depended on to survive. Glancing around before heading through the double doors, Elyse was assaulted by bright lights. She hated coming to the mall because of its blatant waste of electricity. Quickly walking toward the dress store, Elyse barely took the time to see who else was around.

She opened the door and found herself smiling as she stepped inside. Several mannequins were wearing gowns. The first one was silver with a high neckline, long sleeves, and a full skirt. The next one was a strapless black cocktail-length dress that was heavily beaded. Elyse ran her fingers under the edge of it, surprised at the weight. She wandered through the store, fingers trailing through the folds of the dresses.

"Can I help you, ma'am?" inquired a bubbly female voice from somewhere behind Elyse.

Elyse turned toward where she thought the woman was and was rewarded with a beaming smile belonging to a curvy woman of medium build with smooth olive skin and short cropped black hair, wearing a silk fuchsia suit with a pale pink shirt. "I'm looking for a dress for the masquerade ball that's coming up."

The saleswoman smiled, showing teeth, and looked at Elyse from head to toe, eyes lingering on her face longer than anywhere else. "I have just the dress."

Elyse followed the woman as she walked to the rack Elyse had already browsed and pulled a green dress off of it. Beckoning Elyse to follow her, the saleswoman led her to a changing room. "Try it on and let me know what you think."

Elyse stepped inside the changing room and quickly undressed before sliding into the gown. She was shocked at how the saleswoman had not only guessed her size right, but she had also gotten everything else perfect too. Elyse posed for herself a few times in the mirror and tested out the skirt before reluctantly sliding out of the dress.

She stepped out of the room. "It's perfect. I'll take it."

A satisfied smile on her face, Elyse waved goodbye to the woman in the dress shop who had helped her and, carefully lifting the bag so it wouldn't drag on the floor, wandered out into the main mall area.

Much to her surprise, the store had not only had a dress that was the exact shade of green as her emerald necklace, they had also had a large selection of masquerade masks and matching shoes, simplifying her task immensely. As she headed back toward the entrance of the mall, Elyse peered through several of the shop windows, curious at what were considered the hottest new trends for the people of Atlanta. A jewelry store caught her eye with a couple of pieces incorporating horses in gold. Her hand hesitated on the door, when out of the corner of her eye she saw a familiar-looking petite blonde. Dropping her hand from the door, Elyse took a few steps away from the jewelry store and turned.

A smile tugged at Elyse's lips as she realized that it was probably Quinn. Hastening her pace, but not wanting to run after her friend, Elyse followed her, until the woman paused at a store window.

"Quinn!" Elyse called with a wave. The woman didn't turn toward her. *How odd.* Just as Elyse reached out her hand to give Quinn's shoulder a squeeze, she turned. Elyse gulped and took a step back. This close, it was clear the woman was not Quinn. Elyse let her hand fall, face flushing in embarrassment. "I'm sorry, I thought you were a friend of mine."

The woman frowned at Elyse. "I do not know you," she said brusquely. She opened the door to the shop and stepped inside.

Taking a deep breath, Elyse clutched her dress bag for a moment before willing herself to relax and continue her way out of the mall.

Ring. Ring. Ring.

Sighing, she stopped walking, sat down on a bench, and pulled out her phone.

"Hello?" she answered, not checking the number first. All she could hear was heavy breathing on the other side of the phone.

"Hello?" she said again. just as she was about to hang up, the phone went dead. Raising her eyebrow, she shook her head. *That was weird.* She shoved her phone back into her purse, stood up, and gathered her bags before heading out to where her car was waiting at the curb. She opened the back door and gently slid the dress bag onto the seat before sitting in the front.

"Take me to Uncle Albert's," Elyse ordered the car. Silently, the car surged forward, merging onto the street, and followed the route to her uncle's condo.

Quinn is going to be so jealous of my dress, Elyse thought. Because of their different body types, Quinn and Elyse rarely wore the same style of clothing. *If that woman at the mall had indeed been Quinn, I could have shown her. Now she'll just have to wait till the masquerade.*

The car pulled into the garage and an older man with a neatly trimmed steel-gray beard and clear French heritage in a black tuxedo stepped forward to open the door for her. Elyse smiled and leaped out of the car to give him a hug. "George!" For as long as Elyse could remember coming to her uncle's, George had always been here, as butler and assistant.

Taking in his tuxedo, Elyse remembered when she was five and had asked him why he wore one. His response had been he liked the way he looked in a tuxedo better than a suit.

George smiled warmly and took a step back. "Good to see you, Elyse."

"How is Uncle Albert?" she queried as her car pulled away to park itself.

George shook his head still smiling. "He is doing well. He wanted to make sure you were greeted properly. You know how he is. Come, let's get you inside." George gently guided Elyse by the elbow toward the elevator.

As the elevator door closed, Elyse turned to look at George. "*Is* everything okay?" she coaxed quietly, knowing once they were in her uncle's presence George would not tell her anything ill about her uncle if she needed to know.

George shrugged and patted her hand. "He is starting to slow down some and has cut back his hours at the lab even more, but

I think he is working on a new project at home…he won't tell me what it is though."

Elyse's interest was piqued by the mention of a new project. Usually, George knew everything her uncle was working on. Something new and secret…*I wonder if Uncle will tell me what he's working on.* Elyse opened her mouth to ask George another question when the elevator door opened.

Uncle Albert's condo never ceased to impress her. Elyse stepped out of the elevator and into the grand foyer. Huge slabs of white Carrera marble sheathed the floor and walls. Large columns of black sandstone lined the hallway until the room opened up to a twelve-foot fireplace framed by a wall of windows. Sometimes the windows showed the glittering lights of the city. That night, they showed the sunset on a beach near Savannah, Georgia.

She took several strides toward the windows showing the beach before she noticed her uncle standing in the shadows by one of the columns. Eyebrow raised, she changed directions and walked toward him.

"Uncle Albert," she stated.

A lean, wiry man with pale, almost transparent skin, a thin patch of white hair on his head, and a small white mustache smiled at her before closing the distance and wrapping Elyse in a hug. Gently, she hugged him back, sadness filling her as she realized how much weight he had lost in the last few months. Concern clear on her face, she opened her mouth to speak.

Uncle Albert shook his head. "Do not fret, my dear, I am fine. Dinner is just about ready. Why don't we go sit, and then we can talk?"

Elyse nodded and smiled warmly at her uncle as they walked arm in arm toward the dining room.

Two hours later, Elyse and her uncle walked into the library. The dinner had been fabulous as it always was. Her uncle's conversation had remained polite, but it seemed like he was holding something back. She hoped that he would talk to her over an evening scotch.

She sat down in one of the big wingback chairs facing the fire, swirling her glass and taking small, tentative sips.

Uncle Albert smiled at her with a tinge of sadness. "I know George told you I have a project. I suppose you want to know what it is I am working on this time, here at my house of all places."

Elyse nodded, afraid if she spoke that he would stop.

"Well, I am working on a project, but it's not really for the lab as George might think. I was just doing some research on our family, and it's not ready yet, but I would like to share it with you at some point. I think you remember from history books that Archibald Cornelius was one of the people who was working in the lab that was responsible for the creation of COVID-50…at least the COVID-50 that was wreaking havoc in the eastern United States."

"What do you mean the COVID-50 in the eastern United States?" Elyse wondered.

She watched her uncle grimace before responding. "I'm sure you know that with illnesses such as the flu there tend to be different strains. When the virus mutates?" She nodded, and he continued, "COVID-50 is no different from the flu in that regard. However, it seemed that certain strains were found in regional locations. This made it difficult to develop a vaccine, and also created some intriguing side effects, if you will."

Unable to resist the tidbit, Elyse asked, "What kind of side effects?"

"Magical talents," he said, voice getting quiet.

Elyse gasped and giggled uncertainly. "Magic isn't real."

"Are you sure about that?" Uncle Albert wheedled, his voice soft.

"Pretty sure…or wouldn't there be people walking around, you know, doing magic?" Elyse replied.

Uncle Albert sighed. "What has historically happened to people in our society who are different?"

Elyse just gazed at him blankly.

"Your mother taught you these things," he chided her.

Elyse shrugged, not recalling any conversations with her mother that would have related to this one.

Clearing his throat, Uncle Albert continued, "Very well then, I'll give you a history lesson too. Historically, in the United States and around the world, people who are perceived as being different—either because they physically are different, or they have different cultures, beliefs, or gender identities—have been persecuted. Even though on the surface everyone is now 'accepted for who they are,' many families still have vivid memories of the times before it was so. Having magic would make an individual be perceived as being someone different—an outsider, if you will. Many times, society as a whole decided that it was easier to mistreat people who were different than to make an effort to include them.

"As soon as it became common knowledge that people with magical talents existed, targets were put on them. Some, such as the government, wanted to learn more about the talents, experiment on them and use them for the government's own agenda. Others felt that people with magic were abominations and sought to find and destroy as many of them as possible. Organizations formed that wanted to create armies of magic users to go against the government and anyone whose ideas are different than their own."

Elyse just sat in her chair, jaw hanging open, hand drooping, her glass of scotch precariously tipped. She hadn't really believed Josh when he said magical talents existed, but now that her uncle was saying the same thing, she was beginning to doubt her beliefs. *Magic is just something made up, a story for people to enjoy, right?* She was still trying to collect her thoughts when she felt her fingers being gently pried off the glass.

"Are you okay?" her uncle coaxed with concern.

Elyse shook her head. "Yes, sorry...I just never realized that magic is something real and not just pretend. What is the project you're working on exactly?"

Uncle Albert shrugged. "I am doing some ancestry tracing for families who are known to have magical talents. To see how it has been passed down from generation to generation. It's just to give me something to do. The lab has been forcing me to decrease my hours, and I haven't yet found a hobby to keep me occupied."

"How far have you gotten on the family tracing?" Elyse inquired.

Uncle Albert gave her a thoughtful look. "Unfortunately, not very far yet. Maybe next time you come for dinner I'll be further along and can show you."

"I'd like that very much," she murmured. She was about to say something else when George rushed in, phone in hand.

Bowing, George said, "Sir, the lab is on the phone. It's urgent."

Uncle Albert sighed. "I'm sorry, Elyse. I had a lovely time tonight. Maybe we should try harder to make this a regular weekly get together?" Elyse nodded in agreement. "Good, then I will see you next week. Have a safe drive home."

With that, her uncle stood up and took the phone from George before disappearing farther into the condo.

Elyse stood up and stretched before peering around the silent great room. *I don't think I can recall a time when Uncle took a phone call, and both he and George disappeared.*

Shrugging and deciding that it probably was nothing, Elyse found the closet George had put her purse in and went to the elevator. Next to the elevator was a table with a vase of fresh flowers and a stack of mail. Elyse glanced around to make sure she was alone before picking up the letter on top. As she did so her eye caught on the family tree that was hanging on the wall above the vase of flowers. She set down the piece of mail and began studying the family tree. At the top was Archibald Cornelius and Renee Dubois, next was Albert Cornelius and Brianna Cornelius Hutchinson. *Archibald Cornelius? Isn't that the name of the man heavily involved in COVID-50?* Eyes wide, Elyse was dumbfounded by this revelation. *What does it mean that Uncle Albert is related to Archibald Cornelius? That I'm related to him?* More questions flooded her thoughts. But her uncle had just been called to the lab. She'd have to remember them for their meeting in a week.

She had a pretty good relationship with her uncle, so she was hoping he would be willing to explain more—maybe even why, if he was a Cornelius, that information had always been kept hidden. Elyse stepped into the elevator and decided that she definitely needed a suitable distraction from what she just learned. It was ten p.m., not too late. Tomorrow was Thursday and Mya had asked for the day off to attend to some personal matters. Which meant she had to do all of the farm chores solo, but there was nothing going on in the morning that she needed to be functional for.

Elyse was reaching for her phone when it rang. She glanced at it curiously and was surprised when she saw Quinn's number. *How odd.*

She answered cheerily. "Hey!" Just then the elevator dinged and the doors opened. Elyse stepped out without really paying attention to what was around her.

"Do you have plans tonight?" purred Quinn.

Elyse giggled. "I just got done at Uncle Albert's earlier than I had expected. I was going to call you when I got in the car, but you beat me to it."

"Perfect. Want to meet me at Three Dragons?" Quinn asked.

"Yes. I can be there in…fifteen minutes or so, if that works?"

"Sounds great. I'll see you then," Quinn replied silkily and then hung up.

Elyse's car pulled up as she was putting away her phone. Sliding into the back seat, she grimaced as she sat on top of her masquerade dress bag. She had forgotten she had laid it across the back seat. Grumbling to herself, she gently slid the dress out of the way before shutting the door. Her car darkened the windows and headed to Three Dragons without being prompted.

Elyse turned on the light in the back seat and searched for her bag of clothes to change into. Quinn would think she was crazy if she arrived in the outfit she was currently wearing; so would most of the people there, for that matter. Conservative apparel was not in their vocabulary.

She quickly got dressed in the clothes, grateful she had brought them in case her plans changed with her uncle. Usually, they would talk for several hours after dinner, not leaving her time to see Quinn or have any other plans.

Stepping out of her car, Elyse took a deep breath, rolled her shoulders back, and ran a hand down her dress to smooth it out. Tonight, she was wearing a simple but chic navy satin strapless dress with a sweetheart neckline and flared skirt that came just above her knees, matching strappy navy flats, and a shiny gold purse.

Quinn rushed out of Three Dragons, smiling, and pulled Elyse into a quick hug. They kissed each other on the cheek.

"Are you ready for some fun?" Quinn queried.

Elyse smiled. "Absolutely."

As the pair headed inside, arm in arm, Elyse glanced around to see if there was anyone she knew there. She spotted a few of their other friends and waved as Quinn led her over to the bar.

"Pick your poison," the bartender said with a raised eyebrow.

"White Russian," Elyse responded promptly.

"Ooooh, I haven't had one of those in a while," Quinn said slyly. "Make that two!"

The glasses clinked as the bartender set them on the counter. Elyse picked up both and headed for one of the tall tables scattered around the bar. She offered Quinn her drink before taking a small sip of her own, savoring the rich coffee flavor of the Kahlúa as it slid down her throat.

After a few more sips, she glanced at Quinn. "How have you been?"

Quinn smiled and set her glass down, waving a waitress over. "Two more white Russians," she said smoothly.

Elyse raised an eyebrow. Quinn usually wasn't quite this quick to order a second drink. "Is something going on?"

Quinn shrugged. "Nothing important."

Elyse took a big swallow of her drink and started coughing, the alcohol burning her throat. Face becoming bright red from coughing, she finally stopped, breathing heavily. With her eyes watering, she took a tentative sip, crossing her fingers that she wouldn't choke again.

"Are you sure?" she asked worriedly. Quinn shook her head. Elyse sighed. If Quinn didn't want to talk right now, she knew there was not much she could do to get her to talk. Elyse swirled around the last bit of her drink and took the final sip. Just then the waitress returned with their refills.

Elyse took hers and decided that to avoid choking again she would just take smaller sips. Quinn clearly didn't have the same concern as Elyse, and she drained her glass in one swallow.

Something must be wrong, Elyse thought. *Quinn rarely just downs her cocktails.* Deciding that maybe Quinn would open up if Elyse went first, she began to speak. "I had dinner with Uncle Albert. He is working on a new project, tracing some random people's family trees."

Quinn looked at her sharply before abruptly changing the topic. "Did you buy your dress for the masquerade yet?"

Elyse smiled. "Yes, I did."

A small smile formed on Quinn's bright pink lips. "Good. I was worried you had decided not to come…*again.* The masquerade is way more fun when you're there."

Much to Elyse's chagrin, the waitress came by again with another pair of drinks for them, but she kept her thoughts to herself. Not that she minded drinking. She just wasn't used to Quinn wanting to so quickly. Elyse glanced at her watch. She'd been in the bar all of twenty minutes and they were already on their third drink. If they kept going at this rate, she was going to pay tomorrow morning when she had to do farm chores with a bad hangover.

As the waitress brought their fourth round, Elyse decided she needed to get Quinn to do something else. "Let's dance!" Elyse suggested, grabbing Quinn's free hand and tugging gently.

Quinn shook her head. "I'd rather just drink."

"Well, I need to move around some. I'm going to go dance." Elyse gave Quinn a quick kiss on the cheek and headed out to the dance floor. Merging with the crowd, Elyse danced to the beat of the music. She'd learned long ago that she didn't need to have a friend with her on a dance floor to have fun. Everyone was here to have a good time.

As Elyse found the rhythm of the music, she found herself relaxing. Her uncle had caught her off guard with his mention of magical talents and then having to abruptly end their evening. The music was finally giving her a chance to let go of her questions and save them for another day.

A featherlight touch on her waist. Elyse almost missed it the first time, but then it happened again. Turning her chin slightly to peer over her shoulder, she was surprised to see Derek behind her. Momentarily closing her eyes, she decided to just dance as though he wasn't there. Maybe he would get the hint and leave her alone.

The song changed to a slow one. Elyse decided it was time to check on Quinn when a hand snagged hers, pulling her back. Elyse gave her hand a swift tug as she spun around to face Derek. "What do you want?"

"Just one dance?" he pleaded.

Elyse hesitated, not sure he would respect her no. Blowing out her breath, she gave a slight nod. "One dance and that's it."

Derek flashed her a brilliant smile and twirled her into his arms. As they danced, he slowly drew her closer to him, so their bodies were pressed tightly together. At first, Elyse didn't mind, until she found that she could barely move because he was being so restrictive. Elyse stopped moving, forcing Derek to stop too. Some of the other couples gave them nasty looks as their lack of movement caused them to bump into her.

"Let go of me," she demanded, twisting her wrists, trying to get him to loosen his grip.

"I need you, Elyse. Can't you see that?" he said, his mouth against her ear.

"No," she hissed. "What I see is a man who is selfish and only considers what he wants."

Derek shifted his grip on her, allowing her arms to fall to her side. She took a slight step away when he grabbed her arm and twisted it behind her. He pushed her forward through the crowd, heading for the door that led into the hallway with the elevators.

"Let me go," she snarled under her breath. She knew there would be bruises on her arm tomorrow. He was twisting it tight enough that she wouldn't be able to get free without hurting herself even more. They burst through the door into the hallway. He released her arm and spun her around so her back was against the wall, planting his arms on either side of her face.

"I can't ever let you go. We're soulmates," he said in a tone that made her realize he believed every word he was saying.

Elyse struggled as he tipped his head down and forced his lips onto hers. She tried biting his tongue as he forced it into her mouth, but she narrowly missed; instead, her teeth grazed her own cheek, filling her mouth with the coppery tang of blood.

"Hey, what are you doing?" shouted a baritone voice from near the elevators.

Elyse closed her eyes, praying that whoever was coming her way would get Derek away from her. When she reopened them, the owner of the baritone voice was only two strides away. She met his eyes over Derek's shoulder and gasped in shock. "Josh?" she blurted out.

Derek ignored Josh and unfortunately kept his focus on her. "You know him?"

"Hey!" shouted Josh again.

Derek, face red in anger, turned toward Josh, but Elyse still didn't have enough space to slip away from him. Josh, however, was close enough to punch Derek hard in the face. Trembling, Elyse stumbled over a collapsed Derek and brushed past Josh. A hand lightly touched her back. Elyse jumped and hit her shoulder hard on the wall.

"Sorry," Josh said, reaching under her arm to help her up. He brushed a strand of loose hair off her cheek. "Are you okay?"

Elyse leaned against him, trying to collect herself. She knew Derek was bad news but hadn't expected him to force her out of Three Dragons. "Yes, no…I don't know."

Josh laughed. "At least you're being honest."

"It has been a strange night," she admitted. "I should probably head home before it gets any stranger."

"Do you want to get a drink?" Josh offered, gesturing toward the doors to Three Dragons.

Elyse smiled at the genuine offer. He truly seemed concerned about her. As much as she wanted to go with Josh, she knew the best place for her was to go home and process everything that she had learned tonight at her uncle's—and hopefully forget the encounter with Derek.

"Rain check?" she replied.

"Sure. Just call me when you're ready." Josh gave her a light kiss on the lips before roughly grabbing Derek and escorting him back into Three Dragons, leaving Elyse alone in the hallway.

Taking a deep breath, Elyse headed for the door outside to where her car was waiting for her.

THIRTEEN

JOSH

Early Thursday morning, just as the dawn light was creeping over the high-rise buildings and reaching his apartment windows, Josh was pacing. His work computer was sitting on the coffee table, open to a map of downtown Atlanta. Yesterday morning, Catrina had delivered Kiara Velez to him as promised, and he had taken her into the FBI headquarters. Gerald surprisingly hadn't said anything about Octavien, and Josh had wisely kept his mouth shut. Kiara would continue to be interrogated over the next few days.

He took out his work computer and opened Kiara Velez's case file. As Catrina had promised, Kiara had confessed during her interrogation to committing all of the crimes they were charging her with, including selling the magical item, the Snowflake, that could hack into solar farms. He was surprised that she had confessed after less than twenty-four hours in FBI custody. Although she did give up Octavien Boutin as the source of the Snowflake and provided details on her three potential buyers *and* the last location she knew Octavien to be at, he had not been there. No one was surprised. Criminals like Octavien kept track of their associates, and if one was captured, then they made sure that the rest of them were impossible to find.

Josh had agreed to Catrina's request to back off from Octavien for the time being. Now he was wondering if the man would even be alive if Josh chose to reach out again, especially after the night at the underground fighting ring. He realized he had almost forgotten about that and the man—or whatever it had been—who had said his name was Dariusz.

When he finished reviewing Kiara's file, Josh shut it and was about to turn off the computer when he saw the file labeled Unidentified #00911. *There's no way. Or is there?* Once again, he found himself reviewing the file and then comparing what was in it to the very little information that came up about Dariusz. Tugging on his lip, Josh became lost in thought.

Blinking his eyes slowly, he realized that he had gotten sidetracked. He needed to focus on what was important: trying to figure out where James Valdez was so that he could make plans to set the second tracker. HAC was not a patient organization. If Catrina was going to hold him to her original one-week deadline, he had until midnight tomorrow or she would return to tell him he was failing at the assignment. He knew she had something violent planned if he failed and was hoping he wouldn't have to find out what. He was surprised that she had not pestered him about placing the other two trackers when she had appeared the other night to warn him away from Octavien.

His phone vibrated in his pocket. Josh pulled it out. "Hello?"

"Hey! I know we don't usually meet up on Thursdays, but would you want to spar some?" asked Todd.

Josh's eyes lit up. Sometimes he found that kickboxing was just what he needed to figure out a particularly tricky part of a case. Maybe it would help with Catrina's assignment too. "Sure. When do you want to meet?" he asked eagerly.

Todd laughed. "Is thirty minutes too soon? I'm about to head out the door, but I could waste time if I need to."

"Thirty minutes is great. I'll see you then." Grinning to himself, Josh ended the call and set his phone down on the counter. With a bounce in his step, he headed into the bedroom to change into his gym clothes and gather his gear bag.

Todd waved to Josh from next to one of the sparring rings. "I wasn't expecting you to say yes. Is something bugging you?" Todd teased. Josh and Todd had met not too long after Josh moved to Atlanta. By now, his friend was used to Josh using kickboxing as a way to clear his head.

Josh ignored the question and set down his bag before starting to stretch.

"So serious…work? Or is Patrice messing with you again?" Todd inquired.

Josh shuddered at the mention of Patrice. "I haven't seen Patrice since we broke up. She made it clear that she never wanted to see me again."

"A different girl, then? Or work?" Todd asked.

Josh considered his answer. It might make tonight go better if he could at least tell Todd something. "Both, I guess. The woman I've been on two dates with…she's now one of my assignments."

Josh glanced over at Todd and saw his friend grimace. "That's rough…and seems like quite a coincidence. I take it you're into her?"

Josh laughed. "You could say that." He stood up, finished stretching, and quickly wrapped his wrists before pulling on his gloves. He slid underneath the ropes around the perimeter of the ring and retreated to one side, throwing some punches to warm up. On the other side of the ring, Todd followed suit.

"Ready?" asked Todd as he stepped toward the middle of the ring.

Josh nodded. "One, two, three!" He ducked as Todd threw a high punch with his left hand and retaliated with a mid-punch of his own. Todd blocked and Josh dodged his next swing before doing a quick right-left combination that didn't get blocked in time. He then pivoted on his back foot and did a lead kick.

Unfortunately, Todd was ready for the kick. He bounced to the left and threw a well-aimed hook kick at Josh's abs. Josh pivoted to avoid getting hit but didn't move quickly enough. Todd's foot connected with his low back in his kidney.

"Ooof," Josh gasped, stumbling forward a few steps.

"Let's take a water break," Todd suggested. Josh nodded, nostrils flared. His reflexes seemed slower than normal. It had been a long time since Todd had been able to get him in the back.

Josh opened his water and took a swig, the cold water sliding down his parched throat. He closed his eyes, forcing himself to relax. When he opened them, he found Todd peering at him curiously.

"I didn't kick you that hard. Do you want to talk about it?" Todd asked.

Josh shrugged. "The woman, her name is Elyse. I wasn't expecting to want more than one date. Quinn introduced us."

At the mention of Quinn, Todd smirked. "Ah, she's one of Quinn's friends. That explains a lot."

"Maybe that's how she ended up on Gerald's list…because of Quinn." Josh paused, considering this information. "Now that I think about it, I think that over the years there have been cases that involve individuals also tied to Quinn." Josh stopped speaking. *How is Quinn tied to this? She must know something about magical talents if she is the link between several of my cases, or perhaps she works for Gerald directly.*

Josh took another drink from his water bottle, attempting to redirect his mind to the task at hand: a kickboxing match with Todd.

"You ready?" he asked Todd, eyebrow raised. Todd was just setting down his water.

"Yep!" Todd grinned at Josh. Josh grinned back, and they began sparring again.

The kickboxing session with Todd was just what Josh had needed to break through his mental roadblock with the trackers. As soon as he got back into his condo, he dumped his gym bag by the couch and pulled out his computer.

He brought up James Valdez's current case list. It appeared as though James was undercover on the west side of downtown, which meant his car would likely be there. He wrote a couple of notes down on a small piece of paper and then typed in Gerald's name. Usually, his boss wasn't working cases; he was overseeing things. But Josh had to be sure. If he had to place the tracker while Gerald's car was at their headquarters, then it would be almost impossible. Perhaps he'd get lucky and his boss would have a meeting away from headquarters.

Scrolling down the page, Josh was in luck. Tomorrow at one p.m., Gerald had a meeting at Smokies. Josh wrote down that information on a different piece of paper. The great thing about Smokies was that it was not usually busy during lunch, when the meeting was scheduled. Which meant there would be fewer people around to notice if Josh was messing with a car that didn't belong to him.

He shut off his computer and tucked it into his work briefcase. Standing up and stretching, Josh decided he should probably shower and before making his preparations to head out to where James was undercover.

Elyse's gaze was hot with desire. Josh tipped he head down ever so slightly, lips brushing against hers…

Ring. Ring. Ring. Josh's eyes snapped open as his ringing phone pulled him out of his daydream. The shower water was still hot. *I need to get my head in my plan to place the tracker or I am going to be in trouble when I get there.* He grimaced, trying to redirect his thoughts to going undercover as Diego—and before that, he was going to have to meet with Gerald. He had to report to his boss in person.

Thirty minutes later, Josh, wearing a black suit and tie, glanced quickly over his shoulder before opening a door to a small, decrepit building in downtown Atlanta.

"You're late. I was wondering if you were going to show at all," said a gruff voice from the end of the hallway.

Josh walked quickly down the hallway and into the room at the end. "Apologies, sir. I was trying to find more information about Elyse Hutchinson and lost track of the time."

Short and lean with curly brown hair, hazel eyes, and a day's scruff, Gerald Fernway, assistant director of the Federal Bureau of Investigation, was not a patient man. "Yet you look like you had time to take a shower." Gerald peered at Josh. "Were you able to get what we need?" Josh could hear his foot tapping.

Josh cleared his throat and handed his boss a file. "Paper, how quaint," Gerald said with a sneer, before skimming through the pages. "I see…so you didn't believe me when I told you that Elyse Hutchinson is the great-granddaughter of Archibald Cornelius. But it looked like you were able to trace the lineage, proving what we already knew. Wasting time."

Josh stayed silent.

Gerald continued, "It's clear that Elyse has no idea who or what she is. Otherwise, she wouldn't be wasting time with those horses. A lot is riding on your ability to convince her to join us before someone else gets to her first, like Hellfire and Chaos. The last thing we need is for HAC to get someone with her potential."

Hands behind his back, Josh kept his face neutral. "I will do everything in my power to convince her to join us."

Gerald walked past Josh and patted him on the shoulder. "You do that. I expect a report every week on your progress. *Email,* please. No more of this paper nonsense." He dropped the folder in the trash can and walked into an office, shutting the door before Josh could follow him.

Shaking in anger and trying to quiet his emotions, Josh grabbed the folder out of the trash and tucked it under his arm before stalking out. Slipping into his car, he muttered, "Go dark. Go home." The windows instantly turned black, making it impossible for anyone looking in to see anything.

I will go ahead with my plan to place the tracker on James's car and then tackle the issue of recruiting Elyse, he planned in the darkened car.

Josh tapped his foot impatiently as the elevator took him up to this apartment. For this undercover task, the stash of clothing in his car would not be good enough. In order for anyone to believe he was Diego, he would have to make more dramatic changes to his appearance than just a set of clothes.

Once in the apartment, Josh pulled out his laptop and logged into the FBI's computer network. Since Fernway had mentioned possibly transferring Josh's case over to Valdez, it wouldn't be considered too strange for Josh to be looking into where exactly Valdez was. Usually, a case handoff would happen in person to ensure all information that could be pertinent was shared.

Josh clicked on the agent map, hoping maybe he'd get lucky and Valdez would be visible. Much to his surprise, there was a square pin labeled "Valdez" on the map. There was also a pin for Fernway and about ten other FBI agents who operated out of the downtown office. Josh zoomed in on the map at Valdez's pin. He thought the location seemed a little out of character for Valdez, but then he wasn't sure if he should be one to judge a person he despised for the most part. They had never really been friends, although when they had both been in training some ten years or more ago, they had gotten along fairly well. Until…

Josh shuddered. Some memories were best left alone. Giving the map a thorough examination, he plugged the address into his phone and then logged out of the FBI site on his computer.

He set the phone back down on the kitchen counter before wandering into his bedroom, making a beeline for the closet. The good part about frequently going undercover was he had a well-rounded selection of clothing to choose from. He was just not sure if it was good enough to let him be invisible where Valdez was. Usually, being a white male with blond hair wouldn't create problems. Today, it would paint a huge red target on his back if he wasn't careful. Valdez was in one of the few neighborhoods where there was still a clear line dividing people by race. It was held by an organization run by a family of Spanish-European descent who had adopted the caballero clothing to remind the local government they were not under their control. Of course, Valdez fit right in with his Spanish heritage and fluency in the language. It was his first language, with English being his second. Josh knew Spanish, but he did not look as though he hailed from any country where it was spoken natively.

Thumbing through the clothing on the hangers, he selected a white collared button-up shirt, a light brown suit with a short jacket and high-waisted matching pants, a woven wool belt of red and white, and a wide brimmed hat that was tan, with a band of brown that matched the suit. To complete the Spanish caballero outfit he had a pair of black leather boots. He tossed the clothing and shoes on the bed before heading into the bathroom. Opening the medicine cabinet, he pushed down on the second shelf, causing the whole interior to swing open, revealing another full-sized cabinet behind it. There was a row of temporary hair dye, boxes of colored contacts, a stack of facial hair pieces, and more. He chose a bottle of brown-black dye, brown contacts, and a dark-brown full mustache.

Stripping his shirt off, Josh dyed his hair, then checked himself in the mirror, verifying that he did get the dye everywhere before washing off his hands with soap. The dye was a brilliant find he'd made a few years back. It would wash out with one shower, but the effect was good enough that he sometimes got compliments about his hair color.

Next, he quickly put the contacts in. They were more difficult because for some reason his magical talent made the contacts dissolve faster than they should. They would hold for about six hours.

Hair done and contacts in, Josh glued the mustache on and then got dressed. Doing a onceover in the mirror, he was satisfied he at least appeared as though he could maybe have a grandparent or great-grandparent from Spain.

Picking his phone up off the counter and stashing it, the device from Frank, and the tracker in a small leather pouch, Josh departed.

"South Peachtree and Eleventh," Josh instructed his car. His plan was to walk the last ten blocks so that no one watching the entrance to the community would get suspicious about the car. He was also hoping he would come across Valdez's car out there. Most of the inhabitants of that part of Atlanta could not afford to have cars. A select few were still known for breeding the prized Lusitano and Pure Raza Española horses, though Josh had never figured out where they kept the horses. He suspected the horses were a front for more illicit operations, but he had never procured proof to support his theory. The inhabitants of this community lived modestly, with many being able to afford moderate amounts of electricity because they didn't have the expense of a vehicle.

The car slowed down. Josh reached down to check the knife sheath strapped to his right ankle. He then realized that he had decided to not wear any weapons, relying on his ability to fight his way out if it came to that. Josh had a backup gun in the car as a precaution. One thing he had learned during his time as an FBI agent was that it never hurt to be overly prepared.

The car came to a halt, and Josh checked his pocket one more time, ensuring the tracker was in its pouch, before slipping out of the car. He shut the door quietly.

As he walked away from the car, he slipped into a rolling gait with his legs slightly bowed that was common for people who spent a lot of time on horseback. His pants were annoyingly tight around his waist, but if he wanted to blend in, then he had to wear this particular outfit.

Josh took his time walking the ten blocks, taking note of the lovely artwork on some of the walls depicting the Spanish caballeros working cattle with their horses, flamenco dancers, and the Spanish flag. When he was three blocks from his destination, he made note of the young girl around eight years old shadowing him on the other side of the street. He was fairly sure there was a teenage boy about a block behind him as well. They didn't seem to be alarmed at his appearance, which meant his disguise was working.

At the next corner, he turned right, and about one hundred or so feet in front of him was the old police barricade. Sometimes older FBI agents would reminisce about the drawn-out fight that led to the governor deciding to give up this section of downtown Atlanta instead of losing more lives.

Government officials had been given an official stand-down order fifteen years ago. Every year, they were told, "Do not go in there. We cannot protect you. The laws of Georgia and the United States do not rule the people who live there."

Yet Josh had found himself passing through that barrier, not just today, but twice before. Today, he was on business for HAC, but the last two times, those had been *government* undercover assignments. He took a deep breath, reminding himself of his task at hand and to focus on the present.

Oozing confidence, Josh strode right up to the barricade and through the gap in the middle. He could feel eyes on his back, but no one stepped forward to challenge him. Josh kept himself moving. He had expected someone to question his presence but found himself relieved when they didn't.

Keeping his face blank, Josh walked for about ten more minutes before halting. Valdez's car was supposed to be in an old parking garage about two blocks from his current position. The problem was someone had been following him since he walked through the barricade.

Josh heard a thud behind him and turned with a sneer. "It's about time."

A short man with dark, almost black skin gave a barking laugh. His outfit was black on black, allowing him to blend into his surroundings. "Did you think you would be able to come in here without me knowing, Diego?"

Josh shrugged, without answering.

"Why are you here, Diego?" the man snapped.

"I am here, *Juan*, for business that doesn't involve you," Josh roared.

Juan smirked. "I'll find out anyway."

"That's your choice. I'm not going to tell you," Josh said, turning on his heel and heading in the opposite direction of where the car was supposed to be. He made it about halfway down the next block when he got shoved from behind, causing him to stumble. Josh caught himself and spun to face his attacker.

"You're wrong. You are going to tell me your business," spat Juan. Juan slid two blades out of their sheaths and lunged forward, aiming for Josh's stomach.

Josh, however, anticipated the move and twisted out of the way, slamming his fist into Juan's ribs before spinning out of reach. Juan gasped for breath. Josh feinted to the left, then did a little hop and pivot before swinging his right leg for a roundhouse kick aimed at Juan's ribs again. Juan fell for the feint and left his side unprotected. As Josh's foot connected, he heard a sickening crunch. A howl escaped from Juan's lips before turning into a gasp.

Josh grinned maliciously at Juan. "I've learned a few things since the last time we met." Josh spat on the ground at Juan's feet before turning around and sprinting around the corner and into the shadows. He drew on his magic to help him fade into the building. For the most part, his magic was useless, or so it seemed to him. He could block his mind from being read by even the strongest vampires, was a *little* bit stronger and faster than most humans, and could sometimes cause himself to fade a little bit into his surroundings—if there were enough shadows.

Josh waited silently in the darkness. He wanted to be sure Juan was gone before trying to locate Valdez's car again. If Juan came hunting for him when he was in the middle of placing the tracker, things would not go well. Josh was glad it had been Juan who found him. Juan didn't get along with Valdez, so the odds of it getting back to him that Diego was back were very slim. At least, not while Josh was still down here.

Now if Mateo got wind of his presence, it would be a whole different ball game. Mateo Jesús Valdez was James's cousin and the leader of Arañas Rojas, the principal gang that ran western half of downtown Atlanta. Josh had seen several of the files Mateo had possession of, one of which included a list of active FBI agents, their descriptions, and any aliases they used. Not only did Mateo know Josh was not Diego, he also was personally responsible for the gruesome murders of two of Josh's coworkers. In a one-on-one fight, Josh felt confident he stood a good chance against Mateo. However, Mateo always had at least four bodyguards.

Josh pushed off of the wall and resumed his walk. He took an indirect route to the garage where Valdez's car was. The old parking garage became a dark apparition looming above the street. Josh tilted his head back to get a better look. The top level was crumbling, and pieces of concrete littered the street. The only entrance he could see had a gate and a lock.

Uncertain, Josh approached the gate, more cautiously than he had been walking down the street. To his relief, the chain and lock were just there to deter people, but they weren't actually closing the gates to each other. He reached out and pushed the gate closest to him. It swung open with the slightest sound. When the opening was wide enough, he slid through it and pushed the gate back to its original position, hoping to make it look as it had before he opened it. Josh slowed his pace, allowing his eyes to adjust to the dimness of the garage.

Directly in front of him was an assortment of vehicles. Most were covered in a thick layer of dust. Josh wandered down the row. When he finally reached the last car, he almost walked right past it. It too was covered in a layer of dust, but it was significantly newer than the other vehicles. Peering around the dim garage, Josh made certain there was no one around before he stepped closer to the car. He covered his mouth with his hand, stifling the laughter bubbling up. Yes, this car was covered in a layer of dust, but it looked more like someone had taken a bucket of dust and carefully dumped it over the car to make it blend in. The wheels, however, had been missed.

Josh confirmed the barcode before he moved up toward the hood of the car and slid Frank's device out of his pocket so it could unlock the hood. Precisely two minutes later, there was a soft click and the hood opened. Swiftly, Josh placed the tracker in the designated spot and shut the hood. Taking a deep breath, he realized his hands were shaking slightly.

Now I just need to get out of here, he thought.

He just barely made it through the gate when he got tackled to the ground, the wind knocked from his chest. He tried to roll the person off his back but started to cough instead. The assailant on his back was grinding their knee into his ribs. Josh gasped, trying to catch his breath. Finally the coughing stopped.

He heard a cold laugh from above him. *Shit! I know that laugh.*

"Diego, so good to see you again," a heavily accented voice said. "Or should I call you Josh?"

Josh tipped his head to the side so he could get his mouth to work. "Mateo," he replied coolly. *I wonder how he found out I was here.*

Mateo tsked. "You should really keep up on what is happening before you try to come into *my* territory. Juan works for me now."

Josh's eyes opened wide in surprise.

"You didn't expect that, did you? Times change. New alliances can often prove more profitable than old rivalries," Mateo stated. "I would think that as an FBI agent, you of all people would know that." Mateo paused. "And yet here you are."

Hands yanked Josh up so he was on his knees and forced to look up at Mateo. Mateo had a mop of curly black hair, dark skin, piercing green eyes, and a jagged scar that ran from his left ear to his right cheek. The tip of spider legs that belonged to the large tattoo that wrapped around Mateo's whole torso were visible under the collar of his white shirt and dark blue short-waisted jacket. Josh gave Mateo a blank look. He had no idea what the man wanted, other than to make trouble.

Mateo laughed. "I have waited a long time for this."

Josh opened his mouth to respond when a lightning-fast fist with brass knuckles connected with his stomach. The punches kept coming, right, left, right, left. Josh tried to refrain from reacting to the beating, but by the fourth punch, it was a struggle. Clearly, Mateo still trained, and whatever this was about, the man wanted to prove his point by conducting the beating himself. Josh could feel the trickle of blood down his abs and wondered if Mateo had even noticed.

The next fist that connected was higher up, at the base of his rib cage. Just as the second punch connected, Josh heard a loud snap, and he hissed as sharp pain lanced through him. Tears streamed unbidden. Mateo grinned even more and punched the other side in the same spot. Another sickening crunch. Josh felt his body sagging to the side. The pain was too intense for him to be able to hold himself up. Every breath was like daggers. He slumped all the way to the ground. Before Josh had time to react, Mateo kicked him in the face. Josh's vision splintered, and he blacked out.

Josh's whole body ached. Taking a breath, he gasped as intense pain rolled through his chest. He was sure he had multiple broken ribs and probably some internal bleeding. Taking a much shallower breath through his nose, Josh opened his eyes, trying to figure out where he was. His hands were bound behind him, and he was attached to some sort of metal post. There were also shackles around his ankles, although Josh was certain with the amount of pain he was in that there was very little he would be able to do to resist anyone.

Josh peered around but found he was having difficulty getting anything into focus. Mostly it was just fuzzy. Grinding his foot into the ground, he found that it crunched like gravel. There also seemed to be lines of raised platforms that were on a slight angle and about eight feet in the air. The platforms were in uniform rows.

Think, Josh, think, he reprimanded himself. He might not be able to see in as much detail as usual, but he was familiar with Atlanta and the surrounding areas. The presence of the platforms ruled out him being in a rural area, like Jackson County, or even in downtown Atlanta. Which left just one other place he could be. "The solar farm."

He jumped, not realizing he had spoken out loud, and instantly regretted moving at all. *There's only one reason they would bring me here,* he thought.

Josh heard a loud click to his side. He slowly turned, keeping his movements slow to not jar himself any more than necessary.

Juan held a pistol aimed at Josh's head.

"Is this what it's come to then?" Josh asked bitterly.

Juan shrugged. "Business is business. I get my orders, same as you. This is not personal."

Josh barked out a laugh. "Not personal? I don't think Mateo does anything that isn't personal."

Juan gave him a disappointed look. "I was hoping you'd fight, at least."

Josh spat on the ground. "You were there when he beat me. How do you think I can fight? There is nothing I can do to make you feel better about killing me."

"But there is something *I* can do," a musical female voice said.

Josh kept his face as blank as possible. He recognized the voice from an undercover case a few years back that had taken him all the way up the California coast and north into Oregon. Terrance Basak. Josh wasn't sure if he should be dancing for joy or cowering in terror. Terrance was from HAC, which meant Catrina had sent her…but Josh wasn't sure which side Catrina considered him to be on anymore—friend or foe.

Terrance stepped forward out of the shadows. Josh could see her skin starting to ripple but wasn't sure if Juan was paying enough attention to notice what was going on. Josh was about to speak when a shot rang out. Terrance staggered back and a bloodstain spread at her shoulder.

"Shit," growled Josh.

Terrance took a flying leap toward Juan and in midair shifted into a massive tiger. Claws flashed in the air as she landed on top of him. Juan's scream was abruptly cut off as the tiger ripped him to shreds.

More shots were fired, and gang members came running from the shadows straight for them.

Josh tugged on his cuffs. Terrance was brilliant when it came to combat in her tiger form, but there were twenty people with guns coming toward him. Josh was unarmed and useless.

"I hope you have help," he shouted over the gunfire. Terrance roared in answer to his question, the firing momentarily paused. *Their mistake.*

Terrance raced through their numbers, slashing with her claws and leaving a bloody mess in her wake.

Even as the gang members were shredded, Josh watched as more filled in the lost spaces. *Mateo must really want me dead.*

Josh was surprised to find that part of him was worried—for Terrance and for himself. When he became an FBI agent, he accepted that he would likely die in the line of duty. It was one of the reasons he tried to not get too attached to people. Why he kept any romantic connections as informal as possible. That way when he died, no one would care. *Yet, now there's Elyse,* he thought. *Does she even care about me the way I care about her?*

I'm just a nobody. If I die, then at least I'll know Elyse will still be safe, he told himself. *But will she be safe, if I'm dead?* A small tidbit of doubt. That the world didn't need him. He was just another number. *My life or death is meaningless.*

A bullet hit the pole, causing it to vibrate. Another one grazed the top of Josh's head. With a roar, Josh tugged again on his restraints. *If I'm going to die, I want to go out fighting, at least—not chained and helpless.*

He heard an ear-piercing shriek, which could only have come from the tiger. *I'm running out of time.*

The air in front of him shimmered and out stepped Catrina and another woman, wreathed in fire.

Catrina was dressed for battle, *mostly.* A black leather corset, set with metal spikes, accentuated her tiny waist and voluptuous breasts to perfection. She also wore tight black leather pants with numerous guns and knives strapped to them.

The woman wreathed in fire was wearing a black long-sleeved turtleneck and black pants. Her blue-black hair was braided tightly down her back. If it hadn't been for the fire around her, she would probably be almost invisible under the solar panels.

A volley of gunfire was aimed their way. Josh closed his eyes, waiting for death, but it never came. He hesitantly opened his eyes and was surprised to find everything on fire. He looked for Catrina and found her smirking at him. The fire mage was bent over what he assumed was Terrance.

"Are you here to save me or kill me?" Josh asked in a monotone voice.

Catrina disappeared and then reappeared next to Josh, brushing her lips against his. She was careful to not push her body into his, as though she knew precisely where all of his injuries were.

Running her tongue along his ear, she purred, "I don't want to kill you…yet."

"Then what do you want?" he asked. Usually, he would push her away, but he couldn't muster the energy needed to do that.

"Am I not allowed to protect my investment?" Catrina replied, kissing him.

Josh felt himself sagging. Her kisses were sucking what little energy he had left right out of him.

With a snap of her fingers, Josh's restraints disappeared. As he sagged even farther, she did the unthinkable. She picked him up. Surprise lit up his eyes. This time he was the one to initiate the kiss.

Catrina pulled back first. "I need to get you to a healer before your internal wounds kill you." She gave Josh one more quick kiss on the lips.

Everything went black.

Josh opened his eyes and was surprised to find himself on a bed, pain free, in a darkened, windowless room. He sat up slowly, testing out his body, not sure how long he'd been out or if he had been healed.

He noticed Terrance sitting in the chair.

"Hi," he croaked.

Terrance smirked and offered him a cup of water. "Hi."

"Who was the mage?" Josh inquired once he could speak clearly.

"Oh, you mean Blaze?" Terrance asked.

"Blaze? What kind of name is that?"

Terrance arched an eyebrow. "I would highly recommend you keep any opinions of her name to yourself. Especially if you want to have full use of your cock." Terrance looked pointedly at his crotch.

Josh gave her a pained look. "I'll do my best to remember." He took another sip of water. "But you didn't really answer my question. Who is she?"

Terrance shrugged. "Who are any of us? I don't know if even Catrina knows how many people are in HAC. The organization is not just here in Georgia. It's all over the United States. Maybe even the whole world."

Josh sighed. Terrance was right, and figuring out who Blaze was should be the least of his concerns. He still had to place the last tracker on Gerald's car. If placing the one on James's car was any indication of how complicated it could be, then he was in trouble. "Are you going home now that you've kept me from dying or are you hanging around Atlanta for a while?"

Terrance shrugged. "Catrina hasn't told me yet. Besides, it's not like I can get back to Idaho easily, unless she or another vampire decided to teleport me there. Horses hate me."

Josh laughed. "Yes, I imagine horses aren't too excited about being around a tiger."

Terrance stuck out her tongue at him. "And do you have any idea how tiring it is on my paws to run that far? It's almost three thousand miles."

"You could borrow a car," Josh suggested.

Terrance started laughing. "A car? Really? You must not get out very much if you think a car would make it all the way to Idaho."

"Has it gotten that bad?" Josh asked, trying not to let concern creep into his voice.

Terrance shook her head. "I don't think it's gotten worse really, but a good portion of our country is very loosely controlled by the government. As long as they are meeting the supply quotas for providing food to the cities, the people are mostly left alone. With the big cities, such as Atlanta, few and far between, it would be too costly to for the government to tightly manage all of the small communities."

Josh heard a click of heels on the floor, followed by a rustling of wings.

"It's better for us that the government is not regulating those areas because it has allowed HAC to gain a much stronger foothold than they suspect," Catrina said from the doorway. "As to your question about what happens next, I want Terrance to help you place the last tracker. As much as I believe you should have been able to complete the assignment yourself, I have been informed that you, Josh, are not as expendable as I was led to believe. If you die, I will be executed. Therefore, Terrance will help you."

Josh leaned back against the pillow to give himself a better view of Catrina, who was not moving any farther into the room. "I don't see why you can't just put the tracker on yourself."

"Because," Catrina replied with a pause. "The FBI cars can unfortunately sense when a vampire—and a few other select creatures—are touching it, which then sends an alert to the owner."

Josh stared at her in shock. This was news to him, and given how many years he'd worked for the FBI, it seemed odd that it was just coming to light. "I've never heard about any sort of technology like that."

"That is because," purred Catrina, "it's above your pay grade. You don't really think that Gerald tells you everything he does?"

Josh opened his mouth, then snapped it shut, deciding he should keep his thoughts to himself before he got on Catrina's bad side.

Josh saw some movement out of the corner of his eye and turned to see Terrance standing up. "When do you want us to place the tracker?"

Catrina smiled. "As soon as possible. It must be done by midnight this Friday." She handed Terrance a phone.

"Everything you need is on there, including the precise location of the car at this very moment, as well as his schedule for the next two days. Now, I must get going. I will leave the two of you to get it sorted out."

Catrina turned and headed out the door before sticking her head back in. "Oh, and before I forget, Terrance knows where everything is in this safehouse that you might need, so feel free to help yourselves to anything necessary to complete your objective."

Then, the vampire vanished.

Josh was still gaping at the space Catrina had occupied when something landed in his lap, causing him to jump. He looked down and saw a pair of jeans, boxers, and a dark-blue polo shirt.

"You should get dressed. Meet me in the hallway when you're done. There is a selection of shoes in the closet. I'm sure you'll find something that will fit," Terrance said, walking out of the room and shutting the door firmly.

Josh slowly stood up. In bed, he had felt fine, but he wasn't sure if they had given him anything for the pain or if he had been fully healed. Carefully, he walked over to the full-length mirror. He set the clothing he had been given on the table next to it. He stripped out of the puke-green hospital scrubs someone had dressed him in.

Taking a deep breath, he stared at himself in the mirror. Fading purple and green bruises covered most of his torso. The darkest ones were over the right side of his rib cage, where there were also several freshly healed scars.

I guess not all the bleeding was internal, he thought. His leg twinged painfully, but it did not seem to have any visible bruises. Turning around, Josh peered over his shoulder to inspect his back, but it wasn't any different than the front.

Inspection complete, he slipped the boxers on, followed by the jeans and the polo shirt. Opening the closet, he found a pair of white athletic shoes that seemed about the correct size and a pair of socks.

Fully dressed, Josh opened the door to find Terrance leaning against the opposite wall, facing him. "Ready?" she asked.

Josh nodded. Terrance took off at a brisk walk before Josh could say anything else. They went down a couple of flights of stairs before heading into a dark room. Josh followed her, wondering why they were in the room, when a light came on.

Row after row of weapons lined the walls. The weapons ranged from modern guns to historical models, knives of various shapes and sizes, and even a few swords. Shelves were full of labeled boxes. Josh stepped toward one and realized that it was ammo. One wall was dedicated to different types of armor as well.

Josh whistled in appreciation. "This is quite the selection." He had never had the privilege of being in one of HAC's armories.

Terrance shrugged. "They have an even larger armory at their headquarters, but this is sufficient for our needs."

"Are you planning on going to war to place a tracker? I am pretty sure Catrina wanted it to be a secret it's on the car," Josh reminded her.

She assessed the situation. "No, I am not planning on going to war, but after what happened to at the solar farm, I am expecting we will run into some sort of trouble. Or I should say that you will run into trouble, and I will have to save you…again."

Josh glared at her in annoyance. "I don't need help. I've gotten myself out of trouble many times without anyone but myself to rely on. While I may not be able to turn into a tiger, I most definitely am not without skills. Besides, most of the thugs that we'd come up against are likely to either have a gun or want to fistfight."

Terrance clamped her lips together. Josh shrugged and walked over to the wall with the handguns. He selected one and then found a box of ammo for it. Once it was loaded, he tucked it into the back of his waistband, with extra clips of ammo in his pocket. Next, he selected two knives and straps, which he then proceeded to attach to his legs so they were hidden by his pants.

"I'm ready when you are," Josh announced.

Terrance, like Josh, had selected a handgun. But she had also chosen a belt full of some sort of grenade.

"Isn't that a little much? And people *will* notice you're wearing it," Josh growled.

Terrance smirked and pushed a small button on the belt. It simply vanished.

"What the hell!" Josh snarled.

"It's still there, but no one can see it. C'mon. Before you get your panties twisted too badly, we need to leave and lie low for a few more hours," Terrance said as she walked over and grabbed Josh's arm, leading him back out into the hallway.

FOURTEEN

ELYSE

Back at home Friday morning, two mornings after the thought-provoking dinner with Uncle Albert, Elyse decided to see if there was anything at her house that might give her some insight into her family history—and Archibald Cornelius.

Farm chores completed for the morning, Elyse spent a couple of hours digging through boxes in the attic and storage shed. Just as she was about to give up, she found a box in the back corner of the shed. Holding her oil lamp up high, she could make out the word "Cornelius" on the box.

"Hmmm," she mused to herself. Carefully setting the lamp on a shelf, she bent over to pick up the box and was surprised by how heavy it was.

"Is it a box of rocks?" she gasped under the weight. She set it back down, deciding to look at the contents before lugging it into the house. Gingerly, she pulled off the lid. Inside were stacks of books. She selected one and gently picked it up. The cover had a thick layer of dust on it. Using her sleeve, she rubbed it off, revealing a neat cursive script: May 2028.

Her eyebrow quirked upward in surprise. She hadn't expected to find a journal that was almost one hundred years old in here. She opened to the first page.

Property of Archibald Cornelius

Elyse's jaw dropped in surprise. *What are the odds…that I have a box of Archibald Cornelius's journals? I suppose he is family.*

Elyse quickly looked through the box and found that there was indeed a rock at the bottom. She picked it up and was surprised by how heavy it was. As she ran her fingers over it, she realized it didn't feel like a normal rock. Maybe it was some other material. *I will leave the rock here and just take the journals.* She set the rock down in the corner the box had been in and replaced the lid on the box before lifting it. It was a much more manageable weight now. Shifting the box onto one arm, she grabbed the lamp off the shelf and made her way awkwardly out of the shed and into the house.

Setting the box on the table, Elyse prepared a sandwich for lunch, then snagged one of Archibald's journals from the box and sat down at the dining room table with it. *The perfect distraction while I eat,* Elyse thought.

She opened the first page and began reading.

May 15, 2028

Today is my eighteenth birthday. Mom and Dad surprised me with a truck. The way they've been carrying on about us needing to save money to buy our own vehicles, it comes as a big shock.
I don't have much time to write now.but in case I don't follow through keeping this journal up to date I want to get a few things down.

In a week, I will graduate from high school.
As valedictorian, I'm supposed to give a speech.
I haven't written it yet. Maybe I'll just wing
it again. In August, I will start at Harvard in
their bioengineering undergraduate program.
Mom's small Arabian horse breeding program
is still going strong. Two days ago, her mir-
acle foal was born, using advanced reproduc-
tive techniques. He's perfect, black with four
socks and a stripe, just like his mother. The
techniques she is using are what piqued my
interest in biology and led me to discover
bioengineering. Strange, huh?

Elyse rubbed her face. *This is from ninety-seven years ago.* Taking a sip of water, she returned her focus to the journal. The writing was neat and easy to read. She found herself rereading the line where he said what he was going to be doing: Harvard and bioengineering. *Do I want to even know what that is? It definitely has nothing to do with breeding horses.* Shaking her head, Elyse's eyes found the next line. The words started to blur. She rubbed her eyes, wondering if something got in them. But it didn't work. The next thing she knew, everything got blurry.

Row after row of folding chairs were slowly filling with people in caps and gowns. Suddenly, someone stepped through her and sat down. Turning, Elyse gasped in shock as the face was vaguely familiar. Like a much younger version of Uncle Albert, it was a boy with a mop of messy, not-quite-curly brown hair, square glasses with green rims, and vibrant hazel eyes. The boy—teenager—was happily talking to his neighbors. Elyse noticed the gold-hued stole. As she gazed around, she realized that this person had to be Archibald Cornelius.

Elyse blinked, trying to make sense of it all, and discovered that her nose was all the way in the journal, the table a solid mass in front of her. *What the hell was that?* Hastily shutting the journal, Elyse thrust it away as though it were hot coals. The journal had more momentum than she intended, and it slid across the table and fell with a thump on the floor.

Elyse pushed back away from the table and paced, trying to digest what had just happened to her. Strange emotions washed through her. Curious but also nervous about what might happen next, Elyse grabbed a couple more journals out of the box, skimming through the pages. The last journal she pulled out was labeled 2047.

She flipped through the pages until she got to:

September 4, 2047

I'm a dad!

October 31, 2047

Albert's first Halloween at almost two months old.
Who knew being a parent was this much work?

The journal fell to the ground with a thud. Elyse stood up, needing to eat or drink or something. Albert Cornelius was Archibald Cornelius's son. The journal just confirmed what she learned at her uncle's, which meant she was a direct descendent of one of the primary people tied to COVID-50. Fumbling with the glasses in the cabinet, she finally grabbed one and was able to hold her hand steady enough to fill it without spilling. Braced against the sink, she took a long gulp of water.

"I should call Aunt Grace. Maybe she knows how this all fits together since she's the one who told me about the journals." Decision made, Elyse picked up her phone and dialed Aunt Grace. The phone rang and rang before going to her voicemail. Sighing in disappointment, Elyse left a message. "Hey, Aunt Grace. It's Elyse. I found Archibald Cornelius's journals and have questions. Please call me when you have a chance."

"I could just keep reading them. I might find the answers I want in the journals," Elyse said aloud. *Maybe…but they won't explain why no one told me anything about my family.*

An idea came to her. Josh worked for the FBI. Maybe he would know more or be able to help her find out. Even though he'd seemed a little off when he came to her rescue at Three Dragons the other night, she still found herself craving his company. She had to be honest with herself though. She was attracted to him, but at the moment she was mostly concerned with understanding this magical talent thing, and whether or not these feelings she'd had most of her life were not feelings at all but some strange kind of magic.

Glancing at a clock, Elyse cursed. It was nearly one o'clock, and she'd told Mya she'd be back by 12:30 to help work the two-year-olds. Mya was sure to be wondering what was taking so long.

Just as Elyse was about to open the door, Mya beat her to it.

"Hey!" Mya said in surprise. "I just wanted to make sure you're okay."

Elyse blushed. She didn't like to make people worry about her. "Sorry, I must have lost track of time when I was reading."

"No problem. I brought all of the two-year-olds up so we can bathe them," Mya said.

"That sounds like a great plan," Elyse said, smiling.

Every two weeks over the summer, the young horses would get a full bath. Not because they were dirty, but to teach them that bathing was a normal fact of life and good behavior was always expected.

Elyse quickly cleaned up her plate, returned the journals to the box, and followed Mya back to the waiting two-year-olds.

Later that afternoon, just as Elyse was washing the forgotten dishes from her morning meal, the landline rang. She hurried into the bedroom to answer it. "Hello?"

A familiar warm voice came over the line. "Hello, my darling."

Elyse smiled at her aunt's greeting. "Aunt Grace, I was hoping you would return my call."

"I am glad you found the journals. I think you are ready to discover what they hold. Uncle Albert and I disagree on that, but since the journals are at the ranch and he is in the city..." Aunt Grace let it hang.

Elyse could imagine her aunt shrugging, before she asked, "Is it true that Archibald Cornelius is my great-grandfather?"

"Yes. Just as he is my grandfather," Aunt Grace confirmed.

"How is that possible?" Elyse inquired, wondering how she could be related to someone like Archibald Cornelius without ever having known.

"Your grandmother was Brianna Cornelius, younger sister to Uncle Albert. When she married, she took the Hutchinson name, hoping to protect her children and grandchildren from any problems that could arise from people knowing we are the direct bloodline of Archibald's due to his ties to COVID-50." Aunt Grace suddenly gasped on the other line, and something fell to the floor. "I need to go, my dear. I promise we will finish this discussion soon."

Eyes narrowing in concern, Elyse wished she was there with her aunt to see what was happening.

"I love you," Elyse said, but she wasn't sure if her aunt had heard her or not. Taking a deep breath, she returned the phone to its cradle. *I wonder if Josh can tell me more about my family? An excuse to see him again*, she mused, liking the idea of asking him for help. Elyse texted Josh to ask if he was available for an early dinner and mentioned she wanted some research help. He replied immediately, and they made plans to meet at six.

Three hours later, Elyse pushed the elevator button again, impatient for it to open. After finding the journals and the brief conversation with Aunt Grace, she was eager for more information on her family and hopeful that Josh could help. Sometimes she got feelings about decisions she was making. Most of the time they were about ranch-related things, like which mare to breed to which stallion. Tonight, she was trying to direct her thoughts to Josh, curious to know more about how their budding relationship would turn out. Much to her disappointment, she didn't get any feelings about Josh. She shouldn't be surprised. They usually happened when she least expected it.

As the elevator approached the thirtieth floor, Elyse realized that she still didn't know much about Josh. On their last date, she'd learned he was an FBI agent, had lived in Atlanta for five years, and went to the gym for fun. Other than that, she also knew he was friends with Quinn…which could mean just about anything, since Quinn knew so many people and lived in Atlanta full time. Laughing out loud and startling herself, Elyse realized that she hadn't told Josh much about herself either. *I guess we both need to open up a little more.*

The door buzzed and opened, revealing her in a dark green mini-dress and high heels.

Josh flashed her a smile from across the room. "It's good to see you again, Elyse."

Elyse crossed the room, heels clicking on the marble floor. She smiled, debating if she should kiss him or if that would be too bold for a greeting on a third date. If her plan for the night was to get to know him, she should probably skip the hello kiss. Making a decision, she replied sweetly, "It's good to see you too."

"Are you ready to go eat?" he asked, stepping closer to her and reaching for her hand.

As he captured her hand and ran his fingers over her knuckles, she started to get another one of those feelings, this time of unease. Thinking quickly, she responded, "I'm famished…but I need to use the bathroom before we head out."

Josh nodded. "Sure. It's through the bedroom."

Elyse followed his directions and found it easily. Once inside, she shut the door and turned on the light, leaning against the wall as she tried to let her emotions settle. When she finally felt under control, she started to wash her hands. Then a feeling came crashing down on her, accompanied with an image of Josh's face.

Josh is going to betray you.

Gasping for breath, she clutched the sides of the sink. Feelings of terror and foreboding washed through her in waves. Even though the feelings were not new, the vision was, and she didn't like it one bit.

How can a person betray you that doesn't even know you? Struggling to regain control, Elyse washed her hands for a second time and reapplied her lip gloss before taking a deep breath and returning to Josh.

Trying to mask that something happened in the bathroom, she forced a smile, hoping he wouldn't see through it.

Unfortunately, Josh noticed. "Is something wrong?" he asked uncertainly.

Elyse shook her head, afraid to tell him what she had seen. "No, I'm fine. I just can't stay out too late. I have another important client meeting tomorrow," she lied.

Shrugging and appearing unconvinced, Josh snagged his keys and wallet from the counter before once again offering a hand to Elyse. Hand in hand, they walked to the elevator. Once inside, Josh turned to face her, searching her eyes. "You know you can tell me if something is wrong or bothering you, right?"

Elyse nodded reluctantly and changed the topic. "Where are we eating?"

"Mmm, I was thinking Equinox. Have you been there before?" Josh asked.

Elyse shook her head. "No, I haven't even heard of it."

"Really? They have amazing steaks. Is that okay?" he said.

The elevator reached the ground floor, and the door opened. Elyse stepped out ahead of Josh and shrugged. "I'm open to whatever sounds good to you. I promise I'm not a picky eater."

Josh smiled and took her hand in his, gently stroking her fingers. A tremor of desire went up her spine before she tugged her hand out of his, reminding herself firmly that she wanted to get his help and learn more about him, not have a romp under the sheets.

They headed down the hallway to a door marked Exit. They stepped outside and a brisk wind hit them, making her shiver. To her surprise, Josh didn't call for his car, and they walked around the building before crossing the street. She glanced over and for a moment was certain there were eyes in the shadows across the street. Josh tugged on her hand, reminding her to keep walking, and then the eyes seemed to disappear. They walked two more blocks, and then they reached Equinox. It appeared to be small and intimate.

A waiter recognized Josh and motioned for them to follow. They were seated at a booth. Josh glanced at the wine menu before looking at Elyse. "You do drink wine, right?" Elyse laughed and nodded.

When the waiter came back, Josh ordered the house wine for both of them. The waiter returned quickly with the bottle and poured it with a flourish. Elyse giggled and took a small sip, then closed her eyes, savoring the taste.

"Good?" asked Josh.

"Mmmm," replied Elyse.

"How was your day?" he asked.

Elyse shrugged. "Not quite as hectic as the weekend was. What about yours?"

"I had to spend most of today behind the computer doing paperwork," he said hesitantly.

Elyse took a sip of her wine, trying to gather her thoughts before she asked the question she really wanted to ask. After reading the journals, she was desperate to know more about her family. With the resources of the FBI at Josh's fingertips, he was a logical person to ask. "I was hoping you might be able to help me with some research."

"What kind of research?" he asked.

She opened her mouth to reply when the waiter walked over. "Are you ready to order?"

"Sure," Josh said, giving her an apologetic look before returning his gaze to the menu. "I would like the rib eye, rare, with the wedge salad…and the lady…would like a filet mignon, medium, with the Caesar salad, light dressing."

Elyse looked at Josh in shock, wondering how he guessed exactly what she wanted.

Josh winked at her. "Did I guess right?"

"Yes, you did," she murmured.

The waiter bowed and departed with the order. Elyse tried to steer them back to her previous question before she got distracted by anything else. "Since you are in the FBI, I thought maybe you could help me find out more about my family."

Josh raised an eyebrow. "I can probably help you with that. We can use my work computer at the apartment after dinner."

Elyse gave him a warm smile. "I'd like that. On our last date, you said you like to go to the gym. What else do you do for fun?"

"Fun? People do things for fun?" he said with a laugh. Elyse waited for him to stop goofing around and reply. "Sometimes I go out into the mountains to hike. Or just out for a drive."

Elyse wrinkled her nose at the last one. "Out for a drive? But our cars are automated. We can't drive them. I don't see how that would be something fun."

"You might not believe me, but I actually have a sports car from before COVID-50, and I can drive it," he replied.

"That would make your car at least ninety years old!" Elyse gasped.

Josh shrugged. "That doesn't mean it doesn't run well. So, what do *you* do for fun?"

"Well, I can tell you I definitely don't drive an old car. Dancing is on the list though," she said, vividly remembering their first date.

"Is that it? Just dancing and painting?" he teased.

She shifted slightly in her seat, unsure how to respond in a way that wouldn't reveal things she wasn't ready to share yet.

Raising her glass for another sip, she replied, "I like your place. It's convenient and close to Three Dragons. Perhaps we can go dancing after our research."

The waiter arrived with their food before Josh could comment. The conversation ended as they both dug into their steaks. The silence stretched on as they savored the perfectly cooked meat.

The filet mignon was larger than Elyse expected. After eating the whole salad, she was getting full. Worried about hurting Josh's feelings, she ate more than she normally would before finally giving up. Regretfully, she set her napkin on the table, picked up her wine glass, and took a small a sip, watching as Josh finished the last bites of his steak.

Letting her thoughts drift, Elyse jumped when Josh began speaking. "I have something else I want to talk to you about…"

"Okay?" she replied, not sure why he was not just telling her outright.

"My boss at the FBI would like to talk to you about your magical talent."

Elyse held up her hand to stop his explanation. "What do you mean 'magical talent'?"

"You have special abilities that you were born with and inherited from your grandmother because she was born to a woman who died of COVID-50 during childbirth," Josh explained patiently.

"I don't have special abilities," Elyse retorted. *Don't I? What about these feelings I get? That Aunt Grace has said Papa had too? And Uncle Albert mentioning doing research tracing families that have magical talents?*

"They may not have manifested all the way, or perhaps they're not as strong as my boss seems to believe," Josh responded quietly.

Elyse just looked at him. "So…let's just say theoretically I have these special abilities. Why is your boss interested in me?"

Josh plowed on with his explanation as Elyse's wariness continued to grow. The conversation last night with Uncle Albert, and now Josh saying almost the same things, made it difficult to believe they were making it up.

"My boss is the assistant director of the FBI. He wants you to join our team so that you can be protected by the government before Hellfire and Chaos discovers you."

She refused to react to the mention of the antigovernment group that was so often in the news. While she knew HAC was real, they also only seemed to interfere with people who lived within the large cities, not the farmers and ranchers in the surrounding counties.

Eyes narrowed, Elyse retorted, "Let me get this straight, the FBI wants to recruit me so they can protect me from HAC? Is that all they're going to do? Protect me? Or do they want something in return? Why do I care what HAC wants with me…and why is this all coming up now?"

Josh sighed and scratched his chin. "I will try to answer all your questions. Essentially, the FBI wants you on our team to help with investigations involving other people with magical talents and to find others like you. HAC wants to destroy the government and is a violent group. They'll do anything they can to get what they want. Do you remember the explosion in Raleigh at the capitol that was on the news? That was HAC. Forty people died in that explosion, just so they could prove a point that the governor of North Carolina signed a bill that he had been warned to veto. Now that the governor is dead, the lieutenant governor will get the position, and she is in HAC's pocket."

"I don't have a magical talent like you think I do…all I have are feelings, premonitions if you will. They're about simple things like what to wear or where to go for the day. Not anything major, and I just get them randomly," Elyse said in a soft, wavering voice. Glancing around, Elyse was on edge, concerned that if Josh and the FBI knew she had some sort of magic, HAC also knew.

"You are admitting you do have something, though…which means you might not have completely unlocked them. Sometimes magical talents manifest as latent abilities and can develop into more. Events involving extreme emotions can cause the magic to unlock," Josh said, reaching across the table to take Elyse's hand.

She snatched her hand back and clutched her purse, anger flaring. "No. I don't want anything to do with the FBI or unlocking my magic, if it's even real."

Josh reached out and grabbed her hand, holding it tight. Eyes flashing in anger, Elyse yanked her hand back again, picked up her glass, and threw the wine in Josh's face. "I don't want any part of you or your FBI plan. Forget I even asked for help figuring out my family. I want you to leave me alone." Elyse stood up and stormed out of the restaurant. Whipping out her phone, she pulled up the app to call her car as she stomped down the street.

When she was far enough away from the restaurant and confident Josh wasn't following her, Elyse took a deep, shaky breath. Her phone buzzed, telling her the car was two minutes out. She glanced around, realizing she went in the opposite direction from where Three Dragons and Josh's apartment were and that she was in an unfamiliar part of town. A chill ran down her spine as she noticed a dark shadow across the street. Her hands shook slightly.

She sighed in relief as a friendly car horn honked at her. Her car glided silently down the street toward her. Just as it came to a stop, rough hands grabbed her from behind. Startled, Elyse dropped her purse.

"Josh!" she gasped in shock, twisting around, expecting to see him. She realized the person was the wrong height to be Josh, but their face was obscured by a mask. Elyse struggled before her instincts kicked in, and she drove her elbow back and stomped on a foot. Her attacker's grip loosened and provided an opportunity for her to run toward her car a very short distance away. Unfortunately, running in six-inch stilettos was almost impossible. Elyse stumbled and the rough hands grabbed her again.

"Let me go!" she screamed, flailing her arms and legs. She tried to get away, but the hold around her tightened.

"Why would I let you go?" a woman hissed menacingly from behind her. "You're right where I want you, where Hellfire and Chaos wants you."

Elyse looked around frantically for anyone. "Help! Help!" she screamed.

A ghostly pale hand reached out to cover her mouth, and she bit it hard, tasting blood in her mouth. She spat. The next time the hand covered her mouth, it shoved a wad of cloth into her mouth first and tied the gag behind her head. The woman laughed.

Suddenly, Elyse could see Josh running down the sidewalk toward her. As angry as she was with him, at least she knew what he wanted. He also had warned her that HAC would be after her. She just hadn't believed him.

As Josh rapidly approached, the woman shifted her grip on Elyse, twisting her arms behind her. Then, she pulled out a knife and held it to Elyse's throat. "Don't come any closer, or she's dead."

Elyse hoped fervently that Josh had a plan as she watched him skid to a halt. He reached a hand behind his back and pulled out a gun.

"I'm pretty sure you don't want to do that. Her powers haven't been unlocked yet," he called, maintaining his distance.

The HAC woman withdrew the knife slightly from Elyse's neck, giving Josh the opening he needed. He fired the gun and shot the woman's shoulder. The knife clattered to the sidewalk. Elyse ran toward Josh, tears streaming down her face, body shaking. She tried to get the gag out but was unable to make her fingers work the way she wanted.

Josh stepped closer to Elyse and untied the gag. Elyse sagged against him. He wrapped one arm around her while keeping the gun trained on the HAC woman, who glared at him from the ground. "If you come after her again, I'll make sure the next bullet is in your head."

The woman slowly got up and took off at a run, disappearing around the corner.

"C'mon, let's get you back to the apartment," Josh said, quietly leading Elyse toward her car and helping her into the back seat. He slid in next to her, pulling her close. The door shut, and he recited his address to the car, which took them there quickly.

As the car came to a halt in front of the side door into the building, Elyse started shaking her head. "I need to go home. I can't be here with you and all of this," she said, voice quivering.

"I don't think you should be alone," Josh whispered reluctantly.

Elyse shook her head firmly. "This is my life, *not* yours. Just because you saved me tonight doesn't mean that I have agreed to join the FBI or that I ever want to see you again. Please get out and let me go home." She pointed to the door, her arm unable to stay straight because she was shaking so hard.

Josh hung his head in defeat, opened the car door, and stepped out. Instead of leaving, he turned back to her. "I am just a phone call away if you change your mind. Good night, Elyse."

Elyse turned away and curled into a ball as the door closed. "Go home," she told the car before sobs wracked her body.

FIFTEEN

JOSH

Bristling in anger, Josh walked into his dark apartment. The faint glimmer of streetlights was too far below to offer much light without the moon. Once the elevator door shut with a click behind him, he let out a scream of frustration. "I was so close."

A figure stepped out of the shadows toward Josh. "Yes, you were. To ruining everything."

Josh stumbled backward, almost tripping on the side table as Catrina Fox glided toward him. She rubbed her shoulder with a hand. "I can't believe you shot me."

Josh continued his retreat backward, desperate to get as far away as he could without angering her more. He stopped moving once the couch was solidly between himself and Catrina. Josh considered his words. He knew if he said the wrong thing, he'd be dead, which would only make things worse for Elyse. "You ordered me to make it believable and then held a knife to her throat. I didn't kill you."

"A bullet won't kill me," Catrina said with a glare.

"A bullet with holy water will," Josh retorted.

Catrina hissed, revealing her fangs. "You wouldn't dare."

152

"Except you can't read my thoughts. So, you have no way of knowing if your assumption is true or not. Care to test it out?" Josh replied, hoping he hadn't just signed his death warrant. He was right the vampire couldn't read his thoughts, but he had first-hand knowledge of the other terrible things she enjoyed doing to her victims. He also knew there was no way he could reach his stash of holy water bullets before she'd be on him.

Catrina turned away and paced, her skintight black leather pants and corset accentuating her perfect curves. Josh quickly averted his eyes, reminding himself that Catrina chose her appearance to lure her prey in. He learned that the hard way a few months ago and had succeeded in getting himself into this mess. Double agent. The FBI would have a field day and he'd be flayed alive if they ever found out.

"You must win the girl back. She is a critical part of our plans. Be warned, your time is running out. If you haven't delivered her in seven days, before the masquerade ball, then you will find yourself suffering a fate far, far worse than death. The clock is ticking. I will allow you two extra nights, by Sunday at midnight, to place the last tracker on Gerald Fernway's car with Terrance's help, but you will not have help with bringing me Elyse," Catrina informed him.

Shuddering, Josh wiped his clammy hands on his pants. The few seconds he stopped watching Catrina, she disappeared.

"How can I be so stupid?" he muttered to himself, regretting not for the first time that he let lust make his choices for him. An image of his first encounter with Catrina Fox came unbidden.

A young woman with pale skin and delicate features, shoulder-length black hair that caressed her bare shoulders. A white floor-length dress that he now realized should have been a red flag, since women wouldn't dress like that in the alley she was in. Instead, his brain disappeared, and his cock led him to that woman. Oh, it had been fun at first, until she told him what she really wanted. His connections

> *to the FBI and all the information he had access to there.
> The information that would enable Hellfire and Chaos to
> remain one vital step ahead of their enemies.*

Josh shook his head, blinking as the memory faded, forcing him to consider the impossible decision he still had to make about Elyse. Betray a woman who was a stranger and should mean nothing to him and his country for an organization he hates, or tell his boss and the FBI about the situation and sign everyone's death warrants.

What if I choose wrong again? he wondered.

Nine years ago, Josh had been given his third assignment involving tracking and recruiting someone with a magical talent. After his first two had gone well, with both individuals agreeing without drama to join the FBI, Josh had mistakenly thought his assignments would be that easy. His third recruit was supposed to be Ben Piro. The name had sounded strangely familiar, but it wasn't until he was face-to-face with Ben Piro that Josh discovered it was his friend Ben from Manhattan, who had set Hugo Everly's apartment on fire.

Just like his first two recruits, Josh went through his prepared script, and Ben flat out refused his offer, forcing Josh to get creative. Josh had even resorted to begging Ben and offering promises of wealth and status. Nothing he did would entice Ben. Josh came to accept that he could not recruit every person he was assigned. That these individuals were still allowed to make their own choices and have free will. He had informed his supervisor, Nate Frost, of Ben's refusal.

The following day, when Josh was walking past the park bench where he had met with Ben, he saw his friend. Deciding to just have a friendly conversation with him, Josh was in complete shock when the pathway by the bench swarmed with FBI agents, guns drawn. His supervisor was the one who handcuffed Ben, leading him away.

As Ben was dragged by, he snarled, flashing the claws that he usually held in check. "You betrayed me."

"No...I...I..." stammered Josh. To his dismay, Nate Frost stopped so that Ben could say whatever he had to say.

Ben, still appearing like a ten-year-old boy, even all these years later, glared daggers at Josh. "I refused your offer and now the FBI are here taking me away. How is that anything but a betrayal? Know this: I do not forget, Josh. You are now my enemy, and someday I will repay you for this."

Josh shuddered. *No, I cannot allow that to happen again, turning over someone I care about, not without a fight, not when they were unwilling to go.* Either way, he was likely going to be dead or wishing he was by the time everything resolved. He just had to decide if he had the balls to stand up to Hellfire and Chaos or if he was a coward.

SIXTEEN
ELYSE

Saturday morning, Elyse trudged out of the house toward Mya, who was standing by the pen where she just put her gelding. After a week jam-packed with activities including an attempted kidnapping and numerous trips into Atlanta, Elyse was ready for a day to just sleep in and relax. Unfortunately, being a rancher meant true days off were few and far between. Unless she decided to give up being a horse breeder completely, this was the life she was committed to.

Mya met her halfway to the barn and glanced appraisingly at Elyse. Elyse sighed deeply and waited for the questions to come. As much as she appreciated Mya's help, the woman tended to be nosy at times.

"Are you okay?" Mya asked.

Elyse shrugged and headed into the feed room and began scooping that morning's grain. "I didn't sleep well." Out of the corner of her eye, she could see Mya staring at her. "We're still going to go to Lake Lanier. I can't change my training schedule based on having one bad night. If I push back even one step a day, it can really mess up months of training. Besides, the weather is going to be wonderful for the next two days, which is exactly what we need for this trip."

As Elyse mentioned the weather, she got a premonition. If they left within the hour, the ride would be uneventful. If they delayed even a couple of hours, the likelihood of complications arising increased. Departing tomorrow guaranteed a disaster of epic proportions would befall them.

After quickly filling the remaining buckets with grain, Elyse loaded them on her arms and almost ran out of the feed room. The urgency to leave as soon as possible crashed down on her. Gulping a breath, she quickly fed her half of the horses in the barn. Elyse noticed Mya giving her an odd look as she fed the rest of the horses.

Elyse paused. "Come on, the sooner we finish, the sooner we get on the trail. Do you really want to lose the coolest hours of the day because we were slow with morning chores?"

Mya shook her head and put away the feed buckets before she snagged the hay wagon and went around to all the dry lots to feed the rest of the horses. While Mya finished up feeding, Elyse tacked up Honey.

Precisely an hour after Elyse's feeling, the two women were riding through field one and then to the gate of field two. Luckily, the two-year-old horses were congregating at the gate. Elyse and Mya both dismounted and tied their horses to the fence post before slowly making their way to the two-year-olds.

"We're going to take Shorty and Beatrice," Elyse said. Mya chuckled at the names, which were characters in one of the locally written comic strips that was in the monthly Jackson County newspaper. Elyse slid through the gate and walked over to a huge black-and-white pinto colt. Standing on her tiptoes, she got the halter on him without any fuss. She passed the lead rope to Mya. "This is Shorty."

Elyse pushed a brown colt out of the way and slipped next to a fine-boned gray filly. With the halter securely on Beatrice, Elyse led the filly through the gate while trying to chase away the other two-year-olds with the end of the lead rope. Successfully through the gate, she secured it, then tied the long rope onto her saddle horn, and Mya did the same. Then, they both mounted. Not wanting to spend any more time than they needed to, Elyse clucked to Honey, and they rode off at a brisk trot with the two-year-olds ponied behind them.

As they settled into the rhythm of the trot, Mya edged closer to Elyse so they could talk.

"How did Shorty get his name when he is *this big*? Are you sure he's only two?" Mya said.

Elyse laughed. "You probably won't believe me, but he was very small as a foal. The smallest of the year, actually. His mother is almost seventeen hands though, so the size is not a surprise."

The first obstacle of the ride was when they reached Brown Creek. Elyse slowed to a walk and gave Honey her head, and they crossed. Beatrice tried initially to fight the tug of the rope and then reluctantly followed them into the water and out the other side. After Elyse was clear, she turned back around to watch as Mya nudged her gelding into the water. Shorty followed along like an old pro.

"You good?" Elyse asked. Mya nodded. Elyse clucked Honey back into a trot.

For a while, it almost seemed like she was not riding with Mya, but instead with her mother, as they had done training rides like this with all the young horses every summer.

Mya broke the silence again. "Did your clients who picked ZuZu up make it home safely?" Elyse nodded, eyes trained on the trail ahead of them. "Are you selling any more horses I need to know about?"

Elyse shook her head. "No, none of the others are ready. They all need at least another six months. Some are closer to twelve. I get calls all the time with people demanding a perfectly trained horse or people complaining about how much I charge. I guess most seem to think they grow on trees and are a dime a dozen. Nowadays, there are tons of breeders, but most of them have no idea what they're doing. They produce foals that can be decent but aren't training them."

"How many foals are you expecting this spring?" Mya asked.

"Five. Although I am considering going above that number for next year. I haven't decided. The problem is that they are such a long-term commitment. It takes six years for me to have something to sell. Seven if you count the time from when you breed the mare and stallion. But they sell for such a high price…it's hard to resist such an amazing market," Elyse explained, thinking back to the moment Brenda handed her the envelope of one hundred thousand dollars. Though her thoughts also hovered over how hard she worked to be able to sell a horse for that much money. Elyse sighed. As much as she truly enjoyed ranching, she wondered if maybe the time was coming to give it all up. *And do what instead? It's not like I can make a living selling my paintings.*

Thankfully Mya stayed silent, allowing Elyse's thoughts to drift to the future and what she wanted do to with herself. *Shit…Josh, last night. How much of what he said should I even believe?*

Suddenly, Beatrice spun, pulling hard against the line, and tried to take off while bucking wildly. Elyse braced herself against the saddle to keep from popping off as Honey dropped her haunches and dug her hooves into the ground. Beatrice twisted and turned, attempting desperately to get loose, but neither Elyse nor Honey gave her an inch. Finally, after what felt like hours but was really only moments later, Beatrice stopped fighting. Sides heaving and lathered in foamy sweat, the two-year-old filly stood, head hanging in defeat.

"That was some spectacular riding!" Mya spoke with awe in her voice.

Elyse reached back for her canteen and took a long sip. "Every so often, one of the two-year-olds will try to get away like Beatrice did. It never works, but they seem to feel obligated to try. I'm sure you can imagine it's a little more challenging to handle when you're ponying two of them at the same time."

"Have you ever lost one?" Mya asked uncertainly.

Elyse laughed. "Sort of. I've had them get loose, but they're young and unsure of themselves. Once they have their moment of freedom, they tend to decide its safer with me than out there," she said, sweeping her hands to indicate the vast forest around them. At that precise moment they heard the yips of a pack of coyotes.

"I know you mentioned before that this is quite the challenging trail for ponying youngsters. So far, we've crossed one creek and a few hills but nothing too remarkable. Can you tell me more about where we're headed?" Mya requested.

"Sure." Elyse nodded. "We have to cross the Oconee River twice to get there, and the second crossing it gets pretty deep. I won't do it with the yearlings, so this is Beatrice and Shorty's first time doing a deep crossing, and it can get a little hairy. Horses can swim. They just don't always want to."

"I can't believe you'd attempt crossing the river with two on your own," Mya responded.

Elyse shrugged. "I just do it. This is what I learned from my mom and how my family has been training the young horses for longer than my lifetime. Our methods work, as you know, in creating well-behaved horses anyone can ride to any destination. At some point, I think my grandmother realized the earlier we get the horses used to going through rivers, the more accepting they are of it. Usually with a total of four river crossings, by the time I return from one of these trips, the young horse is completely comfortable going through water." Elyse paused to take a breath. "I don't always have the choice to bring help with me. Sometimes I get a feeling that going a certain route is going to be good or bad. If I follow those feelings, nothing bad ever happens. It's when I ignore them that I get into trouble. Like the time my mother and I got caught in the middle of a giant thunderstorm. The river swelled so high we had to camp for two nights until the water dropped to a crossable level with a much slower flow."

Looking at Elyse, Mya said skeptically, "You get feelings?"

Elyse shrugged nonchalantly. "Yes…but not just about where to go on a trail ride. I also get them when making breeding decisions." She glanced toward Mya to see if she was going to question her further but saw Mya gazing blankly into the trees and made the decision to drop the discussion. She welcomed the silence because it allowed her to listen to the whisper of wings as a hawk soared overhead, the buzzing of bees in a nearby tree, and the distant sound of the Oconee River as they drew closer to it.

The rest of the ride to the lake was uneventful. The horses were all tied to trees on long ropes, allowing them to graze and have access to the water. Elyse took a sip of water before stretching. Her arm brushed her saddle bag and the edge of something. *The journal.* Elyse gave Mya a glance, deciding there wouldn't be any harm in reading one or two journal entries. They needed a break just as much as the young horses did before going back.

Elyse tugged the journal out of the bag and into her lap.

"What's that?" asked Mya.

"A family member's journal," Elyse explained.

Mya nodded and lay back down to presumably continue napping.

Elyse still wasn't sure what had happened the last time she read the journal. But she had been reluctant to go back to reading it. *If I want to know more about my family, the journals very well might have the answers. I just need to be brave enough to read them.*

She flipped through the journal looking for the entry after the one she read last time. "Hmm…May and then November, I guess he did not write very often."

November 1, 2028

I have made a lot of new friends at
Harvard. The core classes are rather boring.
I did join the soccer club. Our first game is
next week.
It has been eight years since the COVID-
19 virus wreaked havoc on the world. Three
years since the economy and supply production
returned to normal. Auto manufacturers are
continuing to push forward toward exclusively
electric vehicles and phase out any gas- or
diesel-powered vehicles.
The truck Mom and Dad got me is electric.
It's kind of cool but also kind of strange. It
can tow decently. Although that's not particularly useful here at school, I have been able to
help friends with transporting bulky items. It
has made me quite popular.

Elyse laughed out loud, startling herself. Glancing at her watch, relief flooded her when she realized she'd only been reading for about five minutes. *I wonder what it would have been like to have a car at eighteen. To not have your own transportation and be dependent upon others for so long. I mean, I got my first horse at six, and by the time I was seven I was allowed to ride over to Jessica's house without supervision.* She continued to mull over how different life was almost one hundred years ago.

"Let's see what happened next," she said to herself. There was evidence of a few pages having been ripped out at some point and a couple of blank pages. Not wanting to dwell on her ancestor's journaling etiquette, Elyse finally found the next journal entry that had more than a date and a doodle.

June 1, 2032

I did it! Yesterday I graduated from Harvard with my undergraduate degree in bioengineering. Johns Hopkins is allowing me to do a deferred entry. Instead of starting immediately in the fall, I get a year off to do a paid internship. There is a lab close to home in Jefferson that I have set up an internship at.

I'll get a year of hands-on work, and then I will start my MD-PhD program in biomedical engineering. I know, this is not originally the path I was intending to go down. A dual degree of all things. After what I learned during undergrad, I feel like this path will let me have the greatest impact. I mean, look at everything we have learned from COVID-19. What If I could prevent a disease like that from happening? Or at the very least develop the ability to treat it more quickly?

I must admit there are days where it feels insane to think I'm going to have another eight years of school. But in 2041, I will be able to do my own research. Instead of having someone telling me what I should be studying, I will be able to make my own choices.

My little sister seems to also have some big ambitions, although not in the same field. Kate is in her junior year at Princeton in mechanical engineering. Right now, she's talking about also pursuing some sort of dual degree for her graduate program, but combining business with engineering. I guess we'll see if she sticks to that.

Elyse was closing the journal when it began to blur. Taking a deep breath, she tried to clear her mind. *I'm just tired.* To prove her point, Elyse yawned, not once but twice. Then, everything faded out.

> *Elyse found herself standing in the pasture with part of the creek at the bottom. She could hear young children laughing and the pounding of hooves. Moments later, a black Arabian mare with a small stripe down her face and four white socks came galloping down the hill toward the creek. A young boy who could have been no more than six and a little girl were on the mare's back. There was no halter, no saddle, nothing, just the two kids and the mare. As Elyse continued to watch, she noticed that although the mare was galloping, one ear was cocked back, and her attention was on her two passengers. As the little girl started to slide one way, the mare shifted her hind end to help the girl balance back out.*
>
> *The threesome reached flat bottom, and the mare slowly decreased her speed, allowing her passengers to stay balanced.*

Elyse's eyes got wide as she realized, I know this mare. *She opened her mouth to say something, then everything went black.*

When her surroundings regained color, Elyse was back on the grass at the side of the lake. Mya was snoring and the horses were quietly grazing.

Filled with confusion, Elyse nervously rubbed her face. "What is happening to me?" she whispered. "Maybe I should call Aunt Grace when we get back." *Or...her aunt would just tell her she's being silly.* There was no such thing as magic objects, and she was just letting her imagination run away with her. Exhaustion could do things like that to people.

Elyse and Mya rode back into the barnyard of the ranch at just about six p.m., later than she had originally planned, but still not the longest time that particular ride had taken. Together, they dismounted and tied their riding horses to the hitching post before untying Beatrice and Shorty.

"Let's give them a quick rubdown and a hot mash in the barn tonight. We can put them back out in pasture with their friends tomorrow," Elyse suggested.

Mya nodded in agreement and led Shorty into the barn. Elyse followed closely behind with Beatrice, who was dragging her hooves along the ground as though they weighed too much. Rolling her eyes at the silly filly, Elyse reached over to grab a handful of towels from the stack before leading Beatrice into the stall at the very end of the barn. Once in the stall, Elyse expertly rubbed down the filly. Glancing up, she made sure Mya was doing the same with Shorty. Beatrice leaned into her hands, thoroughly enjoying the attention. Elyse gave her one last pat before sliding the halter off and stepping into the aisleway.

Elyse glanced over to check Mya's progress before heading back down to the feed room to start preparing the hot mash. The door opened behind Elyse, and Mya set out the feed buckets for the other horses. Stretching her arms and rolling her head, trying to get her body to loosen up, Elyse sighed.

"If you want to take over the grain, I can do the stalls really quick," Mya offered, covering her mouth to stifle a yawn.

Elyse yawned too. "Sure." She retrieved the feed scoop from one of the bins and started filling the rest of the buckets. In the aisleway, she heard Mya put the pitchfork in the wheelbarrow and rattle down to the first stall. Since most of the horses were still outside in anticipation of their late return, the stalls should be fast, since they wouldn't have to maneuver around the horses.

Elyse dropped the last bucket on the stack just as Mya returned with an empty wheelbarrow.

"Whew, done for the day!" Mya said tiredly.

Elyse smiled. "Thank you for staying to help. I'm going to go take a shower and go to sleep."

Mya sighed and slowly walked over to her gelding, still tied to the hitching post. She still had to ride thirty minutes home before she could crash into bed.

Turning her attention toward the house, Elyse trudged up the path, struggling to keep her eyes open. Between the events of last night and her crazy idea to still take the two-year-olds to Lake Lanier, she was in desperate need of a good night's sleep.

The next morning, Elyse decided maybe she should have Jessica come help her go through the journals. Then, she'd have someone she knew almost as well as she knew herself there to tell her if any funny business was happening when she was reading the journals.

Picking up the phone, she started to dial Jessica's parents' house, then realized that her friend had a new number. She hung up the phone and reentered the number. Crossing her fingers that Jessica hadn't left for the ranch yet, Elyse was about to give up hope.

"Hello?" Jessica's voice came over the line.

"Hey, Jessica! I was wondering if maybe on your midday break you wanted to come over. I thought you might be able to help me look at some of the journals," Elyse asked hopefully.

"Sure! Besides your house stays cooler than ours does. I'd rather be at your place for my break," Jessica said happily.

"Great. I'll see you in a few hours! I'll make us lunch too," Elyse said, grinning and hanging up.

Elyse was grateful Jessica had agreed to help her go through the journals, certain that with another person helping her she would hopefully find more useful information and that she wouldn't hallucinate again. She was almost done making their lunch. She had decided to surprise her friend with steak and eggs.

"It smells amazing!" Jessica exclaimed as she walked into the house.

"I thought you'd like a treat," Elyse said, grinning over her shoulder. "I was thinking maybe you could take the journal I've been going through, and I'll try one of the later ones. If you find anything other than a description of whatever class he is taking that could be useful, just let me know."

Jessica smiled. "Sure thing."

They sat in companionable silence with the occasional sound of pages turning.

"Oh, listen to this," Jessica said excitedly.

October 3, 2036

> I finally got the guts to ask my professor the question I've had at the back of my mind. What happened with the COVID-19 virus? The answer I got is that it is ancient history and to move on. I know I was just a kid at the time, but I remember the missed school, everyone getting sick, and people dying. I don't get how society can just pretend like it never happened.

"So, his question was dismissed. Like they didn't care about it because it was in the past?" Elyse asked incredulously.

Jessica nodded. "It seems that way. I guess now we know it was their carelessness we must thank for the COVID-50 mess."

Elyse turned her attention back to the journal.

"I think I found something…maybe," she said a few minutes later.

January 3, 2048

> I was in a conference today with the board of directors at the lab. You know what came

up? COVID-19. I was shocked. Not only did it come up, but they are also asking me to investigate it. I am excited. They believe that some of the discoveries I made while at Johns Hopkins could help further our understanding of COVID-19 and hopefully aid in preventing a similar disease from having as large of an impact on our country and the world.
 Renee is concerned.
 I also get a new high-tech lab dedicated to the COVID-19 research and class IV safety protocols. I was impressed when they gave me the initial job offer and a new lab, and now I get an even better lab.

Elyse looked up at Jessica's face, when it began to fade. She was apprehensive about this happening again, when her friend was there, and she still had no understanding of what was going on. She found herself bracing for whatever she would see.

A man in his late thirties with short brown hair, hazel eyes, and a day's stubble covering his face was bent over a microscope next to a woman. The woman was average in stature with light brown hair. She glanced up, seeming to look right at Elyse, and Elyse discovered the woman's eyes were green, the same shade of green as hers. Their shoulders touched in a way that made it seem as though they were more than just coworkers.

"What do you think, Renee?" the man asked.

"We did it, Archie! We really did it!" Renee replied, excitement in her voice.

A cough behind them made all three turn toward the door. A tall, elegant man in a tailored navy suit with short white hair and a neatly trimmed white beard arched an eyebrow.

"Good evening, sir," Archie said with a bow. Elyse was shocked at the formality. Who was this man?

"What is it that you did?" the elegant man asked.

"Mr. Davidson, we have confirmed that we successfully identified when the COVID-19 virus mutates and what steps can be taken to prevent it from mutating," Renee explained.

"Excellent news. The board will be thrilled with the progress," Mr. Davidson replied. "Don't stay too late! I know little Albert misses you both."

Renee nodded in thanks, and as Mr. Davidson departed, the room faded away.

Elyse blinked and saw Jessica staring at her. "What's wrong?" Elyse asked in alarm.

Jessica opened and shut her mouth a few times before she could get the words out. "You faded. Faded till I could see through you."

"I did what?" Elyse asked, confused.

"You faded…like you weren't completely here. I don't know how else to explain it," Jessica said.

"You're sure?" Elyse asked.

Nodding, Jessica replied, "Yes, I am sure. Is there anything you need to tell me?"

Elyse took a deep breath. "I don't know. The past couple times I have read the journals some strange things have happened, but I just thought I was imagining it."

"Strange how?" Jessica inquired.

"I have seen things…Archibald Cornelius graduating. Two kids galloping down one of my pastures on that mare," Elyse pointed to the photograph of Silk, "but they were bareback with no tack at all."

"That sounds crazy," Jessica replied quietly.

"I *know*! That's why I didn't say anything, because people will think I'm crazy," Elyse said, throwing up her hands. Tugging on her lip, she considered her next words carefully. "What if I told you that recently not just one, but several people told me that magic exists in our world and that I possess it in the form of a magical talent?"

Jessica gave her an appraising look. "Well, my first thought is that you're completely insane. But my second one is that magic would be a logical explanation for why you seem to fade out when you read the journal."

Elyse raised her eyebrow. "You're ready to just believe magic exists and isn't a fairy story?"

Jessica shrugged. "I mean, it sounds strange, but I can't think of any other reason why you would have just faded. I mean, it's not like you were doing some sort of science experiment at the time or messing with the lighting in the room. Do you remember my Grams?"

Elyse nodded. "I remember what she looked like."

"Well, Grams would sometimes tell me this story. About how one year Bri came out to the ranch a week before the calves were due. She walked around the pasture with a marker and drew Xs on all of the cows in blue or pink. Every cow she marked with blue had a bull calf, and every one marked with pink had a heifer. I always thought it had been a made-up story since she told it a lot and then would ramble on about Bri. But I wonder if Bri is your grandmother, Brianna, and if she somehow had this magic too," Jessica explained.

"It is possible. My uncle and I've had a few conversations lately where he said things that he shouldn't have known, but he did. Maybe the whole family was somehow affected. I just am having trouble wrapping my mind around the fact that I have magic and that magic is a real thing in this world. Are we going to suddenly start coming across magic users now that we know? Has a veil been lifted?" Elyse asked Jessica, knowing her friend likely didn't have any more answers than she did.

"I have no idea. Maybe the journals will tell us more? Or your FBI guy, Josh?" Jessica suggested.

170

Elyse grimaced at the mention of Josh. "Things didn't go so well on our last date. I might have told him I never ever wanted to see him again."

Jessica giggled. "I am pretty sure you could just call him up and ask him on a date and he'd say yes."

Elyse rolled her eyes. "I haven't slept with him."

Jessica stuck out her tongue. "Yet," she said with a wicked grin. "So, are we reading more journals or…moving on to something else?" Jessica asked, lifting up a journal and shaking it for emphasis.

Elyse let out a breath. "What if I fade completely and can't come back?"

Jessica patted Elyse's knee. "How about this: I will keep one hand on you and we can read the next entry together?"

Elyse nodded somewhat reluctantly. She did want to know more, but what if she got stuck in the journal? She opened the one she had been reading last and skimmed a few entries before stopping on one and reading it out loud.

May 15, 2050

Today I turned forty. What an adventure this has been. I also got some of the best news I've had in a long time. We're expecting again! We got to visit Mom and Dad in April, and Albert rode his first horse. The sheer joy on his face. I cannot wait to share that with this next baby too.

July 1, 2050

Shit. There's a new coronavirus.

Elyse glanced over at Jessica before continuing to read out loud.

July 10, 2050

The board of directors is begging us to get
a set of samples from the state hospitals and
see if we can be the first to figure it out. I
don't know if I want to be on the forefront
of this research. A virus without a cure.

July 15, 2050

We agreed to work on the new virus. Renee
is going to stay home with Albert and work
remotely. I will rotate with my three colleagues.
We'll take two-week shifts, with two of us
always in there at the same time. Forty-eight
hours of quarantine and then twelve days home.

Elyse was about to look at Jessica again when everything started to fade. This time she could feel Jessica squeezing her leg. When things lightened up, she found herself in the same lab where she had encountered Archibald and Renee before.

Archibald was in a heated discussion with another person in a lab coat. Elyse edged closer to hear the conversation.

"Eighty percent of the mice are dying! The fluids are not making much of a difference. We need to come up with another solution," Archibald said vehemently.

The other person in a lab coat was another man with a deep bass voice. "Your concern is noted, but you of all people should know that things like this take time. This project has been going for a mere two weeks. We don't make breakthroughs in virus research overnight. I will remind you that we are close to having the virus completely sequenced. It should be done tonight. Then, Renee can work her magic and hopefully we'll make progress once we can identify where to start with our modifications to the virus."

Archibald sighed. "I hope you're right."

The lab faded out. Elyse was expecting to be back in her house, but when it lightened up again, she was behind Archibald as he walked up to a large brick house with a tidy front yard and a bright red front door. The door opened, and a little boy shrieked in excitement.

Jessica gave Elyse's hand a squeeze, causing Elyse to jump. She hadn't noticed that Jessica was with her in the lab. Together, they followed Archibald into the house.

A young boy, who looked to be about three years old, leaped into Archibald's arms and hung on like he was never going to let go. Archibald walked farther into the house. Sniffing the air, he changed course and entered the kitchen, where Renee was stirring a pot of something.

"You're home," Renee said simply and continued stirring the pot. Elyse noticed that Renee was indeed pregnant. She had a lovely round baby bump.

Archibald set his son down and went over to his wife, pulling her in for a tight hug. "I missed you," he whispered and kissed her.

Renee pulled back, uncertain. "You followed protocol?"

"Yes, of course. I would never endanger you or Albert. You know that," Archibald said firmly.

"Okay, I just had to ask. I've missed you so much, but there are so many people dying. It scares me knowing you're at the lab working with this new virus, deliberately putting yourself at risk," Renee said softly.

"The lab spared no expense on equipment. We are as safe as possible," Archibald reminded her.

Just as they embraced warmly and kissed in a much more frantic way, everything faded out.

Elyse took a deep breath. When she opened her eyes, she was back in her house.

"Wow!" exclaimed Jessica. "That was wild."

"Did you see all of it? The lab and the house?" Elyse asked.

Jessica nodded fervently. "Yes. I could see you. Could you not see me?"

"I saw you with me in the house, but not in the lab," Elyse replied.

Jessica pursed her lips in thought. "That is strange that you could see me in one but not the other. But…you're not crazy. The journal and your magical talent are doing something, allowing you to see the past, beyond what's in the journal entries."

"The journal entry was dated 2050, and Archibald is talking about a virus. Do you think it's the COVID-50 virus?" Elyse asked uncertainly. *I wonder if that's why no one says anything. Because he was involved in the creation or mutation of COVID-50.*

Jessica shrugged. "It would make sense if it's COVID-50. The timeline would be correct."

Elyse shut the journal and shoved it to the side, raising her arms over her head to stretch. "Do you want some water?" she offered, needing to stand up and move around some. Without waiting for an answer, Elyse walked into the kitchen and filled two glasses with water. She set them at the dining room table but remained standing to drink hers.

"You have a look of deep thought. Is there something else you want to tell me?" Jessica asked, grabbing her cup and taking a sip of water.

I told her about the possibility of magic. I guess there would be no harm in telling her the rest. "Maybe," Elyse replied, trying to figure out the best way to explain things. "You know how I told you that Josh is in the FBI?"

"Mmmhmm." Jessica murmured.

"Well, the FBI wants to recruit me. There is also this other organization, Hellfire and Chaos, and they apparently want to recruit or capture me also. My last date with Josh…well, it went badly partly because HAC tried to kidnap me." Elyse's voice got softer the further she got into the explanation.

"You were almost kidnapped?" Jessica gasped in shock.

Elyse nodded. "Yes, but Josh shot the woman, and she took off running."

"Why do two organizations want you?" Jessica paused, realization clear on her face. "Because of your magical talent?"

Elyse shrugged. "That's what Josh said. He was also talking about how it needs to be unlocked, which can cause my magic to change. If you ask me, it all sounds like bullshit. I don't want to be a part of either organization. I just want to run my ranch."

"You declined, so now what?" Jessica asked.

Elyse shook her head. "Honestly, I have no idea. Everyone knows about the FBI. Or at least whatever small amount of information is out there. I don't know anything about HAC. Josh seemed to think that saying no would not be an option. I can start carrying my handgun as an extra precaution, I suppose."

"I would feel better if you did. What if they try to kidnap you again?" Jessica said.

"I will be ready," Elyse said firmly.

Later that evening, after Jessica had left, Elyse was preparing to head into Atlanta for dinner with Uncle Albert when her phone rang.

Elyse picked up the phone without looking at it and assumed he was calling to confirm. She hadn't seen him since she had the weird magic experiences with the journals, and she had loads of questions for him.

"Elyse Hutchinson?" an unfamiliar voice spoke on the other end. Elyse could hear strange beeping and clicking sounds in the background.

"Yes, who is this?" she said, shifting the bags onto her lap.

"Albert Cornelius was just admitted to the hospital. He is asking for you. Please come soon," the voice said neutrally.

Gasping, Elyse took in the information. *Uncle Albert in the hospital?* "Which hospital?" she asked, trying to collect her thoughts. While waiting for a response, she began collecting some items in a bag. A spare set of clothes, a spare toothbrush, and an apple. She wanted to be prepared if she was going to have to stay at the hospital overnight with him.

"Atlanta North Hospital. We're on—"

"I know where it is," she said, cutting the nurse off. "I will be there shortly."

"See you soon," came the reply. There was a click and the line went dead.

Elyse gathered her bag and rushed out of her house and to the car, the wind gusts plucking at her clothing. Worry flooded her mind. Albert had sounded good on the phone a few hours ago. *What had changed?*

At her approach her car turned on and began hovering. She quickly slipped inside, setting her bag on the seat next to her. "Take me to Atlanta North Hospital," she ordered the car.

Leaning back, Elyse closed her eyes as the car effortlessly made its way down the dirt road and onto old Highway 124 to take her to the hospital. Sinking into the seat and trying to prepare herself for what she would learn, Elyse jumped when a feeling of foreboding hit her. "Now what?" she muttered to herself. She took a few deep breaths to calm herself down.

"I must just be worried that he is not going to be okay. The nurse or whoever I spoke to only said to come, not what had happened," she said quietly to herself.

The car slowed down, and Elyse looked up apprehensively at the large neon sign with Atlanta North Hospital scrawled across it in blue and white letters. The car smoothly glided to a halt at the curb a few feet away from the automatic doors. Elyse pocketed her phone. "Wait nearby," she told the car, before shutting the door and walking into the hospital.

The bright lights momentarily blinded her as she stepped into the foyer of the hospital. She squinted, tears trickling down her cheeks as she waited for her eyes to adjust. She took one step toward the front desk, where a young man with a bored expression was staring at the counter.

"Excuse me," she said, trying to get his attention. The young man continued to stare at the counter. "Can you help me? I got a phone call that my uncle is here."

Finally, the young man peered up at her in confusion, blinking rapidly. "What was the name?" he asked.

"I'm looking for Albert Cornelius," she said, trying to keep the impatience from her voice. The person she'd spoken to had made it sound extremely urgent.

The man peered at his computer. "Go sit in that waiting room over there," he said and waved his arm around in a giant circle.

"Over where?" Elyse asked.

"There, like I just said," he repeated, pointing to the left, his arm steadier this time. "Someone will come get you."

Elyse exhaled in relief. "Thank you." She quickly walked over to the indicated waiting area and sat down in one of the hard orange chairs. She had barely sat down when a woman holding a clipboard opened the door.

"The family of Albert Cornelius," the woman announced in a nasally voice.

Elyse leaped out of her seat and it tipped over, clattering to the ground. Blushing in embarrassment, she righted the chair before heading over to the woman. "I'm here for Albert Cornelius."

The woman nodded. "Follow me." She turned on her heel and headed down the hallway.

Elyse followed her, a little surprised that they continued to pass room after room. "How much farther?" she asked.

Much to her surprise the woman ignored the question. Elyse shivered as the feeling of foreboding hit her yet again. She stopped moving and waited for the woman to notice.

"We're not there yet. Why did you stop?" the woman asked, raising an eyebrow.

"Are you sure you're taking me to Albert Cornelius?" Elyse asked in a concerned voice.

"Yes. He is just this way. It's a little bit farther." The woman gently slid her hand under Elyse's elbow and guided her down the hallway. When they reached the elevator, the nurse pushed the button. When it arrived, they stepped in. They went up two levels and then got out, heading to the end of the hallway to a door with a small sign marked "Stairs." They went up two flights before there was another door. This staircase seemed to only connect the third floor and whatever floor they were about to enter. Elyse thought it was strange, but it wasn't like she was an expert on hospital construction.

When they entered the hallway, a male nurse with curly red hair and a scruffy beard in pale orange scrubs came out of a room on the left with an angry expression. Elyse could hear shouting from inside the room he had just vacated. The woman leading her was heading straight for the nurse. Elyse watched his face change from anger to relief when he spotted them.

"Finally! What took you so long?" he said.

Out of the corner of her eye, Elyse could see the warning look and slight head shake the woman gave to the nurse.

"Here we are," said the woman, waving her hand toward the door where the shouting had come from. "Your uncle is in there." The woman released Elyse's elbow.

Elyse took a hesitant step toward the door and then another. As she stretched her hand out to grab the doorknob, she realized that she was visibly shaking. She pulled her hand back quickly and inhaled a breath through her nose, trying to calm her nerves and not let the nurse and doctor see how scared she was. *It's just Uncle Albert inside. Why am I nervous?*

"He's just inside," said the woman with a reassuring smile.

Hand on the doorknob, Elyse turned it and gave a push. "Uncle Albert?" she called, projecting her voice so that he could hear her if he was awake as she stepped into the dark room.

As soon as she was fully in the room, a shape loomed out of the dimness on her left side and something came down toward her face, then everything was black.

Elyse woke up to find herself handcuffed to a hospital bed with an IV line in her arm. Her whole body ached. She remembered being hit on the head, but that wouldn't explain why she felt as though she'd been beaten too. She sat up, wanting to evaluate herself, and caught a glimpse of herself in the mirror over the sink. She gasped. Her face and arms were black and blue with smudges of blood here and there. She was wearing a hospital gown and loosely covered in a blood-smeared sheet. Glancing down, she saw the bruises were also on her legs and torso. Shuddering, a cramp hit her stomach hard, and she barely got her mouth over the side of the bed in time before she threw up.

Bits and pieces of what had happened were coming back. They had asked her many questions about Archibald Cornelius. The olive-skinned nurse with dyed-red hair and an accent of some sort had been the one interrogating her. He seemed to believe she knew far more than she did. When it had become clear she didn't know anything, Elyse had hoped they would just leave her alone. Everyone left. Even the hallway went dark.

Except then he came back, shoved a gag in her mouth so no one could hear her screams, and beat her, claiming she was lying about what she knew and would pay dearly for doing so. She slipped in and out of consciousness after that. To her dismay, her body would not listen to any commands she gave it. She was helpless against him, unable to even bring her arms up to protect her face.

Elyse curled up into a small ball on the bed and rocked herself. Her stomach clenched again, but she fought hard to keep from throwing up, to keep from being overwhelmed by feeling so utterly helpless. *I need to get cleaned up and get out of here.*

Trembling—whether from vomiting or fear she wasn't sure—Elyse inspected the handcuffs, hoping maybe she could get them off. But there didn't appear to be any weak links as she'd hoped. Looking around the dim room, she prayed that there would be something within reach that she could use to pick the lock.

Elyse heard heavy footsteps in the hallway. Her shaking became more pronounced, and she curled into as small of a ball as she could, hoping that whoever it was would rescue her, since it didn't seem to be possible for her to rescue herself. The person hesitated at her door before pushing it open wide, letting the fluorescent light spill in from the hallway.

"Oh good, you're awake," a short man with wavy salt-and-pepper hair said with a smile.

Elyse eyed him warily. He was wearing blue hospital scrubs and had a stethoscope around his neck.

Maybe he will rescue me, she thought.

He took small steps toward her like a predator approaching its prey.

"Now…I want to know everything you know about Archibald Cornelius," he ordered in a no-nonsense tone, then proceeded to remove the gag.

Elyse stared at him bleary-eyed. "I already told the nurse in orange scrubs everything I know."

"Ah, ah, ah…now. Let's not play this game. I know you know more than what you've said." The man wagged his finger at her as if admonishing a naughty child.

Clearing her throat, Elyse shook her head. "I told him everything I know."

The man had been slowly getting closer to Elyse. She hadn't realized how close he was until he slapped her across the face. Elyse felt her lip split and a trickle of blood ran down her chin.

Closing her eyes in pain, she was caught completely off guard when he slapped her again. She slumped forward, shaking uncontrollably.

"I will ask you again. Tell me what you know about Archibald Cornelius," the man ordered.

Elyse couldn't move. Everything hurt too much. Hoping he wouldn't hit her again for not answering, she just focused on trying to breathe. *In...out...in...out...* The shaking lessened, and she could feel her muscles loosening a little. The pain was not going away, but she thought maybe she could sit back up again. Taking her time, she slowly straightened so she was in a sitting position.

Afraid to meet his eyes, Elyse spoke quietly. "I can tell you what I told the nurse." She then repeated all the information she had said earlier, recounting the few journal entries she had read. She omitted the visions she'd had, not completely sure if they had been real or just her imagination and magical talent playing tricks on her.

"I was told that your magical talent had shown you some additional information." The man picked up a clipboard off the table next to the bed and flipped through the pages. "Archibald Cornelius is your great-grandfather and is the man who was responsible for COVID-50."

Apprehension flooded Elyse. Did he really think she was going to confirm what he was saying? That her great-grandfather created COVID-50? Elyse hadn't found any direct evidence proving Archibald had in fact created COVID-50. Everything she had learned so far only mentioned a new coronavirus. It hadn't been identified by a name. *Aunt Grace mentioned COVID-50 though...* She rocked herself back and forth, arms wrapped around her knees. Out of the corner of her eye, she could see the doctor fiddling with her IV bag. Elyse fervently hoped someone would save her or that this man would leave and she could maybe find a way out herself. As she was rocking, her eyes began to slide shut. She tipped to the side and fell asleep.

SEVENTEEN

JOSH

Now that Josh had placed two of the three trackers, all he had left was the one on Gerald Fernway's car. His plan to use the lunch meeting at Smokies had been a bust. But when he checked Gerald's schedule for Monday, he had noticed that his boss was supposed to be visiting Victoria Babit at the hospital. Last time, he had been successful at the hospital, and he saw no reason to doubt that it wouldn't work a second time.

Josh was at the rear of the hospital with his left hand on the handle of one of the employee doors. In his right hand was a small glasses pouch. Terrance was supposed to be meeting him, but she was nowhere to be found. Josh was tired of waiting and decided to just go ahead without her. She could catch up to him or not. Shrugging, he turned the doorknob, and surprisingly, it opened. His excitement was short-lived as he heard the rapid footfall of someone coming his way. Glancing at the doors in the hallway, he took a guess and chose one. Once again luck was with him, and the door opened. Stepping inside what appeared to be a supply closet, Josh shut the door behind him and glanced around. The shelves were full of basic supplies a hospital would need—blankets, pillows, sheets, few bins of bandages and gauze. He was about to give up on this room having anything useful when he noticed a stack of unopened rust-orange scrubs.

"Jackpot," he muttered.

Pulling off his faded blue baseball cap, he quickly slid the scrubs over his white T-shirt. He tugged off his jeans and replaced them with the scrub pants, knowing that he likely would not have a chance to retrieve them again. Taking a deep breath, he stashed his hat and jeans under a stack of gauze. Then he pulled his glasses with thin black rims out of the pouch and stashed that too. Grabbing the clipboard and a stethoscope that was on a hook by the door, he headed out of the supply room.

Josh decided to stick to the hallways instead of going into the lobby, hoping he could locate Hector's wife and check on her to see if Gerald was even here before hunting down Gerald's car.

After wandering the hallways, Josh finally decided he needed to ask someone. He walked up to the nurses' station with an air of authority he had witnessed doctors use. "Excuse me. I am looking for a patient in the ICU. The Babit family has called for an update on Victoria Babit, and I promised I would find out the most up-to-date information."

The nurse at the station looked at him. "Are you new here?" she asked as she proceeded to inspect him from head to foot, taking in the messy hair and crooked glasses. *Shit, I didn't check a mirror.* Berating himself, Josh almost missed her next words.

"The ICU is on the sixth floor, south wing." She looked at him again, as though assessing him. "The stairs would be quickest if you're up to it."

Josh nodded. "Thank you so much!" He took off at a jog, ready to get away from the nurse before she asked him too many more questions. True to her word, the stairs were very close.

Josh reached the sixth floor and opened the door, peering out cautiously into the hallway. It was empty and the far end was dark. *How odd.* Shaking his head, he proceeded down to the right. Once he rounded the corner, he could see the entrance to the ICU ahead. Unfortunately for him, a nurses' station was at the entrance. The nurse was presumably screening people coming through, which made sense since it was an intensive care unit. But it still threw a kink in Josh's plan of just going right up to Victoria Babit's room.

Taking a deep breath, he stepped into an empty room on his left, trying to decide how to proceed. When he heard first Hector Babit's voice and then Gerald's, he cautiously peered out of the room he was in, past the nurses' station. Sure enough, the doors into the ICU had just swung open, allowing Hector and Gerald to leave.

Now I have the confirmation I need that the car is here. I just have to get to it before Gerald makes it to the parking garage. Josh waited for them to get around the bend in the hallway before he headed back toward the stairs, walking as fast as he dared without drawing attention to himself. He went down one flight and paused at the door to the next level. The window showed the hallway on the other side was completely dark.

I should mind my own business and complete this task for Catrina before she punishes me for failing. But…why is the hallway dark? He rolled his eyes at himself in disgust. He would never get the third tracker placed if he didn't stick to his plan. Curiosity getting the better of him, Josh opened the door and started down the dark hallway. He could hear some sounds farther down. Reaching into his back pocket, Josh pulled out a small flashlight and turned it on.

Slowly, he worked his way down the hallway, opening each door and shining the light inside. At the very last door, he heard a muffled whimper. Reaching back with his right hand, Josh pulled his gun out of the back of his pants. Opening the door, he took a step inside and then another. As he took a third step, a shape leaped toward him. Without hesitation, Josh fired his gun twice. The shape shrieked and fell to the ground.

I really hope that was someone I should have been shooting.

A higher-pitched whimper came from the corner. Using the flashlight, he found the light switch and turned it on, ready to shoot anything else that decided to attack him.

The whimpering in the corner was coming from underneath the desk. Kneeling, Josh checked his assailant. Dead. The face seemed vaguely familiar, but he wasn't sure why. Whipping out his phone, he took a photo of the man's face, intending to look him up once he returned to the apartment.

Another whimper from the corner had Josh edging closer, gun ready, not sure if it was a trick or someone who needed help.

"You're safe now. He's dead," he called in a soothing voice, hoping to draw out whoever it was. The whimpering got louder. "I need you to come out now. People will be coming soon because of the gunshots. It will be better for both of us if we are not here when they show up." Taking a deep breath, Josh tucked his gun back into his waistband, hoping this wasn't another trap, before kneeling by the desk and offering an outstretched hand.

A shaking hand grabbed his. The trembling grip was familiar. *It can't be!*

"Elyse?" he said softly.

A gasp from under the table followed by a sob. Then, almost inaudible: "Josh?"

He gave her hand gentle tug, trying to draw her out. *I really don't want to have to explain this to my boss if I'm caught here.*

An anguished sob and Elyse finally scooted out from underneath the desk. Josh dropped her hand in shock and stumbled backward.

Elyse was barely recognizable. Her lips were swollen and bleeding, her face completely covered with fresh black-and-purple bruises. A large cut was on her forehead. Her left arm dangled at her side as though dislocated or broken. She attempted to stand but couldn't put weight on her right leg.

Squeezing his eyes shut and then opening them, Josh tried to collect himself. *I'm the professional. She's relying on me to help her and get her out of whatever mess this is.*

"Let me carry you?" he asked, reaching for her.

Elyse stared at the floor, trembling, and tried to back away from him. She was shaking so hard, he thought she might have tipped over if she hadn't had the wall to brace against.

"There's a chair," she whispered and started coughing. Looking around, not sure what kind of chair she thought would be better than him carrying her, his gaze finally fell on a folded wheelchair. Yep, that would be faster—and would keep him from having to hold her. Not wanting to dwell on why Elyse would be afraid to be touched, other than intense pain, he quickly grabbed the wheelchair and unfolded it before rolling it over to her. Elyse gave him another fearful glance before slowly lowering herself into the chair.

Josh grabbed a blanket from the bed, then rummaged through a cabinet. He found a bottle that had some fast-acting pain meds. He handed her the blanket, then a tiny cup of water and the small pill. "Here, take this. The meds should hold you over till I can get you to a doctor or healer. We need to go."

Elyse took the offered items without comment, and once he was sure she had taken the pill, he grabbed the handles of the chair, spun it around, and headed at a run down the hallway toward the lights, hoping he could make it to an elevator without getting stopped.

They got lucky—almost too lucky. No one came across them in the hallway before they got on the elevator. Once inside, Josh turned the wheelchair around so Elyse was facing him. He kneeled in front of her so she wouldn't have to look up, which she seemed to be avoiding doing.

"Can you tell me what happened?" he said, placing a hand gently on her knee.

Elyse looked away, face flushing. "I'm so stupid. I got a call from someone who said they were a doctor and to come to the hospital immediately because Uncle Albert was here…" A tear dripped slowly down her cheek. She brushed it away gingerly. "I still don't know if he's okay or not."

Josh took a deep breath, trying to quell his desire to interrogate her to get the answers he wanted faster. He needed to know if Hellfire and Chaos were behind the attack or not. If they were, it would explain why Terrance hadn't been there to help him. Swallowing, Josh rubbed his face, wanting to touch her but afraid to scare her more. He hit the emergency stop button on the elevator, trying to buy more time before they had hospital staff interrupting their discussion.

"Did they ask you for information?" he inquired.

Elyse finally looked him in the eyes. "Yes, about my great-grandfather. But I don't know much."

"Hmmm…" Josh pondered, scratching his chin.

"Isn't this your area of expertise? You're an FBI agent, right?" Elyse said in a stronger voice.

Josh stopped pacing. "Yes…but you haven't told me anything useful."

Elyse took a shaky breath. "You haven't really asked any questions other than what they wanted to know about."

Josh coughed and avoided her eyes. She was right. He hadn't asked any questions that could give him information. "Okay… what did they look like?"

"One was wearing orange scrubs like you are. He…had…dyed red hair and an accent, Spanish maybe," she finally got out. He watched as she closed her eyes. Moments ticked by, and he wondered if she was going to be able to tell him anything else. "There was another man, he had salt-and-pepper hair and seemed like he was a doctor, or at least as though he had authority."

"I need more than just hair color and accent," Josh muttered. She was clearly not in a state to give him any additional information. He hit the button and the elevator rumbled back to descending to the ground floor.

Elyse glared at him. He could see her anger bubbling to the surface. Anger was good, better than no emotion at all. "You could… INVESTIGATE!"

Josh opened his mouth to respond when the elevator door dinged and opened, revealing, much to Josh's chagrin, Hector Babit Gerald Fernway. Of course—he had seen them on the sixth floor coming out of the ICU and had forgotten in his concern for Elyse. Now Gerald knew he was here. This was not going to go well.

Josh quickly grabbed the handles of the wheelchair and rolled Elyse out of the elevator and down the hallway.

"Not so fast," Gerald called after him.

"Shit," Josh muttered under his breath, turning Elyse around.

"Is something else going on?" Elyse murmured.

Josh chose to ignore her, worried that they were close enough that Gerald would hear any answer he gave and that it could further implicate him. He stopped a few feet in front of his boss and waited expectantly.

Instead of ripping Josh a new one, Gerald gazed in concern at Elyse. "Ms. Hutchinson, I'm Gerald Fernway, assistant director of the FBI. We should get you a doctor."

Josh couldn't see Elyse's face, but he could feel her shaking again as the chair rattled. Guessing why the comment had set her off, he had another solution in mind, *if* Gerald would sign off on it.

"What about having Celine see her?" Josh said loud enough that even Hector could hear the question.

"Celine? Why?" Gerald asked.

Josh sighed. He should have known Gerald would require an explanation to use one of the FBI's healers. "Elyse is here because she was tricked into coming and then brutally beaten, just upstairs in one of the wings that seemed to be under renovation. I was here undercover, tracking a possible suspect in the black-market case, and happened to come across her."

"Beaten?" Gerald echoed. "That would explain why she has so many bruises…I had thought perhaps she had a mishap with a horse. If I agree to let a healer see you, will you at least give the FBI's offer more consideration than you have?" implored Gerald.

Elyse stayed silent.

Josh let go of the wheelchair and took Gerald's elbow to guide him to the side to have a more private conversation. "You have impressed upon me how important she is to us. Do you really think she would consider taking the offer if we don't at the very least heal her? Besides, what about when she goes back to the ranch? Questions will be raised. You know that HAC has people everywhere. What if we paint an even larger target on her back by not having Celine see her? In her current state, I doubt Elyse could even hold a gun."

Gerald pulled his elbow out of Josh's grasp and straightened out his suit jacket sleeve. "Fine, take her to see Celine. But I am running out of patience, Josh. Finish your assignment, or I will relocate you back to California and have James Valdez take over with Elyse. You have three days."

Josh walked away without waiting for dismissal. He pulled out his phone and sent a message to his car before grabbing Elyse's wheelchair and guiding her away from the FBI agents. The last thing he wanted was for any of his assignments that dealt with women to be turned over to James Valdez.

EIGHTEEN

ELYSE

Josh rolled Elyse down the hallway, away from Gerald and the other FBI agent who hadn't been introduced to her.

"Where are we going?" she asked as she realized they were heading toward the exit of the hospital. The pain pill Josh had given her had worked remarkably fast at turning what had been sharp, jabbing pain into a dull ache.

"To see Celine. She's a healer," Josh said curtly.

"A healer?" Elyse waggled her fingers. "That uses magic?" Sitting in the chair with Josh behind her pushing, she could not see his face, but she could hear the amusement in his voice.

"Yes, a healer that uses magic. She will be more effective than a doctor here."

Elyse kept silent, not sure what else to say. Tremors still ran through her. At times, she thought she could feel hands hitting her over and over. Her breathing became more rapid as more detailed images of the numerous beatings invaded her mind. Closing her eyes, she willed her mind to stop. She was safe. Or safe enough with Josh. Regardless of whatever feelings they might or might not have for each other, he was at least proving he was still a decent human being. He wanted her to be healed, not just treated at the hospital.

They emerged out onto the sidewalk, and Josh's car was waiting for them at the curb. The back door popped open. As though he'd done it before, Josh quickly set the brakes on the wheelchair before picking her up and settling her into the back seat.

"I can walk, you know," Elyse said in barely a whisper as he shut the door.

Josh slid into the front seat. "I'm sure you can manage something that resembles a walk, but it was faster to pick you up. I'd rather not hang around the hospital any longer than we must."

All but the front window darkened and the car picked up speed as they went down the road. Elyse tried unsuccessfully to look out of the window to figure out where they were going. "Where is this healer?"

"She actually lives in my building," Josh replied.

Elyse was surprised that a healer lived in Josh's building, but then again it was one of the larger buildings in downtown Atlanta. It had Three Dragons, expensive condos on the top ten floors, and a wide range of business offices on lower floors.

"Then why do you have the windows blacked so I can't see out?" Elyse asked.

Josh glanced back at her. "It isn't so you can't see where we're going. It is so people can't see you are in the car. The hope is that any HAC watching will assume you are still in the hospital. I don't want to draw any more unnecessary attention to you."

Elyse pressed her lips together. She understood, but she couldn't decide whether she was pleased that Josh wanted to make sure she was safe, or annoyed with him.

Instead of dropping them off at the front of the building, the car proceeded to enter the parking garage. It pulled into what seemed to be a small room barely large enough for the car. A door slammed shut behind them, causing Elyse to jump. Minutes ticked by as they waited. Finally, the wall in front of them slid open, revealing another room.

Josh hopped out of the car and opened Elyse's door.

Elyse peeled herself off the car seat. Since she wasn't wearing pants, just two hospital gowns, her legs stuck uncomfortably to the leather. She finally extracted herself from the car and stood up, wobbling unsteadily. Josh reached out as though to help her, but she ignored his hand, using the car to stabilize herself. When she got to the front of the car where she'd have to let go of it, her first step was sketchy, but she didn't fall. Taking a deep breath, Elyse slowly walked forward until she was standing in the middle of the room.

"Now what?" she asked, peering around.

"The elevator," Josh said as he came up beside her.

"I don't see an elevator," muttered Elyse.

Josh winked at her before pulling his phone out of his pocket. He walked over to the wall in front of them and placed the phone against it. There was a click and a hiss and a seam appeared, then the wall split in half horizontally.

"The elevator, madam," he said with a sweeping bow before taking her arm and gently guiding her over the line in the floor.

Elyse glanced around at the so-called elevator. It looked exactly as the other room had, especially once the doors shut and the car was no longer visible.

"Now what?" Elyse asked. *Surely there must be a button or something he has to press to make it go.*

Instead of answering the question, Josh just pointed. The door split in half again, revealing to Elyse's astonishment a large room that looked like most traditional doctors' offices: a front desk with a waiting area holding some uncomfortable-looking chairs and a hallway off to the left with several doors.

"How did we get up here? I didn't feel the elevator move," Elyse asked.

Josh shrugged. "It's magic. Not all of Celine's clients want their presence known. She has a contract with the FBI but mostly does freelance work. It pays better than being under one organization's thumb."

"Ah," Elyse said, nodding as though she understood, even though she had no clue what Josh was talking about.

As soon as they were all the way in the room, a young woman came over. "Josh, Celine is expecting you. This way please."

Before Josh could answer, the woman was leading them down the hallway and into a room. To Elyse's surprise, instead of a typical exam table, there was a bed that might be fairly comfortable, a large overstuffed chair, and a counter with a sink and cabinets over it.

As they all stepped into the room, the young woman turned to face Elyse. "Do you want Josh in here during the exam?"

Elyse was surprised and grateful for the question. It hadn't occurred to her than Josh might stay in the room during an exam.

"No, I don't," Elyse replied softly, keeping her eyes on the nurse so she wouldn't have to see Josh's reaction to being shut out. *I don't owe him anything,* she reminded herself.

The nurse nodded and opened one of the cabinets, pulling out a loose-fitting oversized shirt and handing it to Elyse. "For the exam, you'll put this on. When Celine is done, if you need to stay here longer, there is a suite you can stay in with a full bathroom."

"Thank you," Elyse murmured, clutching the shirt to her chest.

The nurse stepped through a door opposite of where they entered. When Elyse turned around to say goodbye to Josh, he was already gone. She shrugged. He must have realized how much she wanted privacy and went out to the waiting room.

Elyse heard a soft knock on the door. An older woman, who appeared to be in her sixties, walked into the room. "Hello, Elyse. I'm Celine."

"Nice to meet you," Elyse murmured.

"Josh told me that he found you this way and that you had been beaten. Is there anything else that was done to you that I should know about?" Celine asked, stepping toward Elyse.

Elyse shook her head and a whimper escaped her lips before she could stifle it. *I suppose I should consider myself lucky; they only beat me and didn't go any further. The red-haired man certainly seemed like he wanted to do more.*

"Hush, you're safe now," Celine said and came close, enveloping her in a comforting hug.

Elyse wasn't sure how long Celine held her for. Slowly Celine released her arms and took a slight step back.

"I am surprised you can even talk," Celine said softly.

Elyse looked at her in confusion. "What do you mean?"

Celine chuckled. "While I was holding you, I was using my magic to evaluate your body. The way my magic works is it shows me how each wound occurred. I do not see it like a movie, more just an impression or feeling. For example, when you were punched in the face, they hit you hard enough that your jaw is fractured in a couple of places."

Elyse gasped. "Your magic can tell you that?"

Celine nodded. "Yes, and now that I know how much damage has been done to your body, I can begin to heal it. I must warn you though, the damage is extensive. I can repair much of the physical, and what I can't, I can at least speed up the healing process. The psychological affects, though—those I cannot erase. I can help you work through them, but it is something you will have to come to terms with. It is easier if you have someone other than me you can talk to. I don't know what kind of relationship you have with Josh, so he may or may not be the right person. If he's not, perhaps you have a close friend who can come stay with you once you go home, at least for a few days."

Elyse took a shaky breath. "Yes, I have a friend at home. Jessica. I can ask her to stay with me, if you think that would help. How soon can you start the healing process? The sharp pain is starting to come back. I guess Josh was right about the pill he gave me being short-lived."

"Right now. I just need you to pick either the chair or the bed, whichever you think will be most comfortable. You will fall asleep for a few hours, and when you wake up, hopefully your most painful body parts will not hurt as much," Celine said.

Elyse decided on the bed. She lowered herself onto it, relieved at how comfortable it was. Celine came over to her side and rested her hands on Elyse's arm. Elyse watched for a few minutes before her eyelids got too heavy. She fell asleep.

NINETEEN

JOSH

Josh fell asleep in the waiting room while Celine examined Elyse. A couple of hours later, a hand shook his arm. Josh jerked awake, reaching for his gun before remembering where he was.

Celine was giving him an amused look. "I wasn't expecting you to stay."

Josh shrugged. "What is your assessment?"

"You must really like her to have brought her here. I know Gerald would not usually sign off on something like this," Celine said, ignoring his question. "I want you to come with me so we can speak more privately."

She said this last bit while glancing around the waiting room. Josh watched as her eyes rested on each occupant of the room for a moment before moving on.

Josh stood up and followed Celine down the hallway. He expected her to take him into one of the patient rooms and was surprised when she took him into her office instead.

It must be pretty bad if she wants to talk in a shielded room.

Celine shut the door firmly behind Josh, and a ripple of magic washed over the room. Josh could feel when the shield settled in place. "Now I'm really curious. Usually, you aren't this secretive. What did you find in the exam?"

Celine sat in a chair at her desk and folded her hands. "I am not sure who is responsible for what happened, and under normal circumstances, you know that I keep patient information confidential. However, this is not usual. I don't know what she's mixed up in, but whoever she tangled with was very thorough and careful. Precise punches that created severe damage, but not enough to kill her." She paused. "It reminds me of some interrogations I've witnessed."

"Interrogations by who? That is not the FBI's style and it's certainly not Catrina's," Josh inquired, wondering if Celine had a particular group in mind or was just tossing ideas at him.

Celine ignored his question. "I'm surprised she tolerated being with a man so soon after one beat her like that. It says something about how strong her mind is."

"Were you able to heal her?" Josh asked.

"Physically, yes. She will have some light bruising in areas that can be covered by clothing. However, mentally…that will depend on her. Some victims of attacks like this don't have any psychological damage, and for others, it takes years to recover. She did say something when she was in the healing sleep that I found intriguing. She kept talking about journals and being inside the journal."

Josh ran a hand through his hair, considering his next words. He could usually trust Celine to be discreet. "Her magical talent hasn't been unlocked yet, and I am not sure what journals she would be referring to. So I'm not sure how she could have gone inside of a journal, or honestly if that is even possible."

Celine shrugged. "I am surprised as an FBI agent you haven't come across any other weird occurrences with journals. What I don't understand is, if it was HAC who had captured Elyse, why did they not just take her to one of their safehouses? Why keep her in a hospital?"

Josh gave her a sharp look, realizing she was on to something. Why *would* HAC have kept Elyse at the hospital? *Is there another player in this mess?*

"I don't know."

Celine spread her hands wide. "Neither do I, but consider this. If there is something about her that makes her a high-value target, then HAC is likely not the only organization to be willing to go to extreme measures to get their hands on her."

Josh pretended to inspect his hands to avoid Celine's piercing gaze. "I know."

"Are you on the right side?" Celine asked quietly.

"I have never had the luxury of choosing. You of all people should know that," Josh replied equally quietly.

Celine might have lived in Atlanta longer than Josh had, but they both grew up in Manhattan, and she had lived in the apartment across the street. She had been watching from her window the day he had been recruited by the government and sent away. Celine never had told him how she had avoided being sent to the school. Although she had clearly received training to heal people magically from somewhere. *Maybe it's better I don't know.*

Josh stood up, then made a quick decision. Bracing his hands on the desk, he leaned over Celine. "Do you know anything about Dariusz Sierżęga?"

Celine's face blanched, and she shoved back from the desk. "Don't ever speak that name aloud," she hissed.

"Why?" Josh said alarmed.

"It is said if you say his name, it gives him the power to come to wherever you are. Most people who encounter him don't survive," Celine said in a hushed voice. She grabbed his shirt, peering up into his face. "Josh, if you are mixed up in something that involves him, then you need to run, and don't look back."

Josh gave her a pained look. "What if I can't?"

"Just leave, while you can. Trust me," Celine said again.

Closing his eyes, Josh took a moment to get his thoughts in order. "I can't leave Elyse."

"I will take care of Elyse. You need to leave," Celine said.

"I appreciate the offer, but…Linney, I think I'm falling in love with her. I can't just abandon her," Josh said softly.

Celine gave him a look he couldn't read, and she sat back down in her chair. "You always did have a talent for complicating things when we were kids. I suppose I shouldn't expect that would have changed over the years."

"Your premature aging is a result of what you're calling my 'talent for complicating things,'" he said softly, before adding in a more assertive voice, "What do I do?"

"I don't know." Celine paused. "Do you know if Elyse even feels the same way? Or, I should say, if she did?" Celine took a deep breath. "How much time have you spent around victims of brutal attacks?"

Josh shook his head. "None of my friends or close acquaintances have ever been attacked in the way Elyse was."

"You must be willing to accept that she might consider the attack your fault or not want to be around you, since she was attacked by a man," Celine said softly.

"I appreciate the warnings, but, Linney, I have to try. Elyse… is different. I just don't know how to explain what I feel for her, how she makes me feel," Josh said, bewildered as he tried to sort through his emotions for Elyse.

Celine shook her head. "You don't need to explain. I can see it in your eyes, in your aura." There was a hard knock on the door.

"Celine, you're needed," a young boy called through the door.

Sighing, Celine stood up, "My duties call. You are welcome to stay. Although if you won't take my advice to run, I would recommend that you go home and figure out what you're doing before you come back. I will give you an update when she wakes up."

Josh nodded solemnly and watched as Celine headed out of her office and disappeared down the hallway. *Celine brought up so many things to consider. Maybe the attack wasn't HAC, but who? And this Dariusz fellow scares the living daylights out of her…and everyone really. But no one will tell me who he even is. She is right. I need to go home and at least give myself a chance to regroup.*

Mind made up, Josh let himself out of the office and to the main entrance, where he could find the elevator that would take him up to his condo. As he was riding the elevator, he remembered that the reason he had gone to the hospital had been to place the tracker on Gerald's car. Once again, he had failed at that task.

When he stepped into his condo, he was surprised to see Terrance sitting on his couch waiting for him. "I was wondering where you went," she purred.

"I could say the same about you," Josh said, walking toward her. "You never showed up at the hospital, and then everything went crazy."

Terrance tsked. "I actually was there, and I placed the tracker for you."

Josh's jaw dropped open. "How?"

Terrance laughed. "You forget that when I'm in tiger form, I can blend into things. You were distracted enough that you didn't notice, and I snagged the tracker out of your pocket and found the car while you were busy talking to Gerald after you found Elyse. Thank you, by the way, for creating such a lovely distraction. It was perfect."

"Was HAC behind the attack on Elyse?" Josh demanded.

Terrance shrugged. "I have no idea. If it was, no one told me about it. But I rarely know about anything going on beyond my own orders."

Josh glanced at the clock. It was five p.m. He still had time left in the day to hit the gym if he could get rid of Terrance. "Is there something else you need from me?" he asked with a pointed glance at the door to the elevator.

"No, I don't need anything else from you. I'll see you around." Terrance stood up and sauntered out his front door.

Josh rubbed his face with both hands. *What a strange day it has been*, he thought.

Once Terrance was gone, Josh remembered that he had taken the photo of the assailant he had shot in the room he found Elyse in. Slipping his computer out of his briefcase, Josh powered it on, then transferred the photo from his phone to the computer.

"Search the database for a match," he ordered the computer. The image of the man was up on the screen. Since he hadn't provided any details other than the photo, there was a chance it would take a while. Setting the computer down, Josh prepared himself a fresh cup of coffee.

Just as he was about to take his first sip, the computer announced, "One hundred percent match found."

He eagerly picked up the computer.

NAME: JAIME TEJERO
AGE: 42
HEIGHT: 5'11"
HAIR: GRAY
KNOWN AFFILIATIONS: NONE
KNOWN ASSOCIATES: ENZO TOLEDANO, JUAN GONZÁLEZ, LUIS CAMACHO

Josh's eyes widened as he read the known associates. *The second name. I know that name.* "Show me information on Juan Gonzalez."

The screen replaced Jaime's information with Juan's.

NAME: JUAN GONZALEZ
AGE: 46
HEIGHT: 5'5"
DESCRIPTION: BLACK HAIR, BLUE-BLACK SKIN
ORIGIN: CORDOBA, SPAIN
OTHER: SPIDER TATTOO ON HIS LEFT SHOULDER
KNOWN AFFILIATIONS: ARAÑAS ROJAS

KNOWN ASSOCIATES: MATEO JESÚS VALDEZ, MIGUEL FIGUEROA

Josh gazed at the screen. *That's why Juan Gonzalez sounded familiar. But it doesn't really make sense that the Arañas Rojas would be involved.* Just for the heck of it, Josh looked up Mateo's information.

NAME: MATEO JESÚS VALDEZ
AGE: 46
HEIGHT: 5'8"
DESCRIPTION: CURLY BLACK HAIR, DARK BROWN SKIN, GREEN EYES, JAGGED SCAR FROM LEFT EAR TO RIGHT CHEEK
ORIGIN: CORDOBA, SPAIN
OTHER: SPIDER TATTOO COVERING WHOLE TORSO FRONT AND BACK; COUSIN OF JAMES VALDEZ
KNOWN AFFILIATIONS: ARAÑAS ROJAS (LEADER)

"Show me Jaime Tejero's known associates," Josh ordered the computer.

It pulled up their information side-by-side. Josh skimmed it, noting that both Enzo Toledano and Luis Camacho were associates of Kiara Velez and had cases being built against them by other FBI agents for selling magic items on the black market. Kiara had not given them up during her interrogation, but Josh did not doubt that with her in custody, they would soon be captured as well. *The Arañas Rojas don't have anything to do with Kiara Velez that I know of.*

Josh tugged on his lip, trying to work out what the connection was between Elyse and the people who had captured her, but could not come up with anything that made sense—at least not with the information he had at his disposal. *Maybe Elyse will remember more and that will help me figure it out.*

His phone rang. "Hello?" Josh answered, eyes still lingering on his computer screen and the Jaime's information.

"Josh, I've been trying to reach Elyse but have not been successful. Do you know where she is?" Quinn said.

Josh was not expecting Quinn to call him. It took him a moment to figure out how to respond. He knew they were close, but he was unsure if he should tell Quinn that Elyse had been attacked at the hospital. "She has been visiting her uncle. I am sure she will call you when she is available," he said, the lie rolling smoothly off his tongue.

"Thanks. See you around," Quinn replied before hanging up.

Josh sighed. The gym still sounded like a great place to end his day. He shut off his computer and returned it to the briefcase, then began his preparations to go to the gym. Normally he'd call Todd to see if he was available, but tonight, he felt like weight training would help him settle better than kickboxing would.

TWENTY

ELYSE

Elyse stayed at Celine's healer suite—or whatever it was called—through Monday afternoon, before she felt as though she could try heading home. She wanted to be home in her own bed. To be able to go for a ride with Honey and just let the memories of the bad things that happened at the hospital wash away.

When Elyse had woken up after the first healing session, late Sunday night, she had called Jessica and given her the barest of details, begging her friend to see if Mya would take care of the ranch on her own for the rest of the week, buying her time to come home and continue her recovery without immediately adding the farm chores to her agenda.

As Elyse's car made its way up the driveway, Elyse realized how nice it was to not have to drive a car like her great-grandfather. She could just take a nap or think about other things while her car navigated its way to the house. She hopped out and pushed open the doors to the shed where her car was stored. The car moved into the shed and then lowered itself to the ground and shut off.

To Elyse's surprise, Jessica was sitting at the dining room table with lunch laid out for two.

"How did you know?" Elyse asked, voice catching.

Jessica smiled and walked over to her, enveloping her in a hug. Elyse felt herself melting into her best friend's arms. "Josh called me. He thought you would need someone here when you got home, and he wasn't sure you would ask for help. Let's eat while the food is still hot."

Elyse reluctantly unwrapped her arms from around Jessica and meekly followed her to the table. Sniffing the air, she was surprised that Jessica had actually made fried chicken and mac and cheese.

"Is that what I think it is? Grams's recipes?"

Jessica laughed throatily. "Yes. I thought you would like your favorite food when you came home. To help you settle better. I brought some steak for tomorrow."

"Tomorrow?" whispered Elyse.

"Yes, silly. I am going to be living here with you for at least the next week while you get back on your feet." Jessica gave Elyse's arm a squeeze before gently pushing her into the chair and placing a fork in her hand. "Now, please eat while it's hot."

Elyse nodded and took a bite, staring at the plate but not really seeing it. At Celine's, there had been constant background noise. Not intrusive, but just enough so she knew that she wasn't alone, someone was just a moment away. Her home had always been quiet, a place for meditation. Now the quiet just felt oppressive.

Jessica brushed a finger over Elyse's hand, and Elyse jumped, recoiling at the touch. Spilling her glass of water all over the table, Elyse fell backward out of her chair. A wave of pure terror went through her, and she curled into a tight ball on the ground, squeezing her eyes shut.

The red-haired man in orange scrubs lightly ran his fingers over her hand before smashing down on her hand as hard as he could with his fist. She had screamed and screamed, but the gag muffled her enough so no one would hear and come to her rescue. Whatever drug they had given her had removed her ability to command her own body.

A feather-soft touch on her arm, and Elyse screamed uncontrollably, squirming out of the way.

"Elyse, it's Jessica," a voice repeated over and over. Slowly, Elyse realized she did have control over her body. She was clenching and unclenching her fists. The hardwood floor was making her freshly healed and still tender ribs ache.

I am not in the hospital, Elyse thought, trying to talk herself into believing it.

Taking a deep breath, she opened her eyes. Jessica was peering at her from a few feet away, her hand outstretched as though to touch Elyse but afraid to do so.

"I'm sorry," Jessica said. "I didn't mean to upset you. I thought…I thought when you were okay after the hug that it would be okay if I touched you."

Elyse sat up and loosened her grip on her legs. "I'm sorry too. I don't know what came over me." She said the last bit without looking into Jessica's eyes, hoping her friend wouldn't pry for details.

"Can I…can I just get in bed?" Elyse asked quietly.

Jessica nodded, standing, then offered Elyse a hand, careful this time to allow Elyse to initiate the contact. "If that is what you want, then of course. I am here for whatever you need me to do."

Elyse took the offered hand to stand, then let it drop. Shoulders slumped, focusing on her feet, she shuffled into the bedroom. She left the door open and turned on the light, jumping slightly when it flickered before turning on all the way.

I need to get a grip. Jessica is not going to attack me, and no one else is here.

The door to the bathroom was ajar, and the shower caught her eye. *Just what I need. A nice hot shower and then some snuggly pajamas and I can get into bed.*

Mind made up, Elyse turned on the shower, cranking it to as hot as it would go. It would take a lot of power from the batteries, but after the past few days, Elyse figured it really didn't matter if she had an extra-hot shower once or twice. *It's not like I have a family of five I need to conserve the energy for. It's just me.*

Elyse yanked the white shirt and gray sweats off. Celine had been kind enough to provide her with clean clothes, but Elyse didn't want the extra reminder of why she had had to use a magical healer. She stepped into the shower, then realized her hair was in a braid. She undid the hair tie and flung it over the top of the glass, not caring where it landed.

Hot water, almost too hot, ran over the top of her head and shoulders. Elyse wasn't sure how long she stood there just letting the water wash over her when a knock came on the open door.

"Are you okay in there?" called Jessica, stepping into the doorway so Elyse could see it was her, but keeping her back politely turned to give Elyse privacy.

"I'm fine," Elyse answered.

"You've been in the shower almost an hour," Jessica said.

"An hour?" she said in shock.

Jessica giggled. "Yes, I can't believe you have enough hot water to do that."

Taking a deep breath, Elyse shut off the water and began wringing out her long hair. When she was done, she stuck her hand out the door for a towel, then noticed there wasn't one.

Elyse coughed in embarrassment. "Would you mind finding me a towel?"

"Absolutely," said Jessica. Elyse could hear the obvious amusement in Jessica's voice.

At least someone thought it was funny.

Jessica returned, back still toward Elyse as she offered a towel. Elyse took it and gave her friend's hand a squeeze before wrapping herself in the towel and stepping out of the shower.

"Thank you," Elyse said. "You can turn around now…I am covered."

"Are you sure?" Jessica asked uncertainly.

"Yes, I am sure," Elyse said with more confidence than she felt. Jessica turned around, and Elyse was surprised to find that even though she was only in a towel, having her friend there with her didn't stir any bad memories. Relief coursed through her. Maybe she would be okay if she took baby steps with letting someone get close to her.

"I will let you get dressed. I'll be out there if you need me," Jessica said, turning and heading toward the living room.

Elyse waited a few moments. She heard the scraping of the dining room chair, then she toweled herself dry and went on a hunt for pajamas. She found a flannel pair that was hot pink with yellow cats on it. She tugged them on, then climbed into bed. Elyse noticed one of the journals was sitting on the nightstand. *Odd, I don't remember leaving one there.* As soon as her head hit the pillow, she was asleep.

Elyse was standing in a strange hallway. The walls on either side were half walls with windows the rest of the way to the ceiling. Lab equipment was in the rooms on both sides. She found herself walking down the hallway, toward the door at the very end. She reached for the doorknob, but when her hand brushed the door, it passed through. What on earth? Elyse took a step and passed through the door. Inside were case after case full of test tubes. Equipment of all sorts—most of it unfamiliar to her—filled every available space. Then she realized she could hear voices.

"The alterations you made to the COVID-50 virus have not done anything to decrease the rate at which the mice are becoming affected by it. In fact, one of the variations seems to have increased the rate of spread," a woman's voice said angrily.

Another voice, a man who seemed vaguely familiar, replied, "You know as well as I do that it takes time. This crazy push for an immediate solution is forcing us to cut corners that we normally wouldn't. As you can see, it is also adding delays because our work is sloppy. While my name might be on the door to the lab, you cannot blame me. Our whole team is working on COVID-50, including my pregnant wife, whom I haven't seen in over a month because I am trying to figure this out."

It dawned on Elyse that she knew the voice. It was Archibald Cornelius. Now I'm dreaming about him too?

The lights flickered in the lab.

"Not again," muttered the woman.

The power went out. A whirring sound could be heard, then the backup generators kicked on, with the lights following moments later.

"See? It came back on, like it always does," Archibald said. He opened the door of the fridge closest to him and gave a satisfied nod that it was still running. Just then, a huge flash of light illuminated the room before everything went black. Archibald let out an unearthly scream as the fridge he had been peering into collapsed on top of him.

Elyse jolted awake as her house shook. She could hear heavy rain, maybe even hail, pelting the metal roof. Her fingers clutched something. Elyse realized it was the journal and let it go in shock. *How did it get in my hands?* Backing away from the journal, Elyse fell off the bed, screaming.

Pounding footsteps came toward her. "Elyse?" called Jessica.

"Jess?" Elyse said from the floor, trying to calm herself. Her breath was coming out in short, ragged bursts.

"What just happened?" Jessica asked as she peered at Elyse on the ground.

"I had a bad dream." Elyse murmured.

"Did it have to do with the journal?" Jessica asked, holding it up. Elyse gasped and backed away until her back hit the wall. "Yes!"

Jessica examined her from head to toe before placing the journal on top of the dresser and returning to Elyse. Instead of offering her a hand to stand up, Jessica sat down beside her. "What did you dream about?"

"Archibald Cornelius…he was in his lab and arguing with someone about COVID-50, and then there was a storm, and a fridge fell on him." Elyse looked away as she realized how ridiculous that sounded.

"A nightmare about a fridge attacking your great-grandfather?" Jessica said in an amused tone.

Elyse giggled slightly. "It does sound rather silly."

"Do you think you can go back to sleep?" Jessica asked.

"I don't know. What time is it?" Elyse asked. The curtains were all drawn and the house was rather dark, but she couldn't tell if that was because it was in the middle of the night or not.

"It's not quite dinner time. How about this? We can go out to say hello to Honey. I know how much just being around her helps when you're stressed out. If you want to ride, we can ride, or you can just go back to sleep," Jessica said.

Elyse glanced down at her pajamas, realizing that Jessica was right. Maybe seeing Honey was exactly what she needed, and no one here would criticize her for wearing silly pajamas to go spend time with her horse.

"Let me just find my boots and raincoat." She didn't have much searching to do since her farm boots were tucked in their usual spot behind the front door. Yanking them on, Elyse headed out to find Honey, desperately hoping Jessica was right and that the horses would help erase any bad dreams she had been having.

A soft nicker called to her. Elyse found a smile tugging at her lips as she followed Honey's call into the barn. Inhaling deeply, Elyse savored the sweet smell of hay and grain as the horses quietly ate their dinners, except for Honey. Honey was hanging her head over the stall door, golden ears pricked forward, waiting for Elyse. Elyse found herself running the last few steps and then throwing her arms around the mare. Taking a deep breath, Elyse felt herself relaxing. Then, a crazy idea came to her. She glanced over her shoulder at Jessica before returning her attention to Honey. Giving the mare a pat, she unlatched the stall door, then let it slide to the side.

Honey stood gazing at her, warm brown eyes meeting bright green ones. Elyse crooked her finger at Honey, and the mare stepped out of the stall and into the aisle. Elyse stepped to the mare's side, wrapped her fingers in her mane, and with one swift jump, pulled herself onto Honey's back.

"Are you sure that's a good idea?" asked Jessica with an amused smile on her face.

"It's probably going to hurt and be very wet, but other than that, yes, I think this is great idea. Besides, *you* suggested I go for a ride," Elyse reminded her.

Jessica laughed. "I meant with full tack, not with nothing at all in pouring rain."

Elyse just shook her head and gave Honey a squeeze with her thighs, relishing the feel of the mare's muscles bunching beneath her. "See you later," Elyse said.

As soon as they departed the barn, Honey moved into a smooth lope. Elyse closed her eyes, her hands balanced lightly on her thighs, and let the mare decide where they were going. Mya would surely think she was crazy going for a ride like this—no bridle, no halter, no saddle, nothing but her and Honey, and the rain. But Jessica understood. When they were younger, there had been many times that they had gone out for rides just like this, much to their parents' chagrin.

They weren't gone for long. Elyse could feel her still-sore muscles protesting. Honey must have felt the shift in her body too, because when Elyse opened her eyes again, they were approaching the front of the barn, where Jessica was waiting.

"Better?" Jessica asked.

Honey stopped just before they reached Jessica, and Elyse slid off with a grimace.

"Yes. Thank you for the idea," Elyse said. Honey nuzzled her hand before stepping around Jessica and walking back into the barn, heading for her stall. Both women watched her. "I guess she wants to finish her dinner."

Jessica's stomach made a gurgling sound. "I guess I'm hungry too. I can go start dinner while you shut Honey's stall door. Oh, before I forget, Uncle Albert called and I told him you're fine. I figured you can call him when you're ready."

Elyse nodded in agreement.

After one and a half days under Jessica's care, Elyse slowly settled back into a routine where she could tolerate another person touching her. Elbows would brush as they passed by each other. Having Jessica brush her hair. Touching hands. Elyse found she could only sleep when Jessica was in the bed with her; otherwise, she dreamed of Archibald Cornelius being attacked by the fridge. Jessica had offered to search the journals, looking for anything mentioning an accident with a fridge, but couldn't find anything. Neither of them was sure what it meant, other than it really was just a figment of Elyse's imagination and the fridge represented something, perhaps the men who had attacked Elyse at the hospital.

Tuesday, they went out for two long trail rides. Elyse found herself opening up to Jessica, telling her bits and pieces of what happened to her. Other times, they reminisced about past adventures they had together. Neither of them mentioned Josh, for which Elyse was glad. She was afraid to examine her feelings for him because of what other emotions it would stir up. Several times, Elyse had almost called Uncle Albert to ask him about Archibald and the journals, but she was afraid to have the conversation on the phone. If she went into Atlanta, she knew he would fuss over her and ask questions about the attack she wasn't ready to answer.

While she was under Celine's care, Josh had confirmed that her uncle was indeed safe at his home and that the whole incident at the hospital had been a trap for her. What he wouldn't tell her was who was behind it. Whether it was because he didn't know or didn't want to tell her, she wasn't sure.

Jessica was planning on returning home Wednesday morning to resume her own duties at her cattle ranch, since Elyse finally felt like she could handle being alone. In the wee hours of the morning, Elyse startled awake and fell out of bed with a loud crash. Groaning, she pulled herself up. She searched for her ringing phone before realizing it was the landline, not her cell phone. Wondering tiredly who would be calling her at whatever ungodly hour this was, she found the phone and answered it. "Hello?"

A shaken voice responded, "Dark people came. I hid…they trashed the whole house. Some scary-looking woman with black hair in all leather was leading the group."

Eyes widening, she gasped, recognizing the voice. "Aunt Grace!"

"I don't know what to do, Elyse…what if they come back and aren't satisfied with what they found this time?" her aunt whispered, terrified.

"You could come here. Stay with me," Elyse offered, though she knew her aunt wasn't comfortable riding anymore and would have difficulty just getting to the ranch.

"I'll think of something," Aunt Grace uttered.

A shiver went down Elyse's spine as a feeling hit her like a sledgehammer. This was going to be the last time she ever spoke to her aunt.

"I could come to you!" Elyse said, alarm in her voice. She felt Jessica squeezing her hand in reassurance.

"Your feelings, your magical talent, are getting stronger, aren't they?" her aunt said. "It's my fault for not telling you about our bloodline before. I wanted to tell you face-to-face. But I waited too long."

Elyse pulled herself onto the bed, shaking. She clenched the phone in her hand, afraid she already knew that her aunt was going to confirm some of the things Josh said. Things she had refused to believe could be possible.

Sucking in a sharp breath, Aunt Grace continued, "I know how busy you are and that you probably haven't had a chance to go through all of Archie's journals. Archibald Cornelius was your great-grandfather. He married Renee Dubois, and she was pregnant with your grandmother when she became infected by COVID-50. Archie did everything in his power to save Renee, but it wasn't enough. The baby girl, though, Brianna, she survived. I am sure you have heard the rumors that babies born from mothers who died in childbirth while infected with COVID-50 developed magical talents. Well, it is not just a rumor, it is the truth. Your grandmother could see the future. This ability passed on to your father and to you. Your Uncle Albert suspected that there could be more to the magical talent than just seeing the future, but your grandmother refused to let him experiment on her or your father, terrified of what could be unleashed if he was right."

Sitting on the bed, mouth hanging open in shock, Elyse struggled to process what her aunt was telling her. *Magical talents? Seeing the future? She is confirming everything I have been told already.*

"Have you ever wondered why every single one of your foals has been perfect? That each generation is better than the one before. Unless you ignore that feeling you get. The two times you ignored it the foal died at birth or was malformed."

Elyse gasped. *That was being able to see the future? These feelings I've had my whole life?*

Aunt Grace continued softly, "You must trust yourself, Elyse. Someone clearly knows enough about our family to have put a target on my back. I can only assume they are coming after you next. After all, what good is an old woman with ancient books?"

"Please come…try, for me, Auntie," Elyse begged.

"I cannot…just know that I love you, and I know you will make the right decision for you."

There was a gasp on the other end of the phone, and the line went dead with a click. Elyse jumped up and tried calling her aunt back, but the line acted as though it had been disconnected.

Terror gripped her. Her aunt was going to die or was already dead. She had just learned that she *could* see the future and potentially had other talents as well. *Maybe that is what is happening with the journals. Some other aspect of my magic.* Shaking, she decided to take a shower, hoping that what she had just learned was part of a bad nightmare and she just had to wake up the rest of the way.

"What is going on?" asked Jessica, propped up on her elbow.

Elyse took a deep breath, trying to settle her nerves. "My Aunt Grace is being attacked, and there is nothing I…we…can do about it."

"What about Josh?" Jessica asked, fully alert now.

Elyse shook her head. "I don't know…part of me wants to ask him for help, and the other part is terrified of what seeing him again is going to do. Until that phone call, I've felt since I've been at the ranch that I've finally gotten myself back. I don't want to lose *me* again."

"I have an idea. Why don't you take a shower and think about it. Let yourself relax a little bit and help your mind clear some. Then you can decide if calling Josh is the best course of action," Jessica suggested.

Elyse nodded. Jessica did have a good idea.

Hot water slid sinuously over her back. Elyse stood in the shower, shoulders hunched, replaying her aunt's words in her head and wondering if she missed something, a hint that her aunt would still be alive if she could reach her.

Her eyes closed, she tilted her head up to let the water run over her face. *She said to trust myself. Is there no one else to trust? What about Josh? He lied…no, that's not fair. He just wasn't upfront that he was trying to recruit me all along.* The third date, he told her about the FBI wanting to recruit her. Hadn't most of the second dates in

Elyse's history gone similar ways? First date decided if the person was fun, and the second date she got to know them better.

Elyse decided that instead of just calling Josh and hoping for the best, she was going to try to deliberately see the future and what the outcome of making that call would be. Even though the idea of seeing the future sounded downright crazy, there wouldn't be any harm in trying, as Aunt Grace had asked.

Taking a deep breath to settle her nerves, she focused her thoughts, picturing herself calling Josh, the way his voice could sounded when he answered the phone. Images formed in her mind: Josh answering the phone, but behind him, smiling viciously, was the woman who had tried to grab her after her their date. The one Josh had shot. The edges of the woman were blurry, as though she wasn't truly there.

The vision disappeared. Elyse sighed. She hadn't gotten any information, only more unanswered questions, including whether her mind was playing tricks on her. She stepped out of the shower and wrapped herself in a towel and headed into the bedroom. A glance at the clock showed that it was four a.m., too early for a typical phone call. But tonight had been anything but typical.

"What did you decide?" Jessica asked from the bed.

"I'm going to call him. Worst case he won't come, and then we still have to figure out if we're doing anything," Elyse explained. She grabbed the phone and dialed Josh.

He answered with a sleepy, "Who's this?"

Elyse was surprised when hearing his voice gave her a feeling of comfort. Elyse cleared her throat. "Josh, it's Elyse," she said urgently. She could hear him fumbling on the other end of the line, presumably for a light; there was a clear click followed by a groan.

"Is something wrong?" he asked, seeming to have woken up more.

"My aunt called me…and…her house was ransacked." Elyse hesitated as tears welled up and finished in a barely audible whisper. "I think she's dead."

"Are you safe?" Josh said in a brisk, businesslike tone. Like an FBI agent.

"I don't know. She seemed to think that they would be coming after me. She also said they were looking for something, but she wasn't sure if they found it or not. And she—" Elyse choked back a sob that tried to escape.

"I should come to you, to protect you," Josh interrupted.

"She told me more about my family," Elyse continued as though Josh hadn't spoken. She decided not to tell him exactly what her aunt had said since she still didn't believe it herself.

"I can be there in thirty minutes," Josh offered again.

She shook her head, then realized he couldn't see her. "If you come here, people will ask questions. You don't come off as a rancher," Elyse informed him.

Josh chuckled. "You might be surprised at the skills I possess. Let me come. My car can go invisible, as long as you have a place I can put it where someone won't bang into it."

"Then yes, I do have a place you can put the car. I guess we can try you being here. I do have a guest cabin where you can stay. But you better be very convincing. No one in Jackson County, other than Jessica, knows that I go into the city. I'm not ready for that to change. The ranch is off of old Highway 124," she said firmly.

"Yes, I have the address. I'll see you soon," Josh said, and then the line went dead.

Elyse returned the phone to the drawer and leaned back on the bed, wondering what on earth she had just done. Josh would be here in less than an hour. Glancing over at Jessica, her mind drifted to Josh, the guy she barely knew, who was coming here, to her home, and inserting himself in her life to protect her from some unknown enemy. How could this end any way but badly?

TWENTY-ONE

JOSH

Josh set down the phone and sighed. He had been surprised by the call, not by the circumstances. He was certain that HAC *wasn't* behind the attack on Elyse in the hospital, that it was a different organization altogether. Probably one that had found out Elyse was a Cornelius and wanted to get their hands on her. The part that still puzzled him though was her description of the man who had primarily been responsible for her beating. The dyed-red hair, olive skin, and the accent. It was oddly familiar, like he'd seen him somewhere, but he hadn't yet been able to place why. This new attack, on Elyse's aunt, felt like HAC too, but without confirmation from Catrina or Terrance, he had no way of being sure. What he did know was that, regardless of who was behind the attacks, the next one would likely be worse, which meant the ranch would most likely take a direct hit.

His decision to keep his distance from Elyse had been working. Since she had returned home from Celine's, he had not heard anything from her or Jessica, which he felt must be a positive sign that some of her psychological wounds were healing.

I'm not sure if that will be the case once I am there. I will have to make sure to keep my distance unless Elyse indicates she wants me to do otherwise. He stood up and walked over to his closet, shoving the row of suits to the side to reveal the back. He placed his hand on the back wall. A blue glow flashed briefly under his hand. There was an audible click and then the back wall slid to the left, revealing a second closet. Josh stepped into the second closet and the light turned, on revealing a lot of clothing: suits and shirts in every color, a large selection of shoes, a wall of belts and accessories. Walking with certainty, Josh headed straight for the back wall. Neatly folded and stacked jeans; an assortment of long-sleeve collared button-up shirts, mostly in some shade of blue or plain white, a few red-and-black plaid. Above the hanging shirts was a rack with several cowboy hats and below were two well-worn pairs of boots.

He shouldn't be surprised Elyse wouldn't believe he could pretend to be a rancher or cowboy. However, just over ten years ago, one of his first undercover assignments had been infiltrating a rodeo circuit. He had had to learn how to ride a horse well, and fast. Returning his thoughts to packing, he pulled out a suitcase and put four shirts and pairs of jeans inside. Then, he pulled on a pair of jeans, a light-blue button-up shirt, dark-brown boots, and a black hat. When he headed back into the bedroom, the secret closet closed on its own. Josh tossed some other necessities in the suitcase. Then, he opened his gun safe and took out his belt holster and two handguns, along with a couple of boxes of ammo. Uncertain what he would be up against if HAC did make a move on Elyse, he wanted to be as prepared as possible.

With one last glance around his apartment, Josh departed. His car had a stealth super-speed mode, making it possible to travel the almost sixty miles to Elyse's ranch in less than twenty minutes.

As he neared the edge of the ranch, Josh told the car to slow down, worried that if there were riders on the gravel road at this hour that the car wouldn't be able to stop in time. He gazed around in the dark pre-dawn. Trees loomed as giant shadows. The car slowed down even further as it went around a curve, and the trees fell away, revealing acres of what he suspected were rolling pastures.

As the sky lightened, he could see the outline of the small farmhouse, barn, and other outbuildings forming just ahead. The car identified a suitable location to park, next to a rather small shed set to the side of the house. Josh opened the door to the car and removed his suitcase. As soon as the door was shut, all traces of his car vanished. Pleased the setting was working as it should, he made his way toward the farmhouse, assuming that was where he would find Elyse.

Josh knocked gently on the door, not sure if Elyse lived alone or if her employee lived here too and afraid to get yelled at for waking anyone up. He waited patiently for the footsteps he knew would come, but they didn't. Minutes ticked by and still the house beyond the door remained silent. Wondering if perhaps Elyse was out in the barn already, Josh decided to try the door before exploring the other buildings. The door opened with a creak. Josh cringed at how loud it sounded and wondered if he should offer to fix it during his stay.

Stepping inside, he peered around before he focused on the couch. At first glance, he had thought it was just a large blanket. Now, he realized a hand was peeking out from the edge and strands of red hair cascaded on the armrest and off the side. Elyse had fallen asleep.

As he debated whether he should head back outside or stay in the house, she stirred. At her small movements, the blanket slid. He watched, entranced, as the blanket partially fell to the floor, revealing her long legs hidden by bright pink pajamas with yellow cats. He took an unbidden step forward as a rush of intense desire ran through him, swiftly followed by apprehension. Another step followed. Hands clenched, Josh struggled to rein himself in. She needed his protection and was a survivor of a brutal attack. He did not need to complicate things any more than they already were. Besides, she had made it quite clear that she was no longer interested in having any sort of relationship with him. And yet, she had called him first for help.

A movement by Elyse's feet caught Josh's attention. Jessica was curled up in tight ball on the opposite end of the couch, almost invisible because of the dark brown blanket covering her that blended in with the couch.

Shaking his head and stepping backward, Josh sighed and decided it was not the time nor place to question the complications of associating with women. He turned back toward the door when he heard a gasp behind him. He whirled back around, hand going to the gun in his holster. Elyse was blinking at him uncertainly. He relaxed his hand and dropped it to his side, taking in the sight of her waking up. The faded black shirt she was wearing had slipped off one shoulder and revealed far more flesh than he was prepared for. Surprising himself, Josh blushed and suddenly felt extremely uncomfortable, as though he was breaching an unspoken boundary by seeing her so vulnerable. Josh spun and walked out of the house, deciding he'd wait outside the front door for Elyse to wake up and get properly dressed.

As he stood on the porch, he listened to the sounds coming out the partially open door. Footsteps followed by doors opening and shutting. He hadn't expected Elyse to fall asleep since he said he could be there so quickly, but she had.

I suppose with everything she's been through, she probably needs sleep whenever she can get it.

The door creaked open behind him. "Hello, I'm Jessica," came a woman's voice from behind him.

Josh turned and took Jessica's offered hand. "Josh. Nice to finally meet you," he said politely.

"It would have been nice if it were under different circumstances. I just started a pot of coffee. Elyse will be out in a moment if you want to come in." Jessica held the door open and gestured toward the table.

Josh entered the house and peered around. On the walls were old faded photographs of horses; many had brass plaques under them, presumably with the name of the horse. The smell of fresh coffee flooded his senses. He took a deep breath, inhaling appreciatively. "The coffee smells divine."

"Thanks. It's grown locally, here in Jackson County," Jessica said and indicated that he should take a seat at the table.

Josh followed her direction and sat down, continuing his evaluation of the house. There was a rifle over the front door and another one over the fireplace. He also saw a quiver full of arrows peeking out from behind a stack of firewood.

"How is she doing?" he inquired as Jessica set a mug of coffee in front of him.

Jessica shrugged. "She's improving. The first day was really rough. If I let her sleep alone, she has nightmares about Archibald Cornelius and a refrigerator."

Josh choked on his coffee, spitting some out before he got his hand over his mouth.

Jessica offered him a cloth napkin with a smirk. "I know, I know, it sounds completely crazy, but…that's what she said."

Josh took a tentative sip of the coffee, trying to make sure this time it stayed in his mouth. "Has she been having a lot of strange dreams about Archibald?"

"I don't know if I would say a lot…did Elyse ever tell you about the journals?" Jessica asked.

"Journals?" Josh said uncertainly.

"Did you have to tell him about the journals?" Elyse said from her bedroom doorway.

Josh peered from Jessica to Elyse, intrigued by their exchange.

"If you want him to help protect you, then he should know everything. Besides, I thought you had already told him," Jessica said matter-of-factly.

Elyse glared at her before slipping into the kitchen, pouring herself a mug of coffee, and joining them at the table. "Fine, I will tell him about the journals." Elyse finally looked at him. She held his eyes for a few moments before looking back at Jessica. "I found a box of my great-grandfather's journals, and I have been reading them. There are times when I see things, visions, or whatever you want to call them, of events that are not in the journals but seem to be related to the written entries."

Josh listened, enthralled. He had heard of many kinds of magic. Journals were frequently used as magical objects. Although with her tale, he was wondering if it had more to do with Elyse's magical talent starting to manifest itself further, where the journals were just a catalyst. Perhaps that was where the dream came in. She had progressed to no longer needing the journals to go into the past.

"When you had the dream, did you fall asleep reading the journal?"

Elyse let her eyes drift back to him. He could tell she was making an effort to stay focused on him. "No, I didn't fall asleep reading the journal. But when I woke up it was in the bed with me." She gave an involuntary shudder. "The people who went after Aunt Grace. Do you think they will come here?"

"There is a good chance of that, yes. My best guess is they are coming after people and places you care about. It would be logical for them to attack the ranch or you directly," Josh explained.

"What about Jessica? Is she safe?" Elyse said softly.

Josh shrugged. He hadn't determined who was behind the attacks for sure and didn't want to scare Elyse any further. "I don't know. If it is HAC who is coming after you, then they likely wouldn't go after Jessica unless she was here and in the way. However, I don't expect her family to be in any danger, unless of course you decided to go hide at their ranch instead of here."

Jessica cleared her throat, ending the stretch of silence. "What is your plan? For today, the next few days? How are you going to keep Elyse safe?"

Josh took a sip of coffee, buying himself a few extra moments before he had to answer the question. "My plan…is just to stay as close to Elyse as possible. That way if an attack does come, I can protect her—and you, if you decide to stay too."

"I need to go home at least for a few hours to check in and make sure everything is fine. I will try to come back." Jessica walked over to Elyse and gave her a quick hug. "Call the house if you need me, and I'll come."

When Jessica passed him, she beckoned her finger, indicating she wanted Josh to follow. He stood up, giving Elyse a quick glance before following Jessica outside. They walked in silence until they were well out of earshot of the house.

"What didn't you want her to overhear?" Josh said, keeping his voice cool.

"I wanted to give you a warning. She is still fragile after the attack, even if she has been saying she is better. I have known her for too long to not see the truth. I know there was something going on between the two of you, before you had to screw it up and try to recruit her. If you hurt her again, I will come after you, and you'll regret it." Jessica was in his face as she snarled the last bit. "She is still healing. Don't push her past the breaking point, Josh."

"I promise, I will not push her to do anything she is not willing to do," Josh said, meeting Jessica's gaze. She gave him a nod and turned on her heel and went in the barn.

Taking a deep breath, Josh adjusted his hat and went back to the house.

TWENTY-TWO
ELYSE

Elyse stared open-mouthed at the spot where Josh had just sat at the table, his abandoned mug of coffee still half-full. A shudder ran through her as another memory from the hospital invaded her mind. The red-haired nurse turned away from her and his shirt had slid up, revealing part of his back that had a giant spider tattoo on it. Wrapping her arms around her middle, she headed into her bedroom. To do what, she wasn't sure. *I should probably tell Josh I remembered a new detail.*

Mya would be showing up soon, and Elyse needed to come up with a reason that Mya would believe as to why Josh was at the ranch. Elyse rarely had visitors unless they were clients picking up a horse.

In the bedroom, she hesitated. She left the door halfway open. She was still afraid to be shut into a small space and was prone to panic attacks when she tried. Muttering to herself, she poked around her room, trying to figure out what she was supposed to be doing.

Jessica has left for a few hours. Mya is coming soon, she reminded herself. She glanced down and realized although she wasn't in her pajamas anymore, she hadn't exactly gotten dressed to do ranch chores either.

She discarded the baggy shirt on the bed, tossed her underwear into the hamper, and opened the dresser, pulling out a pair of dark jeans and a black long-sleeve high-collar blouse that would hide what was left of the bruises. Lost in her thoughts on the agenda for the day, she absently ran a finger over the blouse. A shadow fell over her, and she started shaking as tremors of fear worked their way through her. Squeezing her eyes shut, she willed the tremors to stop.

I am home. I am safe, she repeated over and over. As she regained control, she slowly opened her eyes and began pulling the clothing on, starting with her pants. About to tug the shirt over her head, a noise caught her attention and Elyse stood there, half-dressed and frozen to the spot, staring at Josh. Another memory of the nurse in orange scrubs relentlessly punching her in her stomach and then in her face assaulted her. She closed her eyes again, trying to force the images away. She had forgotten that Josh was here and had not been prepared for him to invade her personal space. Instead of her nerves settling, she could feel her mind unraveling more. The memories came faster and faster. She felt herself sink to the floor, and the tears were streaming freely down her cheeks. Curling into a tight ball, Elyse stopped fighting and let the memories take over.

Elyse had no idea how long she was on the floor, when she felt calloused fingers run over her arm, then face. A weight settled around her shoulders. *A blanket*, her mind supplied. Her breathing was raspy, as though she had been running for a long, long time without catching her breath.

"Elyse, are you okay?" Josh asked in a worried tone.

Her eyes snapped open and locked onto his blue ones. "Blue," she murmured. "Blue, not brown."

"What?" Josh said.

"His eyes were brown. Yours are blue," she said as though Josh should understand her.

"Yes, my eyes are blue," he confirmed.

"The nurse in orange scrubs, his eyes are brown. His hair is dyed red. Spider tattoo." Elyse blinked. "Josh?"

"I'm here, Elyse," Josh said softly as he hesitantly ran his finger along her jaw.

Her eyes fluttered shut, and she leaned into his featherlight touch on her jaw. Instead of memories of the nurse in orange scrubs, this time when her eyes shut, Elyse saw herself and Josh dancing on their first date at Three Dragons. She could feel him crouched beside her and felt her body leaning into his. Part of her wanted to replace the bad memories from the hospital with good memories of her and Josh.

Her position on the floor was awkward. She couldn't imagine how uncomfortable Josh was. Elyse had no idea how long they sat there on the floor together, but she was impressed that he had been willing to just sit with her, just as Jessica had, to help her heal. Except she was lifelong friends with Jessica, and Josh…she had been on three dates and then told him she never wanted to see him again. *So why is he here?*

"I don't know," she whispered, burying her head her hands when she realized she had answered her own question aloud.

"Don't know what?" Josh asked.

"It's not important. But…I need to finish getting dressed. Mya is coming soon." The statement was intended to motivate herself to get up, to move past whatever had just happened and get on with the day.

"Okay, I will let you get dressed." Josh scooted a few feet away from her before standing up.

Elyse stood up. As she teetered, the blanket started to fall off her shoulders, but she stopped it just in time and clutched it tightly to her. She gulped and waited for the panic attack or old memories to hit her again. Nothing happened. Sighing in relief, she gave Josh a tentative smile, which he returned. She found herself wanting to be in his arms. Shaking her head, she took a step back toward the dresser.

"I'd like to get dressed now," Elyse said in what she hoped was a calm voice.

To her relief, Josh nodded and walked out of the bedroom, pulling the door halfway closed behind him.

A while later, a fully dressed Elyse emerged from the bedroom just as a woman called through the screen door, "Hello?"

"I'll be there in a few minutes, Mya!" called Elyse.

Josh raised an eyebrow at her. Elyse held a finger up to her lips.

"Okay!" replied Mya, followed by booted footsteps heading back off the porch.

As Mya headed back to the barn to start the chores, Elyse's stomach rumbled. "Shoot, I didn't eat. I guess I need to go tell Mya I'll be more than a few minutes."

Elyse rushed past Josh and out the door. "Hey, Mya!" she called, jogging down the gravel in her bare feet. Mya turned back around, giving Elyse an amused look. "I forgot to eat. So, I'll be a little longer than I thought. But...we are going to have extra help for a few days."

"Extra help?" echoed Mya.

Elyse smiled. "Yep. A friend of mine is visiting and has offered to let me put him to work."

"I look forward to meeting him," Mya said with a smile, heading back toward the barn.

After breakfast, Elyse headed out to the barn, desperately wanting to throw herself into chores. Maybe then she could sort out her feelings for Josh. Grabbing a wheelbarrow and pitchfork, Elyse went into the stall at the far end and began cleaning it, her mind churning.

I can't deny that I am attracted to Josh, and yes, he should not have tried to force me to join the FBI, but since then all he has done has been there for me. He rescued me from the kidnapping, from the hospital, and now once again he has come to my aid. How can I dislike someone for caring that much about me?

Humming to herself, she settled into the rhythm of cleaning the stalls, letting all of the confusing and conflicting thoughts disappear. Elyse was surprised when Mya came over to her.

"Can you tell me what was actually happening in your house this morning?" she asked, eyebrow raised.

Elyse rolled her eyes. She should have known better than to think Mya would not be suspicious. "I got a call from Aunt Grace last night," she said, deciding to start with the truth, even if it was not the whole truth. "Her house was hit by robbers. She is going to temporarily relocate for a while and will be difficult to reach."

Mya gasped. "Oh! I'm so sorry. Can't you go help her? I would be happy to take care of the horses while you're gone."

Elyse gave Mya a grateful smile. "You know how stubborn she can be. She insisted that she can handle it herself without my help." Mya nodded in understanding, having met Aunt Grace once. "For today, I was thinking we could start the annual fence check? You could head out and start with the fence along the creek. That one is the trickiest to keep intact and almost always needs repairs. I'll start with the stallion pasture," Elyse continued, deciding that the best way to handle having Josh here and introducing him to Mya was if they didn't have many opportunities to see each other. The stallion pasture was on the opposite end of the property from the creek.

Mya nodded in acknowledgement. "I'll take some basic supplies with me and come back for the cart if I end up needing anything big."

"Sounds like a plan. I will finish up here and then head out too." Elyse returned her attention to the last pile of manure in the stall, hoping that Mya would be on her way. She heard departing footsteps down the aisle.

An hour later, all ten stalls had been cleaned and new shavings added. Elyse put the wheelbarrow away and was debating whether she should pick a horse for Josh before talking to him about his riding skills or after, when in the distance, the door to the guest cabin opened, and he emerged. Black cowboy hat, light blue shirt, faded jeans, and brown boots. Shaking her head, Elyse realized that he did indeed know how to dress properly to blend in on a ranch. Now, she just had to find out if he could ride as well as he dressed.

She raised her hand in a casual greeting. Josh sped up his steps, but Elyse turned away and walked over to one of the dry lot pens before he could reach her. She opened the gate and waited for him. "Come on."

Josh looked at her uncertainly before stepping through the gate and latching it.

"Can you ride?" she asked, doubt clear in her voice.

Josh laughed. "Yes, I can ride. I have even competed some in team roping."

Elyse, eyes wide, looked at him in surprise. "How skilled would you say you are…beginner, intermediate, or advanced?" she asked, so she wouldn't pick the wrong horse for him. Josh shrugged. "I do need an answer." She made a clicking sound with her tongue.

"Intermediate, I guess," he replied. Elyse walked farther into the dry lot, making a beeline for a black horse with a big blaze and four socks. Halter in hand, she ran her hands over the gelding, giving him a once-over before putting the halter on. He gently nibbled on her hand before quietly following her back to where Josh was standing. She offered him the lead rope. "This is Fork."

"Do you have a Spoon too?" he teased.

Elyse shook her head. "Not at this time. But I had a Knife a few years back," she offered.

Josh chuckled. "What happened to Knife?"

"Sold him…that is my business, raising and training horses to sell," she chided him, knowing he should know this already since he was an FBI agent. *I doubt there's much about me he doesn't know.*

Leading Josh and Fork back toward the barn, Elyse paused long enough to retrieve Honey from her turnout pen. "Let's tie them here, and we will carry the tack out."

After Elyse had double-checked Josh's rope-tying skills, they headed into the tack room in the barn. She directed him to grab a pad and saddle off the rack, and she snagged a girth and bridle. Josh carried the saddle over to Fork. He tried to balance the saddle while flinging the pad onto Fork's back. Giggling at his awkwardness, Elyse snatched the pad out of his hand and skillfully set it on Fork's back in the proper position. Josh swung the saddle up next and settled it over the pad.

Elyse held up the girth. "Can you do this?"

Rolling his eyes, Josh swiped the girth out of her hand and began to buckle it. "Yes...I did tell you I spent time on the rodeo circuit."

Elyse shrugged and headed back into the barn to grab her own saddle, girth, and bridle.

"Okay, a few quick tips for you with Fork," Elyse said as Josh slid the bit into Fork's mouth. "He steers by neck reining with one hand. If you want to turn to the left, move your hand to the left. To go right, move your hand right. Don't use two hands or you're going to regret it, especially if we're in the pasture with the stallions...that's not a good place to get into an argument with Fork." Elyse gave Honey's neck a scratch as she remembered the last time she decided to work with Fork on using two hands. He had flipped over on her, and then Rocko and Harris had almost run her over while she was on the ground in their need to put the young gelding in his place.

"Okay, I will make sure to keep only one hand on the reins. How is he with gunfire?" Josh asked.

Elyse shrugged. "None of my horses have an issue with it. They learn as two-year-olds when I pony them through the major life lessons. I won't shoot from them until they're four, but he's almost six. If he were to react, it would be because you were doing something I told you not to."

Josh coughed and looked away before Elyse continued her explanation. "If you lose your balance and start tipping, Fork will stop."

"That's easy enough," Josh replied.

Elyse shook her head. "Sort of…if you're loping and you start losing your balance, he will stop, abruptly and usually with some amount of slide. You're almost guaranteed to fall off unless you get lucky. He hasn't learned to slow down gradually. He will, but for now it is abrupt." Peering at Josh over the top of Honey's saddle, she was surprised to see him gaping at her. "What?"

"I can't believe that you teach them all of this. In stages, clearly, but train them nonetheless." Josh's voice was laced with awe.

Elyse shrugged again and slid her foot into the stirrup before swinging her leg over the saddle. "You didn't think people would pay me over a hundred thousand dollars for a horse that dumped them every time they lost their balance, did you?"

Josh mounted Fork and toyed with his black mane before replying. "I honestly hadn't thought much about it. I'm an FBI agent… remember? I own a car and live in downtown Atlanta. The lifestyle and needs of your clients are not something I have spent much time considering."

Unsure of how to respond, Elyse clucked to Honey, and they took off at a trot.

TWENTY-THREE

JOSH

Side by side with the horses almost evenly matched, Josh and Elyse loped up the last hill to the highest point in the stallion pasture. He found himself watching Elyse, the way she rode her horse effortlessly. Just as Elyse had said, Fork was a simple horse with comfortable gaits and an easygoing personality. Josh knew he was treading a delicate line out here with Elyse. The only way to protect her was to be wherever she was on the ranch. But out here in the pasture, although he should be able to see anyone coming long before they attacked, he still felt too vulnerable.

Or maybe it's just that I'm out of my element. On a horse, of all things.

When they reached the top of the hill, they halted and looked out over the pasture. "Harris and Rocko are over there under the oak trees," Elyse explained, pointing to the far corner of the pasture. Josh nodded, not able to distinguish the horses from the shadows under the trees.

"Do we need to worry about them, since they are stallions?" he asked lightly.

Elyse shrugged her shoulders. "No…they know Honey is off limits. Unless you do something stupid, they would have no reason to bother us. They are lazy, and it's hot today."

"This seems rather large for just two horses?" Josh asked.

Elyse waved her hand in dismissal. "They're out here together for about two months in the fall before they move closer to the house for the winter. Depending on the year, this is also one of the pastures I will put a stallion in with his mares. I have to be careful with how many horses and the frequency I put them in a particular pasture, otherwise over time it will kill the pasture. Through careful management I have been quite successful. Every third year, I typically close a pasture for a growing season and will hay it instead."

"Sounds complicated," murmured Josh.

"It's only complicated if you're not familiar with it. Given that you live in Atlanta…I imagine you don't concern yourself with how to grow grass for hay and pastures," Elyse said with a smile. She turned Honey and nudged her closer to the fence, wanting to inspect the corner. Josh just watched. He preferred to stay on Fork so that he could have the advantage of the horse's height just in case someone decided to attack.

They spent the rest of the day going through the same routine. Josh rode Fork and Elyse rode Honey. They inspected fence line, making minor repairs with the equipment they were easily able to pack in the saddle bags and noting any larger repairs to tackle on another day.

On the second day at Elyse's house, Josh was piddling around in the kitchen. He had two mugs of steaming coffee and two plates of scrambled eggs with bacon sitting on the table when Elyse finally emerged from her bedroom.

He glanced over his shoulder from his place at the sink, where he was cleaning the pan he used for the eggs. "I figured I could at least make us breakfast."

She gave him a grateful smile and sat down at the end farthest away from Josh, eating her breakfast quickly.

Josh finished cleaning the pan and dried it, then returned it to the hook it was on before joining her at the table. To his surprise, Elyse finished the eggs and set down her now-empty mug of coffee.

"Thanks for breakfast. I need to go help Mya," she said, rushing out the door.

Mouth open, Josh stared blankly at the door as it shut. *I thought she was finally trusting me again, but she just ran out the door without me,* he thought. Josh shrugged. He would finish cleaning up from making breakfast, and if Elyse didn't come back to retrieve him, then he would go find her in the barn.

While cleaning up, Josh realized he hadn't looked at his work computer since he'd arrived. He decided he should probably at least add the new details Elyse had mentioned to the file he had started on the attack in the hospital.

In the guest cabin, Josh entered Elyse's additional notes when it dawned on him that she had said the nurse who had beaten her had a spider tattoo on his back. Eyes wide in shock, Josh almost lost his grip on the computer. *The accent and skin color alone, it could be anyone, but when a spider tattoo is added into the mix…I think she was attacked by Arañas Rojas. Which would also explain Jaime Tejero as a known associate of Juan Gonzalez. I also only got a photo of his face. I didn't bother to inspect him to see if he had a spider tattoo, and who knows what happened to the body.*

"Show me all known members of Arañas Rojas," he commanded the computer. His open file disappeared and was replaced by thumbnail headshots of known members of the gang. Josh meticulously went through each file, searching for male members with the spider tattoo on their backs. Nothing came up, which wasn't unexpected.

"It must be someone who goes undercover for them, who wouldn't want the tattoo flashing around." Unfortunately, Josh had not been involved with the gang long enough to know of

236

anyone like that. Shaking his head and deciding he could worry about that another time, Josh put away his computer and headed out to the barn.

Josh was expecting for them to go back to inspecting fence line. The sight of Fork and Honey hitched to a cart stopped him in his tracks. The cart had a roll of fence and some fence posts along with an assortment of shovels and other tools.

Elyse saw him and came toward him, smiling. "Today we do the major repairs. Are you up for that?"

Josh nodded. "Absolutely."

"Great, just hop on back and we'll head out." Elyse gestured to the back of the cart, and she headed around to the front.

Josh sat on the back of the cart and almost tipped off as it started forward. The movement was smoother than he expected, but not very fast. He assumed she wanted him to sit in the back so he could open the gates, but he quickly discovered that Elyse must have opened them earlier because they didn't have to make any stops.

A while later, the cart slowed to a stop. Josh hopped out and surveyed where they were. It was the stretch of fence that had three posts that needed to be replaced. Elyse had parked in a nice flat area, but they would have to carry the posts to the section of fence about fifty feet away.

He picked up two posts as though they weighed nothing and took off at a jog to the section of fence. He set them down, then sprinted back and grabbed the last post, which was longer and heavier than the others. He took off at a run with it. When he came back to the cart again, Elyse was staring at him.

"What?" he asked.

"I didn't realize you have a magical talent," Elyse blurted out.

Josh chuckled. "Yes, I do. Strength and speed mostly."

Elyse picked up the shovel and tossed it at him. Josh caught it smoothly out of the air. "Does that mean you can dig super fast?"

"Maybe. I don't spend much time digging," Josh said with a shrug. Carrying the shovel, he ran back to the posts.

Elyse made her way over, grabbed one of the posts they were replacing, and rocked it back and forth. "See how this is so loose? I'm going to cut the wire fence and then we can just roll it back, pull all three posts out and then put the new ones in, and replace the wire with a new section. The corner post you're going to have to dig. The other two you may not need to."

Josh watched as she cut the wire at each of the staples on the first post and then started to roll the fence. Once she headed to the second post, he wrapped his hands around the first post and applied a little bit of pressure. It popped right out of the hole, then broke in half.

"Oops, I guess I squeezed too hard," he muttered under his breath.

Using the shovel, he removed the excess dirt before putting the new post in and packing the dirt back around it. Josh quickly did the same for the next post and then picked up the big corner post and met Elyse.

She was just finishing rolling up the old fence. "You're done already?"

Josh laughed. "Yes. See, I told you I'm fast."

"Maybe I should hire you full time for fence repairs. I was expecting to spend a couple of hours fixing these posts," Elyse said gratefully.

When they finished repairing the first section of fence, they loaded the tools, broken posts, and wire onto the cart and moved on to the next section, working until they ran out of fresh fence materials.

Josh's stomach rumbled as he was loading the last broken post into the cart. Elyse was putting the tools back in the bucket and giggled. "Are you used to eating on a strict schedule or something?"

Josh shrugged, wondering why she thought being hungry was funny. "Don't you eat breakfast, lunch, and dinner?"

"Usually I eat breakfast, a snack at some point, and dinner. It's a working ranch. Days I do fence repairs, I load everything I think

I can get to in one day and head out. When I'm done, then I go back, and usually that's at the end of the day. You are in luck though. Since your magical talent has allowed us to work more than twice as fast as I was expecting, we need to go back and get more fence supplies. So, we can have lunch too," Elyse said, grinning. She made a light jab at his still-gurgling stomach.

Josh loosely grabbed her hand. His first instinct had been to kiss her, but he was still afraid to push her too fast. Instead, he brought it up to his lips and gently kissed it. "I am at your service, mademoiselle," he replied with a flourishing bow, which sent Elyse into a fit of giggles.

"Let's go get lunch," Elyse said and gave his hand a gentle tug as she led the way to the driver's seat. Josh was a little surprised there was space for two people, since she had insisted he sit in the back. He wondered what had changed her mind. Before he could ask, she clucked to Fork and Honey and slapped the reins, sending them into an ambling walk in the direction of the barn.

He let the silence go for a few minutes before he remembered a question he had been refraining from asking. Now that Elyse seemed to be able to relax around him, he thought it would be a prime opportunity. "When I first showed up, Jessica mentioned something about journals. Would you mind telling me about those?"

Elyse gave him a sideways glance before returning her eyes to the path they were following. "Sure. I found a box of journals that belong to Archibald Cornelius. Sometimes when I'm reading them—and once or twice when I was not reading them—I have had visions of things that are related to the journal entries but not necessarily written in the journals."

Josh tugged on his lip in thought. *They don't sound like normal journals.* "I wonder if your magical talent is somehow using the journals as an amplifier or something. Letting you see the past?"

"Can people do that? See the past?" Elyse said.

"I have heard rumors that type of talent exists. It would be even rarer than seeing the future," Josh answered.

"You also mentioned that journals can have their own magic. How do we know that these are not that kind of journal?" Elyse inquired.

Josh sighed. "I can try examining them, but unless they look out of the ordinary, I probably won't be able to tell if they do or don't have their own magic." He thought, *Catrina might be able to tell if she were here, since vampires are able to see if inanimate objects have magical properties.* But he didn't want to say that to Elyse, or he would have to explain how he knew a vampire and his ties to HAC. Just then, they pulled up in front of the barn.

"If we're going to have lunch, what do we do with the horses?" Josh asked uncertainly.

Elyse jumped out of the cart and disappeared into the barn, returning with two bags that had straps on them. "I will give them a snack while we eat lunch."

He watched as she attached the grain bags to each horse so their muzzles were inside. He could hear the quiet crunching sound as the two horses munched on their snack.

"C'mon, let's go inside for that bite to eat," Elyse said before briskly heading toward the house.

TWENTY-FOUR

ELYSE

To Elyse's surprise, after lunch, they continued the fast pace of plowing through all of the major fence repairs. Josh's speed was saving her hours and hours of work, maybe even days. Since they finished the major fence repairs so quickly, they had time to go back out and continue fence checks. Glancing over at Josh as they rode side by side through the pastures, she realized that she finally felt comfortable around him again. He had stayed true to his word and had not pushed any boundaries between them, giving her the time she needed to feel confident around him again after the attack. It had also provided her the opportunity to examine her feelings for him. As much as she was frustrated that he had tried to recruit her for the FBI, she also realized that it was his job, which he had told her. She was not the only person with a magical talent the FBI had assigned him to recruit. Perhaps it had just been bad luck they had gone on two dates first.

Can I let go of that anger and let us continue where we left off? She glanced at him in what she hoped was a subtle manner and realized that the feelings she had been ignoring were still there. She was still attracted to him. Just as she was about to look away, he caught her gaze and held it for a moment before focusing on where they were going.

They reached one of the lowest points of the pasture, where the grass was almost as tall as the fence. Making a mental note that she would need to come out and trim it back, Elyse's focus was only on inspecting the fence. She had decided to walk this section because she already knew it needed some minor repairs. Tools in hand, she worked her way down the line, pausing here and there to hammer in a staple or pull the fence back up in a spot where it had sagged.

The fence repairs used to be a family affair with Elyse and both of her parents working together. Her father would replace the broken fence posts, and Elyse and her mother would attach the new fencing. With three people, the work had gone fast. The past five years, doing it with just two, the repairs became tedious and a dreaded part of the year. She was surprised that with Josh at her side, the monotonous chore was once again enjoyable.

Behind her, she heard a whinny and Josh yell. Spinning away from the fence, Elyse saw Fork rear and Josh slide off backward. Eyes wide in shock, Elyse dropped her tools and ran toward Josh.

"Are you okay?" she gasped, almost tripping and falling in her rush. He lay unmoving in the tall grass. Fork stood nearby, ears flicking uncertainly. Elyse threw herself on the ground next to Josh, fingers gently probing him, when suddenly his arms wrapped around her and pulled her on top of him. She froze in shock.

"I was worried you hit your head! Why didn't you say something?" Elyse said, concern still fresh in her thoughts.

Josh shook his head and smiled. "I'm fine. Promise. I had the wind knocked out of me, but I'm much better now."

Peering into his face, Elyse wasn't sure what to think. He wasn't complaining that her lying on top of him was causing any discomfort, so maybe he was telling the truth. Then, she realized that this was the most she had touched anyone other than Jessica since the attack at the hospital. Over the past few days, they had brushed hands a few times, but that was it.

Josh's eyes searched hers, then he slowly lifted his head and very gently brushed his lips against hers before letting his head fall back on the grass.

After the light kiss, Elyse became more aware of Josh's body beneath hers and realized that instead of fear, she felt desire. Deciding to test out her reaction to Josh, she tentatively placed her lips on his. A featherlight kiss, the barest of touches. The fear was staying away. Gaining more confidence, Elyse kissed Josh again, letting her lips linger.

Josh wrapped his arms around her and rolled so that Elyse was now beneath him. He kept his weight off of her, but she was still trapped. Her heart beat faster, and she tried to fight off the fear that was flooding her mind, but it wasn't working.

"Fuck," she gasped, eyes squeezed shut.

To her surprise, Josh rolled back onto the grass beside her and started laughing.

Elyse's eyes popped open, and she lifted herself up on her elbow. "What?"

"Well, we definitely…didn't get to fuck," he uttered, causing Elyse to blush.

"Is that what you were hoping for?" Elyse demanded.

Josh shook his head. "No, I wasn't hoping for any particular outcome. I just found your word choice amusing. But you were fine with the kisses until I rolled us over, which is a significant improvement."

"I know. I just…I don't understand these reactions. How can I be okay straddling you, but panic if you are on top of me?"

Josh sat up, studying her. "I am not a doctor. I don't have answers." He leaned down, giving her a light kiss as though to prove his point.

Elyse took a deep breath and sat up. "Josh, we are supposed to be checking the fence line."

Josh nodded and raised his hand. "I solemnly swear I will behave."

Elyse rolled her eyes and lightly punched him in the arm. "I will hold you to that."

Standing up and straightening her shirt, she was not prepared when a wave of pain rolled across her body, causing her to fall to her knees. Nostrils flaring, she inhaled deeply, struggling to breathe through the pain. She smelled smoke.

"Elyse!" Josh yelled as she fell.

She groaned, holding her head in her hands. "It's burning," she sobbed.

"What is burning?" he asked. She felt his warm arms as they wrapped around her, holding her close.

"The barn!" she gasped as an image slammed into her of the barn engulfed in flames and horses screaming. "We need to go to save them!"

Josh wouldn't loosen his grip. She struggled, needing to save her precious horses, her livelihood. "Let me go!"

"Listen to me…your magical talent is to get visions of the future. Can you tell if what you're feeling is happening right now, in this moment? Or if it's something that could happen, minutes, hours, or days from now?" Josh said quietly. His logical response shocked her but made her realize that he could be right and what she was feeling might not be happening right now. But what if it was? She couldn't abandon her horses to a barn fire that she knew could be happening less than a mile away.

"I don't know. But it would kill me to find out that the fire is happening right now, and I did nothing," Elyse whispered, yanking her arm out of Josh's grip and standing up. Honey chose that precise moment to walk over and nibble on her shoulder. "C'mon, girl. We need to go home."

Honey's ears pricked at the word home. Elyse wrapped a handful of mane in her hand and pulled herself up into the saddle. Looking down at Josh, she wasn't sure how to read his expression. "Are you coming or not?"

Josh sighed and threw up his arms in defeat. "I will come, but only because if the barn is on fire you are going to need all the hands you can get."

"Just don't fall off," Elyse called over her shoulder. Then, she asked Honey to lope with a kissing sound. Keeping her eyes forward to watch out for anything that could injure Honey, Elyse shivered, praying that her vision was wrong and that not only would the barn not be on fire, that it wouldn't ever catch fire. One of her worst fears as a rancher was to have a barn fire with horses trapped inside, unable to be rescued. Honey sensed Elyse's urgency, and without being asked, accelerated from a lope to a gallop.

Sliding to a stop, Honey threw a cloud of dust in front of the barn. Shaking in relief that the barn was not on fire, Elyse jumped when Mya started coughing.

"Geez, Elyse," Mya said between coughs. "Did you have to almost slide into me?"

Face already flushed from the ride, Elyse turned an even darker red in embarrassment. A clatter of hooves and a thump sounded behind her. Elyse turned to look over her shoulder and saw Josh on the ground in a heap by Fork's feet. She exchanged an amused look with Mya.

"Oops," Elyse giggled. "I suppose I should make sure he's okay. Find anything needing major repairs?"

Mya shook her head and gathered the few pieces of wood she dropped. "No, just small stuff. I came back because I needed a few pieces to brace things, but I think Scooter can carry these easily in a sack."

"Okay. I think we're going to grab a snack and then head back out. Give the horses a chance to get some water," Elyse stated. She let Honey's reins rest on her neck and walked over to where Josh was pulling himself off the ground.

"I warned you he stops fast," Elyse said with a smile.

Josh dusted off his pants and looked at her. "Yeah...I just was tilted a little too far forward. His stop was rather enthusiastic. What's the plan?"

"Snack…and then we go back out. Now that we know the barn isn't on fire, there shouldn't be a reason to not finish checking that fence line," Elyse explained. Josh nodded.

Josh had been on the ranch for not quite two full days. Much to Elyse's surprise, he knew how to help with most of the ranch work and was not too bad of a rider either. Before they called it quits for the evening, she decided to take advantage of having another rider and had Josh ride some of the young horses who needed to get used to having more than her as a rider.

So far it was going pretty well. Elyse was standing on the railing of the round pen observing as he rode Twizzler, a red four-year-old mare.

To Elyse's pleasure, being around Josh no longer seemed to be stirring up fear or memories from the hospital attack. *I guess everyone recovers at a different pace. Or…because I'm home and not in Atlanta, I am recovering faster.*

She shrugged before focusing on Josh again. A wave of desire coursed through her as she watched how easily he asked Twizzler to canter. The young mare decided to throw in a couple of bucks, and Josh stayed on and then put her back to work as though nothing had happened.

Elyse jumped off the railing and headed back into the barn, intending to dunk her head in a cold bucket of water. The last thing she needed was to be distracted from her list of tasks to do today.

"You have a bit of chocolate on your lip," Josh observed before reaching over and ever so gently caressing her lip with his thumb, presumably to wipe it off. Sure enough, he pulled his thumb away and showed it to her, a smear of chocolate. Smirking, he took his finger and slowly stuck it in his mouth and sucked on it.

Elyse watched him, mouth slightly parted. She could feel desire rising up within her. Josh gave her a knowing look and leaned forward to kiss her. Elyse could taste the chocolate on his lips.

Slowly, Josh wrapped his arms around her waist and pulled her closer to him until she was tight against his chest. Josh tilted his head back to look at her. "Am I going too fast?"

Instead of answering, Elyse ran her fingers through his hair and kissed him, exploring his mouth with her tongue. That seemed to be all the encouragement he needed, because Josh ran his hands under her shirt and tugged it over her head in one smooth motion. Next, he unclasped her bra and let it fall onto the ground with her shirt. He captured her lips with his and while keeping her mouth busy, he gently massaged her breasts.

A gasp escaped from her lips. Josh abruptly stopped everything, concern flickering in his eyes. "I don't want to hurt you, Elyse. If this is too much for you to handle this soon, just tell me. I can be patient."

Elyse tried to give him a reassuring smile, but from his expression, she didn't think she was successful. "I'm fine, I promise," she uttered, before grabbing his belt and pulling him a few steps forward. When he was close enough, she slowly slid her hand down his pants, cupping his cock and running her hand along its impressive length. Before she could do anything else, Josh kissed her again.

Elyse was eagerly returning the kiss when she thought she heard something from outside. She paused. Josh tried to get her attention, but she heard the noise again. Almost like a crackling sound.

Elyse's eyes flew open and she sat up, realizing she was in her bed, alone. Her eyes began to flutter closed again when she caught a whiff of something, and then it registered. She could smell smoke. Since no one was cooking anything, that could only mean one thing. Something was on fire.

Elyse stood up and ran to the door for her boots. As she shoved out the front door, she saw Josh running toward her from the guest cabin. She skidded to a stop, tilted forward, and face-planted in the gravel pathway. Hissing in annoyance, she slapped away Josh's hand as he tried to help her up. Her attention was riveted to the barn.

Smoke was billowing out the big open doors and the open tops of the Dutch doors where the stalls were. Elyse stood up and realized she was shaking. Fear snaked through her as every horse owner's worst nightmare was happening. Barn fires were usually devastating. Without a thought for herself, Elyse ran to the barn.

"Wait!" yelled Josh.

She ignored him. He wouldn't understand why she'd run into a burning building and risk herself for one of her horses.

She was surprised when Josh grabbed her arm and yanked her to a halt. "Stop and listen to me, Elyse," Josh demanded.

She gave him a scalding look. "I need to get the horses out before it's too late!" she shouted.

"Remember, we put everyone out for the night? There's no one in the barn," Josh explained patiently.

"We did?" Elyse said finally, turning to look him in the eyes.

"Yes, we did. I asked you why we were changing it up, and you had said that when it gets as hot as it has been that sometimes you put them on a reverse schedule, so they're in during the worst of the heat and out when it's cooler," Josh replied, his voice cool and calm even though the barn was on fire.

"I still…I need to go get my stuff out of the barn, to save what I can," Elyse said, taking a few steps toward the barn before Josh stopped her again.

"No, the only thing you need to do right now is make sure that the fire doesn't have anywhere to go other than the barn." Josh said.

Sighing, Elyse realized that Josh was right. There was nothing in the barn that was worth risking her life for. "Hardpacked dirt, with some areas covered in gravel, goes around the whole perimeter of the barn. About a ten-foot-wide pathway."

"Will your neighbors help? Is there a fire department?" Josh asked.

Elyse stared at him. He clearly had no idea what it was like to live out here. "The only help I might get is Jessica's family. But unless they happen to have a cart currently loaded with a full water tank, I don't know how much help they will be. Other than Jessica, none of the neighbors are close enough to be any help. By the time they show up it would just be to help clean up. How about I call Jessica, and you can use the hose and see if you can start working on putting the fire out."

Elyse jogged back into the house and made a beeline for her phone. *Ring. Ring. Ring.* She waited for someone to pick up. *Ring. Ring. Ring.* "Fuck!" she grumbled when she realized if they weren't answering, it meant likely they were handling their own emergency with the cattle. "I guess we're on our own."

Anger bubbled up as she headed back to Josh. "This is all your fault," she shouted, running at him, fist swinging. Instead of blocking her punch, he let it land. She swung again. "If you hadn't gotten me involved in the FBI and HAC mess, then my barn wouldn't be on fire right now." The second punch connected too, although her fist was protesting at how hard his abs were when she connected with them.

Josh gave her a sympathetic look. "Elyse. I am truly sorry about your barn. But it's not my fault. If you'll let me help you, we can see what we can save."

Hot tears streamed down her face, and she shook. *I wish you were here, Mom. To tell me what to do.* Wrapping her arms around herself, Elyse stood there, shaking and sobbing. She could hear the crunching of gravel and then the gush of water as Josh turned on the hose.

Sobs wracked her body. In the distance, she heard the horses panicking from the smoke. Whinnies pierced the air, snapping her back to the present. *I'm here. I can do something.* Elyse quickly jogged toward the pasture fence. She had another water hydrant and a long hose over there. Turning it on, she grabbed the hose and sprayed down the wood fence, hoping if she saturated it enough that the fence would be safe if the fire jumped. The horses all ran toward the fence, wanting comfort. She could see the whites of their eyes even as they jostled for the position closest to her. Keeping the hose in her right hand, she reached out with her left and gave them all reassuring pats, whispering soothing words. When she withdrew her hand, they walked off calmer than when they had approached.

Finished, Elyse decided to see how Josh was faring in the barn. She gave the building a wide berth but was thrilled to see no evidence of flames trying to emerge, just lots and lots of smoke. As the sun was long gone, the darkness and minimal moonlight made it difficult to see inside and what the damage could be. She took a deep breath in through her nose and started coughing. She bent over, trying to catch her breath, but struggled to stop the coughs from coming.

Josh found her that way. Luckily, he had a canteen of water, which he offered. "This should help."

Elyse took the canteen and tentatively took a sip, hoping it would go down her throat and not come right back out in another coughing fit. As the water trickled down her throat and the coughing abated, she took a few more sips.

"Did you get the fire out?" she asked.

"There are still some spots that are smoldering, but I drenched everything in there that hadn't burned yet, so I think it will burn itself out. But…it's not a pretty sight in there," Josh warned.

Elyse nodded. Over the years, her neighbors had had a few barn fires on their ranches. Elyse had seen the aftermath and knew how fast everything in a barn could burn up. She wasn't sure if she was lucky or not that the barn had metal sides and a metal roof. *I suppose that helped contain it inside.*

"I want to see it," Elyse said firmly, not wanting Josh to object. *It is my ranch after all. He is just a guest that I invited.*

Josh nodded, although she could tell he wanted to refuse. Taking the lead, she walked around the corner and to the doors of the barn. She could not believe what she saw. Everything was black. The stalls that had had some old metal parts from before COVID-50 were collapsing. Several of the beams supporting the roof had fallen into the middle of the aisleway. The tack room was just *gone*.

TWENTY-FIVE

JOSH

Josh followed Elyse, worried about her reaction. When he originally said it was pretty bad, he had been underselling the damage. He didn't think there was anything they would be able to save from the building. In fact, he was not sure they should even be standing inside of it because of how compromised the supporting beams were.

"Who would have done this?" Elyse asked as tears fell freely down her sooty face, leaving streaks.

Josh sighed and ran a hand over his face, debating what to say. "I think it's safe to assume it is HAC. They want you and will use any means necessary to get you. I wouldn't be surprised if they'd rather see you dead than in the custody of the FBI."

Elyse stepped back from him and hit the wall, which shook. Ashes cascaded around them.

"We need to go now. It's not safe in here!" Josh shouted over the sound of the groaning metal. He reached out a hand to Elyse, which thankfully she took.

There was a loud *pop, pop, pop.* "Run!" He tugged hard on her hand, praying she would run and not force him to pick her up and pack her out.

252

They were almost out of the barn when they heard a huge *BOOM*. A huge red flash, and suddenly, he found himself thrown in the air. Elyse's hand was yanked out of his and everything went black.

Josh groaned. He could feel hard gravel digging into his arms and legs. Something heavy was on his torso. Cautiously opening his eyes, he could see metal pieces scattered around him. Across the yard, he thought he saw a boot, but he wasn't sure with all of the smoke.

"Elyse!" he tried to yell, but it came out more like a croak. Swallowing to see if he could yell again, he coughed instead. His throat felt like sandpaper. *I wonder where the canteen went,* he thought.

Taking a breath through his nose, he tried to shift slightly. Whatever was on top of him did not want to budge. Since he was flat on his back, he couldn't really see what it was. Carefully he ran his fingers on it. The shape seemed oddly familiar. Then, it dawned on him. *It's a car door.* That realization made him pause. *Why would a car door be on me?* As he mulled over this piece of information, using one arm to push and one to lift the car door slightly, he was able to shimmy out from underneath it.

Free, he stood up and looked around in disbelief. Pieces of the car, including the other doors and bits of windshield, were strewn across what had been the barnyard. The shed that had been hiding Elyse's car was obliterated, which meant only one thing. *HAC put a bomb on her car.* He hadn't thought Catrina was that cold, or that she would risk killing Elyse when she seemed to want to control her magical talent so badly. But she could teleport, and she was already tracking Josh's every move somehow. He knew she answered to someone else, higher up in HAC. Josh had learned long ago that orders were orders, and sometimes no matter how much you hated them, not obeying would be even worse.

A wave of terror washed over him. "Elyse!" he yelled. He lifted all of the pieces of debris, searching for her. The search became more frantic as he kept failing to find her. *We were holding hands. Where on earth could she be?* Then he heard a soft nicker. Uncertain why one of the horses would be this close to the explosion, he hesitated. Then, the nicker became louder. Rolling his eyes at himself and the idea of a horse deliberately calling to him to come, he followed the sounds. Sure enough, there was Honey, near the fence. Between her legs was Elyse, curled in a ball.

Josh dropped to his knees beside the horse and let out his breath in relief when he found Elyse's pulse. She had just passed out. He carefully extracted her from beneath the horse, gave Honey an awkward pat of thanks, and carried Elyse into the house.

Josh laid Elyse down on the couch and blew out his breath, then headed to the cabin to see if he had any urgent messages. Just as he shut the door to the cabin, his phone started to ring from inside his suitcase. *Now what?* he wondered, frustrated at himself for how he'd been handling his interactions with Elyse.

"Hel—" he started to answer.

"Shut up and listen," shouted his boss. "You disappeared without a word two days ago, and since then I have been getting all kinds of crazy reports of HAC attacks. What did you do?"

Josh took a deep breath. "I didn't do anything. Elyse called me, scared…HAC attacked her aunt, and I offered to go to her ranch to protect her. Which is what I am doing. Didn't you tell me she isn't any good to the FBI if she's dead?"

Sputtering on the other end of the line, Gerald took a moment to reply. "You should have brought her here to headquarters. Out there, you are too far away for us to provide additional support if HAC does attack Elyse outright. You *know* this, and yet you went ahead and did it anyway. I think it's time to pull you off the case. You're too close to her and are not thinking straight. There's no other explanation for why you'd be this stupid."

Josh decided staying silent was smarter than responding. When his boss made up his mind about something, that was the end of it. Besides, if Josh told him the real reason he came out here—that he was a double agent working for HAC—he'd be in jail, or worse, dead for treason.

"I'm going to send James Valdez out there to collect Elyse and bring her back. When he has her in custody, you will report back to headquarters and explain yourself," Gerald said angrily.

Josh bowed his head. "Yes, sir." He knew any other response would cause more problems. The phone went silent. Josh returned it to the pocket on his suitcase. Of all the agents Gerald could have assigned, why did it have to be James Valdez? The man was ruthless and known for taking what he wanted from those he was assigned to protect. James would deny it till he was blue in the face, but there had been whispers about how the women he was assigned to protect were often more damaged after he turned them over than before, and it wasn't because they were attacked by whomever they were running from.

Josh sat down on the couch with his head in his hands. *Would it matter anyhow?* The deadline Catrina had given him to turn Elyse over was only hours away. If it passed and she wasn't in HAC's hands, that surely would be the end of his life, and then who knew what was in store for Elyse...unless they ran, but he wasn't sure Elyse would agree to that either.

Perhaps this was the opportunity he needed, as much as he detested it. James would have to transport Elyse into the city. What if Josh called Catrina and notified her that Elyse would be on the move and an easy target in a car that HAC had a tracker on already? Even though he couldn't stand the thought of turning over someone he cared about unwillingly to another organization, he also was worried about what James would do to Elyse. As twisted as Catrina could be, he did not believe she would rape Elyse. *But she raped me. Why would Elyse be any different?*

Before he had time to change his mind, Josh pulled out his phone and called Catrina.

"Joshie," she answered, sending unwanted shivers down his spine.

"Catrina," he replied, trying and failing to keep his voice level. "My boss has decided to move Elyse into the city. James Valdez is on his way here now. You could intercept them just before they cross the bridge into Atlanta."

In a silky voice, Catrina replied, "Very well done, Joshie. Now you must ensure she actually is in his car, and I will take care of the rest. Your debt will be paid when she is in my custody." *Click.* The line went dead.

Does nobody ever say goodbye anymore? Wondering how badly Elyse would take the announcement that she must go to the city to be under the FBI's protection, and thrilled it was not his job to inform her, Josh stood up and made his way to Elyse's house to prepare a quick breakfast for both of them.

TWENTY-SIX

ELYSE

Humming to herself, trying to channel the calmness her mother had always been so skilled at, even when the world was falling apart, Elyse wrapped her hair in the towel on her head and meandered over to her dresser. After her car exploded and Josh had brought her into the house, he had refused to let her go back outside again. She couldn't be too angry with him for wanting to protect her. The explosion had been terrifying. Although she was confident there wasn't anything else on her farm that could explode like that, she wasn't sure she wanted to venture back outside to find out if she was correct.

Tugging clean clothes on, Elyse decided to broach the safe topic of her family research. They hadn't really had a chance to have a proper conversation about it. It would be a good distraction from the destruction that awaited her outside.

Mind made up, Elyse pushed open the bedroom door and saw Josh standing with his back to her, stirring something on the stove.

He has helped me when I asked without wanting anything from me. I should trust him until he gives me a reason to not. Mind made up, Elyse walked up behind Josh and tentatively wrapped her arms around his waist.

"Smells delicious," she said into his ear.

She felt him stiffen. She released her hold on him and took a step backward. "Is something wrong?"

Josh turned around to face her after setting down the wooden spoon. "Nothing is wrong, per se. The assistant director of the FBI is sending another agent, James Valdez, out here to keep you safe."

Eyes narrowing, Elyse took another step backward and caught her hip on the dining room table. Wincing, she waited for Josh to finish explaining, but he stayed silent.

"Keep me safe how?" she questioned. His behavior had her questioning her decision moments before to trust him.

Josh dragged his fingers through his hair a few times, avoiding her eyes, before finally responding. "My boss does not think I can protect you adequately. As soon as James comes, I will be going home."

"I see..." she replied, even though she didn't. *So much for Josh helping me learn about who I am.*

Much sooner than she expected, she heard a car door slam and the *crunch, crunch* of feet on gravel. Elyse gave Josh one last look before she headed over to open the door for Agent James Valdez.

As soon as she saw James Valdez, she wished hadn't. A medium-height man stood there, clearly of Spanish heritage, with olive skin, broad shoulders, slicked-back black hair, and dark eyes. He was wearing the standard FBI black suit, white shirt, and tie. Something about him made her skin crawl, and he also seemed strangely familiar, although she wasn't sure why. She threw a look over her shoulder at Josh, but his back was to her, his attention on the stove.

Plastering a smile on her face and hoping it would be enough to mask her fear, Elyse held open the door. "Good morning, sir."

James Valdez gave her a slight smile that almost looked like a grimace, "Good morning, Miss Hutchinson." His voice was oily with a heavy Spanish accent, as though English wasn't his first language.

Stepping aside so that James could get through the door, Elyse realized that her hand was trembling. Yanking it tight to her side, she hoped he didn't notice. She threw another furtive look Josh's way, but his back was still turned. Straightening her spine, she took a deep breath, reminding herself she didn't know James, and not all her first impressions were correct.

Since when have they ever been wrong? her mind informed her.

Elyse walked away from James, wanting to put some distance between them. Her hand hovered over the back of the chair next to the couch. "I have a guest house you can stay in. It will be free once Josh leaves," Elyse offered, even though she was cringing at the thought of him even being in the guest house.

James laughed, a harsh barking sound. "He didn't tell you."

"Who didn't tell me what?" she asked, annoyed.

"*Josh…*" he said, emphasis heavy on the name, "was supposed to tell you to pack a bag. You're coming with me back to Atlanta, for your protection."

Elyse brought her hand up to cover her mouth, unable to mask her surprise. Running her tongue over her lip nervously and trying to figure out how to respond, she glanced again in Josh's direction. Unfortunately, James seemed to have caught the glance this time. "Josh has his orders too—to go home and stay away from you."

"And if I refuse to come with you?" she asked, eyebrow raised. Everything about this man had her on edge. She didn't want to go anywhere with him, let alone into Atlanta. *Why does his voice sound so familiar?* Biting her lip hard enough to draw blood, Elyse felt a panic attack creeping up on her and prayed she could keep it at bay.

"Then I'll tie you up and throw you in the trunk of my car," he said maliciously.

"You wouldn't!" she gasped, backing up until she hit the wall to her bedroom.

"Do you want to find out?" James shot back at her, reaching into his back pocket and pulling out a set of handcuffs. He let them unfold and shook them.

A shudder went through her, and she shook her head. "No, I'll go pack." She turned on her heel and slowly walked into her bedroom. Once in the room, she shut the door hard and leaned against it, shaking. Her legs gave out, and she slid to the floor, gasping for breath, her sides heaving.

Minutes passed, and slowly her fear was replaced by anger and annoyance at being told she had to go back to Atlanta by this James Valdez fellow. Elyse finally peeled herself off the floor and packed a small suitcase, angrily shoving an assortment of things into it. A quick phone call to Mya assured her that Mya would hold down the fort at the ranch, yet again, but Elyse still couldn't believe that the FBI had the nerve to require her to go anywhere.

Valdez gave her a creepy feeling whenever she thought of him, followed by a flashback of the nurse in the orange scrubs with the spider tattoo peeking out on his back, which didn't make any sense. Josh had said the attack wasn't HAC or FBI, so why would James Valdez remind her of it? When she finished packing the suitcase, she zipped it up and set it by the door. Then, she went over to the dresser and opened the lid on the jewelry box. On top, was her mother's wedding ring. Elyse picked it up and stared at it. *I wish you were here.* She kissed the ring and set it back in the jewelry box, then closed the lid. Just then, she heard a soft tap on the door.

"It's me," said Josh. Then, he opened the door and came in.

"Go away," she spat, but kept her back toward Josh, not really wanting any company.

When the door clicked shut, she turned. "Why do you think I want you in here?"

Holding up his hands defensively, he replied. "I just wanted to talk for a few minutes."

Elyse turned and looked at him eyes blazing with anger. "Why bother? You're not stopping Valdez from escorting me into Atlanta.

I thought…" she said, searching his face and realizing that she had been stupid, thinking that she and Josh could find a way to make their relationship work. "I guess I was wrong. You are who I thought you were all along."

Josh opened his mouth, jaw working, but no words come out. Elyse glanced at him before pulling on a pair of short black boots and grabbing her suitcase.

"Goodbye, Josh," Elyse said quietly before walking out of the bedroom. She turned to Valdez. "I'm ready to go when you are."

Valdez gave her a silky smile that made Elyse shudder in revulsion and led the way out to his car. She was surprised when he opened her door to the back seat for her. As she slid onto the seat right past him, an image of a spider entered her mind, then vanished. As she blinked rapidly, unsure if she should ask Valdez about it, he shut the door practically in her face and then climbed into the front seat. She hadn't been sure what she would have done if he'd sat next to her. Trying to keep her eyes on the edge of the road, Elyse was afraid to let her guard slip, sure that if she did, Valdez would take advantage of her.

They were halfway over the bridge into Atlanta. Usually, Elyse wouldn't pay much attention to it, but this time she did and realized how beautiful and terrifying it seemed. As they drew closer to the city, she could see the buildings on the outskirts that had been abandoned and were beginning to crumble. In a cluster in the middle of the city were the well-maintained skyscrapers. Sunlight reflecting off the glass windows. Fingers twitching, Elyse imagined picking up her paintbrush to capture the scene before her.

Boom!

The car shuddered as something crashed into it. Elyse slammed into the car door. Biting her lip, she attempted to brace herself as the car spun from the impact—one, two, three full spins. Waves of nausea washed over her, and jabs of sharp pain. Elyse gazed down at her arm and saw blood seeping out of it. Looking up to see if

Valdez was okay, she saw the other car heading straight for them again.

"Implement evasive maneuvers!" Elyse screamed at his car, praying an FBI agent's car was programmed to take orders from someone other than the agent.

"Ghiii…grrrrr," the car speakers sputtered.

"Implement evasive maneuvers now!" she screamed again, terror on her face. The oncoming car collided with the front of Valdez's car, and a blast of pure power rolled out of Elyse, through the FBI car and into the other one, blowing what remained of both vehicles apart. For a split second, she felt as though she were encased in a warm bubble of air and her mother was touching her face. Then, she had a sense of falling through the air and sinking in water before she blacked out.

TWENTY-SEVEN

JOSH

Ring, ring. Josh glanced up from his suitcase and opened his briefcase, looking for his phone. He was still collecting all of his things at Elyse's ranch before heading back into Atlanta. He answered it without checking who the caller was. "Hello?"

"Are you with Elyse right now?" Gerald asked with urgency in his voice.

Josh narrowed his eyes. "No…you ordered me to let Valdez escort her to headquarters. I am just getting into my car to head that way now from her ranch."

"Shit!" Gerald muttered.

"What? Did something happen?" Josh asked, unable to hide the genuine concern in his voice.

"Valdez's car just disappeared and so did he," Gerald sputtered.

"What do you mean it disappeared? Like they went off grid?" Josh asked.

"No…like it no longer exists. Valdez drove an agency car, which, as you know, has multiple ways of being tracked. But none of them are putting out any sort of signal. Valdez's phone was being tracked, and it's gone too. Which shouldn't be possible unless they were obliterated. Which makes it highly likely…" Gerald left it hanging.

Words failed Josh. *Elyse dead? No way.* Catrina wanted her alive, not dead. "Are you sure the car is gone?"

Gerald cleared his throat. "I deployed a team right before I called you to investigate the last known location of the car. I'm sure if there is something to find they will find it."

Josh zipped up his suitcase and hastily shoved it into his car. A quick glance in the early dawn light showed him the destruction from the fire and explosion last night. Elyse would be devastated all over again when she got home and saw the damage. Josh got into the car, and it turned on when the door shut. The phone transferred instantly to the car.

"I want to go check it out," Josh said firmly. Gerald had no reason to say no since he would be returning using the same route Valdez was supposed to take.

"Just make sure you call me as soon as you know anything. See you soon," Gerald ordered, and hung up.

Josh ran his hands through his hair. Something had to have gone wrong…or Catrina lied to him and her plan all along had been to kill Elyse. He punched the dashboard of the car in his anger, and it crumpled under his fist. He punched it a second time with less power behind it, realizing that Gerald would likely charge him to repair the dash. One of the disadvantages of the enhanced strength from his magic…things that shouldn't be flimsy were. The car slowly drove down Elyse's road and picked up speed as it got onto the old highway.

Since the cars of 2125 did not have wheels or tires, they simply hovered over a road. Josh had Frank hack into his car and reprogram it so that Josh could have it go faster than the limits the FBI set. Part of him had suspected that Gerald was aware of his modifications to the car but didn't care. Either way, what mattered at the present was that his car could reach Atlanta in a quarter of the time James's could. Which meant he could still make it to the crash before anyone else got there. *Maybe.*

"Maximum speed. Stop when we reach the collision site," Josh commanded his car. Thrust back into the seat as the car propelled itself forward at over two hundred miles per hour, he kept his eyes forward. He learned the hard way after he had the modification done to not look out the side windows or he'd get motion sick.

Sooner than he expected, the car slowed down, then stopped abruptly. Josh checked his gun in the holster and the one tucked into the top of his boot before stepping out of the car warily.

As the sun climbed toward its zenith, he saw the grim scene before him. A big black-rimmed hole was in the middle of the bridge with scorch marks darkening the pavement. Bits and pieces of what he assumed was James's black car were scattered, as were a few pieces with green paint on them. *So, they were hit by another car. Interesting.* He peered into the murky water, visible through the hole in the bridge, but couldn't see any movement.

He pulled out his phone and called his boss. "You're going to need a boat," he said matter-of-factly.

"A boat?" Gerald replied in a baffled voice.

"Yeah…there is a hole that goes all the way through the bridge down to the water." Josh could hear his boss's breathing get heavier.

"Do you think they survived?" Gerald asked.

Josh ran a hand through his hair. "Maybe…I don't know."

"Can you tell what caused the explosion? My team is still about ten minutes out," Gerald inquired.

"James's car was hit by another car. As to the explosion…I don't know. Last night, Elyse's barn caught on fire, and then her car exploded too. It's possible it was just the car if the impact was in the right spot." He held his breath, hoping that Gerald would accept the explanation he provided and not ask about the alternative option.

"That sounds plausible. We will have to see what the team determines when they get there. Feel free to call me if there is anything else you notice before they arrive," Gerald ordered, then hung up.

Josh pocketed his phone and walked around the hole, crouching down to inspect the scorch marks. Marks he was certain were the result of a magical explosion, such as the ones sometimes caused by a talent being unlocked. *If I am right…then Elyse's magical talent is now unlocked, which makes her more valuable to HAC than she was.* As an afterthought, he added, *And more valuable to any organization who has her in their sights.*

Josh was standing next to his car with his computer propped on top of it when he heard footsteps behind him.

A throat cleared, then Gerald Fernway spoke. "You're sure it's HAC?"

Josh shut off his computer and turned around. He hadn't told Gerald about his suspicions that Arañas Rojas were behind the attack on Elyse at the hospital. If that was the case, they could theoretically have caused the accident on the bridge as well. "Pretty sure. It seems like it would be rather strange for any trace of Elyse and James to disappear if this were just an ordinary car accident. The marsh isn't deep enough for the cars to sink far enough to be invisible in the water."

Gerald nodded. "Yes, I have come to the same conclusion." His hands were behind his back.

Josh kept his eyes on his boss's face. "Did you order a boat?"

"Yes, I did, but what I'm wondering is how HAC knew where James was. I mean, don't get me wrong, I know they monitor the FBI's doings, just as we keep track of them. It just seems…odd, that I would send James to bring Elyse back, and then almost immediately they have an accident and disappear," Gerald said. Two other FBI agents came up beside Gerald, flanking him.

Gerald reached into his pocket and pulled something small out. Josh gasped audibly at the HAC tracker in Gerald's hand.

"Ah, you do recognize this." Gerald waved his hands at the two agents, and they stepped forward and grabbed Josh's arms tightly.

"Don't do this, Gerald," Josh said, struggling against the grip of the agents.

"It's too late for that, Josh. I thought you trusted me as I have trusted you. Instead, you've been going behind my back working for HAC. I had this tested, and it definitely has traces of Catrina Fox, who is a known high-ranking member of HAC. Well, your involvement with them and your time as a double agent ends tonight. Take him back to headquarters. I want two agents with him at all times."

One of the agents, Finn, grinned viciously at Josh and pushed him hard against the car as the other one roughly put handcuffs on him.

"Don't do this, Finn," Josh murmured, hoping that one of them would listen and let him go before everything got even more out of hand.

Finn spun Josh around so they were facing each other and punched Josh in the jaw.

Wincing in pain, Josh rasped, "You don't know what you're getting mixed up in."

"Are you so sure about that?" Finn snarled low in his throat. "Gerald is not as oblivious to your actions as you seem to believe. He was just waiting for the right moment to lock you up."

Josh clamped his mouth shut, refusing to give Finn the satisfaction of an answer. But Finn had succeeded in causing Josh to doubt himself. *How long has Gerald known? Which car did the tracker he has come off? Did Catrina set me up as a way to get me off the playing field now that she has her hands on Elyse?*

Finn and the other agent shoved Josh into the back seat of another FBI car. He narrowly missed hitting his head on the door frame. As soon as they shut the door, bars went up over the windows, doors, and as a barrier between the front seat and back seat. He kept himself low on the seat, waiting for them to walk away. When he was sure they were gone he dug his fingers into his front pocket and pulled out a thin wire. With some careful maneuvering, he used the wire to unlock the handcuffs. Rubbing his wrists together and trying to get the feeling of the metal digging into them off his mind, he looked around the car. With the bars up, the odds of him getting out without help were slim. Undoing handcuffs was one thing. The bars operated with a combination of magic and a computer and were entirely a different matter.

Gerald had witnessed him using his magical talents enough to know the full extent and limitations of his abilities. Since Gerald had come to the bridge with a plan already in place, there was no way he'd be stupid enough to leave Josh unattended in a vehicle, unless he knew Josh wouldn't be able to escape.

Idiot, there might still be something you can do. Closing his eyes, Josh slowed his breathing, forcing himself to into a much calmer state. The primary magic he had was what everyone knew about, but the secondary abilities…he kept those to himself unless absolutely necessary. Other than vampires, to his knowledge very few people could also read minds. His magical talent primarily allowed him to block his mind from being read and gave him extra strength. Sometimes he could also deflect magical attacks. He could also see magic. The ability to see magic was helpful if he was trying to understand a spell and wanted to unravel it, but he didn't have the kind of magical talent that would just allow him to blast through another spell with a bolt of pure magic.

When Josh opened his eyes, he could see threads of magic woven throughout the car. Numerous spells were at work. While he might be able to undo one spell if he had the time, there were too many on the car for him to even attempt it. The only thing he would do was draw attention to the fact he could see the magic. Resigning himself to his fate in the hands of the FBI, Josh shut his eyes and fell into a light sleep.

Rough hands grabbed him and yanked Josh out of the car and onto cement.

"What was that for?" he growled.

Instead of an answer, he got a kick to the ribs. Then he was lifted to his feet and shoved from behind.

"Walk," ordered Finn. Letting his head hang and shoulders slump, Josh started walking, letting them think they had hurt him with the kick. Maybe they would leave him alone on the trek to the holding cells at the bottom of the building.

Josh's ploy worked. Neither agent guarding him tried to hit or kick him. Finn unlocked the door to the empty cell, and the other one placed his hands on the small of Josh's back and shoved as hard as he could. Josh allowed himself to be propelled into the cell. He could have easily resisted, but instead of fighting, he decided to see if he could glean any information from the FBI. He had obviously misjudged Gerald and was wondering what other mistakes he had made.

A few hours later, Finn came and removed Josh's handcuffs. He also brought him a plate of unidentifiable vegetables and some sort of mush. As Josh reached for it, his fingers just barely brushed the plate when Finn let go. Josh was not in the correct position to save his plate. It fell upside down onto the floor.

"Pick it up," Finn ordered.

Josh looked at him, eyebrow raised. "No."

"Pick it up," Finn repeated.

Josh turned his back on Finn and walked to the corner of his cell. He heard the whisper of Finn's boots just before the fist came for his head. Josh ducked and spun, coming up behind Finn. He did a quick jab, jab, right straight punch, and was shifting his weight to follow through with a roundhouse kick when arms wrapped around him from behind. *Shit.* He'd been so focused on getting Finn back for the kick earlier, he hadn't heard the other agents slip in behind him. He struggled against his captors and was about to jab one with his elbow when he heard Gerald's voice.

"I guess you want to do this the hard way. I was hoping you would work with me so that I could acquire the information I need without harming you further."

Josh twisted so he could see Gerald and spit on his former boss's shoes. "There's no way I'm giving you any information, not after you sent Valdez to take Elyse."

"I am sure you will change your mind, eventually," Gerald said in a silky voice.

"Never," growled Josh.

"We'll see," Gerald replied, flicking his fingers in some sort of signal and then turning on his heel and heading back upstairs.

The two agents restraining him pinned Josh to the floor, and Finn beat him. Finally, the three of them let go, and Josh heard the clank of the door shutting. Josh just lay there, letting the cool concrete soothe him. His back, legs, and arms were on fire. He knew the pain would subside soon enough, but Finn had been nothing if not thorough. Josh wasn't sure what the purpose of the beating was though. Gerald had to know it would take more than physical torture for Josh to give him any information. Hell, the man had read his file. He knew all the tests Josh had been through, including multiple SERE (Survival, Evasion, Resistance, and Escape) sessions, both while he had been at the academy and since then.

Josh lost track of how much time had passed. Finn, accompanied by two agents, came in three more times to beat him. The third time, Josh blacked out, and afterward they left him alone. No one else was down here that he could tell. Which was just as well. He didn't feel like talking and was worried anything he did say would be used against him.

Pulling himself up to standing, Josh walked to the corner of the cell and emptied his bladder in the corner. There was no toilet, and they hadn't provided him with any container to pee into, so he just went in the most out-of-the-way place he could.

When he was sure no one was coming, Josh ran through a series of stretches. Testing his body, trying to determine how badly he was injured. The stretches hurt. If he was being honest, his whole body ached almost unbearably. He was surprised that they hadn't yet demanded he give any information and wasn't sure what to make of Gerald's strategy. Or maybe it wasn't a strategy. Maybe he was just buying time until he acquired the information he needed from a different source.

Sliding to a sitting position against the wall, Josh decided to meditate. Then he heard heavy footsteps and the clanking of keys.

"Get up," the agent shouted at Josh.

Josh looked up in surprise. It wasn't Finn this time; it was someone he had never met before. Deciding he would cooperate for the moment, Josh stood up and walked over to the gate.

"Put your hands out."

Josh did, and cuffs were slid onto his wrists. Then, the gate opened.

"Now come with me. If you do try anything, I've been authorized to shoot you."

Josh nodded in understanding and walked side by side with the agent down the hallway. They stopped at the first room on the left. Josh had been in that room before. It was an interrogation room.

"Sit," the agent said, motioning for Josh to take the chair closest to them.

Josh sat and waited. The agent sat across from him. "I'm Agent Myers," he announced. Josh just stared at him. Agent Myers cleared his throat. "Where is Elyse Hutchinson?"

Josh shrugged. "I have no idea."

Agent Myers wrote a note on a piece of paper. "Where is Catrina Fox?"

"I don't know," Josh replied.

Agent Myers wrote another note before giving Josh an appraising look. "Who do you work for?"

Josh smiled. "The FBI."

Agent Myers frowned. "Who *else* do you work for?"

"I work for the FBI. Who do you think I work for?" Josh asked.

Agent Myers coughed. "I'm the one asking questions today, not you, Josh. You deny that you work for anyone other than the FBI?"

"Yes, I just said that I only work for the FBI. How many ways do you need to hear the same thing?" Josh hissed. *Don't let him get under your skin,* he chided himself.

"What can you tell me about Elyse Hutchinson?" Agent Myers asked.

"Everything I know about Ms. Hutchinson is in her file on my FBI account," Josh said, keeping his voice calm.

"What kind of relationship do you have with Elyse?" Agent Myers asked.

"She was just another one of my potential recruits," Josh said with a shrug.

"Then why were you at her ranch?"

"Gerald Fernway told me to recruit her. She called asking for help, so I thought I should go help her. Since doing so, you know, might convince her to allow me to bring her under the FBI's wing. She was still undecided at the time she made the call," Josh explained.

"I see," remarked the agent as he made more notes on his paper. "Wait here."

Josh glared at him, wondering where Agent Myers thought he was going. Raising his hands, he ran them awkwardly over his face. There was a lump on his nose. He realized he was lucky it hadn't been broken.

Agent Myers exited through a different door than the one they had come through, and when the door opened again, it was Dwayne. They hadn't ever gotten along since they met at the government's magical talent training school, and Josh did his best to keep out of Dwayne's way.

Dwayne gave Josh a vicious smile and cracked his knuckles eagerly. "Hello, Josh. Where is Elyse Hutchinson?"

"I already told Agent Myers I don't know," Josh replied.

"Wrong answer." Dwayne clicked his tongue in disapproval and slugged Josh in the gut. There was enough power behind the punch that Josh toppled backward in the chair and onto the ground. Wheezing, he struggled to get untangled from the chair.

"Where is Catrina Fox?" Dwayne said, slinking closer to Josh, who hadn't gotten up yet.

Josh clamped his mouth shut. He knew it wouldn't matter if he spoke or not. Unless he had the answer Dwayne wanted—which he honestly didn't—then what happened next would be the same. Dwayne was going to hit him until he got what he wanted. If he didn't then, he would change strategies. While Josh did sometimes resort to exclusively brutal tactics when questioning someone, he had discovered that usually it didn't provide the outcome he wanted, unless combined with some psychological aspect as well. Dwayne excelled at beating people, but he was not good at manipulating their minds.

A while later, the door opened. "Enough of that, Dwayne. He clearly isn't going to tell us anything else," Agent Myers stated.

Josh gave him an annoyed look. Blood dripped down his face from a gash on his forehead. On the floor was a puddle of blood dripping from his left arm, which dangled uselessly at his side.

Agent Myers tossed a file on the table. "Go ahead and take a look."

Josh ignored the file and picked a spot on the wall, focusing on that.

"Trust me, you're going to want to look."

Frowning, Josh flipped open the file. Inside were photos of Elyse, photos when she had been attacked at the hospital. One of them clearly showed a man in orange scrubs as he was beating Elyse. In the shadows, he could make out what looked like Catrina watching. He spread out the photos. Several showed Catrina in the background as Elyse was beaten.

"You see, Catrina Fox was there when Elyse was attacked at the hospital. Why would you protect a vampire and an organization who think so little of human life?" Agent Myers asked. He then slid the photos back into the folder and closed it.

Josh lifted his hands, trying to wipe away the blood threatening to drip into his eyes. He was exhausted, and Agent Myers had a valid point. *Why would I turn over Elyse, a woman I care about, to Catrina Fox, when she was there watching Elyse getting beaten and did nothing about it?*

"I will give you some time to think it over. If you decide you are ready to tell us everything you know about Catrina Fox, then I will tell you what the FBI can do to ensure Elyse's safety," Agent Myers informed Josh.

A wave of exhaustion hit Josh, causing him to sway in the chair. He thought he nodded in agreement, but he wasn't sure. The next time he was aware of his surroundings, he was back in his cell, flat on his back.

TWENTY-EIGHT

ELYSE

Head rolling to the side, Elyse groaned as every inch of her body throbbed in pain. Her soggy clothes clung to her, adding to her discomfort. Slowly opening first one eye, then the other, Elyse discovered she couldn't see anything. Wherever she was, it was pitch-black with no light source. Taking a deep breath, she tried to sort out what she could feel. A rough rope was tied tightly around her wrists. She brought her hands up to her face and gingerly touched it. Her fingers came away sticky with blood.

Lowering her hands, she tried to awkwardly feel the ground around her. Some sort of stone or concrete on the walls and floor. *I wonder what happened? There was another car and then...*

She gasped as she remembered the feeling of some sort of power rolling out of her as she blacked out. *I caused the accident...this is my fault.* A sob escaped her lips before she could stop herself. Hot tears fell unbidden. Blinking them back, one moment she was staring into darkness, the next she was blinded by a bright white light.

Blinking rapidly, she tried to make her eyes focus on whoever was in front of her. Moments ticked by, and a person who looked strangely familiar slowly materialized. Elyse gasped. *Why does she look familiar?*

"Oh, good, you're awake," Catrina purred.

Elyse felt her chest tighten at the familiar voice. The voice that was under the mask of the woman who had grabbed her…just after Josh had told her he wanted to recruit her.

"You're supposed to be dead! I watched Josh shoot you," she blurted out.

The woman laughed. "I'm not that easy to kill."

Elyse slowly looked the woman over from head to toe, taking in the pale skin, bright red lips, sharp nails, slightly pointed teeth, and strange eyes.

"What are you?" she whispered and tried to scoot backward, away from the woman who was likely not human at all.

Catrina laughed again. "Vampire." Baring her teeth, she flared her wings wide.

Elyse shook. "V…vvvv…ampire?" *Those aren't real…I must be dreaming.*

"It's not a dream, Elyse. I am very real." Catrina reached out and grabbed Elyse by the arm and pulled her up to standing.

Elyse swayed, and her legs buckled from the pain. "How…how did you know I was thinking that?" she said in barely a whisper.

"I am Catrina Fox, one of the first vampires. There is not much I can't do," the vampire retorted, oozing confidence.

Elyse realized that it was only Catrina's grip that was keeping her from collapsing. The car accident and explosion had obviously done more damage to her than she thought.

"Can you heal?" she questioned, hoping to at least make Catrina aware that she was badly injured. Maybe the vampire wouldn't want her to die from her injuries and had a way to heal her.

Catrina's eyes locked with Elyse's. "No. You're not going to die from your injuries. I've already inspected them. But…you're not going to be able to escape either."

Everything hurt. Elyse could feel some blood trickling down her leg as well as her forehead. Catrina thrust Elyse away from her, and Elyse collapsed to the ground and curled into a ball, whimpering.

Eventually, she heard Catrina's high heels clicking on the floor as the vampire walked away. Elyse carefully opened her eyes. She took a shaky breath and counted backward from ten, trying to settle her mind. The deep breaths were surprisingly helping to control her pain too.

Letting her eyes flutter shut, Elyse tried to remember what Josh had told her. Magical talents need to be unlocked. *Did I cause the explosion?* Taking another deep breath, Elyse continued counting, hoping that if she could convince her body to relax, she would come up with a way out of a seemingly impossible situation.

As her body began to relax, the events of the past few hours came flooding back. Gasping, she realized that James had come and taken her away before she was able to ensure all the horses were fine after the fire. The director of the FBI had just ordered her away, completely disregarding what she wanted. She struggled to breathe as she considered what might happen to the horses. Then everything went black.

When things became light again, Elyse was no longer in the room. It took her a moment to realize she was at her ranch.

How did I get here? she wondered.

Suddenly, Jessica appeared, followed by her father. They were walking around. Jessica had a notepad and was writing things on it as her father was telling her something. Try as she might, Elyse could not hear what they were saying. Elyse couldn't recall any time when Jessica and her father had been taking notes at the ranch, when she realized that there were pieces of debris scattered everywhere, including an oddly familiar metal door.

This is now? Confusion filled Elyse, wondering how and why she was seeing this. Her vision went black again and then lightened and the scene had shifted.

Jessica was riding her horse and her father was on his, and they were driving about ten horses through a pasture gate.

Elyse was relieved as she recognized each horse. *These are my horses.*

A hand was shaking her. Elyse mumbled something, and the hand shook her harder.

"Hello, Elyse," Catrina said in a surprisingly pleasant voice. "Since it is obvious your magical talent does not involve self-healing…I have brought you a healer." Catrina waved her hand and a very old man with clear Asian heritage tottered over to her. He reached out and set his fingers on Elyse's temples.

Recoiling from the touch, Elyse scooted backward along the ground until her back hit the wall.

"Now, now," tsked Catrina. "That is no way to react to a healer. Chen needs to touch your face to heal you. Now, let him do it, or there will be consequences."

Chen slowly made his way over to Elyse again and settled his fingers on her temple. This time Elyse forced herself to think of something else. *Horses…*her mind drifted to the feel of galloping Honey over the hills at the ranch. Eventually, Chen removed his hands from her face.

"How do you feel now?" Catrina asked.

Elyse blinked rapidly, trying to pull herself back to the present. Nothing hurt; the pain that had been wracking her body was somehow gone. "He really healed me?" she whispered.

Catrina nodded. "Yes, of course. I told you I had a healer. Why would I lie?"

"Because you have no reason to tell me the truth. Nor do I have a reason to believe anything you say. First, you threatened me when I was having dinner with Josh. Then, you had someone trick me into going to the hospital, and you had me beaten. Next, you had my Aunt Grace murdered. And most recently, you tried to kill me in a car accident," Elyse said, glaring at Catrina.

"How on earth do any of those things make you think I would want to trust you?"

Catrina shrugged. "Fine, don't trust me. But…I was not responsible for all the events you just cited."

"If not you, then who?" Elyse shot back.

Catrina ignored the question. "Today, I want to find out what your magic does now that it has been unlocked. Before, you had feelings about events or decisions that you were about to make. In my experience, individuals with that particular talent tend to be upgraded—if you will—to getting actual visions of the future. Sometimes there are other skills as well."

"You want me to predict the future?" Elyse asked incredulously.

Catrina nodded. "Of course. If I know the future, then if I don't like the outcome, I can change it."

"It works like that?" Elyse said, uncertain. She knew nothing about people with magical talents, let alone how to predict the future. She also knew there was no way she was going to tell Catrina she'd just had some sort of vision.

"Usually," murmured Catrina, peering at her phone.

"Okay, so what do I have to do?" Although Elyse had no desire to help Catrina or Hellfire and Chaos, she did want to know more about her magical talent and how to make it work or control it.

"That, my dear, is the tricky part. To start with, you're going to come with me, and we will go someplace more pleasant."

Catrina gently snagged Elyse's hand and tugged her out the door, down a hallway, and up several flights of stairs. When they finally stopped moving, they were in a vastly different room than where they had started.

Elyse gazed around, taking everything in. The room was fairly large with a dark oak floor. At the center of the room was a large animal skin rug of some sort, possibly a zebra. Two oversized brown leather sofas were placed around the animal skin. Huge paintings of African animals were on the beige walls. As refreshing as it was to be in a room with this level of comfort, Elyse also took note of the lack of any windows.

Are we underground? Or do they think I will escape through a window? Elyse thought.

Catrina turned to face Elyse. "This room is magic-proof." The statement came out as though Catrina had heard Elyse's thoughts. *Which wasn't possible, was it?*

Catrina continued, "This is the strongest room I have here. Magic can't get in or out once the door is shut. Which means that any magic you do will stay contained within the room, and no one can attack us with magic from outside. Come sit, and we will begin." She gestured to the sofas and then stood waiting.

Elyse decided to sit down on the sofa on Catrina's left. Much to her chagrin, the vampire sat down next to her. Biting the tip of her tongue, Elyse refrained from saying anything, hoping Catrina would explain sooner rather than later what they were doing. Being so close to the vampire made Elyse nervous.

"We will start with the least complicated way of telling the future. I want you to think of something you'd like to know that could happen in the future," Catrina commanded.

"And then?" Elyse asked.

"And then hopefully, you will get a vision showing you what will happen."

Elyse closed her eyes and let her mind drift, trying to think of something simple that she would like to know.

How many fillies will I have born next year? she thought and put as much of her willpower behind the question as possible. She started off by holding her breath, but nothing was happening, and she was getting lightheaded. Sucking in some air, her eyes fluttered open for a moment, and she caught Catrina's expression of annoyance.

"Did you get a vision?"

Elyse shook her head. "No. Nothing happened."

"Maybe you should think about something other than horses? Don't you have a fifty-fifty chance already of a boy or a girl?"

Drumming her fingers on her thigh but wisely keeping her mouth shut, Elyse tried to come up with something else. *Josh…do I date Josh?* Taking a deep breath, she let the question flow through her and attempted to keep her mind relaxed. She decided to not hold her breath this time, but minutes ticked by and nothing happened.

She could feel Catrina shifting her weight on the couch. "It seems like this way is not going to work for you. Sometimes it is necessary to have an item to focus on. A personal possession is the best if the actual person is not available." Catrina's eyes dropped to Elyse's neck. "Perhaps your necklace?"

Elyse started to protest; the necklace had been her sister's. She didn't think using an object that belonged to a dead person would help her predict the future, but what did she know? Nodding, she wrapped her hand around the pendant and closed her eyes.

Brilliant white light flashed, and Elyse's eyes opened. To her shock, she was no longer in the room with Catrina. Looking around, she found that she recognized the woods. They were on the ranch near one of the creeks.

She could hear the heavy breathing of a running horse. A horse and rider galloped by, almost running through Elyse, but she didn't feel anything, and they didn't seem to notice her. As the horse passed, Elyse gasped. White mane and tail, black body…

"Sonora?" she whispered, a tear trickling down her cheek. The rider had a long blonde braid trailing down her back and a hot-pink shirt. "Tory!" she called as a shudder ran through her. Her sister had been dead for fifteen years. Why was she seeing her running through the woods?

Elyse started to run after her sister, hoping to catch her. And then what? She could feel the ground shaking from hooves coming up behind her. Not one but two riders came galloping through the woods. Both were armed with rifles, and one was getting ready to take aim.

"No!" she whispered.

The gun went off once, twice. A loud crashing ahead. Sobbing, Elyse took off at a dead run, weaving through the trees. She had been told it was a horrible accident. Which, as she slid to a halt, she realized was only half of the truth.

Sonora was on her side, blood trickling out of her mouth; the wound in her neck must have hit the carotid artery. As Elyse watched, she died. Tearing her eyes away from Sonora, Elyse searched for her sister before turning and noticing a tan arm under Sonora. She stumbled backward a step as what she was seeing registered. Playing out what happened and what she had been told. The men who had been after her sister shot Sonora, and they both fell. The weight of the horse combined with the proximity to the tree had killed her sister.

Elyse fell to her knees, sobbing.

A hand shook her, gently at first, then more firmly. "Elyse, wake up."

Body shaking with grief, Elyse opened her eyes and was startled to find herself back in the room with Catrina.

"Tell me what you saw," Catrina ordered.

Elyse looked away. Sharp fingers gripped her chin and pulled her face back so she was looking at Catrina. "Tell me now."

"I saw Tory die," she whispered.

"Who is Tory?" Catrina asked uncertainly.

"My sister," Elyse replied.

"Maybe we can prevent it from happening," Catrina offered.

Elyse glared at her through her tears. "You can't prevent what already happened. Tory died fifteen years ago. I was told it was an accident, but two men were pursuing her."

Elyse could feel Catrina getting up from the couch and hear the clicking of her heels on the oak as she paced. Wiping the tears off her face, Elyse tried to collect her thoughts. *I just saw the past... what does that mean? Tory was murdered...by who?*

"If she can see the past, then she should be able to see the future," Catrina said behind her, although she didn't seem to be talking to Elyse. Elyse stood up, looking around for something to drink. Her throat felt dry and her mind was still reeling from finding out the truth about Tory's death. *But who would want her sister dead? Why had it been covered up?*

Finally, she spotted a sink and a selection of glasses on the counter next to it. She headed over and filled up a glass of water, taking a slow sip and savoring the feeling of the cool water going down her throat. Refilling the glass again, Elyse finally felt as though her thirst had been quenched. Holding the glass, she wandered around the room, getting a closer look at the paintings on the wall.

"Ahem," a throat cleared behind her.

Whirling around, Elyse narrowly missed sloshing water out of her glass. "Yes?"

"I am going to have you try it with me. So, this time you're going to hold my hand and then focus on finding out what is in my future," Catrina explained. The vampire motioned for Elyse to join her back on the couch.

Settled on the couch, Elyse took Catrina's hand in hers and closed her eyes again. *I want to know what Catrina's future holds,* she ordered herself. Counting to three and then letting out her breath, inhaling and repeating, she tried to get into a more meditative state while keeping her mind focused on learning about Catrina's future.

A white light flashed, and Elyse found herself in a room almost identical to the one they were in, except the animal skin on the floor was definitely not a zebra. Standing up,

Elyse peered around. Everything had a slight haze to it. The room seemed empty at first, and then as she moved around, images began to appear slowly.

Catrina was cowering on her knees, wings spread out as though they could shield her from the man standing in front of her.

Not a man. Elyse gasped as the huge creature in front of Catrina, arm raised as though to strike her, turned his attention on her, as though he could see her. His eyes were bright blood-red, and he had huge bloody fangs. She could see the shadow of leathery black wings. As his gaze intensified, the white light flashed again.

"Elyse?" Catrina asked eagerly.

Rubbing her arms as though to warm herself up, Elyse took a moment to sort through what she saw. "I don't know if that was past or future," she started.

"What did you see?" Catrina asked again.

Elyse was surprised that the vampire who could so easily read her thoughts about other things did not seem to be able to pluck her vision out of her head. "You were cowering on the ground and this man…no, not a man. This scary possible vampire was standing over you as though to hit you…and then…he saw me." Elyse watched as Catrina's face blanched. "What? Does my vision mean something to you?"

Catrina pinched her lips together and shook her head, refusing to answer, but Elyse could sense her fear. *Who was that man?*

"Can you at least tell me if it was past or future?" Elyse asked, wanting to know if they had been successful or not.

Catrina shook her head. "I don't know…There are more rooms like this one in this compound as well as at other HAC locations throughout the country."

"Who was that creature?" Elyse pushed, hoping for an actual answer.

Catrina shook her head again. "I won't tell you."

"He scares you. Why?" Elyse commented.

"Just pray you never meet him yourself," Catrina said, standing up and walking away from Elyse.

Tired of waiting for Catrina to say anything, Elyse stood up and walked over to her, grabbing her arm. "Are we done here?"

Catrina hissed at her, fangs bared. Elyse hastily dropped her arm and backed up a few steps, hands raised. "When you brought me up here, you said we were going to figure out how to get me to see the future. Is there anything else we're doing? I'm tired and hungry." Her stomach let out a ridiculously loud gurgle.

Elyse met Catrina's eyes again. This time the vampire didn't hiss.

"We can take a break and get you some food." Catrina raised her phone to her ear and spoke in a tone too low for Elyse to hear any of the words clearly. Shrugging, Elyse wandered around the room again. She wasn't really sure how much time had passed since the accident on the bridge. *James Valdez!* She shuddered, realizing that she had been in the car with someone else, and she didn't know what happened to him. *Do I care? He gave me the creeps. Even Josh seemed to not like him, and they're coworkers.*

When Catrina hung up the phone, Elyse cleared her throat to draw her attention.

"Yes?" Catrina said impatiently.

"What happened to the FBI agent, the one who was with me in the car?"

"He was taken care of," Catrina replied shortly.

"Taken care of?" Elyse repeated, not liking the sound of that. Like they had disposed of him as though he was garbage, not a human being.

"What's it to you?" Catrina queried, eyebrow arched.

"I just wanted to make sure he's okay. You know, like a decent human being would be concerned about other people."

Tapping her finger on her lips, Catrina responded. "Do you have any idea what sort of person he was? No...Josh probably didn't tell you the details. Well…let's just say that any female that was left in James's care for too long…was never the same again."

"Never the same how?" Overcome by curiosity, Elyse wondered why Catrina was drawing this out. Another game?

"Most of them died. Not that he killed them. They just no longer wanted to be alive, and found…let's just say they found ways to die."

A knock on the door interrupted Catrina's monologue.

Elyse took a deep breath. She had been right. James Valdez was not a good man, but she still couldn't find it in herself to wish even someone as terrible as he was to suffer or die. She turned as the door shut and saw Catrina holding a couple of bags. Sniffing the air, Elyse smiled as she inhaled the scent of fried chicken and French fries. Catrina laid out the contents of the bags on a square table with four chairs in the corner of the room. There was a stack of paper plates and several containers of food, and a thermos of something.

Elyse reached out to grab the thermos, curiosity getting the better of her, when Catrina snatched it. "That is not for you."

"What is it?" Elyse asked.

Catrina ignored the question and retreated to the opposite end of the room.

How odd, thought Elyse. Her stomach rumbled again and made the decision for her. She sat down in a chair and started piling steaming food on a plate before digging in. The chicken was really good. She had not been expecting Catrina to care enough to have food that would be enjoyable to eat. *But what do I know about Catrina?* She paused chewing to mull over her question. *Nothing… other than she has a high rank within HAC and that Catrina and Josh have some sort of history. And Catrina is a vampire.* Elyse sucked in a breath and started coughing, a piece of chicken lodged in the back of her throat. Face turning bright red, Elyse grabbed a cup of something and took a small sip, sighing in relief as the chicken finally came loose. Then, it clicked. *Catrina is a vampire. Vampires need blood. That must be what's in the thermos.* Curiosity satisfied, Elyse dug into her food voraciously.

Food finished and cleared away, Catrina turned her attention back to Elyse. Elyse shivered under the vampire's gaze. The way Catrina was looking at her, Elyse started to wonder if the vampire was going to take a bite out of her, not help her learn to use her magic.

"How close were you and Josh?" Catrina finally asked. Elyse blushed at the question, causing Catrina to smirk. "I see."

"Are you reading my thoughts?" Elyse demanded.

Catrina shrugged. "Yes. I read everyone's thoughts."

"Can you turn it off, so you don't know what everyone is thinking all the time?" Elyse asked.

"I can tune it out, if I try hard enough. But usually knowing what people are thinking is too useful to want to shut it off. For example, when I asked you the question, you didn't have to answer aloud. I was able to see exactly what you and Josh were doing just before the barn caught on fire."

Elyse found herself blushing even more. "It was a dream. That didn't happen. Why did you want to know about Josh?" she squeaked.

"Because if your necklace made you see the past, if I helped you see an unidentifiable time, then maybe focusing on Josh will help you see the future. Since your history with each other is so short, there won't be much for you to see of your past." The vampire paused. "Or at least that is what I am hoping. As I said earlier, everyone's magic operates differently."

"You want me to focus on my future with Josh?"

Catrina nodded. "Yes, please."

Elyse took a deep breath and closed her eyes, counting to ten. She thought about Josh, how respectful he had been while at the ranch, allowing her to determine what path their relationship would take, and if she wanted to try to be intimate.

A bright light flashed, and Elyse opened her eyes.

> *She was standing in a meadow with oak trees, their leaves in brilliant fall foliage spreading out behind a wood trellis decorated in rust-colored roses. In front of the trellis, she saw herself, in a simple but elegant white A-line satin wedding gown. Her red hair cascaded down her back with tiny white flowers and crystals adorning it. She was able to pick out the faces of her close friends and a few family members filling the seats. Uncle Albert was there. Whenever Elyse tried to focus on the person she was facing, though, all that was there was emptiness. She knew someone was there, but she could not identify who it was.*

The bright light flashed again, and Elyse opened her eyes, realizing she was still frowning. Catrina was looking at her optimistically. "Well?"

Elyse sighed. "It was my future. I haven't gotten married yet, and I saw my wedding. The strange part was that I couldn't see who I was marrying at all. It was as though the person wasn't there."

"Perhaps because that part of your future is undecided. You will get married, but who you marry will depend on choices that you make and their outcomes."

"Have you had that happen before? A giant hole where a person belongs in a future vision?" Elyse asked, wanting to know if Catrina had experience or was just making things up.

Catrina shrugged. "I can't see the future myself. So no, I do not know for sure. But the people I am acquainted with have told me that sometimes when they are trying to determine a particular event, it appears completely blurry. As though that particular future could exist but doesn't yet."

"Is there something in it for you personally if I can tell the future?" Elyse asked. *Am I doing this for HAC or for Catrina herself?*

"Wouldn't you like to know what the winning lotto numbers are, so you could be the winner of millions?" Catrina fired back.

Elyse giggled. "The lottery still exists?"

Catrina gave her a strange look. "I forget that you live *out there* in Jackson County and wouldn't be well-versed in all the luxuries of the city. Yes, the lotto still exists…or at least it mostly does. The wealthy seem to find it entertaining to gamble. So once a month, they pick a winner of the lotto and then make a big deal out of it."

Elyse contemplated the lottery. It still felt like a strange thing to her, but what did she know of the hobbies of the super-rich?

"We have determined that you can see the past and the future. I knew you would be able to see the future. I did not anticipate you would be strong enough to see the past too." Catrina spoke as though she were distracted. "It makes training you even more critical. You need to learn how to control what you do. It is possible there are other skills that we will identify as you progress."

Elyse pressed her lips together in thought. "How do I train?"

"Trying to make the visions come intentionally. Eventually, you will be able to have them without needing an object to focus on. For some, control of a magical talent comes easily. For others it takes months, years even. Hopefully you are the former type of individual," Catrina said resolutely.

"Okay, then I will try again," Elyse murmured before closing her eyes. She knew learning more about her parents' deaths would be even more devastating than what she'd learned about Tory, but perhaps she could focus on something else, less raw. *Josh was not able to confirm who attacked me. Maybe I can find out.*

Taking a deep breath, Elyse focused on how the beating had felt, what the hospital room looked like.

A bright light flashed, and she opened her eyes, blinking.

She was standing in the hospital hallway, outside of the room she had been held prisoner in. The nurse in the orange

*scrubs with dyed-red hair and a Spanish accent was stand-
ing in the hallway, talking to the gray-haired doctor.*

*"This is a fool's errand," hissed the doctor. "She doesn't
know anything useful."*

*The nurse bared his teeth at the doctor. "Mateo wants her.
This," he waved his hand in the air between them, "is just to
break her so when we take her to him, she will do whatever
it is he wants."*

*"We should not be holding her here. It is too exposed in the
hospital," the doctor warned.*

*The nurse just glowered at him. "You are too paranoid.
James Valdez is making sure the FBI stay out of our way.
He is loyal only to Mateo. There is nothing for you to worry
about. Besides, are you so weak that you fear the FBI's little
agents?"*

"I just—" the doctor began, but was cut off.

*"Just shut up. Do as you're told. I can't believe they thought
you could handle a task this important." The nurse spit on
the floor at the doctor's feet in disgust before squaring his
shoulders and stomping into the room where Elyse was.*

The bright light flashed, and Elyse found Catrina's face way too close for her comfort. Standing up and wanting some distance between herself and the vampire, Elyse blew out her breath. "You said that you had taken care of James Valdez...did you know he was associated with an organization other than the FBI?"

Catrina gave her a sharp glance. "No...but it makes sense, now that you mention it. The Arañas Rojas is run by his cousin, Mateo Jesús Valdez."

"The Arañas Rojas?" Elyse repeated, remembering the edge of the spider tattoo she'd seen. "Why would they want me?"

Catrina threw back her head and laughed. "Who wouldn't want you? Many people would do anything to get their hands on some-one who can see the future. Let's pray no one finds out you can also see the past." The vampire smoothed out her face till it was once again void of emotion. "But now we know another player is in the game, and perhaps why they attacked Josh at the solar farm."

"Josh was attacked?" Elyse gasped. He hadn't said anything about being attacked, even after all the time they spent together.

Catrina shrugged. "Yes, but he's an FBI agent. He gets in fights all the time. It's nothing to worry about."

Elyse wasn't sure if she believed Catrina about the attack on Josh being nothing to worry about, but she was curious about the Arañas Rojas. "What about the Arañas Rojas, should I be worried about them?"

"No, we wiped out most of them when rescuing Josh from the solar farm. I doubt there's enough of them left to muster any sort of retaliation," Catrina said with a smirk.

Biting her lip, not wanting to know what Catrina was planning for any Arañas Rojas members who might try coming after her or Josh again any time soon, she decided to change the subject. "Any suggestion for what I should try to focus on to see the future?"

"What about the masquerade ball?" Catrina offered.

Elyse nodded. She had forgotten about the ball. She closed her eyes and focused on what Quinn would be wearing. This time there was no flash of light, but an image of Quinn formed in her mind. Her friend was wearing a long, deep purple, almost black dress that shimmered in flickering candlelight. Quinn's hair was in an elegant chignon, held up with a delicate comb encrusted in amethysts.

Elyse took a deep breath and opened her eyes. "I saw what Quinn is wearing, but this time it was different than the others. No light flashed, but all I saw was Quinn, not anything else around her."

Catrina shrugged. "I can't see the future, so I am not sure what to tell you about the differences between types of visions, but it seems as though they are coming more easily as you spend more practicing."

Lips pressed together, Elyse took a moment to review the visions she had just had. It dawned on her then that although Catrina was teaching her how to control the magical talent, she still had no idea what the vampire's motives were. For all she knew, Catrina was going to force her to work for HAC, just as the FBI was wanting to do. "Then let's continue and see what I can predict," Elyse said with a forced smile.

TWENTY-NINE

JOSH

"This is a bad plan," Josh said from the back wall of his cell under the FBI headquarters in Atlanta. He wasn't sure how many days he had been there, but he knew it was at least one or two.

Gerald ignored the comment and continued speaking. "The exchange will happen at the masquerade ball tonight. You for Elyse. I am not sure what caused Catrina to change her mind, but…you have proven that you're expendable. Elyse's ability to see the future is too valuable for the FBI to allow HAC to keep her."

Josh pushed off the wall and stood within arm's reach of Gerald, who was on the other side of his cell. "Why are you being this stupid? HAC would *never* give Elyse up willingly."

Gerald shrugged. "My orders are coming directly from the president of the United States. You have been in the FBI long enough to know if the orders are coming from that high up, the only thing we can do is ensure they are fulfilled."

Josh closed his fist in anger, wishing he could shake some sense into Gerald. "What about the people attending the masquerade, the ones who are just innocent bystanders?"

Gerald started to pace. "What about them?"

Josh blew his breath out slowly, surprised Gerald was being this dense. "Are you going to protect them when your plan backfires? Or are they just collateral damage that no one cares about?"

Gerald glanced sharply at Josh and took a quick step forward before stopping himself. "I told you already, it will be a simple exchange, you for Elyse. Nothing is going to happen to the people attending the masquerade." Gerald waved his hand to someone Josh couldn't see. "Now, you stink and need to take a shower and get cleaned up. Do not mess this up, Josh."

Finn came out of the darkness. He tapped something onto the keypad next to the cell and the door popped open. "Remember what Gerald said. Don't do anything stupid, Josh."

Josh bowed his head in defeat. As much as he didn't believe that HAC would ever do a trade for Elyse, he also didn't want to jeopardize what might be his last chance to see her. Maybe he would think of a plan to save her.

Finn grabbed his arm and roughly hauled him to the bathroom with a shower at the other end of the basement. Although he spent as little time at the FBI headquarters in Atlanta as possible, Josh was familiar enough with the basement where they were holding him. He'd brought in enough suspects to be held down here. He also knew the odds of breaking out were nonexistent. Security was too good for one man who was locked up to get through on his own.

They reached the bathroom. The room itself was not overly large, about six by six with a shower head on one side, sink, and toilet. The tile was sloped so the water would stay on the shower side. Cameras were positioned in all four corners, ensuring there was no privacy, and nothing a prisoner did would go unnoticed. Finn opened the door and then pushed Josh inside.

"Your tuxedo is here." Finn waved his hands to indicate the garment bag hanging on the back of the door. "Toiletries are also here. You've got twenty minutes to make yourself presentable, and then we'll be leaving." Without a backward glance, Finn departed. The bolt on the outside of the door slid home with a hiss.

Josh took a deep breath and gazed around the room. He unzipped the garment bag, wanting to make sure of its contents before he discarded all his clothes. Inside was a pristine white tux, white shirt, bowtie, and white mask. At the bottom was a pair of boxers, undershirt, white socks, and white dress shoes. After zipping the bag back up, Josh stripped, dropping all his clothing in a heap in the corner behind the door. He looked mournfully at his leather jacket, one of his favorites. *I probably won't see that again.*

The tile was cool under his bare feet but not as cold as he had expected. He reached over to turn on the water. While waiting for it to heat up, he stood, hands braced on the sink, gazing at himself in the mirror. His face had some smudges of dirt and soot, probably from touching his face after inspecting the explosion, not realizing his hands had been dirty. His hair looked like it could use a wash and he had two days' worth of stubble on his face. Rummaging through the toiletries, he found a toothbrush and toothpaste, shampoo, and deodorant. No razor to shave with... just the bare basics. The stubble would have to stay.

Not that it matters. I'm being traded to HAC. Who knows what Catrina will do with me?

He got a nagging feeling, like he was missing something important. Deciding the water had had long enough to heat up, Josh stepped into the shower. The water that should have been steaming hot was lukewarm.

So much for a relaxing shower. He grabbed the shampoo and made quick work of washing his hair and body, not wanting to be in the water any longer than necessary.

"At least it's not ice cold," he muttered to himself, shutting off the water and reaching for the towel.

Josh was just finishing buttoning the cuffs on his shirt sleeves when the bathroom door opened and Finn stuck his head inside. "Good, you're ready. We're out of time."

This time he said "we." Interesting, Josh thought. He snagged the tuxedo jacket out of the garment bag and followed Finn into the hallway. As they walked past some of the cells, a few people cat-called. Rolling his eyes, Josh stuffed down any retorts he would normally give.

Finn glanced over at Josh. "Behave. I would hate to have to ruin your tux before you even get to the ball. Gerald would not be happy."

"If all you're worried about is Gerald, then you are stupider than you look," growled Josh. He leaped backward, narrowly missing Finn's fist in his jaw.

"Let's go!" shouted Gerald from the door.

Nostrils flaring, Josh focused on Gerald and ignored Finn and whatever facial expression he had. Finn wasn't worth his time. If he was going to escape from the FBI and HAC tonight, he couldn't risk being on Finn's death list.

THIRTY

ELYSE

Elyse took a hesitant step into the ballroom. Everything that had happened the past couple of days felt almost surreal. She still couldn't believe that she was at the masquerade ball. It felt like such an odd place to do a prisoner exchange. However, it also provided a lot of hostages should things go sideways. Perhaps that was why Catrina had decided it would be the ideal place.

People mingled around the edges of the large dance floor. Most of the women wore elegant floor-length ballgowns with masks made from a variety of materials. Some covered their faces entirely, while others were barely a mask at all. Elyse ran a hand down the soft emerald velvet of her dress. Somehow, Catrina had been able to retrieve her dress and mask.

Servers were working their way through with trays of various hors d'oeuvres and what might be champagne. When one came close enough, Elyse reached out and took a glass of champagne, downing it in one gulp.

"You look ravishing," a voice said from behind her.

Elyse slowly turned to see Derek. A small part of her had been hoping it was Josh, but she knew it would be better for both if it wasn't. The trade would happen, HAC would get Josh and the

FBI would get her, and then who knew what would happen to them.

Elyse put a smile on her face. "Hello, Derek." She had to admit he was handsome in his black-on-black tuxedo. A waiter passed by and she set her glass on his tray. Behind Derek, the orchestra played.

Derek, an eager look in his eyes, gently took her hand and bowed over it. "May I have the first dance, Elyse?"

She glanced around, wondering if she would be able to spot Quinn in this huge crowd of people, before giving up. She didn't recognize anyone near enough to rescue her.

I need to blend in and not cause a scene, she reminded herself. Unfortunately, if she just walked away from Derek as she was itching to do, it would most definitely turn into a scene.

Offering Derek a small smile, she curtsied and took his hand, inwardly cringing. The panic attacks had virtually disappeared, but she still had to be careful, especially with a man she had a sketchy history with already. Derek led her onto the dance floor. The press of bodies around them was making her fear rise. Elyse forced herself to focus on placing her feet and appearing as though she were enjoying herself. One dance turned into two, then three.

The next song was a slow one. Elyse hesitated, uncertain if getting closer to him would trigger a panic attack. She decided not to risk it, wishing fervently she were dancing with Josh. *At least Derek is behaving properly tonight.* She opened her mouth to say something, then she stiffened as a voice that sounded strangely familiar entered her mind.

Run! the voice ordered her. She withdrew some from Derek, although she kept her hands on his shoulders, trying to hide that something was wrong. It didn't work.

"Are you okay?" he asked, genuine concern in his voice and worry in his eyes.

Elyse bit her lip, afraid that if she told him a voice was in her head telling her to run, either he'd think she was crazy, or it would tip off one of Catrina's minions that were sure to be nearby that something was going to happen. "I'm fine," she lied. "I just…I was remembering the first masquerade I went to, where we met." The lie came out smoothly and would hopefully distract Derek from questioning her further.

Derek pulled Elyse back toward him, so his mouth was by her ear as he whispered. She started shaking, which only seemed to encourage him more. "Mmm, I remember that night. You were wearing a black dress and were much less sure of yourself than you are now."

Closing her eyes and trying to relax, Elyse ignored the comment about her dress. As much as she was cringing inside, her fear of Catrina and what might happen if things didn't go well tonight was greater. Josh wasn't here yet. That she was certain of. She needed him to be here for the exchange to work. Then everything would return to normal.

After a few minutes, Elyse couldn't take it anymore. "I need a drink."

"Okay," Derek said with a nod and led her off the dance floor. As they passed a waiter, he slid his hand out of hers and snagged two champagne flutes off the tray, offering her one. "Let's go somewhere quieter."

Elyse stopped walking. She had no interest in going anywhere with Derek. "I can't," she said, coming to a complete stop.

It took Derek several steps to notice that she had stopped following him. He returned to her, searching her face. "I thought…" His voice trailed away.

Elyse shook her head. "No." Taking a deep breath, she decided maybe the truth, or part of the truth, would help her. "I am not ready to go anywhere with you." She shuddered and almost dropped her glass.

Derek quickly rescued it from her. "Elyse, I need you to come with me," he said more firmly.

Taken aback by his tone, Elyse looked around, trying to see if anyone was close enough to overhear them. "I don't trust you anymore. Not after the other night at Three Dragons."

A waiter passed by, and Derek deposited their glasses on it. Then, he stepped closer to Elyse. She felt her body stiffen. Her breathing increased and started coming out in gasps. He put his lips to her neck, although he refrained from letting them touch her.

"Elyse…it's Derek. Don't panic, please," Derek's voice sounded in her head. She gasped in surprise and their heads knocked together.

"Ow!" Derek muttered with a grimace. As he was rubbing his head, his voice spoke in her mind again. *"Come with me. We need to make this believable, as though we're going to the corner to make out. I swear on my life that I will not hurt you and that we can just pretend."*

Elyse shook her head vehemently. "No." She tried to step away from him again, but he grabbed her arm.

"Let go of me, or I am going to scream," she snarled under her breath.

Taking a deep breath, Derek released his fingers on her arm. "What if we go back to dancing?"

Elyse arched an eyebrow. *Why hadn't we just kept dancing in the first place if he needed to talk to me? Why all the secrecy?* Instead of answering, she lightly took his hand and led him back to the dance floor. Even more people were there than when they'd gone for a drink. It was hard to find enough space for the two of them. Finally, near the center, there was enough room to move without hitting someone. As she turned to face Derek, a slow song started. Elyse delicately placed her hands on his shoulders.

"Please…just do as I ask, and trust me. I will explain everything," his voice sounded again in her mind.

Biting back a sharp retort, Elyse tried to relax and move with the music. It was hard to focus on dancing while worrying about whether he was going to talk in her mind again. *Another type of magical talent that exists.*

"How is this?" she asked him mind-to-mind, not sure if such a thing were possible. If it was a magical talent that was common, Catrina had not said anything to her about talking mind to mind, only that she might get instructions in an unexpected way, and she should follow them explicitly.

"You need to relax more," Derek chided her. *"Hellfire and Chaos are not the evil organization that the FBI wants you to believe they are."*

"How do you know that?" questioned Elyse.

"Because I am a member of HAC. I have been for years," Derek explained.

"What does this mean? If HAC is not the bad guy, then what about the exchange?" she asked as worry and concern for Josh pulled her attention from Derek.

"The FBI is playing you. They want you to be a prisoner. Especially now that your magical talent is unlocked," Derek said.

"What about Josh?" Elyse asked, uncertainty flooding her.

"We can protect him, but he must be willing to drop all ties to the FBI. He has been working for HAC for the past three months but is still under the FBI's control, or at least Catrina believes he is," explained Derek.

"And if I don't believe you?" Elyse asked and rocked back some, searching Derek's eyes for some hint of the truth.

"Your Uncle Albert believes us. You could call him and ask," Derek suggested, his hand slowly running down her back.

A shudder of revulsion ran through her. Elyse took a step backward, trying to get away from his touch. Instead, she felt her stiletto hit something squishy and heard a squeal of anger.

"Watch where you're going!" shouted a woman behind her.

"Sorry," mumbled Elyse. Derek carefully moved them away from the woman she'd just stepped on while Elyse considered his words. *If* she were willing to believe him, then everything she had been told was wrong. But why would HAC have attacked Aunt Grace? Why did they start by threatening her? Another tremor of fear ran through her. She was always so sure about her path and decisions, but now…she wasn't sure who or what to believe.

The music changed to a faster song, and Elyse felt like she needed a moment to herself, away from Derek and the throng of people. Elyse dropped her hands from his shoulders and stepped sideways, trying to not trample anyone this time.

"I need time to think about this," she spoke aloud, wanting Derek out of her head.

He gave her a reluctant nod, and she started to walk away. She made it to the edge of the dance floor before a searing pain ripped through her head. She crumpled to the ground, holding her head in her hands. Moaning in pain, Elyse squeezed her eyes shut, wanting desperately to make it stop.

A cool hand touched her forehead and immediately the pain stopped. Elyse opened her eyes and was surprised to see Catrina kneeling in front of her. The vampire was wearing a deep red satin ball gown with a long flowing skirt and matching gloves. Instead of a mask, her face had been painted with black swirls. Catrina offered her a hand. Elyse took it and was helped to stand. She opened her mouth to speak, but Catrina put a finger to her lips.

"You don't have much time. I have blocked the attack on you for the moment, but I need to know you believe Derek, or I won't be able to protect you anymore." Catrina's words flowed through Elyse's mind the same way Derek's had earlier.

Am I ever going to get used to this? she wondered.

"Yes," Catrina answered her question as though it had been spoken.

Elyse narrowed her eyes. She didn't like the idea of people being able to pluck her thoughts out of her head. Catrina arched an eyebrow and tapped her foot impatiently, waiting for her answer.

Elyse shook her head, not sure that a few minutes was long enough to make a decision that would change everything. *"What about Josh?"* she asked, trying to buy herself a few more moments. She thought she knew what she was going to do.

Catrina shrugged. *"It might be possible to get him out from the FBI's thumb. But he has to want it. He has been working as a double agent for several months."* The vampire reiterated what Derek had said only minutes before.

"But if I agree to join HAC, Josh will be allowed to come too," Elyse demanded.

Catrina's gaze pulled away from Elyse's face to something behind her. Elyse jumped slightly when the vampire leaned over and gave her a quick kiss on the lips, before disappearing. Elyse's fingers went to her lips that were still tingling from the kiss.

What was that? she wondered.

"There you are!" called Derek from behind a group of people.

Elyse turned toward his voice and flashed him a stunning smile. "How about another dance?"

THIRTY-ONE

JOSH

Finn was at Josh's elbow while they stood at the bar in the corner. "Remember, don't try anything, or you're not going to like the consequences," Finn hissed in Josh's ear before disappearing into the crowd.

Josh picked up the shot glass the bartender set in front of him and drained it before motioning for another. He downed the second one just as quickly before placing a tip on the counter and pushing off into the crowd. In a sea of people dressed mostly in dark or jewel tones, Josh stuck out like a sore thumb in his white-on-white tuxedo. He wasn't sure if this was Gerald's idea of a joke or his plan for how to keep track of Josh's whereabouts. He knew Frank was somewhere in the crowd. If he could find Frank, he could get out of this ridiculous white tuxedo and into something that would allow him to blend in better.

Unless of course they stuck a tracker in me. Then it won't matter what I'm wearing. He paused his thoughts. *But I'll feel better about not being the most visible person at the ball.* Mind made up, Josh weaved his way through the people, peering intently at some and hoping that Frank would spot him and make this go that much faster.

He brushed past Terrance, elegant in a rust-orange dress that went well with her golden eyes.

If only the people here knew, he thought, then shook his head. *I probably don't want to know what would happen if she shifted in the middle of the ball.* He recognized several FBI agents, including Dwayne. They were all wearing very traditional black tuxedos and basic black satin masks. They looked rather uncomfortable in their finery and were easy to spot since he knew what to look for.

Finally, Josh thought he caught a glimpse of Frank in a deep purple suit with a mask made from peacock feathers. He shoved a couple of people out of the way when a flash of green caught his attention. Forgetting about the purple suit, Josh looked around for whoever was wearing the green.

Unfortunately, whoever it had been in the green dress had disappeared into the crowd. Instead, he found himself gazing at the back of a petite blonde with her hair up in some sort of elaborate twist. Her not-quite-black dress left most of the skin on her back bare, save for a few slender straps. The woman was laughing at something the person she was with was saying.

That laugh is so familiar, he thought.

Taking a step forward, he accidentally bumped her arm, not realizing he had gotten that close. "Sorry," he muttered.

The woman turned toward him, eyebrows raised in surprise. "Josh?"

Jaw dropping open, Josh hastily shut it. "Quinn?" He knew she loved attending the masquerade ball every year and was close friends with Elyse. He just had not put it together that she would be at the ball tonight.

He opened his mouth to say something to her, but she shook her head to silence him before turning back to the person she had been talking to. Josh peered at the person and realized it was Dwayne. Wondering why on earth Quinn would be associating with him, he realized he was glaring at Dwayne and hastily schooled his face into a mask of indifference. He jumped as he felt Quinn's hand slide into his.

"Let's dance," she said and tugged on his hand to lead him onto the dance floor.

Josh followed her, confusion flooding him. *What is going on?* The orchestra started a slow song. Quinn settled one hand on his shoulder and used the other one to place one of his on her waist.

"Josh," she said quietly, glancing around as though worried someone was going to overhear them.

"Why are we dancing?" He refrained from adding, *I thought the whole point of this was to do an exchange.* Quinn was to his knowledge not part of HAC or the FBI; the last thing he wanted to do was entangle her in this mess.

Quinn laughed. "Did you forget dancing is my favorite thing to do?" she teased, smirking at him.

Unsure of where this was going, Josh settled his hands around her waist and did as she wanted. They danced and danced. For a while, Josh was able to forget why he was here and just focus on the attractive woman in front of him, before he realized how much he wished Quinn was Elyse. *I am such an idiot. I should just tell Elyse how I feel,* he realized. *The next time I see her.*

Lost in his thoughts about Elyse, he twirled Quinn, and the movement caused light to shimmer across her shoulders. Unable to resist, his eyes followed her hair to the top of her dress, and they settled on the curves of her breasts, which he realized with a jolt were not Elyse's. When she completed her spin and was facing him again, he realized she was angry.

"Men are all the same, aren't they? You either think that every woman is a damsel in distress that needs you to rescue them, or your mind is on sex. There is no middle ground." She pushed Josh away from her, causing him to bump into someone behind him and stumble.

"I don't know why we're still friends, Josh," Quinn said, louder this time, causing the dancers around them to stop and stare at the commotion they were creating.

Then, she spit on him. Eyes wide in shock, he watched as she stomped off the dance floor.

"What the hell!" he muttered under his breath. Just then, a hand coming out of a deep purple suit was offered to him.

Josh took the hand before looking up at the person it belonged to in relief. *Frank found me.*

"Come with me…and be quiet. We don't have much time," whispered Frank as he dragged Josh along with him, weaving expertly in and out of the crowd until they ended up in front of a door that blended in with the wood panels of the wall so well that it was almost invisible. Frank opened the door and shoved Josh in ahead of him.

Josh raised his hands, feeling around him in the dark. His foot caught on a step, and he fell, rolling to a stop at the bottom of a four-step staircase.

"What was that for, Frank?" he said in annoyance.

"Your own good," retorted Frank from somewhere above him. A dim light turned on, bathing the room in a yellow glow. Frank had a bag in his hand, and he quickly descended the steps and shoved the bag into Josh's face. "Here, put this on."

"While I change, will you please tell me what the hell is going on?" Josh stood up and began undressing, eager to get out of his white, now spit-covered tuxedo and into something less visible.

"More is going on than you think. Everything you have been told is wrong," Frank declared.

"Everything I know about what is wrong?" Josh asked.

"About the FBI and HAC," Frank clarified.

Josh mulled over that tidbit while he buttoned his shirt up and tugged the coat on. A navy-blue suit and a navy satin mask. Not exactly what he'd had in mind, but at least it was dark and would allow him to blend in more than all-white would.

"Care to elaborate?" Josh stepped closer so he could see Frank's face better.

"No, but you'll find out soon enough." Frank checked his wristwatch. "We're out of time. Let's go."

"Not until you tell me what's going on," Josh said, stepping back from Frank.

Sighing, Frank tapped his foot impatiently. "When they do the exchange, don't fight it. Other than that, you don't need to know anything."

Josh clamped his mouth shut. He wasn't sure what to believe now. *Frank just dropped a bomb on him, and now he was expecting him to blindly trust him? What about Elyse?* He followed Frank back up the stairs, and just as Frank was about to slip back out the door, Josh spoke, not able to leave without knowing. "What about Elyse?"

Frank gave him a surprisingly vicious smile. "It's being taken care of." Frank turned on his heel and slipped out the door. When Josh got through the door, Frank was nowhere in sight. Josh hadn't felt completely helpless in a long time, but that was how he felt at that moment. Something was going on. He had not been planning on letting the exchange go smoothly. Now he wasn't sure if he should follow his original plan, relying only on himself, or if he should take Frank's word that something bigger was being orchestrated and all he needed to do was cooperate and everything would end well.

Josh laughed. Nothing with HAC ever ended well. There were always casualties. Even if Frank was right and everything he knew about HAC and the FBI was wrong, there was no denying the deaths he had seen HAC cause with his very own eyes.

But are all aspects of every organization always following the same agenda? he thought. *Frank has been working with me since I first moved to Atlanta over five years ago. He's never burned me before, and I've trusted him with all sorts of things he could use against me. What reason do I have to not believe him?* Josh took a deep breath as it hit him. *None. I have no reason to not believe Frank.*

Decision made, he started to search the big ballroom for Elyse again. The exchange required both of them to be in the same place. And then he wasn't sure what would happen. Hopefully, when he found her, she wouldn't be so quick to send him on his way. *Not that I deserve her.*

THIRTY-TWO

ELYSE

Are you okay?" Derek asked for the third time. They were back on the dance floor, although Elyse was getting more annoyed at Derek's pestering by the moment.

"Do you really want the truth?" she asked angrily.

Derek's eyebrow raised. "Of course."

"I want tonight to be over…so that tomorrow I will wake up and can just do normal things," she retorted.

Derek threw back his head and let out a deep, throaty laugh.

"What?" she asked, temper flaring.

"You will never just be 'normal,' Elyse." Eyes dancing, he leaned in, and just before his lips touched hers, Quinn shoved Derek out of the way.

Elyse giggled in relief as Quinn snagged her hand and dragged her away from Derek. "I can't believe that creep is still trying to get into your pants," Quinn said.

"I wasn't sure if you were here," Elyse replied, following Quinn to the opposite side of the room, as far away from Derek as possible. As they were walking, she realized that Quinn was wearing the exact same dress she'd seen in the vision. The light flickering in the ballroom made the dark purple shimmer. It was tightly fitting,

310

accentuating Quinn's large breasts and tiny waist before it flared out at the bottom. *I guess they are genuine visions of the future.*

Quinn shrugged. "I got here later than I was planning, but I wouldn't miss it for anything. Not since you said you were coming. Your dress is stunning."

Elyse glanced down at her green dress and ran her fingers along the fabric. "Thanks. Now that you've rescued me from Derek, do you have a plan?"

"Elyse…you are going to mess everything up. Where did you go?" huffed Derek's voice in her head. Elyse jumped.

"What's wrong?" asked Quinn.

Elyse shook her head. There was no way she could tell Quinn about talking mind-to-mind with Derek. "I just can't stand Derek."

"What about Josh?" Quinn asked with a smirk.

Elyse pursed her lips. "I'm not sure. Our relationship has definitely had a bumpy start, but I'd like to think he's in my future."

A waiter came by with a tray of champagne. Elyse snagged one. As she did, she saw a blond man in a navy suit with a navy satin mask heading their way through the crowd. Two other people were trailing him who were obviously FBI agents with their stiff manner and black standard-issue suits. She also noticed another man. He was wearing a black-on-black tuxedo with a full black face mask and a black velvet cape. She was certain it was a man because of his tall, muscular build. That was clear when he moved. Elyse was about to look away when he caught her gaze and she jumped in surprise.

He has red eyes!

"Just keep talking to Quinn," Derek's voice once more invaded her mind, distracting her from the red eyes. *"When Josh reaches us, you will walk past him toward the FBI agents."*

"But—" Elyse started.

"There will be a distraction, don't worry," Derek consoled her.

Nodding, she drained her glass of champagne and put it back on the waiter's tray. She was ready for this to be over with, the subterfuge and uncertainty. When she opened her eyes, she was peering straight into Josh's blue eyes through his mask.

Josh gave Elyse a smile. "Can I have a dance?"

Elyse took a deep breath to settle her nerves, hoping she wouldn't give anything away. A dance was not what Derek had instructed her to do. *Derek can go fuck himself,* she thought.

"Very well." She gave Quinn an apologetic look. "If you'll excuse me, Quinn."

Quinn gave her a wicked grin before moving off into the crowd.

Josh gently took Elyse's hand in his and settled his other lightly on her waist. Elyse avoided his gaze and kept her eyes fixed on the crowd, trying to not screw things up any more than she already had. She felt his hand stiffen on her waist. Her deep emerald-green dress left her broad, muscular shoulders and back bare; around her waist was a diamond belt, and the dress cascaded down into a long train around her feet. Her red hair was elaborately curled and sideswept over her right shoulder.

"You look beautiful tonight," Josh said, quietly leaning forward so his mouth was by her ear. "Are you okay?"

A shiver ran down Elyse's spine. Biting her lip, she tried to ignore her body's reaction to Josh. Unlike Derek, who brought back upsetting memories, Josh's hands on her sent her back to her dream before the fire. The last thing she needed was to screw up whatever was going to happen because she couldn't control her desire for him. Instead of responding, Elyse kept dancing, making sure she was not touching him anywhere that would give him the wrong idea, or allow her to lose focus more than she already had.

Finally getting the courage to speak, she chose a topic that would hopefully keep her thoughts away from the danger zone. "What happened to the white tuxedo?" She thought she'd seen him come through wearing one but had only gotten a quick glimpse.

Josh shrugged. "I found someone who was already passed out and relieved him of his suit. I think Gerald thought it was funny to make me wear white."

"Are you okay?" she asked hesitantly. From what Catrina had told her, she knew that Josh had been held captive by the FBI. What she didn't know is what they had done to him during that captivity. The vampire either hadn't known or hadn't felt like sharing the information with Elyse. As she studied his face, she couldn't see any evidence that he was hurt, but given that Catrina's healer Chen had erased all evidence of the car accident and any other bruises on her body, it was possible the FBI had done the same for Josh.

Josh settled his hands around her waist and did as she wanted. They danced and danced. She was wondering if he would even answer the question when, after he twirled her, he finally spoke.

"I've survived worse before," Josh replied.

Elyse blew out a breath, annoyed at his decision to dodge the question instead of being straightforward. "If you don't want to tell me, then don't." She lowered her voice to barely a whisper. "I don't know why I even care." She shut her eyes for a moment as she tried to steady herself. Suddenly, she was falling backward with Josh on top of her.

She let go of his hands, hoping she could catch herself and that he would not actually crush her. Hands grabbed her elbows and dragged her backward. Elyse drew one arm forward, attempting to shake off the hands, but they refused to let go. Allowing herself to go limp, Elyse decided to try a different tactic. She could feel the person holding her shift as she became dead weight. As he adjusted his grip on her elbows, she pulled up her leg in a quick motion and slammed her heel down on the man's foot. He let out a screech as the sharp point of her stiletto ground against his toes. The hand dropped, and she sprinted away. Glancing behind her, she was surprised when she collided with someone.

"Shit!"

"Stop struggling, Elyse. It'll only get worse if you do," a somewhat familiar voice spoke into her ear. Twisting awkwardly, she finally got a look at the person who was holding her captive.

Gerald Fernway, assistant director of the FBI. "Now you're going to come with me, and Josh is going to go with HAC. Catrina has him even now, as we speak."

Elyse followed his hand with her eyes as he motioned to the other side of the dance floor, where Catrina had her hands wrapped around Josh's arm.

What about the plan? We had a plan…Derek was going to provide a distraction and…

"What are you thinking about, my dear?" Gerald queried, brushing a stray strand of her hair out of her eyes. "Hmm, let me guess…one of Catrina's followers made up some story about how they were going to rescue you and Josh at the same time and that the FBI are the bad guys?"

Elyse averted her eyes, refusing to answer him.

"I'll take that as a yes. Well, Catrina lied…about the plan, that is," Gerald huffed.

Her back was still to him. He was holding her rooted in place at the edge of the dance floor. Her body stiffened as Gerald moved her hair from her shoulder and trailed his finger along her neck. "She was right, though…about the FBI."

Suddenly, the room went dark. Gerald's grip on her tightened as the room erupted in chaos. Elyse struggled.

Not again. Never again will I allow myself to be captured, she vowed. It didn't matter how she twisted. Gerald kept his iron grip on her arm. In the darkness, a bright light flashed, and she fell forward, free of Gerald. Unlike the times when Catrina had been trying to get Elyse to use her magical talent, Elyse found herself in an odd white space.

She held her hands up in front of her face, and she looked solid enough, but nothing else was there. The ballroom was gone. She could hear someone calling her name, but it sounded far off. Gerald's arms were no longer restraining her, nor were his slimy fingers on her neck. She shuddered involuntarily, then took one step forward, then another. Wherever she was did not change with her movements. It continued to be a white, empty space.

"Hello?" Elyse called uncertainly. It felt very strange to be calling for someone in this white nothing space. But she wasn't sure what else to do. She didn't know where she was. Somewhere in the past or future, or a new place entirely?

Or…am I dead? she wondered. It would explain why there was nothing around her.

THIRTY-THREE

JOSH

Josh still felt somewhat dazed as he looked across the dance floor to where his boss—*No, my former boss*, he corrected himself—was standing with Elyse. When Gerald caught his eye and trailed his hand possessively down Elyse's neck, Josh shuddered and averted his eyes. He really didn't want to watch Gerald kiss Elyse.

"Are we going to leave?" he asked Catrina, looking pointedly at her fingers gripping his arm. "The exchange is done. No need to linger. Gerald might change his mind." He tried shifting his weight on his feet to move away from Catrina, but she wouldn't budge. Then, the whole room went dark, and people screamed in panic.

"Catrina?" he asked slightly louder.

Her grip tightened around his arm, but she remained silent. His anger started to rise. He was tired of the games that HAC and the FBI were playing. He spun around so that he was standing in front of the vampire. Even in the darkness, he could see Catrina's eyes had gone completely black.

"What the hell?" he growled, yanking his arm out of her grip. Her fingers released easily enough, but his arm had enough momentum that he ended up swinging it into the poor person behind him.

"Watch it," came Derek's voice from behind Josh.

Josh turned to toward where he thought Derek was standing. "What are *you* doing here?"

"We need to get Catrina out of here. So we can examine her someplace we can see," Derek replied.

"What about Elyse?" Josh countered.

Josh could hear the sneer in Derek's tone. "How sweet. You do actually care about her."

Josh raised his eyebrow. "And you don't?"

Derek didn't reply and gathered Catrina up in his arms, her red dress cascading around his arms. "C'mon, follow me." Derek's tone made it sound more like an order than a suggestion. Josh wasn't sure if he wanted to follow Derek. "I can make you come by force or you can come of your own free will. Either way you will come. *NOW.*"

Josh sighed, following Derek's weaving way out of the crowd. Even though the room was still dark, enough light filtered in for him to see where Derek was leading. When they got into a lit hallway, Derek paused at a chair and gently sat Catrina down in it.

"What's wrong with her?" Josh asked, not sure if he cared or not.

Derek glanced up at him. "She was supposed to get Elyse away from Gerald. But…I'm not sure what's happening. We had a couple of different plans that we could implement depending on what move the FBI made. None of them involved her doing this." He waved a hand, indicating her black eyes.

The door to the ballroom opened and shut. Josh whirled, hand going to the holster that he wasn't wearing.

Frank strode forward, a no-nonsense look on his face. "How is she?" he asked, completely ignoring Josh and kneeling in front of Catrina.

Frank's actions had Josh reeling with many questions floating through his head. *Derek works for HAC and so does Frank…and they are both part of this plan. A plan I still don't understand.*

"Frank, can you explain what the hell is going on?" Josh said in what he hoped was a voice that would command an answer.

Frank just gave him a droll stare. "The FBI are the bad guys."

"No shit, Sherlock," Josh growled. "Do you have any information you want to share that I don't already know?"

Instead of giving Josh an answer, Frank returned his attention to Catrina. He put his hands on her temples and closed his eyes, whispering words in a language Josh had never heard before. Suddenly, Frank snatched his hands back as though they were burning.

"Well?" questioned Josh.

"She kicked me out," Frank said and shared a look with Derek.

"Can you please explain?"

Frank looked at Derek again before focusing on Josh. "Fine, I will explain. Catrina was supposed to retrieve Elyse using magic. You know that she can teleport, right?" Josh nodded. "The retrieval was supposed to be similar to how she teleports, but different. Kind of like plucking someone from one place and depositing them somewhere else. But something happened, and it's taking longer than she expected. It's possible that Elyse's own magic was triggered and was somehow preventing Catrina from using her magic." Frank shrugged. "I'm sure Catrina will get her. She just needs more time than we were anticipating. Which brings me back to why I found you three. Gerald has agents flooding the room looking for Catrina."

THIRTY-FOUR

ELYSE

Elyse was stumbling around the strange white space, still clueless to where she was or how to get out.

Then, a voice drifted toward her. "Elyse."

"Catrina?" Elyse whispered, afraid to hope that the vampire was there with her and was going to rescue her. Everything that had happened the past couple of hours—let alone the past few days—was so hard to wrap her mind around. But Gerald had confirmed what Catrina had said: the FBI were the bad guys.

"Follow my voice," Catrina called to her through the white.

Listening to the words, she felt as though perhaps the voice was coming from the left. Looking down at her feet, she shuffled them to the left at a forty-five-degree angle to where she had been facing and started walking in that direction.

"Keep coming this way," Catrina instructed.

Elyse marveled at how calm the vampire's voice was and wondered if it had been the plan for her to go into this strange white space to get away from Gerald. Or had something gone awry? Derek had told her he was going to be a distraction, and yet he had disappeared completely after she began dancing with Josh.

As Elyse continued to walk in the same direction, she realized that she could hear things other than her own breathing, like the click of her stilettos on a stone surface. The whiteness began to take on a tint of brown.

"Just a little bit farther," Catrina said. This time her voice sounded much closer, as though they were in a room together.

Elyse found herself humming one of her favorite songs, trying to keep her hopes up that she was almost out. Peering around, Elyse realized that she could see a doorway and a shape that could quite possibly be Catrina on the other side. As Elyse reached the doorway, she glanced over her shoulder and saw bright red eyes floating in the space behind her. Screaming, she stepped through. A bright white light flashed again and she stumbled forward and out of the white space.

She was still screaming when strong arms caught her as she fell. Terror gripped her and Elyse struggled before she peered up through the strands of red hair now covering her eyes and into the face of the person holding her.

"Josh?" she gasped.

Her eyes locked with Josh's, and she could tell how concerned he was before he pulled a mask of indifference on. "Yes, it's me."

"It worked?" she asked.

He nodded. "Yeah, it worked."

Elyse took her eyes from Josh and looked around, trying to figure out where they were. They were in a nondescript room with a long sofa that Catrina was lying on and a couple of folding chairs.

"What happened?" Elyse asked, eyes on the unmoving vampire. She could hear Josh pull one of the chairs over and the scraping of it as he sat down.

"I don't really know everything. Catrina has been asleep or in a trance for about thirty minutes. She had to find you, but now that you're here I am not sure why she hasn't woken up. Frank thinks she might just need more time to rest since it took a lot of power to find you. Hopefully, he's right," Josh explained. "What I don't understand is why you wanted me to be rescued too."

Elyse pulled her eyes away from Catrina and back to Josh. "I like you, Josh. Is there something wrong with that? To want to see where this goes?" she said, waving her hand between the two of them.

Josh shook his head. "No, I would like to see where it goes too. But…we need to get out of here first."

"What do you mean?" Elyse asked.

Frank coughed from behind Josh. "We are still essentially at the masquerade ball. I have warded this hallway from most things that can be sent our way, but it is temporary. Now that you are here, we must find a way to escape."

"But…" Elyse said, glancing at Catrina.

Frank shook his head. "Yes, I know the original plan was for her to pull you out and then to teleport everyone to the safehouse. This operation was kept pretty tight-knit. Derek, myself, Catrina, and Elyse were in on it. I know Terrance is here, but I am not sure if she will help us."

Josh growled. "Why wouldn't she help us? She is part of HAC."

Frank gave a sharp, barking laugh. "You really have no under-standing of what HAC is, do you?"

Josh shook his head.

"Let me educate you. Catrina Fox is one of HAC's lieutenants. Some even refer to her as second in command. She answers to Dariusz, and he sometimes finds it amusing to pit his lieutenants against one another," Frank explained.

"What does that have to do with Terrance?" Josh said.

Frank rolled his eyes. "I shouldn't be surprised she didn't tell you. Terrance is another lieutenant and…" Frank dropped his voice to the barest of whispers. "Dariusz is here."

"Wouldn't that mean that he would want me to be rescued? I thought HAC wanted to use my ability to see the future," Elyse questioned.

"Perhaps," Frank replied with a shrug. "He is a vampire. Who am I to know what his agenda is—"

Derek interrupted. "That is beside the point. We are on our own, and we need to leave before someone breaks through. I'll carry Catrina."

At that moment, the doors back into the ballroom shook and shuddered as someone body-slammed them.

"Run!" Derek shouted, gathering Catrina into his arms.

Josh drew the gun Derek had given him and Elyse stayed close to him as they headed farther down the hallway. As they rounded the corner, they heard a loud blast as the doors were finally breached.

Josh picked up the pace, but Elyse couldn't keep up. Stilettos were not made for running. Elyse stopped, balanced against the wall, and yanked them off. She glanced at her dress. It was not really made for running either. She could hear pounding feet and realized she was out of time. Dropping the shoes, she gathered as much of her dress in each of her hands as she could and took off. They seemed to be gaining ground, until her stockinged foot caught on the edge of her dress. Elyse tumbled to the ground. Josh was far enough ahead of her that he didn't realize she had fallen.

Frank knelt beside her. "Hurry up!" he hissed, hauling Elyse to her feet. Frank looked at her dress. "I'm sorry." He grabbed the fabric, and with a few deft tugs, it ripped as he pulled.

The lovely skirt and train fell away, leaving her with a shockingly short green satin dress. It was so short that it didn't cover much past the top of her thighs. She opened her mouth to protest, but Frank grabbed her hand and dragged her down the hallway. Unhindered by the dress, Elyse was able to run ahead of Frank.

Ahead she could see Josh and Derek, but they weren't moving.

"Keep going!" she shouted, wondering why they had stopped. When she slid to a stop, she understood why. The hallway ended, and there was only one door. It conveniently had a plaque next to it. Grand Ballroom A.

"We don't have a choice," Derek announced.

Elyse knew he was right. "We go through the doors and what?"

Josh shrugged. "We don't know what is on the other side. It might be full of agents, or it could still be guests. On the count of three. One…two…three." He pushed the door open and slowly, gun ready, stepped through the door.

Chaos reigned on the other side. A huge tiger was snarling and swatting at anyone that got too close to the hooded man Elyse had seen earlier. The hooded man was holding someone and sucking on their neck. As though he could feel Elyse's gaze, he looked up and grinned. She could clearly see his fangs dripping with blood, as though she were standing directly in front of him rather than across the room.

Tearing her eyes away from who she could only assume was Dariusz, she realized that there were bodies everywhere. Most of them had been mauled by the tiger.

"Hurry, let's go while we can," murmured Frank, leading the way. weaving through the bodies and aiming for the exit.

"Not so fast," came a deep voice that vibrated through Elyse's very core. She froze in place. She knew even without looking that the voice could only belong to one person and that was Dariusz. "You wouldn't want to leave before the fun is over, would you?"

Against her will, Elyse found her body turning so she was facing Dariusz. The face mask from earlier was gone. For a moment, she thought she saw a skull instead of a face, but then the face became slightly more visible. He had dark brown skin, almost black. His hood fell back, revealing a thick black beard flecked with blood and a bald head covered in tattoos.

Elyse struggled against whatever magic he was using to hold her in place, but it was useless. She was unable to move.

"Now, I thought you would like to see Uncle Albert one last time." With a wave of Dariusz's hand, Elyse's uncle appeared, bound to a chair.

"I'm sorry," Uncle Albert mouthed to her.

Elyse was confused. "You have nothing to be sorry for."

"Oh, yes. Yes, he does, Elyse. You see, the lab your uncle works for…I own it," Dariusz announced.

Elyse was appalled. *My uncle works for HAC?*

"No, not for HAC, for me," Dariusz explained, plucking the thought out of her head. "You see, all those years ago I got rather lonely, and I decided that the world would be a better place if there was more magic. Your great-grandfather, Archibald Cornelius, was working for my lab, so it was a simple matter of a few spells to enhance the COVID-50 virus that he was researching. And voilà, a magically enhanced virus got loose and created more magical creatures. If it hadn't been for me, you would not be able to see the future."

"You created COVID-50 because you were bored?" she shouted, anger bubbling up within her. *Maybe if I keep him focused on me, Josh can do something for my uncle.*

"I suppose you could explain it that way," Dariusz replied in a calm voice. "But you see, now that I have you in my possession, I don't need Albert anymore." He slowly approached her uncle, like a predator stalking its prey.

Elyse shuddered, glancing over at Josh, but another FBI agent was brawling with him, fists and feet flying. She tipped her head toward her uncle, hoping he would catch her meaning and do something, but knowing that he likely wasn't aware of anything other than the man he was fighting. She tried moving, but she was still rooted in place. Out of the corner over her eye she noticed that Dariusz stopped circling her uncle and positioned himself behind the chair. He tipped Albert's head to the side, revealing the bulging carotid artery in his neck. Elyse could hear Albert murmuring over and over again, "I'm sorry." Dariusz licked his lips in anticipation, his eyes locked with Elyse's he tipped his head down, opening his mouth. The fangs glistening in the light as they got closer and closer to her uncle's artery.

A blur of motion and suddenly the tiger was on top of Dariusz. The vampire threw out his arm, sending the chair toppling. Vampire and tiger rolled and tumbled, blood spraying everywhere.

Elyse flexed her fingers, then realized she was free of Dariusz's hold, at least for the moment. She lunged toward her uncle, trying desperately to untie him.

"Leave me. Save yourself," he whispered to her.

"I can't leave you. You're the only family I have left, I won't lose you too." Elyse sobbed. The knots were not coming undone. She looked around for something sharp to help her cut the ropes, but nothing was close enough that could be useful. She had no idea where Josh or the others had gone.

Behind her, she could hear the tiger roaring as she tangled with Dariusz, but Elyse could not let herself focus on anything but saving her uncle. Not if she wanted him to live.

A clammy hand reached out and gripped her arm. Elyse stopped messing with the ropes and peered up into her uncle's face. "You must save yourself, Elyse. Dariusz cannot be allowed to get control of you or your magic."

"I would rather die than lose you," she sobbed.

Uncle Albert shook his head, tears streaming down his face. "He is not going to kill you, my dear. He is going to turn you into a slave."

Elyse froze at her uncle's words. *Slave?*

THIRTY-FIVE

JOSH

Josh gazed around the room, trying to come up with a plan, when Dwayne came out of the darkness and launched himself at Josh.

Josh shrugged out of his navy jacket and set his feet in a fighting stance, grinning just as viciously as Dwayne was. Dwayne paused for a second and Josh made a "come here" motion with his right hand.

Dwayne lunged at Josh, a blur of fists, jab, jab, with a straight right punch aiming for Josh's stomach. But Josh was ready for it. He blocked and retaliated with a left roundhouse, forcing Dwayne to drop his arms. Josh then quickly came in with a jab right hand combination. Josh's finishing move was a right foot jab.

Unfortunately for Josh, Dwayne reached out, grabbed his right foot in both of his hands, and twisted, slamming Josh into the ground. Josh grunted, trying to dislodge Dwayne's hands from his foot. With a thrust, Josh levered himself up enough to bring his left leg up and kicked Dwayne in his unprotected groin. Groaning, Dwayne let go of Josh's foot and backed away.

Knowing he would only have this advantage momentarily, Josh didn't waste any time. He leaped toward Dwayne with a left jab, straight right hand, left hook. Dwayne's eyes opened wide in surprise as Josh finished his move with a spinning back kick that connected soundly with his jaw. Dwayne's head snapped back and he collapsed to the floor.

Josh was panting and his lip was split. He glanced around, trying to assess what had happened while Dwayne was distracting him. His eyes found Elyse. She was still being held in place by Dariusz's magic, which was not was affecting him or anyone else. It was fascinating, but also complicated things. He had vowed to get Elyse out, and now, just when he had thought for a moment they would make it, the tables turned once again. As he crept behind Dariusz, Josh lost track of what Frank and Derek, who was still carrying Catrina, were doing.

Then, Dariusz spoke. Pieces of the puzzle clicked in place. Catrina's fear of Dariusz and unwillingness to go into details about who and what he was. The mastermind behind the unleashing of magic across the United States.

What about the rest of the world? Josh pondered. *If Dariusz existed before COVID-50, did other vampires exist too?*

Suddenly there was a roar, and Terrance came flying through the air, leaping on top of Dariusz. The vampire and tiger rolled, fangs and claws flashing. Not wanting to waste his opportunity, Josh ran, giving the pair a wide berth, and skidded to a halt when he found Elyse trying to untie her uncle.

"Let me help you," he said, removing her hands from the knots.

He pulled a knife he had pilfered from one of the appetizer trays earlier out of his sock and sawed at the ropes. Just as he cut through the last one, the ropes reappeared, as though he had never cut them at all.

"What the hell," he growled.

Moving to the front of the chair, he tapped lightly on Albert's face, trying to wake him up. "Albert, what did he do to your ropes?" Josh asked, hoping the old man would give him a coherent answer.

"You can't free me," Albert rasped. "Don't waste your time. Take Elyse while he is distracted and go."

Josh frowned. "I could carry you." Elyse had taken his knife and was sawing at the ropes again.

"If you carry me, he will track me to wherever you are. It is what he wants," Albert replied. He started coughing. A trickle of blood escaped from his mouth.

"Why?" Josh asked.

"She can see the future and the past…maybe even more with training. One of a kind." Albert stopped as a coughing fit consumed him. "The best way to be the most powerful player in a game is to have the exclusive pieces and know how to use them."

Elyse cried next to him. He could feel the sobs wracking her body as once again the ropes fixed themselves. "We can defeat him. I can't lose you too. I have no one left." She wrapped her arms around her uncle, burying her head in his shoulder.

Albert peered up at Josh imploringly. Josh frowned. *If I do what he is asking, she will never forgive me for abandoning her uncle.* His thoughts paused. *But she will be alive. Isn't that more important?*

Josh watched indecisively as Elyse hugged her uncle hard, clearly not intending to let him go. Albert coughed again. More blood dribbled out of his mouth.

He is dying already, and he knows it.

"Elyse, come on, we need to go," Josh said, wrapping a hand around her arm and gently tugging.

"No," came her firm reply.

"If we don't leave while Terrance has him distracted, we will lose our chance. He wants you for your magic. If you stay here, you are playing right into his hands," Josh replied, his patience wearing thin.

He gently slid her fingers from the chair and tugged her back one step at a time. He wrapped his arms around her—to restrain or protect her, he wasn't really sure. Albert gave him a grateful look. Then everything vanished.

Josh stumbled sideways with his arms still around Elyse, and they fell in a heap on a cold tile floor. He peered around and immediately recognized the hallway. One of the HAC safehouses. Catrina was leaning against the wall a little ways off. Her eyes were back to their normal red color, although she still didn't look as perky as usual.

"You woke up," he said, just as Elyse yanked out of his grip and scooted out of his reach on the floor.

"You didn't let me save him," Elyse shouted angrily at Josh.

"He told me to save you," Josh responded softly.

"I don't care. He's my uncle, my last living family. How could you just abandon him to that monster?" Elyse shouted, shaking.

Josh ached to wrap his arms back around her and comfort her, but her anger was directed at him. He knew the only thing those actions would do now is likely encourage her to hit him. "I obeyed his last wish," Josh replied, standing up. He reached out to offer her a hand but withdrew it when she ignored him. Glancing at Catrina, he said, "I'm going to go change."

Catrina nodded and pointed toward a door in the hallway.

Josh gave Elyse one more glance before walking into the room. He shut the door and leaned against it. "I am free," he whispered. "Am I?" Rubbing his hands over his face, Josh headed to the closet and opened it to find an assortment of men's clothing: T-shirts, long-sleeve button-ups, slacks, and jeans. Deciding there was no reason to dress like an FBI agent since he no longer was one, Josh picked a green T-shirt and jeans in his size.

He discarded his navy suit in what seemed to be a clothing hamper, then sat down in a large gold velvet chair with too many pillows, trying to figure out what he should do next.

He must have dozed off in the chair. He awoke when he heard a scraping sound, causing him to jump out of the chair and reach for his gun. A piece of paper had been slid under the door. He cautiously walked over to it. His name was on top.

The letter said:

> Josh,
>
> While I know you think you acted in my best interests by saving me instead of my uncle, I strongly disagree. I realize that it has been a crazy few weeks since we met, and I will be forever grateful for the help you have given me.
> However, at this time, I do not feel as though I can date or continue to have a relationship with a person who would not allow me to save someone I love.
> I wish you well in your future endeavors.
>
> Goodbye,
> Elyse Hutchinson

The letter fluttered to the ground out of his hand. Emotions roiling. He knew something like this had a strong probability of happening when he chose to save Elyse over Albert. But he wasn't expecting how much it hurt. She didn't want to see him again. Everything he had done today had been for her and now that was it—over. He sucked in a shaky breath. His mind whirled. *When did I fall in love with her?*

Bristling with anger mostly at himself, Josh knew he couldn't stay in this room any longer. Throwing open the door, he startled Frank, who was on the other side, preparing to knock.

"What's wrong with you?" Frank inquired.

"I need to get out of here," Josh grumbled, heading briskly down the hallway, not waiting for Frank.

"You can leave if that's what you want. I wouldn't advise it, but… no one is forcing you to stay," Frank said, trying to keep up.

"Good. Then I'm going to go home," Josh said and reached for the door to the stairwell that he knew would take him into the garage.

"If you would at least stop for a moment, please," Frank said.

Josh dropped his hand away from the door and turned. "What?"

"Well, for starters, you no longer have a car or phone. Here." Frank offered Josh a backpack. "Everything you need is in there. A car is waiting for you as well. Oh, and I took the liberty of ensuring that your apartment is safe, so you can go back there."

"Thanks," Josh said gruffly. He took the backpack and swiftly went through the door and down the stairs.

THIRTY-SIX
ELYSE

When Elyse got home midmorning on Sunday, she was emotionally raw from everything that had happened since she left the house. As the car she was in slowed down in her driveway, she gasped in shock. She had forgotten when she had left that she had not cleaned up any of the mess from the fire or her car exploding. There were still pieces of debris here and there, although someone had clearly been making an effort to get things back in order. She could see new boards on part of the fence.

As she stepped out of the car, familiar whinnies greeted her. Elyse closed her eyes and inhaled. *Home.*

She ran over to the fence where the horses were jostling for a place to see who would be first. Honey was there, Fork, and some of the other youngsters. But there were many missing. She wasn't sure if that was because they were somewhere else or if they had been casualties.

"Who's there?" came a familiar voice from far off.

"Mya!" Elyse shouted, grinning.

Mya came running toward her arms outstretched. "You're alive!" Mya gasped.

They embraced. "Yes, I'm alive."

"Thank goodness!" Mya shrieked. "No one was sure what happened to you. You've been gone not quite three days."

Elyse wrinkled her nose. "I know. I'm fine though. I think if I told you everything that had happened you probably wouldn't believe me. So, let's just leave it at: I'm alive and will be forever grateful to you for taking care of my ranch while I was indisposed." Elyse released Mya and stepped back, peering around.

Mya sighed. "The barn, as I'm sure you expected, is going to need to be replaced. I'm not sure I'd trust anything in there. Even if we replace the beams, I think it's too risky. Ultimately, it's your choice, of course."

Elyse nodded and walked around, lifting pieces of debris here and there, starting a pile to one side for the metal and the other for the wood. "What about the horses?"

Mya smiled. "They all survived. Some of them got pretty banged up, and the ones that need stall rest are over at Jessica's, since you won't have a barn for a while. But I was surprised. The barn and your shed are gone, but the horses are not. I have no idea how you got so lucky. When I saw the barn that first day, I think the morning of the fire, I thought for sure horses had been lost."

Elyse let out her breath. "That is a huge relief. I have been preparing myself for bad news when I got here. I don't know if you've seen it before, but in the back acreage, we actually have an old chicken house."

Mya looked at her uncertainly. "You mean the building that looks half collapsed?"

Elyse laughed. "Yes, that one. I will admit about half of it is in bad shape, but the front half is fine. We should ride down there in a bit and see what it looks like."

"Is there a reason you want to use that building versus building a new one?" Mya inquired.

Elyse sighed. "Yes, cost and time. You should be well aware of how difficult it is to get construction supplies out here. With everything that has been going on, I think it would be prudent to use what resources I have available first."

A couple of hours later, Elyse was swaying in the saddle from exhaustion. She hadn't stayed at Catrina's safehouse for very long before insisting she should come home.

"You don't need to be out here, Elyse. Why don't you go inside. Just stick Honey in the round pen and I'll do the rest."

Arching her eyebrow, Elyse peered at Mya uncertainly. "Are you sure?"

"Absolutely. I usually do fine without you. Tonight won't be any different," Mya reminded her.

Elyse sighed and turned Honey back toward the house. She asked her mare to trot and almost slowed her right back down to a walk. The usually comfortable trot was almost more than she could bear with how tired she was.

Leading Honey into the round pen, Elyse pulled off the mare's bridle and gave her a big hug. "I'm so glad you're okay. We're okay," she whispered. Honey nickered and nuzzled Elyse's back as though in agreement.

The landline was ringing. Elyse jumped, startled, and realized she was in bed. *I guess I made it to bed, at least.* Elyse grabbed the phone and held it to her ear groggily. "Hello?" she said, not sure it had come out properly.

"Oh, good. You're finally awake," Jessica said in a bubbly tone.

Elyse stayed in bed, staring at the ceiling with the phone held to her ear. "What do you mean, finally awake?"

"Mya knocked at the front door twice, and I also called already. It's almost one p.m.," Jessica said smoothly.

"One p.m.!" Elyse shouted in shock.

"Yes, no big deal. Mya said she had you covered with the farm chores. I was just wondering if you wanted some company. Mya said you didn't want to tell her what had happened, but given that

I already know a lot more than she does, I'm hoping you will tell me," Jessica suggested.

Elyse sighed and sat up. "Fine. Come over..." She paused. "Maybe you can bring some food? And I will do my best to tell you what happened."

A couple of hours later, Jessica scooted her chair back from the table. Elyse could tell her friend was having trouble processing everything she had just told her. Since Jessica knew about the magic, journals, and her mixed feelings for Josh, Elyse hadn't held anything back.

"I know you may never forgive Josh for leaving your uncle. But did you consider that your uncle might have been dying anyway and that you surely wouldn't have survived if you had stayed any longer in the ballroom?" Jessica twirled a piece of her black hair in her fingers. "I would have probably done the same thing Josh had done. Your uncle was old. Can you blame him for being willing to sacrifice himself so you could survive?"

Elyse sighed. "Maybe what you're saying is something I can consider. But Uncle Albert is...was...my last living relative. It's just me now. How am I supposed to do this all by myself?" Lip trembling, she fought back the tears threatening to spill over.

Jessica stood up and enveloped Elyse in a big hug. "You're not alone. I promise."

THIRTY-SEVEN

JOSH

Josh leaned back into the seat of his vintage, candy-apple-red Corvette, relishing how the sport seat hugged his body. He was probably on a fool's errand. The last time he had seen Elyse on Sunday, three days prior, the morning after the masquerade, they had parted ways, with her unable to forgive him for leaving her uncle behind. But Josh had found that the only thing he wanted was her company. He concluded it would be better to see her in person than it would be to call, and it would keep them both off Dariusz's radar for as long as possible.

Which was why he was driving down the poorly maintained old Highway 124 that wound its way through Jackson County. A safe distance from the highway on the right side was a well-maintained riding and walking path that butted up against the forest. On the left side was farmland.

Sometimes it surprised him how fast everything outside of downtown Atlanta had just fallen apart. The crazy growth the greater metro area had seen from 2020 until 2050, when COVID-50 hit, had been unreal. Farmlands were almost non-existent. Those who owned land had to fend off developers frequently and with a big show of force. After COVID-50, it all went away. Josh blew out his breath. He'd always assumed it had been because eighty percent of the population died in the first year of COVID-50, but maybe something else had been at work. Either way, it wasn't relevant.

He had seen old photos from those early years after COVID-50 showing how rapidly this area had gone back to what it had once been, farmland and forest. The huge housing developments were abandoned and then just started to disappear altogether, with lush grazing land in their place.

Likely, he pondered, *someone had magic and was able to make the houses disappear much faster than they would have decomposed.*

Drumming his fingers on the steering wheel in time to his music, Josh glanced around. He was fairly certain he was close to Elyse's property line, and this stretch of road was smooth. Grinning to himself, Josh pressed his foot down on the gas pedal. The Corvette purred as it rapidly sped up to 150 mph. Adrenaline coursing through him, he kept his eyes glued to the road. This stretch was not terribly long. There was a curve up ahead. Josh expertly navigated around it, and then to his surprise there was a black thing, possibly a large Angus steer or bull, in the middle of the road. He slammed his foot on the brakes and nothing happened. He pressed his foot down harder, but again nothing happened. His right hand went for the emergency brake, but it wouldn't budge either. *Someone tampered with my car!* As a last resort he tried to turn his steering wheel to go around it, but it barely turned, not nearly enough. The black thing was too close.

"Goodbye, Elyse," he whispered to himself as the car plowed with a sickening crunch into the black thing. Josh bit back a scream as the car crumpled around him and he blacked out.

Every inch of him screamed in protest. Josh blinked and groaned in pain. *Smoke. I need to get out.* The thought flickered in his mind, but he couldn't do anything about it. Josh passed out again.

He thought he might be able to hear Elyse's voice calling out, "Are you okay?" But he couldn't figure out why she would be calling for him.

Josh's eyes cracked open. Someone was dragging him across the road. He saw the fire licking at his Corvette and the spreading puddle under the gas tank. The explosion threw them both backward, and he lost consciousness again.

Someone was gently running their fingers over his face. He opened his eyes and was having trouble making sense of the fuzzy white and black shapes.

"Oh, good. You're waking up," said the person touching his face. *A man. That was a man's voice,* Josh told himself.

"Josh, it's Frank," the man said.

Josh tried to move, but he couldn't feel any of his body at all, other than his face. A beige-colored blob bobbed into his line of sight. He tried to open his mouth, but that wouldn't work either.

"Hush. You were in a car accident. I'm not sure why you decided to drive that stupid old car of yours, but anyhow…the car was tampered with, making your brakes fail and forcing you headlong into a fake black Angus steer made of solid steel. It had to have weighed as much as a Holstein bull," Frank explained patiently.

Josh must have made a sound that he couldn't hear because Frank spoke again in a more soothing tone, as though Josh were a child. "Catrina suspects that the FBI set it to take you out. They must have had a tracker on your car or on you somehow and known that you would be driving on Highway 124. As to why it was a cow, my assumption is that they wanted to catch you by surprise, and they would be in deep shit if they had knowingly sacrificed a real cow, given how critical Jackson County is for beef production to the country."

Josh's vision blacked out again. Sighing, he allowed his eyes to drift shut.

When his eyes opened again, he quickly shut them against the harsh fluorescent lights and bright white of the room he was in. Running his tongue over his lips, he realized that he could feel more than just his face. A moan escaped from his lips before he could stop it.

He could hear the scraping of a chair on the floor, and then someone was standing next to him, touching his arm. He shook; even the featherlight touch was excruciating.

"Josh." Catrina's silky voice was a surprise. He would not have expected her to care enough about him to be here, wherever that was. Josh opened one eye and found that the overhead lights had been shut off, and there was only a lamp in the corner. He opened both eyes, and to his delight realized that he could see this time. It wasn't just fuzzy shapes.

"Mrrrppp," Josh said, grimacing as the word he wanted to say came out as a jumbled mess.

Licking his lips, he tried again, "Mmrrrp lsss." Eyes narrowing as it didn't come out right again, he was surprised when Catrina shoved a cup with a straw in his face.

"Maybe some water will help?" the vampire said encouragingly. "I cannot translate whatever it is that you want to say."

Josh nodded and opened his mouth, grabbing the straw with his tongue. He took a tentative sip and a cool trickle of water ran down his throat. Satisfied that it was indeed water in the cup, his second sip was much heartier. When the cup was almost empty, he let go of the straw. Taking a deep breath, Josh tried again, voice raspy—from what, he wasn't sure.

"Who pulled me out of the car?"

Instead of looking at him, Catrina fiddled with the edge of the blanket covering him. "Elyse pulled you out."

Josh gasped. Sweat broke out on his forehead as he tried and failed to sit up. It felt like his whole body was filled with lead weights.

"Is she okay?" he asked, staring angrily at Catrina, willing her to look at him.

Catrina did look at him this time. "She will be fine. You know that we had to pry the two of you apart. You just would not let go of each other. Yet, when you both woke up, neither one of you was aware it had been the other at the explosion."

Josh gazed at her, waiting for a further explanation. Catrina sucked in a sharp breath. "I've never seen anything like it. Almost as though…" She paused uncertainly. "There's no way."

Josh gave her a puzzled look. "No way what? What aren't you telling me?"

Catrina hesitated before taking a breath. "I suppose there is no harm in telling you. It's not like it is a secret or anything." Josh raised his eyebrow at the secret comment, hoping she would just get on with the explanation. His energy levels were dropping again. "It has come up a couple of times among the groups of magic users that there is something called a soulmate."

Josh shrugged, not understanding. He'd heard stories of people who were supposedly fated to be together, soulmates.

Catrina plowed on with her explanation. "Two people who have magic can become true soulmates. Where you are linked not only by your feelings for each other, but your magic becomes linked too."

"Sounds strange. Are you sure it's a real thing?" he asked, no longer able to fight off the sleepiness. His eyes drooped closed before Catrina could answer.

THIRTY-EIGHT

ELYSE

Elyse woke with a start and almost fell out of the bed she was on. Only the cold, hard metal railing kept her in. Peering around, worry flooded her as she realized she was in another hospital room, just like before. Panic gripped her, and her body shook. Pulling her legs up to her chest, Elyse whimpered.

A clicking of heels on the linoleum floor snapped her out of her panic. She turned her head so she could see the door and was surprised when Catrina walked through. Slowly, Elyse lowered her legs on the bed and straightened out the blanket. She was not sure that she completely trusted the vampire, but at least Elyse knew they were on the same side.

"What are you doing here?" Elyse asked.

"What kind of person would I be if I abandoned my allies to the FBI after all the work I've already put in trying to keep you out of their hands?" Catrina snapped at her.

Elyse was taken aback by Catrina's tone. "The FBI orchestrated the crash, not D…?" Her hands shook as she thought of Dariusz, but she could not bring herself to say his name aloud.

Catrina nodded before she began pacing. "Yes."

"Who was in the car?" Elyse questioned.

Catrina stopped pacing to stare at Elyse. "You don't know?"

"Know what?" Elyse asked, annoyance starting to creep into her voice. *I'm the one in the hospital bed. How am I supposed to know everything?*

"Sorry, I just assumed when you pulled him out of the car that you knew. Josh. It was Josh in the car," Catrina said in a soft, almost apologetic voice.

Eyes widening, Elyse opened and closed her mouth, not sure what to say. When she pulled the man out of the car, she hadn't known it was Josh. There was too much smoke. Unable to control it, a tear slowly slid down her cheek. Elyse wiped it away angrily.

"Josh is dead," she said. Honestly, she was surprised she was alive after the explosion.

Catrina sat down on the edge of the bed and took Elyse's hand in hers. "He's not dead. He did have to have surgery, but he is alive."

"How?" Elyse asked in bewilderment, lifting her arms and turning them from side to side. They were mottled in purple bruises, and she could feel the scrape on her cheek, but otherwise she seemed unharmed.

Catrina spread her hands. "Honestly, I don't really know. But if you hadn't been there when you were, he would be dead."

"Can I see Josh?" As she said his name, she felt this odd tugging in her mind that hadn't been there before.

"Of course." Catrina paused, considering Elyse's face for a moment. "We're not at the hospital. We're at the safehouse, the one I had you at when I was teaching you how to use your magical talent."

Elyse's nostrils flared, and she let out a breath she hadn't known she was holding as relief flooded her. The safehouse. She knew HAC had doctors, surgeons, and magical healers at their beck and call. She should have realized that they would have never taken her to a real hospital, not if the FBI and Dariusz were after her and Josh.

Elyse slid her legs to the edge of the bed on the opposite side of where Catrina was sitting. Her bare feet hit the cold linoleum, and she hissed as the cold seeped up her legs. Muttering nonsense words, she stood up, trying her best to ignore the cold floor. Then, she discovered that she was in a hospital gown with nothing underneath as a draft hit her backside.

She cleared her throat. "Do you have any *real* clothing I can wear?"

Catrina laughed. "Yes." She pointed to the closet on the other side of the room. "There is a selection in there. I will step out so you can get dressed. When you're done, just open the door."

Elyse shuffled over to the closet, deliberately going at an angle to keep Catrina from having a view of her butt. Normally, she wasn't overly worried about being modest, but she wasn't sure what to make of the vampire. Although she thought perhaps they might have a budding friendship. She knew very little about vampires.

She waited until Catrina pulled the door shut before opening the closet. While Catrina was right—there was clothing in the closet—it was a very limited selection. Checking the tags, she found an extra-large pair of gray sweatpants that she thought would probably fit, a pair of socks, and a large green T-shirt. Tossing the hospital gown in a heap on the floor, she pulled the T-shirt on first. It fit and was almost too tight as it stretched across her breasts. She ignored the shirt and pulled on the sweatpants, wishing there was also underwear in there. Giving herself a once-over in the mirror, Elyse was satisfied that there wasn't much else she could do right now about the rest of her appearance.

Elyse pulled the door open and stepped out into the hallway. She had thought that Catrina was going to wait for her, but the vampire was nowhere to be found. *How strange.*

She decided she could find Josh on her own. If they were in the safehouse, as far as she knew there was only the one hallway with rooms. He should be easy to find. Her sock-covered feet made no sound at all, adding to the eerie silence.

There was a room with a door slightly ajar, and she could hear Josh's voice, and then Catrina's. Elyse stepped forward, preparing to knock on the door when everything went completely black for a moment.

The door disappeared as though it had never been there. Elyse took a hesitant step forward, then wished she hadn't.

The room had heavy red and black drapes decorating the walls and covering the windows. Lit candles added a golden glow to the room and covered every available surface. In the middle of the room was a massive four-poster bed. The room was empty. Elyse blinked. Now it was almost as though she was perched on top of the headboard of the bed.

Josh walked into the room naked. His muscles rippled in the candlelight. As Elyse ran her eyes down every inch of his body, she jumped when a hand appeared and wrapped itself around Josh's cock and began stroking. Catrina stepped out from behind Josh. The vampire had black leather straps crisscrossing her pale body, and her black hair was up in an intricate braid. Catrina smiled in Elyse's direction before facing Josh and kissing him, starting with his lips and slowly working her way down.

Elyse didn't want to watch but couldn't tear her eyes away. What astonished her the most was how obvious it was they were both enjoying the interaction. Josh was clearly not being tortured for information by Catrina. That belief was cemented when Josh gently picked Catrina up. She wrapped her legs around his waist like they had done this before, and he thrust himself into her.

Elyse closed her eyes, hoping whatever this was would go away. She waited, and it felt like an hour had ticked by when she opened her eyes. The door to Josh's room was in front of her and still slightly ajar. Josh and Catrina were still talking.

Elyse looked down at her hand and realized it was shaking. Feeling queasy and out of sorts, she ran back down the hallway to her room, barely making it in time before she threw up into the toilet. Wiping her mouth with the back of her hand, she slowly straightened herself until she was standing upright. She turned on the sink, and cupping her hand, scooped up some water to rinse out her mouth.

With the nausea seemingly gone, she headed back into her room and sat down on the bed, trying to figure out what on earth had just happened.

Whether that was past or future, it's clear that Josh and Catrina have something between them—far more than just friends or leader and follower. Elyse sighed. *I wonder how soon I can go home and just leave this all behind me.*

Elyse heard a soft knock on the door before it was pushed open, and a woman with golden eyes, dark hair, and an assortment of weapons strapped to her walked in. "Would you like to go home?"

Elyse narrowed her eyes. *What is wrong with these people and their introduction skills?* "Yes, I would like to go home. But first, who the hell are you?" Elyse was not sure how the woman would react. She was not expecting a very convincing animal snarl to escape from the woman's lips. Elyse took a step back and the back of her knees bumped into the bed. She sat down. Gripping the edge of the bed, she had a momentary flash, and instead of the woman she saw a huge Siberian tiger. Blinking uncertainly, Elyse saw the woman glaring at her.

"My name is Terrance. We met, sort of, at the masquerade," Terrance stated.

"Are you a tiger?" Elyse asked warily.

"Yes, I can shapeshift to become a Siberian tiger," Terrance confirmed.

Taking a deep breath, Elyse stood up. "I would like to go home."

Terrance gave her a smile that almost looked like a grimace. "Then follow me."

The drive back to the ranch was quick. It seemed Terrance was not one for conversation, leaving Elyse alone with her thoughts. *I*

know I can forgive Josh for not saving Uncle Albert, but clearly there is something between him and Catrina. If I throw myself in the middle of them, am I going to make an enemy out of her?

The familiar crunch of gravel drove Elyse out of her thoughts about Josh and Catrina and back to the ranch. "Home," she whispered.

Terrance glanced at her and Elyse realized she had spoken aloud. "Enjoy it while you can," the shapeshifter murmured.

Elyse wasn't sure what to think of that comment as she opened the door and stepped out of the car.

Terrance offered her a small bag. "Your new phone is programmed with the phone numbers of everyone who it is safe for you to contact. Oh, and in case you're wondering, today is Friday."

Elyse took the bag, riffling through it. Sure enough there was a cell phone, a small notepad, and a house key. As she looked up to offer Terrance thanks, she realized that the car and Terrance were already gone. With a deep sigh, Elyse trudged toward the house, exhaustion from the chaos of the past couple of days hitting her like a sledgehammer.

Nudging open the front door with her foot, she made her way inside. She deposited the bag from Terrance on the table and saw a note.

ELYSE,
THE HORSES HAVE BEEN TAKEN CARE OF. JUST GET
SOME REST, AND I'LL SEE YOU IN THE MORNING.
-MYA

Elyse smiled at Mya's thoughtfulness. She wasn't sure who had informed Mya she was on her way home, but she was thankful that she could just take a shower and climb into bed without having to worry about the farm chores for a few more hours.

Elyse woke with a start and almost fell out of bed. It took her a moment to realize she was in her bed at the ranch. "What a strange dream," she spoke aloud, startling herself. Running her hands over her face, she tried to make sense of what had happened. The dream had started with her checking the fence. Although some people might think it was odd to dream about chores, that was fairly normal for her. Then, though, it had shifted so that she was galloping side by side with Josh through the pastures, and it just felt right, as though he was meant to be there by her side.

Shaking her head, she decided the best thing she could do was get dressed and throw herself into chores. Swinging her legs out of bed, her eye caught on the nightstand drawer, making her hesitate. *My phone isn't even in the drawer. It's sitting in the bag on the dining room table,* she thought.

Elyse went through the motions of getting dressed and eating breakfast before heading out the door. She was jolted from her thoughts when a black pile of charred ash greeted her where the barn had once stood. Tears threatened to spill as memories from the barn catching fire flooded her mind.

A soft whinny from her left, over and over, finally caught her attention. Elyse turned and saw Honey and Fork waiting eagerly for her at the gate, ears pricked forward and eyes intently focused on her every move. Wiping at her eyes, Elyse ran over to the two horses and hugged both of them. Honey seemed content, but after a few moments, Fork got bored with being hugged and started moving his lips over her arms, shoulders, and finally her hair, as though searching for his breakfast.

"Silly Fork. Your food is not in my hair," she said with a giggle, giving Fork's black chin a scratch before stepping back out of his reach. Glancing around, she spotted a wheelbarrow with two bales of hay.

Gripping the handles, she maneuvered the wheelbarrow as close as she could get to the hay manger and began tossing flakes in. When Honey and Fork were happily munching on their breakfast, she made her way down the line, feeding the other horses before filling their water troughs.

As she dried her hands off on her jeans, Elyse realized with a pang how much she missed Josh. Those two days they had on the ranch had felt so right. *If I want him to come back here, I need to tell him he is forgiven. He can't read my mind.* Decision made, Elyse strode back into the house and pulled her new cell phone out of the bag. Taking a deep breath, Elyse selected Josh's name from the list of contacts.

As the phone rang, Elyse's heart began to pound and her hands became moist. Even though she knew it was ridiculous to be nervous, she could not control her body's reaction.

"Hello?" Josh's voice came over the phone.

Elyse blew out her breath. "I forgive you."

"Elyse?" Josh replied.

"Yes, it's me, Elyse. I guess I should have started with that," Elyse replied shakily.

Josh chuckled. "Thank you for your forgiveness. How are you?"

Twisting a piece of hair around her finger, Elyse debated how to answer. "I'm still adjusting. The barn is…the barn is just gone now, debris cleaned up. It feels strange since that barn has been here for over one hundred years. It's like another piece of me has died." She let the piece of hair fall. "I know it's just a building, but…I guess I'm rambling."

Josh chuckled again. "It's good to hear your voice again. I've missed you."

Before she could bite her tongue to keep the words in, Elyse blurted, "I miss you too." Rushing on to the next thing she wanted to tell him and hoping to not give him time to question her feelings, she said, "Catrina wants me to leave the ranch, since *he* knows where it is and is likely to try again. I just…I don't know if I can bear to give this all up. Even with the old barn missing, there is just so much of my history here."

"I can come out for a few days and help if you'd like," Josh offered.

As soon as he said the words, she got a strong feeling that she should accept his offer. Since her talent had been unlocked, she was not getting feelings as much anymore; most of the time she got visions instead. Now that she knew the feelings were a manifestation of her talent, she also understood why following them was important.

"That would be wonderful," Elyse replied.

"I will get my stuff together and head that way shortly," Josh said and hung up.

Elyse put her phone back on the table. A shiver of excitement went through her at the prospect of seeing Josh again.

She still wasn't sure if she had completely wrapped her mind around what had happened at the ball, just a mere week ago, and to realize that her uncle and Josh had been right. The only way for her to survive was to leave the ballroom without her uncle. It just hurt. He had never not been in her life and now she had no family left. Which was part of her reluctance to just leave the ranch as Catrina was recommending. *How do I abandon over one hundred years of family history without a second thought?*

A couple of hours later, as Elyse was hammering the last new board back in place on one of the paddocks behind the barn, she heard a car door shut, followed by a second one. *How odd.* She set down her tools and walked around the remains of the barn to figure out who had arrived. As soon as she rounded the corner, she stopped dead in her tracks. Josh was standing next to his car with Aunt Grace.

Tears began to fall freely as Elyse ran over to her aunt. "You're alive!" she sobbed, hugging her. Aunt Grace returned the hug equally fiercely.

"I'm alive," Aunt Grace confirmed.

"How?" Elyse said, pulling back but not removing her arms from her aunt.

"Catrina was able to get me to safety," Aunt Grace explained.

Which probably means Dariusz was behind it, Elyse thought.

Aunt Grace gave her a squeeze before dropping her arms and surveying the destroyed barn. "Looks like I have a lot of work ahead of me."

"*We* have a lot of work," corrected Elyse.

Aunt Grace looked at her. "No, *I* do, my dear. You can stay for a few more days if you'd like, but I must insist that you leave and go into hiding. I couldn't bear it if you were caught," she said with a shudder.

Elyse glanced at Josh, who shrugged, before returning her attention to her aunt. "You are going to run the ranch?"

Aunt Grace laughed. "You say that like I'm an incapable old lady. You, miss, have forgotten how much time I used to spend on the ranch. I do know how to run it. I also won't be alone."

"You won't?" Elyse asked.

Her aunt grinned. "No, silly. I have been talking to Jessica and her parents. They are going to help too. The business will continue, and if you are ever able to return, then you are welcome to have it back."

"Was this your plan when you said you'd come?" Elyse asked Josh.

Josh held up his hands defensively. "I had no idea what your aunt was going to do, only that Catrina had asked me to bring her whenever you got around to inviting me out."

"How about we get your stuff into the house and then we can talk about it over lunch?" Aunt Grace suggested.

Elyse nodded—it was a reasonable request—and led the way into the house.

THIRTY-NINE

JOSH

Hours later, Josh, Elyse, and Aunt Grace were sitting on the porch watching the starry night sky. Over lunch, they had figured out the plan, and afterward had ridden out to the old chicken house that was going to be renovated for the horses. Aunt Grace had made a list of everything that was stored in the old chicken house so they could take supplies out there in the cart the next morning. Elyse hadn't known how ancient some of the things in there really were or how much work they had cut out for them.

Three days? Jessica and Aunt Grace are still going to have a ton of work left to do. He paused in his thoughts. *But I will do as much as I can every day till we leave to ensure they have as little as possible to finish.*

Aunt Grace cleared her throat. "I'm going to bed. I'll see you two in the morning."

Josh turned toward them and watched as Elyse stood up and gave her aunt a hug, before returning to her chair and gazing out at the night sky. Taking a deep breath, Josh inhaled and smelled rain, which wouldn't help them with renovating the barn.

His gaze lingered on Elyse's face, and he realized how desperately he wanted to fix whatever had happened between them. He hadn't been lying earlier when he said how much he missed her. Hesitantly he reached out and set his hand on top of hers.

"Can we talk?" Josh said.

Elyse finally turned to face him, meeting his blue eyes with her vibrant green ones. "Of course."

"I know we have both been through a lot. I am sorry for the part I played with the FBI, but I am not sorry that Quinn introduced us. I felt on our first and second date as I feel now, like there is something between us that is worth seeing where it takes us." Josh spoke in a smooth, even tone and then found himself holding his breath, waiting for her answer.

"What about Catrina?" Elyse replied.

Josh opened his mouth and then shut it. *That is not what I expected her to say.* "What do you mean, what about Catrina?"

Elyse shut her eyes and then opened them, as though she were debating what to say. "I had a vision of the two of you having sex, and contrary to what you told me about her torturing you, it looked very consensual. I have no interest in getting in between whatever is going on with you and Catrina."

Josh let his fingers fall from the top of Elyse's hand, eyes wide in shock. "The only time Catrina and I had consensual sex was when we first met." He shuddered involuntarily. "Yes, she is beautiful, and since I'm sure you want me to be honest, she was pretty damn good in bed, but after she tortured me using sex as her weapon— some would go so far as to claim she raped me—I don't think I would ever be able to willingly have sex with her again."

Elyse seemed to search his face, for what he wasn't sure. He shuddered again, remembering when Catrina had decided to be particularly vicious and had strapped him naked to a chair, shredding his arms and chest with her claws while she straddled him, and using some of her magical talent, somehow forced his body to respond against his will. She rode him over and over, until he'd passed out from blood loss and exhaustion.

"I believe you," she said softly and took his hand in hers. "I think we should follow Aunt Grace's example and go to sleep."

Josh nodded in agreement. She was right, of course. He could feel exhaustion dragging at him from all the work they'd done today. He stood up, keeping their hands together, then lifted her hand to his lips. "Good night, Elyse."

Their eyes met. Elyse scooted closer, so their bodies were almost brushing, and gave him a kiss on the lips.

"Good night, Josh." Smiling, Elyse turned and went back into her house, leaving him standing on the porch.

Maybe there is a future for the two of us after all.

The next two days passed way faster than Josh expected. The three of them fell into an easy rhythm of work. Sometimes, they were content to be silent, and others Aunt Grace would regale them with stories from her wild days as a young girl on the ranch. When Josh got the encrypted text from Catrina telling him she would be there at eight p.m., it dawned on him that he was going to miss the ranch, working side by side with Elyse and Aunt Grace and the ease at which he fit in with them. He didn't have to hide who he was from them.

"We need to get ready to go—not just us but the horses too," he informed them as they made their way back to the house. A sideways glance showed him Elyse pressing her lips together in a thin line. They had kissed once or twice since the night on the porch, but Elyse seemed content to take things slow with him. *At least she is willing to try and hasn't thrown me out.*

"I'm already packed," Elyse informed him. "Everything we need for Honey and Fork is just in front of their paddock. It will only take a few minutes to tack them up."

"Good," he replied, giving her hand a light squeeze. "We have time to eat, and then Catrina will be here."

Just as he had predicted, as he was washing the last dish, Catrina appeared in the dining room. Aunt Grace jumped instead of grabbing the plate Josh handed her to dry, and it fell to the floor and shattered.

"Sorry," Josh said, backing out of the way as Aunt Grace grabbed the broom and began sweeping up the mess.

"It's just a plate," Aunt Grace said under her breath, even though she was clearly flustered by Catrina's sudden appearance.

"It's time," Catrina announced firmly.

"Can't I at least help clean up the mess you just caused us to make?" Elyse retorted, voice accusing.

Josh looked from Catrina to Elyse without saying anything.

Catrina shook her head. "No, we don't have time. He has been tracking my movements, and if I am here for too long, he is going to send someone after me. Grab your things and say your goodbyes."

Josh sighed, knowing that Catrina was right and Dariusz likely could easily track her to them if she lingered too long. He went over to the couch and grabbed his backpack and Elyse's. Before moving to Catrina's side, he watched Elyse as she gave Aunt Grace a long hug. When they let go of each other, he could see a hint of tears glinting on Elyse's cheeks. *I hope someday she'll get the time she deserves with her aunt.*

"I'm ready," Elyse said, facing Catrina.

"Let's go grab the horses," the vampire replied, leading them out the door. Less than ten minutes later, both horses were tacked up with saddle bags full of grain and extra supplies tied behind the saddles.

"Very well, take your reins in one hand and then grab my hand with your free one."

Josh took Fork's reins as Elyse offered them and then gripped them in his left hand while holding on to Catrina's with his right. Elyse did the same on the vampire's other side with Honey's reins.

"You didn't tell us where we're going," Elyse said softly.

As the air shimmered and twisted, then the darkness sucked them in.

ABOUT THE AUTHOR

Elizabeth R. Jensen is an award-winning author and Arabian horse and German Riding pony breeder in Atlanta, GA. This is her fifth book. All four of her previous books have won awards in numerous categories including Best Series, Cover Illustration, and Audiobook Production.

E. R. has a bachelor's degree in animal science, a master's of business administration and a master's of organizational leadership. In elementary school, E. R. was introduced to creative writing in an after-school poetry class for gifted students. Since then, she has continued to write poetry.

9 7 9 8 9 8 8 5 9 7 1 2 4